Someone Else's Wedding

Tamar Cohen

Doubleday

LONDON · TORONTO · SYDNEY · AUCKLAND · JOHANNESBURG

TRANSWORLD PUBLISHERS
61–63 Uxbridge Road, London W5 5SA
A Random House Group Company
www.transworldbooks.co.uk

First published in Great Britain
in 2013 by Doubleday
an imprint of Transworld Publishers

A CIP catalogue record for this book
is available from the British Library.

ISBNs 9780857521705 (hb)
9780857521712 (tpb)

Addresses for Random House Group Ltd companies outside the UK
can be found at: www.randomhouse.co.uk
The Random House Group Ltd Reg. No. 954009

The Random House Group Limited supports the Forest Stewardship Council®
(FSC®), the leading international forest-certification organisation. Our books
carrying the FSC label are printed on FSC®-certified paper. FSC is the only forest-
certification scheme supported by the leading environmental organisations,
including Greenpeace. Our paper procurement policy can be found
at www.randomhouse.co.uk/environment

Typeset in 11/14pt Sabon by
Kestrel Data, Exeter, Devon.
Printed and bound in Great Britain by
Clays Ltd, Bungay, Suffolk.

2 4 6 8 10 9 7 5 3 1

MIX
Paper from
responsible sources
FSC
www.fsc.org   FSC® C016897

Someone Else's Wedding

www.transworldbooks.co.uk

Also by Tamar Cohen

The Mistress's Revenge
The War of the Wives

For Sara and Simon

Saturday, 8 a.m.

Everything happens for a reason. Can there be a stupider phrase in the English language?

Paper cuts, tissues in the washing machine, children with bizarre syndromes that age them prematurely, frozen computer screens, perfectly sound motorway lanes randomly closed to traffic, rained-off barbecues, split ends, tsunamis in far-flung places, parking fines, cold sores, lifeless babies born too early, their fingers and toes perfect, their eyes closed as if at any moment they might cough themselves awake.

As far as I can see, the universe is a great big dirty-laundry basket heaped with pointless occurrences.

'Sometimes things happen for a reason,' well-meaning people told me. And I'd smile and nod like you do when you're pretending to agree with something profound, all the time feeling as if there was a great big stone inside me, in that empty place where my baby should have been, and they were kicking it around like a football.

Occasionally I wouldn't smile and nod. I'd say something like 'The dry rot in your downstairs loo? Or your senile mother always thinking you're the woman from the Council? Is there a reason for these, too? Are they all part of some grander plan?'

Actually I didn't say those things at all. But I definitely thought them.

Saul didn't say that things happen for a reason. Or 'Well, I did warn you . . .' Or any of the other things he might have said. Which is a shame in a way, because in the two years since I gave a final scream and Molly emerged perfect in every way except the one that most matters, the words he didn't say (but must have thought) have grown between us like a phantom child, getting bigger, stronger, louder.

In obstetric terms, the words Saul didn't say have thrived.

Only when he's not here are they silent. Which is how, even before I open my eyes in this vast, unfamiliar hotel bed, I know I'm alone.

For a moment I luxuriate in my solitude, stretching out my legs and arms and pressing them into the mattress as if I might some-how grow organically into the sheet, weaving tissue and fibre and hair and silver-painted nail into the wheat-coloured cotton thread. When I finally open my eyes, I see that the space where Saul once was is neatly smoothed and patted, the duvet pulled taut over the pillow.

From my position on the left side of the mattress, I gaze across at his unoccupied domain. In theory the hotel room is neutral territory where we can do as we want, free from what Louise, our marital counsellor, calls 'the unhealthy power-struggle patterns of the long-term relationship', but still the idea of me venturing over the invisible middle line is unthinkable. Like crossing over to the Dark Side. I might say that at our next session. Phrases like 'the Dark Side' wind Saul up. 'I wish Fran would take this more seriously,' he'd say to Louise, his eyebrows raised in a 'see what I have to put up with' way.

Amazing to think it's just eight months since the first time we went to see Louise, arranged elbow to elbow on the sofa opposite her, united against this stranger prying into our lives; yet now we fight over her allegiance, each courting her approval, alert to signs of favouritism.

It makes me smile, remembering that first visit to her comfort-able red-brick home in a quiet no-through road in one of the more affluent areas of south-west London. After what was mostly a fact-finding initial session, Saul turned to me as we walked away, his face light with relief.

'Thank God that's over. It wasn't as bad as I thought.'

I stopped then, incredulous.

'You do know that was just the beginning, don't you? You are aware it's not a one-off?'

We laughed about it later – the dawning horror on his face.

Funny how quickly Louise has become the most important person in our lives. The last time we went to see her, just three days ago, we arrived twenty minutes early and took a walk in the small park in front of her house. We'd just had a light dinner together in the garden, something wholesome involving salmon and vine-grown tomatoes, and for once our conversation felt unforced. As we strolled across the freshly mown grass, Saul took my hand and I allowed my own fingers to curl around his. We didn't speak much, I remember, but it was a lightweight sort of silence that settled easily over us like a fine mist, and I'd felt hopeful for the first time in weeks.

'How are you both this evening?' Louise smiled as we took our customary seats on the sofa in front of her. Louise has a lazy eye, so even while she's looking at me I sometimes have the disconcerting impression that she's actually addressing Saul.

'Fine.' I smiled back, still bathed in the glow of unexpected closeness.

Louise turned her good eye to Saul. 'And you, Saul? How have you been feeling?'

Saul looked at her, and I saw a dark flush crawl out from the hollow of his collarbone, where it had been hiding all this time. 'Actually, I'm angry,' he said. 'Really bloody angry.'

I roll on to my back, my head propped up on a multitude of over-stuffed pillows so that my neck feels bent at an unnatural angle. The hotel room is done out in what was described on the website as 'neutrals'. For 'neutrals' read 'beige'. Who knew there were so many shades of beige? Even the abstract prints on the walls are beige. I have woken up inside a giant surgical stocking.

Without warning, I'm reminded of the first hotel room I ever stayed in (although I suppose 'stayed' might be too grand a word for two hours on a drizzly Wednesday afternoon). I was sixteen years old and horribly naive. For the next few years I truly believed all hotels had greying net curtains and a thick plastic cover over the mattress so that every movement was accompanied by a loud crackling sound, and the smell of sex was a citrus air-freshener tree.

Why am I thinking of that now, after all these years?

My handbag – large and battered and stuffed with rubbish, old receipts and fluff-covered throat pastilles, a lightweight umbrella with a broken spindle, a couple of fraying tampons – squats on the dressing table in front of me and I deliberately don't look at it. Just knowing that the letter is tucked away inside gives me an uncomfortable, fluttery feeling. Instead I focus on Saul's nylon sports bag, which is open next to it. When I saw him loading it into the car boot yesterday evening, something popped inside me.

'Please tell me you're not,' I said. Pointless, when it was so obvious that he was. With the benefit of hindsight, I see I could have handled it better. *Make it about how you feel, not about what the other person has done*, Louise is forever saying. 'Your sports bag makes me feel superfluous,' I could have said. No, that's not the word. Lonely. 'Your sports bag makes me feel lonely.'

Saul didn't even look up. 'Course I am. The marathon's next weekend. It'd be suicide to interrupt my training schedule.'

Suicide? Not that he could ever be accused of being grandiose, my husband.

'So that means you'll be not-drinking, and stuffing yourself with carbs and protein. Even though it's a *wedding*?'

'What's the big deal, Fran? It's not as if I expect you to do the same.'

Since turning forty, Saul has run thirteen marathons and done six triathlons. My husband is a walking, talking sinew.

The first marathon he completed was, I'll admit, quite magical. The girls and I went early to secure a spot near the finishing line and spent hours craning our necks as the runners began to dribble in, the first hundred or so still taking easy strides, the rest in varying degrees of discomfort. I'll never forget that first glimpse of him, mouth stretched back in pain, legs visibly shaking, eyes scanning the crowd wildly. As he came near, we all jumped up and down, waving madly, and as soon as he saw us something switched in his face and, miraculously, he managed a smile. Incredibly, his whole body seemed to straighten and his eyes focused on the finish. When he staggered over the line, we were right there to meet him and he collapsed into my arms.

'I'm so proud of you,' I whispered. And I really was. It was one of the closest moments we've had in recent years. That evening I threw him a surprise party, with a cake in the shape of a running shoe that looked more like a submarine.

But with every marathon he does, more of the shine seems to go out of it. It's not the race itself, it's the endless preparation: the early nights, the special diet, the way the races eat into his holiday allowance – a day here, two days there, Paris, New York. His focus is all on that, and not on me or our life together.

No, that's not it, either. Really it's just us and the way we are with each other now, the petty resentments that bubble like blisters under the surface.

'I just thought we could relax together for once. Louise is always saying we need to get out of our usual environment and unwind.'

'Yes, but by "unwind", she doesn't mean drink, Fran. You're getting the two things confused. Anyway, I'll go for a run first thing in the morning while you're asleep. You won't even know I'm gone.'

But I do know he's gone. I know it from the lightness in the air and the way my muscles feel relaxed and my limbs freely spread. I wonder where he'll run. This close to a marathon he often runs twenty miles in a morning, using a special gadget to tell him how far he's gone. The hotel is eleven miles from Bath. Arriving last night, we drove along mile upon mile of tree-canopied country roads, through quaint villages. I imagine Saul running there now, listening to Snow Patrol through his iPod headphones, a tall, lean rasher of a man in a black vest and shorts, and the running shoes he had custom-made at a special place in north London.

Saul will be in the mood for sex when he gets back, it occurs to me now. All that adrenaline charging around his system, looking for release. The illicitness of an anonymous hotel room, the whiff of borrowed romance. Maybe I'll get up before he comes back. Pip is in the room opposite. I can knock on her door, sit myself down in the armchair and we can chat the way we used to when she was still living at home. Maybe Katy will wander in from her own room next door. My daughters can show me what they've brought to wear to the wedding – knowing Katy, she'll have at least five potential outfits.

I look at my phone on the bedside table. Eight fifteen. The girls won't thank me for waking them up this early. I suppose I could always go downstairs to the hotel lounge, and see if any of the other guests are around. But we don't know many people at this wedding. And what if Jamie is there? My stomach lurches at the thought of him – a flash of green-flecked eyes, and soft blond hairs on a lightly tanned forearm – and I know I won't go down.

So I'm still here when Saul returns. 'I was asleep,' I tell him, opening the door a crack and heading back to bed.

'Sorry, darling. Fantastic run. Eighteen miles. Bit hilly, but breathtaking scenery.'

He unclips his iPod from the waistband of his shorts and places it carefully back in a pocket of his sports bag. His curly salt-and-pepper hair is plastered to his skull and I can see the sweat patches on the back of his vest.

'It's going to be a scorcher today,' he calls from the en suite. I hear the shower running, the sound of honest, healthy physical exertion being washed away. It makes me feel dissolute by contrast, and flabby around the edges. Now the electric toothbrush whirs into life. Saul has always been proud of his teeth, flossing religiously and using a special brand of whitening toothpaste that costs twice as much as any other kind. He reappears in the doorway, a white towel wrapped around his waist, hair still dripping. He's in good shape, my husband. His torso is narrow but well-defined, whorls of black hair forming a neat T-shape over his chest and abdomen.

I close my eyes, feigning sleep. Over the last two years, I reckon I've feigned more sleep than I've actually had. I wonder if all marriages are like that.

Now Saul is back in bed, moving towards me. He crosses the line into my territory and I tense. Louise has been trying to get me to talk about my ambivalence about having sex with my husband. 'Is it about fear, I wonder?' she asks, leaning forward in her chair, as she does whenever we discuss anything intimate. 'Are you scared about what you're giving up?'

But it's not about fear. It's about anger. I'm not scared, I'm furious.

It's not about what I'm giving up, it's about what he's taking.

Saul has his hand on my hip. There's a strict order about sex, as far as Saul is concerned, just as there's a strict order about running and a strict order about work. Saul is Head of Product Development at Premstock, the UK's third-largest stationery company. He's been in that job for six years and with the company for eleven. They love him there. He's what is known as A Safe Pair of Hands. I've met most of the staff over the years at one event or another. At one Christmas lunch, Saul's secretary got drunk and did an impression of his routine when he arrives at work in the mornings.

'First he fills up a plastic water bottle from the cooler in reception, then he hangs his jacket on the back of his office door, then he puts the bottle down on the desk, sits down and does this,' she'd said, closing her eyes and pressing two fingers to her temples while taking a long inhalation. 'And then he does *this*.' Suddenly her eyes popped wide open and a slightly deranged smile sprang, fully formed, to her face. 'And *voilà* – the day begins.'

Saul had laughed louder than anyone but I'd found it quite disturbing – this external verification of Saul as a creature of habit.

We've never exactly been swinging-from-the-chandelier types, but when we first got together, sex was at least varied. On the top, on the bottom, on the knees and rotate (so to speak). I sound like a rotisserie chicken! The main thing was, sex was good-natured. We were rooting for each other, like repertoire actors wanting to bring out the best in each other's performances. Then the girls

13

were born, just eighteen months apart, and we got into the habit of sex by numbers. Do this, do that – the quickest route to orgasm and sleep. But still, sex was pleasant, it was something we did to relax.

Now Saul and I have all the time in the world for sex, but still we stick doggedly to the templates of twenty years ago, as if scared to deviate from what we know, as if deviation would be . . . well, deviant.

While Saul's hand traces its well-worn route around my body – I'm surprised I don't have indentations in my flesh by now, like a muddy footpath trodden into the grass by constant use – I close my eyes, placing my hands where years of experience of my husband's body has taught me produces the fastest results. He moans softly. With my eyes still shut, I relax into the familiar, pleasurable rhythm – until suddenly I feel his mouth on mine, tongue probing to get in.

Immediately my hands stop their stroking and I freeze, turning my head to one side so his mouth falls slack and wet on my cheek.

'I don't mind the sex,' I once tried to explain to Louise. 'It's the kissing I find so difficult.'

She'd nodded, her shiny, conker-coloured hair shimmering in the lamp-light. 'You're frightened of intimacy,' she told me. 'It's very common, I'm afraid. Particularly where resentment has been allowed to build up.'

She made it sound like plaque.

We'd talked a little bit then about when it started, this aversion. It was right around when I read those emails and texts between my husband and his old university girlfriend in Edinburgh. As usual, the subject had sent Saul into an orgy of self-recrimination.

'You feel guilty, Saul?' Louise asked.

'Of course I feel guilty. I've felt guilty every day.'

I've never doubted that Saul feels guilty. Even while it was still going on, Saul's guilt practically moved into the house with us – though at the time I didn't know that's what it was, just that there was something else lodging with us, something I hadn't invited in.

And after it all came out, Saul was almost paralysed by it.

14

Watching television, I'd be aware of his eyes boring into me as he sat, stricken, in the armchair opposite.

'I'm sorry,' he'd say when I finally looked up. 'I'm so sorry.'

Saul's guilt was such a constant presence, it ought to have been paying rent!

'Why won't you kiss me?' Saul murmurs now into my ear. But my hands are moving again, and soon his breath comes in gasps and he doesn't speak at all.

Afterwards, he is cheerful. Pleased with himself and me and the world in general.

I feel a twinge of guilt at how little it takes to make him happy.

'It's really very beautiful around here,' he says, walking to the window and holding open the curtain to look outside. 'You know, we should think about moving somewhere like this. Maybe not quite so far out of London, but it's silly to stay in the city now we're not tied to schools any more. We could get something smaller. Cosier. It's not as if we need the space any more.'

I get into the shower and run the water as hot as I can make it, tipping my face up so it pours over my cheeks and neck. The screen door opens and Saul steps in beside me.

'You know, you are beautiful,' he murmurs.

For a split second we lean against each other under the running water. I imagine relaxing into him, allowing us to comfort each other as we used to.

'We'll miss breakfast,' I say, stepping out and wrapping a towel tightly around me, like a bandage. 'I'm starving.'

I can hear Saul singing to himself as I sit down at the dressing table to dry my hair, which takes a shockingly short amount of time, following yesterday's disastrous haircut.

I'd gone in clutching a photo of Cate Blanchett.

'Could you do something like that?' I asked Becki, who has been cutting my hair consistently badly for the past seven years.

She peered at the photo and then at me and then back at the photo again.

'I'll see what I can do,' she said doubtfully. 'The thing is though, I'm not being funny but she has very good hair.'

As Becki started cutting, I felt the first twinges of alarm.

'Make sure you leave the back long enough to still see hair behind my ears,' I said. 'Otherwise the balance is wrong for my face.'

After she'd finished we both surveyed the result in silence.

'I did say I wanted to be able to see hair behind my ears.'

'Yeah, but, not being funny, you haven't got the right jawline for that.'

Of course, I still paid her, and tipped her, while vowing never to go back. I felt like a mug, remembering all the other times I'd made the same vow, only to waver at the last minute. 'Better the devil you know . . .' I told Saul when he asked why I kept going back.

'Did you know the Japanese have a word for when you look worse after a haircut?' he'd said brightly, then backtracked madly when he saw my face. 'Not that you look worse, darling. You look lovely. You always look lovely.'

Now I gaze flatly at my new haircut in the hotel-room mirror. Becki insisted on 'running a few highlights through' to disguise the few strands of grey that have sprung up almost overnight, like a Banksy mural. So now my usual dull brown is streaked with deep red and burnt orange.

'Crikey,' Katy said last night when we met them in the hotel bar. 'Who needs the Olympic Flame?'

Pip was more complimentary. 'It's taken years off you,' she said, giving me a hug.

But the woman who looks back at me from the mirror is some-one I don't recognize – a stranger with a stranger's hair.

I put on the clothes from last night – tight, slim-fitting jeans with silver flip-flops and a white top. Then I fetch my make-up bag and begin painting myself a face.

'Darling, we're only going down to breakfast,' says Saul, stand-ing behind me, his hands, with their surprisingly broad fingers, gripping my shoulders. 'You really don't need all that stuff on yet.'

I shrug and carry on, applying tinted moisturizer, under-eye concealer, eyeshadow, kohl, mascara, while Saul stands by the door, tapping his foot with impatience.

There's a tightness in my stomach, as if someone has threaded a drawstring through and is pulling on it hard.

Yes, it's only breakfast, but there'll be new people to meet and make small talk to, about how lucky we've been with the weather and the arrangements for the day. And then there'll be Lynn and Max, and Pip and Katy, of course.

And Jamie. My heart bursts with his name.

But Jamie is getting married.

Saturday, 9 a.m.

The hotel lounge is vast and modern, with cream leather seating and dark wood tables. Lynn and Max are at the far end, at a table with five people we don't know. A quick glance around reveals no one else I recognize. I am at once relieved and deflated.

'Ah, there you are,' says Max, getting to his feet and pumping Saul's hand vigorously.

Lynn half stands so I can plant a dry peck some inches from her cheek, but Max sweeps me into a bear hug.

'Fran and Saul, everyone,' he announces as we sit down. 'I like your hair, Fran. It's very gamine.'

'Very gammon? That's not very nice – I'd take umbrage if I were you, Mum,' says Katy, coming up behind.

She and Pip have clearly just got out of bed, but their skin glows and their eyes are bright in their fresh, make-up-free faces. They are effortlessly lovely, with my blue eyes, only bigger and purer, and Saul's dark curls. I wonder if all mothers end up feeling like drag versions of their own daughters.

Now that the girls are here, there is a lot of moving about of seats and adding of tables. I'm glad of the distraction.

'Why don't we have champagne?' I say, suddenly inspired. 'A champagne breakfast. It is a wedding, after all.'

'Darling,' protests Saul, 'it's only half nine.'

I smile to show I was joking. But I wasn't.

We are introduced to the two other couples, whose names I instantly forget, and an elderly woman called Christine. The couples look to be in their mid fifties, like Lynn and Max. I wonder if they are academics as well. They have that same vaguely cerebral air, and each has a pair of reading glasses either folded up next to their plate or tucked into a cleavage or the top pocket of a shirt, like the latest fashion accessory.

'It's lovely to meet you all,' I tell them, making a point of pressing each of their hands. 'Now we won't feel like such Billy No Mates.'

There are smiles then, and a perceptible warming.

'You're looking wonderful, Lynn,' says Saul, and I notice that she, too, has done something different to her hair. It seems to have hardened around her head like a helmet. She shoots him a grateful smile and her usually stern features soften.

'Mustn't let the side down,' she says.

'Just so long as you don't outshine the Mother of the Bride,' says one of the other women, raising her eyebrows meaningfully. 'Having met her in her so-called casual clothes, I can't wait to see her when she's dressed up. The mind boggles!'

'Lucy and her mother were at ours for a barbecue last week,' Lynn explains to Saul and me, before leaning back towards the original speaker and saying, 'Don't worry. As Mother of the Groom, I know my place in the pecking order.'

'Speaking of order, tell us how things are going to pan out today.' Pip's voice cuts in, steering the conversation away from the direction it was going, and I feel a rush of gratitude towards her.

While Lynn explains the itinerary for the day, Max and Saul discuss routes and driving times.

'I'm thinking of getting a hybrid,' Max announces, and for a thrilling moment I imagine he is talking about some wildly exotic cross-breed pet, before I realize – *of course* – they're still discussing cars.

'Where's Jammy?' Katy asks suddenly.

Jammy! The nickname, so easily tossed out, shouldn't shock me, but it does. I'm always forgetting how much the girls see of Jamie now they've all moved away from home and are living and working independently in London. They've forged new relationships between themselves that I have no control over. It should make me happy. It *does* make me happy, but anxious, too. So much happening just beyond my reach.

'He'll be down in a minute,' says Max. 'Sleeping off last night's excesses, I expect.'

'You must be so proud,' says the woman who made the Mother-of-the Bride comment.

Lynn shoots me a glance, then immediately looks away again.

'We are,' she says. 'Very proud.'

'Rosie's a bit put out, I think,' says Max. 'She's always been so possessive of her brother. I think she worries about losing him. I told her he's not that easy to mislay. Not like an old chequebook or something.'

'Do chequebooks even exist any more?' wonders one of the Maybe Academics. 'I thought they'd been phased out.'

Lynn ignores the interruption.

'Well, things are bound to be different from now on, for all of us,' she says, quickly adding, 'Not worse – just different.'

'Where is Rosie?' I ask. 'I didn't see her last night.'

'She was out with Jamie and Liam,' says Lynn. 'Liam is Jamie's best man. Jamie said he was sorry to miss you, by the way.'

I feel my face burning.

Now Katy is pouting. She wants to know why she and Pip weren't invited to go out with Jamie and the others.

'I think they wanted to do something quiet,' says Max.

'Just family,' adds Lynn.

The waiter comes round for our orders. I'm not hungry but I order a croissant anyway and then, on impulse, a Bucks Fizz.

Saul is sitting to my left and I'm aware of his disapproval lodging itself between us like a bolster cushion. I'm grateful when Katy says, 'What a good idea. Make that two.' You can never tell with Katy which way she's going to go. She could just as easily have raised her eyebrows at Saul in that conspiratorial way those two have.

I try to strike up a conversation with the elderly woman, Christine, who seems to be some kind of relative of Lynn's. She has a mobile phone in her hand and is jabbing at the keyboard with unsteady fingers, a frown furrowing her already creased face.

'Do you need any help with that? These new smartphones can be terribly confusing, can't they?'

Christine looks up, amused. Her eyes are surprisingly beautiful, the blue of a swimming pool shimmering under a Mediterranean sun, and the smile that ripples gently across her skin is so warm that I can't help smiling back. Sometimes it unnerves me to look into an older person's face and get a glimpse of the beauty they once had, marooned there amidst the wreckage, but Christine's allure belongs to the here and now, to the folds around her eyes and the soft powderiness of her skin and the marshmallow-white hair held back by two large tortoiseshell combs.

'Don't worry, dear. It's all under control. I'm just blogging.'

'Blogging?'

'I promised my followers a live update from the wedding. I need to keep the numbers up or I'll lose my ad revenue.'

I try to disguise my surprise. 'I've never really understood how that works.'

Christine waves a hand in front of her face in a dismissive gesture. 'There's no mystery. It's just like the newsletters I used to write at Christmas, except now I do it every week instead of every year. You know, there's nothing new under the sun, my dear.'

All of a sudden, a murmur goes up from the people opposite, facing the door. Without thinking, I turn and – wham! – my heart slams straight into my ribcage. I turn back immediately, but I know he saw me look. There's a rushing in my ears and I try to concentrate on my breathing to calm myself.

Rosie comes around first, kissing everyone on the cheek, making a particular fuss of Pip and Katy. She looks tiny next to them, her shiny blonde bob coming only to Pip's shoulder.

'Oh my *God*!' she squeals, grabbing Katy by the arm and peering at her wrist. 'I absolutely *love* your tat.'

Tat?

Saul and I exchange mystified glances, and Katy looks embarrassed. Now that her sleeve is pushed up, I can see she has a delicate tattoo near her wrist. A sea horse, it looks like. My baby has marked herself for life. I'm shocked at how much it bothers me.

'You know you've just consigned yourself to a lifetime of long sleeves at job interviews?'

Saul is trying to joke, but I know that as soon as he gets a chance he'll Google 'septicaemia' and other unpleasant infections our younger daughter may have contracted. But Katy's tattoo is forgotten as a figure looms beside me. Jamie, who has been busying himself down the other end of the table, patting shoulders and shaking hands, has now reached us. I steel myself before looking into his face, pulling my stomach muscles in so they form a rigid core at the heart of me, a frame to keep me upright while the rest of me crumples around it.

'Hello, Fran,' he says, and I turn around.

His eyes are watermelon green flecked with hazel and amber, and fringed with thick, sooty lashes. I'd forgotten how he looks at me as if he's reading me. I'd forgotten the perfect teardrop shape between his nose and upper lip. I'd forgotten the way the centre of me dissolves when I'm with him. I give him an awkward hug.

Now he is shaking hands with Saul, and Saul covers both their hands with his free hand to emphasize his sincerity, fixing his gaze directly on Jamie's. There's often a self-consciousness about the way Saul behaves in company, a staginess, as if an inner monologue might be saying, *And here I am setting people at ease*, or, *Now here I am joshing with my daughters*. In a way it's endearing, this need to make a good impression, like catching someone moving their lips while reading a book and realizing how hard they are concentrating on something that ought to come naturally.

More seats are brought over, more places shifted around. Rosie has squeezed herself in between Pip and Katy and is complaining about the monumentalness of her hangover.

'I feel fine,' says Jamie, sitting at the top end next to Lynn. 'You're such a lightweight.'

'I should hope you *do* feel fine,' says Lynn, mock sternly. 'It is your wedding day, after all.'

'I can't wait to meet Lucy,' says Saul. 'It's rather sweet that she's so traditional about staying somewhere else the night before the wedding.'

'I'm not sure Lucy would appreciate being called sweet,' says Rosie. 'She's quite touchy about things like that. She prefers to see herself as edgy.'

'Rosie.' Lynn's voice is low with warning.

'What? It wasn't a criticism.'

My Bucks Fizz has arrived and suddenly I wish I hadn't ordered it. I take a sip and then worry that the juice will have left an orange mark like egg yolk around my mouth. I dab my lips with the corner of my napkin, hoping no one is watching.

'Are you excited about today – or shitting yourself?' Katy asks Jamie. My younger daughter believes in telling it like it is.

'I'm ready – bring it on!' says Jamie. Then he smiles. 'Not really. I'm shitting myself.'

'You'll be fine,' says Lynn, and she lays her helmet head on Jamie's arm, just for a fraction of a second.

I take a large gulp of my Bucks Fizz. Such tiny glasses they put this stuff in. Two sips and you've practically finished the lot.

I get up to go to the loo. All the way across the room, my legs feel stiff, my walk laboured, as I imagine his eyes watching me.

'*Stupid*,' I tell my reflection in the greenish overhead glare of the Ladies'. My hair looks crazily multicoloured, as if a child has crayoned it in.

In the cubicle I sit down and put my head in my hands. I'm being ridiculous, I know. Emotions lurching all over the place. Could I be menopausal already? Peri-menopausal? It's not impossible, even at my age.

The beeping of my phone in my bag jolts me out of my musings. A text. As soon as I see his name on the screen, everything inside me freezes. 'Can I see you?' I stare at the message as if its four words might conceal some deeper meaning. My heart is exploding.

He wants to see me. But he is getting married. Perched on the seat of the toilet, I lurch queasily between excitement and guilt. Calling up the reply box, I type 'When?' My finger hovers, trembling, over the Send icon. I think about my daughters sitting outside. I think about Saul and how his brown eyes will track my progress back across the room.

I erase the message angrily and click my phone off, hurrying out of the toilets before I have time to change my mind.

As I sit back down, Saul takes my hand and squeezes it under the table. 'All right, darling?'

'Of course. Why wouldn't I be?'

'Have you known Lynn and Max long?' asks the man opposite, one of those heavy types with prematurely white hair and a florid complexion that makes him look curiously infantile.

'Oh, we go back donkey's years,' I say. 'We lost touch for a while – it happens sometimes, doesn't it? – but we're back in each other's lives now. The wonders of Facebook and all that!'

'They're a lovely couple,' he says. 'Wonderful family.'

He's an oncologist, he tells us, specializing in paediatric cancers. There's a mobile phone sitting on the table next to him. Every few seconds it vibrates, convulsing alarmingly and rattling the plate of Danish pastries in front of him.

'I raised nearly a grand last year for childhood leukaemia by trekking Hadrian's Wall,' Saul announces.

The man smiles politely. To his credit, his smile stays gamely in place even after he asks Saul what he does for a living.

Saul sells paper and pens.

When we first met, he was midway through an architecture degree, on work placement in an office near the bistro where I was temping at the time. He brought his drawings in once to show me. He's colour blind and said he needed me to tell him whether the browns he'd used were actually purple, but I could tell he wanted me to see his work, in that way you do at the start of something, when you want to be fully known. His drawings were beautiful, so delicate, and there was such pride in his face as he looked from the drawings to me and back again, waiting for my reaction. He always said he didn't mind giving it up when Pip was conceived not long after – the product of a surfeit of desire coupled with an empty box of condoms – but I never saw that look again.

Now Saul gets up every morning and drives to the station and catches the same train, sitting in the same carriage because he knows exactly which one aligns with the exit for the Tube.

Louise, our relationship counsellor, asked me once if I felt compromised by my marriage.

'It's not . . . how I'd envisaged things,' I said.

Saul had grown incensed by that. By the things he felt I wasn't saying.

'You think it's easy?' He'd appealed directly to Louise, as if I wasn't even there, sitting on the other end of the sofa in Louise's perfectly pleasant, muted consulting room. 'You think it's easy living with someone who is constitutionally disappointed?'

'That's why you had an affair, I suppose?' I flung at him, knowing it would stop him in his tracks.

'It wasn't an affair. How many times do I have to say it? We never met.'

'There are many different types of affair, Saul,' Louise reminded him.

The oncologist turns his attention to me, and I brace myself, knowing what's coming.

'And what do you do, Fiona?'

'It's Fran, actually,' I say. 'Well, I used to be an SEN support worker in a primary school, until quite recently.' What I mean, but can't bring myself to say, is *until Molly*. 'That's working with schoolchildren with special educational needs.'

It sounds so dry when I say it, so worthy. Impossible to convey the unique frustration of working with a child who can't or won't grasp something – or the elation when he finally does. Impossible to explain how sometimes Sue, the SEN coordinator, and I would only just hold it together till we made it to the staffroom door, before collapsing with laughter at something one of the children had said or done.

'Fran's having a bit of a sabbatical at the moment,' Saul tells him now. He's making it sound jolly, like a holiday, although he's often tried to cajole me back to work.

'You could get something full time, now the girls have left home,' he keeps telling me. 'Something more challenging. Or go back to the school. You liked it there.'

I did like it there, and Sue and the others still regularly ask when I'm coming back. I don't tell them I wish *I* knew when I was coming back. I say I'll return when the time feels right. But it never does. The truth is, the job was stressful – all those children, all those problems – and after nine years I was feeling burnt out and relieved to be giving it up to go on maternity leave.

The last two years, by contrast, have been full of nothing. A vast football stadium full of nothing. I don't tell Saul that though. Saul likes to imagine my newly freed-up domestic life as a mosaic of yoga classes and white-wine lunches and edifying trips to the library to hear local writers reading from their new novels. He doesn't know about the times I put on an aerobics CD and lie on the sofa watching *Cash in the Attic* with the sound down, or when I scroll through my phone, looking for someone to call. I have 219 contacts in my phone. No shortage of people I could ring to change a meeting from eleven to twelve, or arrange a dental appointment or an insurance valuation. There are people I could call to wax my bikini line or insert a speculum into my cervix. But no one I could phone on a rainy Wednesday afternoon and simply say, 'I'm lonely.'

Saul would see loneliness as a preventable failing – like astigmatism or oily skin. He'd see it as something to be fixed. And in a way he'd be right. I could go back to work. But I don't, and Saul doesn't understand what stops me. Nor does he understand how life can open up like a chasm on a midweek afternoon, time stretched tightly across the top like clingfilm. Or how it's possible to spend a whole morning looking in the mirror, pulling back the skin of your face over your cheekbones, trying to recapture something lost. But even though Saul doesn't understand, in front of these strangers he seems compelled to fight my corner.

'I think Fran would enjoy setting up her own business,' he tells the oncologist. 'It's never too late.'

When Saul says that about business, I feel a stab of guilt about the letter in the handbag by my feet. An offer of a year's contract in an international school in southern Spain, not far from where my brother and his family now live.

'You lucky cow!' Sue exclaimed when I told her about it last week. 'But will Saul be able to get the time off?'

'Saul doesn't know. I'd be going alone.'

Her mouth fell open then with shock. 'But you have to tell him.'

'I will – when I'm sure. I haven't decided yet.'

I shoo away the memory of Sue's stricken, doubting eyes and try to focus on Pip, who has also weighed in to the conversation.

'Mum's got loads of experience that'd be a great asset in business.'

'If you use the phrase "transferable skills" I might actually have to kill you,' I tell her.

The oncologist smiles and glances at his vibrating phone. I wonder what it must be like to be so in demand.

If Molly had survived, there wouldn't be this question mark over my future – although Saul might say it's the question mark over my future that led to Molly in the first place.

'But you're forty-three,' he pointed out, when I first mooted the idea of another baby. As if any woman over forty needs reminding how old she is. As if I might have mistaken myself for someone ten years younger, labouring happily under the illusion of having my life spread out in front of me like a market stall, heaped with promise.

I couldn't explain to him how I felt, that sense of things shutting down around me and inside me.

'If you had a new job, a new challenge, you wouldn't think about having a baby,' said Saul.

I was incensed.

'You think I want a baby because I'm fed up with work?'

'So explain it, then. Explain why, twenty years after celebrating the end of the nappy years, you suddenly want to do it all again.

27

The sleepless nights, the endless paraphernalia. No impromptu trips to the cinema or weekends away. Explain that.'

Of course, I couldn't. And, of course, he was right in a way. A baby would give a ready-made structure to the next two decades. The future would no longer be a holding pattern, but a neatly mapped-out progression of years, from winter afternoons in the park, breath emerging in white clouds, to school cake sales, to teenage taxi service.

But that wasn't it. Or rather, that wasn't just it. Nor, contrary to what Louise believes, was my need to have another baby somehow linked to that earlier episode, Saul's 'moment of madness', as he grew to call it. Of course, I was angry with him for a long time. I'm still angry with him now – for the intimacies he shared with the architect in Edinburgh and the things he told her that weren't his to tell (the colour of our duvet cover, the way our dishwasher backs up from time to time – the domestic details that make up a home, a family, a marriage).

But there was more to it than that. In the years since first Pip, then Katy, left home, I'd felt myself increasingly unmoored from real life. It was as if the girls were the ropes tying me to the world. Without them, I blew this way and that like a discarded paper bag. Saul didn't know that I felt as if at any moment I could be swept away. A baby wasn't just a way to fill time. A baby would tether me back to my life.

'Sometimes I think Fran loves the girls too much,' Saul once said to Louise, and I remember feeling as if he'd taken a giant sack of potatoes and slammed it into my chest. Instantly I'd turned to Louise for vindication and was astonished when, instead of challenging Saul, she looked at me, head cocked to the side. 'Maybe what Saul means, Fran, is that you love your daughters so much there's nothing left for him?'

'What does Lucy do?' Saul has turned away from me, so he is facing Jamie head-on.

Under the table I grip my hands tightly together, pressing my fingernails into my palms.

'She works for the same TV company as Jamie,' Max butts

in proudly. 'On the production side. Real high-flyer, apparently. Jamie had better pull his socks up if he wants to keep pace with the missus.'

I look up and catch the eye of the waiter across the room.

'Another Bucks Fizz,' I say when he comes over.

I don't look at anyone else, but I know what they're thinking.

Saturday, 10 a.m.

My bikini, a khaki-coloured halter neck, is laid out on the bed, next to what my mother used to call a 'one-piece'. At forty-five I am on the cusp between the two. I look from one to the other in despair.

'You can still rock a bikini, Mum,' says Pip. 'You've got the body of a woman ten years younger.'

'Then it's high time you gave it back,' quips Saul.

Saul doesn't do humour often and has a way of finishing each joke with a quizzically expectant expression, as if he's said something in a foreign language and is waiting to see if he's been understood.

He comes up behind me and gives me a hug. 'Seriously, though, you can definitely pull off a bikini, Fran.'

In one of our recent counselling sessions, Saul complained that I don't 'validate' him enough. Having been against counselling at first, Saul has quickly embraced it, even adopting therapy jargon. 'I hold my hands up,' he sometimes tells friends. 'I didn't have much time for it in the beginning. Now I realize it was classic fear of confrontation.' Validation is one of his favourite counselling terms. As in, he validates me by telling me I look nice, and in return I'm supposed to validate him by complimenting him back. Even after twenty-five years of contradictory evidence, Saul still believes that marriage is a game of two equal halves and I'm just not doing my bit.

'Come on, Mum,' urges Katy, who has come over from her own room and seems put out to find us not all ready and awaiting her arrival. Katy has such a big sense of herself. I envy her certainty about her own importance in the world.

'Why don't you come?' I ask Saul.

'No, you girls go and enjoy yourselves. I've already done an eighteen-miler this morning, so I think I'm excused!'

'Cool,' says Katy. 'What was your time?'

Saul shoots me a look, the significance of which is obvious. I haven't exhibited the slightest interest in how fast Saul completed his morning run. Come to think of it, I can't remember the last time I asked him about his times.

'Your father's on course to do very well next weekend,' I say, trying to make amends. 'In the veterans' class obviously.'

The last bit came out before I could even think.

'Why are you always putting him down?' Katy's face is red.

Luckily Saul steps in. 'It's not a put-down, Catkin. I *am* classed as a veteran. I just intend to be the fastest veteran they've ever seen.'

Pip, Katy and I make our way down in the lift to the health spa in the basement. The girls are in high spirits, and I'm trying to join in, but my hand keeps going to the phone in my pocket. I've erased the other text message that arrived earlier as we made our way out from breakfast. Unlike the one from Jamie, this one scared me and remains imprinted on my mind.

Stay away from us.

The number was withheld, which only added to the sense of menace.

I haven't told Saul about it. He'd only start asking questions, and there are some things I don't want to talk about at the moment. And still more things I don't want to talk about ever.

But who could it be from? In the lift down to the hotel spa, my mind casts through the possibilities. My first thought was that it

31

was from one of the children I used to support at school. Perhaps their idea of a joke. It's not inconceivable that one of them could have got hold of my mobile number – I used to give it out freely to anxious parents wanting the reassurance of a direct line to the person in charge of their child, even though it ran counter to school policy. But now I'm wondering whether it might be someone closer to home. Someone here at the wedding, even. Lucy? Jamie? The thought makes my mouth feel suddenly dry.

'I don't believe you!' Katie has swooped down on the plastic bag I'm carrying, into which I've stuffed my bikini and sundry toiletries, and is holding up a novel, its pages turned down halfway through. 'Look, she thinks she's going to be so bored with our company she'll need to read!'

I don't know why I put it in there. Though Katy is laughing, she's likely to store this up for future use, evidence of another maternal transgression. I wish things weren't like this with my younger daughter, so confrontational, but Katy has always needed to place herself at the centre of every thought I have, every action I take. I wonder what she is compensating for. Did I not give her enough attention? Does she not know how much she is loved?

'It's probably just an insurance policy,' says Pip. 'For when you start bitching about Rob.'

'I do not!' Katy's mouth is a thin line of displeasure as she glares at her sister in the lift mirror. A look passes between them that I've learned to recognize over the years. *Not in front of Mum* is what that look says – a mirror image of the *Not in front of the children* one Saul and I used to share.

I don't mind. In fact, it would be a relief not to hear anything negative about Rob, Katy's long-term boyfriend, who will be meeting us at the church and staying the rest of the weekend. After three years of coupledom, Katy – who as a girl was always flitting from one intense friendship to the next – is getting itchy feet. But I'm fond of Rob. There's something very calming about him.

It's hot in the lift and the idea of going into a steam room or a sauna seems suddenly ridiculous. At the health spa reception, we are given towels and dressing gowns. I've been hoping for something white and fluffy, but my dressing gown is too big and the pile feels hardened by too many washes. We also get nasty brown rubber shoes – one size fits all.

'Will you be wanting a treatment?' asks the receptionist. She has long purple nails studded with silver stars and an orange face, at the top of which her tattooed eyebrows arch like migrating birds silhouetted against a sunset sky.

'No, I don't think so,' I say, and the woman peers at me doubtfully.

'Well, if you change your mind . . .'

As we walk away, we all start giggling.

'She thinks I'm in denial,' I say.

'Just a quick facial peel, Modom,' says Katy.

The changing rooms are communal and I feel suddenly shy undressing in front of my daughters. I attempt to wriggle discreetly out of my clothes under my towel, but end up trapping my left arm in one of my bra straps, the towel falling in a heap on the floor as I attempt to extricate myself.

'You're a class act, Mum,' says Pip, giving me an impulsive hug, and I pat her back stiffly with my free arm.

'Just look at me,' says Katy, pouting and pulling at a non-existent roll of flesh at her waist. 'I'm like one of those huge, fat women men pay to watch on webcam stuffing themselves with cream cakes and squashing people.'

I look down at my own midriff, the indentation from my jeans waistband scored into my flesh, and think with regret of my one-piece still lying on the bed.

'I wonder if they do vajazzling here,' says Katy loudly as the three of us flap our way to the small, irregularly shaped pool in our rubber shoes. 'I could get a special weddingy one done.'

All of us have ditched the dressing gowns and Pip and I have our towels tucked around our waists like sarongs, but Katy's is still rolled up under her arm. She is wearing a pink 1950s style polka-dot bikini with frills on the bottom part and a lot of cleavage. With her long dark wavy hair, she looks like a burlesque model. I try to avoid looking at the inky-blue mark of the tattoo on her wrist.

Pip, meanwhile, has on something sensible and black. I glance over at her as we spread our towels out on white plastic loungers. She is very thin, I notice, ribs like razor clams pushing out through her skin, above a belly that appears swollen, like a malnourished child's. My heart contracts with worry. Pip has always been subdued, at least compared with her sister, but there's a definite sense of something not being right. I ought to find out what it is, but you have to be careful with Pip. Approach her directly and she is apt to curl in on herself like a caterpillar poked with a twig.

There's a shriek and a splash and Katy is in already, thrashing about happily like the child she so recently was.

'Come on!' she yells, flicking water at us as we hover doubtfully on the lip of the pool. 'Let's be having you!'

With just a toe dipped in, the pool feels horribly cold, but once we're fully immersed the water is tepid and clammy, like a bath you've been sitting in slightly too long. We attempt to swim, but the size and shape of the pool means we're forever hitting hands and knees and shoulders against hard tiles.

'Are you looking forward to meeting Lucy?' Katy asks me, out of the blue, as the three of us lie lined up in a row along one side, our legs trailing in front of us like seaweed.

'Of course,' I lie. 'I can't wait.'

'I've met her, actually.' Pip's remark takes Katy and me by surprise. 'Earlier in the week, Jamie brought her round for a quick drink on their way out somewhere.'

Katy is outraged.

'Why didn't you tell me he was coming round? What day was it? I could have come, too.'

Pip leans her head back so she's looking up at the tongue-and-groove pine ceiling.

'It was impromptu,' she says. 'He rang and said he and Lucy were going to a pub near me, and asked if they could pop in. It's no big deal.'

Katy seems mollified. The shabby Victorian house she and Rob share with three others is in south London, the opposite side of the city to her sister's tiny studio flat, so it makes sense that she wouldn't have been invited.

'And is she pretty?'

My voice sounds croaky to my own ears. But Pip replies as if she hasn't noticed anything amiss.

''Fraid she's pretty gorgeous.'

Katy has pushed herself out to the middle of the pool and turns back to face us. I hope she can't see my cheeks burning.

'I *knew* she'd be gorgeous. Jammy is such a walking cliché.'

She sounds put out, jealous even.

Ducking down, I enjoy the coolness of the water closing over my head. I won't think about Jamie. Generally I've become quite expert in not thinking about him, constructing walls around my thoughts to stop them from wandering. Only occasionally, usually when I'm lying awake at night, do I let myself go there, dragging my scruples behind me like a gammy leg. But freed from thoughts of Jamie, my mind wanders back to the threatening text and I feel a jolt of panic that sends me rushing up to the surface.

When I've shaken the water from my ears, I hear that Katy is still quizzing Pip on the mysterious Lucy. Desperate to change the subject, I say, 'I'm starting to shrivel in here. Shall we go boil ourselves?'

As I push open the door of the steam room, we are greeted by a solid bank of white vapour. There is much hilarity as we stumble about trying to find the bench, and it takes us a while to realize we are not alone.

'Oh my *God*!'

My heart sinks as I recognize Rosie's unmistakeable high-pitched squeal. Now that my eyes are growing accustomed to the hot fug, I can make out two shapes over on the opposite bench.

'Is that you, Fran?'

No matter how many times I hear him say my name, it never loses its power to unnerve me. I struggle to keep my voice light.

'Yes, we're all here. The entire female Friedman line.'

'I *love* it!' says Rosie. 'I know, let's all just skulk in here all day and skip the bloody wedding. What do you say?'

Rosie has a way of speaking as if she is constantly colluding, either with or against you.

I tip my head back and close my eyes, one hand over my belly in an instinctive, protective gesture that refuses to be unlearned. Impossible to believe that just two years ago there was a baby in there, growing under my doughy, yielding skin.

Saul had held out against it for longer than I'd expected – and even when he gave in, I think he secretly believed it wouldn't happen. What were the chances, after all, at our age? I think Saul imagined my eggs had long since packed up their things and, quietly and without fuss, taken up watercolour painting in St Ives or tending their own vegetable gardens. They certainly weren't still actively doing the things eggs are supposed to do.

'I've had my coil taken out,' I informed him a few days after the initial baby conversation. He was sitting on the sofa at the time, watching a documentary about wildlife in the Antarctic, and he raised his eyes to me, brown and reproachful, before shaking his head briefly. Then he returned to the mating patterns of emperor penguins, with only a stiffness around his shoulders and a twitch of his mouth betraying that anything momentous had been said.

Two days later, or three or four, when we were lying in bed and the usual overtures of sex began, he stopped, his hand on my thigh.

'So you're not using anything?'

I shook my head in the dark. There was a pause that strung itself out like a washing line across a few long seconds, and then his hand started moving again. But like I say, I don't think he really believed it was possible.

Only when, a few weeks later, I shoved under his nose the white plastic stick with the thick blue line across the little window did he really give proper consideration to the idea of having a third child. 'Oh shit,' he said. But by then it was too late.

I open my eyes to stop myself thinking of Molly. The steam is uncomfortable and clammy and I hate not being able to see anyone's expression. Rosie and Katy are talking about an ex-boyfriend of Rosie's. 'He ironed his pants,' Rosie is saying. 'Don't you think that's *creepy*?'

I can't see Jamie, but I'm conscious of every move he makes, every breath.

Closing my eyes again, I try to focus on something else. The letter in my handbag, now hanging on a hook in the locker, with its offer of a year's contract in Spain, for example. I hadn't even meant to apply. I'd been idly perusing a website offering jobs in schools abroad, indulging in the usual escape fantasies, when I'd noticed that the international school near my brother was advertising for staff. *No harm looking.* I clicked on the link, and then a second, and one thing led to another until, seemingly by chance, I'd dashed off an application. *It's fine,* I told myself. *I won't even hear back.* But I hadn't reckoned on how great a deterrent the paltry salary and non-existent benefits package would be, because almost by return I received an invitation to a Skype interview. *It'll be good practice,* I reasoned. *I'm not committing to anything.* True, I'd almost backed out when the deputy head had asked me in heavily accented English, 'Are you insane?' It was only after she'd repeated it three times that I worked out she was actually wondering if I was in Spain.

Only the arrival of the letter in the post yesterday, the paper thick and embossed with the name of the school, accompanied by a contract for me to sign, jolted me back to reality. It is tangible, this door into another world. It exists, and it's open.

'Too hot,' I say, suddenly pushing myself up from the tiled bench and making for the door. It has occurred to me that if Jamie exits first, he might see me emerging from the steam room, all lobster-red face and foldy-over tummy.

Outside, I am suddenly freezing. My towel is hanging on a peg on the opposite wall, but just as I reach it there's a fresh waft of scalding steam as the door opens again behind me.

'Are you OK, Fran?'

I grab the towel, wrap it around me and whirl round in one almost fluid movement, regretting having discarded the more forgiving dressing gown in the changing room. Jamie is standing behind me, a towel wrapped around his waist, his hair wet with sweat, his lightly tanned skin mottled from the heat. I keep my eyes fixed on his.

'I'm fine,' I say. 'Just got a bit hot in there.'

'Me too. Why don't we have a shower?'

There are a couple of showers just along the wall and I'm desperate to cool off, but not if it means relinquishing my towel.

'Oh no, I'll have one back in the room.'

I expect him to turn then, but he remains in front of me, just inches away.

My body is still hot from the steam, my face still burning. But at the same time I'm shivering in the cooler air. My internal thermometer is going haywire. Jamie's eyes look even greener against his skin which is pinkened by the heat, and beads of sweat have gathered along his collar bone. I'm hot and cold and burning at the same time.

He steps forward. 'Fran, I need to talk to you.' He's so close I can feel the heat coming off his body. 'I think about you all the time.'

His eyes are boring into mine, making it impossible for me to turn away, and I can hardly breathe.

All of a sudden there's another blast of heat as the steam-room door bursts open behind me. The others pile out and bundle into the shower, a giggling mass of damp hair and lovely smooth skin.

I clutch my towel more tightly around me and look down, conscious of my own mottled feet in the ugly brown rubber shoes.

'Sauna next.' Katy bounds up to me, tossing her long hair so that Jamie and I are sprayed with water.

'Wimps!' she cries, as we flinch.

For a terrible moment, I think that Jamie will come too. The thought of sitting alongside him in the clean, clear heat of the sauna, drowning in sweat, is too much. I am trying to formulate an excuse when Rosie unwittingly rescues me.

'No way, José!' she says, linking one arm through her brother's as if he might be on the verge of escaping somewhere. 'You have way too many duties for that. Get used to it, Jam: your life is going to be nothing but responsibilities and commitments from now on.'

In the sauna with the girls, the mood is subdued. Katy seems suddenly out of sorts. When I'm away from her for any length of time I forget about these mood swings, how she can lurch from up to down in the blink of an eye. She gazes into the distance, frowning. Pip is bent over, inspecting her legs for stray hairs. The ridges on her back are pronounced and remind me of baby teeth pushing under the gums. Unhappiness rises off her like steam.

'What's the matter?' I ask her.

Katy looks over at her sister. 'You might as well tell her,' she says irritably.

'Tell me what?'

Pip glares at her sister, then glances at me before returning to studying her legs.

'I'm pregnant.'

Saturday, 11 a.m.

I'm already regretting my promise not to tell Saul about Pip. In part it's because the childish side of me wants Saul to know I was the one she told first. So often over the years it's been me getting information about the girls secondhand, and Saul puffed up with his news. But mostly it's because of worry – why won't Pip tell me who the father is? She is not the one-night-stand type. I am terrified for her and, selfishly, grief-stricken for myself and this fresh reminder of what I've lost.

The girls were horrified when they discovered I was pregnant.

'Have you completely lost your mind?' demanded Katy over the Sunday lunch I'd invited them both to, specifically so we could break the happy news. 'What if it has something wrong with it? What if it has two heads? The risks at your age are *massive*.'

Pip was more worried about the risks for me. She had a friend whose mother had a stroke in her mid fifties. 'They're sure it's from having kids late in life.' Useless to point out I was still only forty-three, still healthy.

Katy, of course, insisted on putting herself right at the centre of this new, unwelcome development. 'It's a reaction to me leaving and the empty nest,' she told me, authoritatively. 'But you know, even this baby will leave home eventually, and then what? Sooner or later, you have to face up to being alone, you and Dad.'

I spent my time nodding and understanding and soothing and

assuaging, but all the time I kept up an inner monologue to the baby inside me. *They'll come around*, I told it. *They'll get used to the idea.* And above all, *You're wanted. You're so wanted.*

Pip's baby isn't wanted. 'I don't know,' she wailed when I asked her what she was going to do. Pip wishes her baby would go away, like a cyst that disappears overnight.

My dress is hanging on the back of the wardrobe door. It seemed so witty and sophisticated in the shop – sleeveless and low-necked with a twist at the front and an asymmetric hem. At nearly £300 it's the most expensive dress I've ever bought (including my wedding dress – although that proved expensive in other ways). Now, though, as I sit on the edge of the bed, wrapped in yet another towel, the dress looks foolish and inappropriate, its splashes of orange on the navy-blue background nothing but a gaudy, tragic mistake.

'Are you intending to wear it, or just look at it?' asks Saul.

He is irritable because we were so long in the health spa.

'If I'd known Jamie would be there, I'd have come too,' he said crossly when I told him about my morning. 'I thought it would be girls only.'

'You make it sound like he was gate-crashing.'

'Don't be silly. But you could have rung up to the room or something to let me know. I was getting bored here on my own. I'd no idea you'd be so long.'

If there was a degree course in Passive-Aggressiveness, Saul would get a first.

Now he is making a big show of getting ready, bustling about the room attaching cuff links and checking the contents of his wallet. Every now and then, he glances over at me and sighs.

'Aren't you going to put that dress on then? I mean, it cost enough. You might as well get maximum wear out of it!'

Impatience spills out of him.

I know Saul doesn't like the dress. He didn't say so, but he didn't have to.

'Very avant garde!' was his verdict when I brought it home.

'It's a dress, Saul, not a bloody school of philosophical thought.'

It annoys me that it still matters to me what Saul thinks, especially when I'm always so critical of his taste in clothes.

'Would it kill you to wear a colour that isn't black or navy blue?' I asked him a few weeks ago, as he got ready for a dinner party in yet another dark jeans and dark-blue shirt combination.

'Black isn't technically a colour,' was his infuriatingly predictable response.

I used to long to see Saul in different clothes, spending hours in upmarket men's shops choosing chunky jumpers in chocolate brown to match his eyes, or long-sleeved T-shirts in bright jewel colours. Clothes to showcase my handsome husband to the world. At first he'd oblige me by wearing them a couple of times before retiring them to the back of a drawer, but after a while he simply asked for the receipt. 'Who is this man you buy these things for?' he asked the last time I attempted to stage an intervention on his wardrobe. 'Because it isn't me.'

There I go again. Louise says I focus too much on the negative memories of Saul and me, and that I need to shift perspective and start remembering the good times. I have to rewrite my own narrative, she tells me. 'Describe to me a happy memory of you and Saul together,' she said a few weeks ago. 'Go on, close your eyes, and now tell me about the first one that comes to mind. What do you see?'

It took a while for the cogs in my brain to shift into a gear that allowed me access to the past, and even with my eyes shut I felt Saul's intense gaze on me as I began speaking.

'OK. We are sitting in a hot tub under the stars in a villa in southern Spain,' I began. 'It's the first night of a two-week holiday, the girls are already in bed, so they must be pretty young, and Saul and I are sipping chilled Cava, and every now and then we burst out laughing and say, "Oh my God, we're actually here."'

'I remember that,' Saul broke in, excitedly. 'It was the year our house was burgled and all our passports stolen just two days before we were due to fly off. We had to spend the entire day before the holiday queueing with the girls in the passport office trying to get new ones rushed through, and even when the office closed they couldn't tell us whether the passports would definitely be ready the next day.'

'God, remember the stress?' I asked him then. 'Packing for the airport, not knowing whether we'd be able to go or not. Bundling the girls into the car and dashing into the centre of London. You waiting on a double yellow line outside the passport office in Victoria while I shot in to find out if they were there.'

'And your face when you came running out, waving the passports above your head! I'll never forget it. Your smile couldn't have been any bigger.'

'We went straight to Gatwick and just caught our flight,' I explained to Louise, my eyes closed again. 'By the time we arrived in Malaga we were semi-hysterical with relief, but we still had to pick up the hire car and find our way to the villa, so it was only later on that it all began to sink in. We'd made it. We were there. Sitting in that hot tub together, I remember feeling all the stress lifting off me. It was like we were teenagers again, giggling together after getting away with something.'

'We made love,' Saul broke in. 'Do you remember?'

But this was one step too far. My eyes snapped open and the moment was broken.

Now, gazing at my new dress, I'm wishing that, despite all my past swipes at Saul's conservative dress sense, I'd played it safe myself. Something plain and classy. With sleeves. And a hemline that didn't look as though someone's toddler had been let loose with a large pair of scissors.

I go to my case and extract the small bag in which my new underwear resides, wrapped in a layer of tissue paper. I glance over at Saul and furtively crumple up the receipt, then stash it in one of the interior pockets of my case. Saul would be horrified to know that the underwear cost nearly as much as my dress.

When I used to go out to work I had a drawer full of nice underwear. Knowing I had decent pants on gave me an extra layer of confidence. But since Molly, I only wear identical black knickers that I buy in multi-packs and that fade to grey at the first wash.

I wonder if Saul would think it odd if I went into the bathroom to get dressed. If I put on the new blue lacy bra and knickers here, might he not think it's all a show for him and get the wrong idea? Instead, I perch back down on the edge of the bed with my back firmly angled to the window, where Saul is scanning the sky for any hint of inclement weather.

The underwear is deceptive. The outer layers of silk and lace conceal a rigid construction of wires and elastic panelling.

'May I suggest you consider this range over here,' the sales assistant had said, gently steering me away from the wisps of chiffon I'd been rifling idly through and towards another display where the underwear seemed to be standing up stiffly by itself. 'Many ladies appreciate the extra support.'

She'd insisted that I try on the bra, dismissing my protestations that by forty-five I should know what size I was. I'd only just strapped myself into my chosen size when she popped her head uninvited through the curtains.

'See,' I said, eyeing my reflection in the mirror with quiet satis-faction. 'This is perfect.'

'What about those pads?' asked the woman, frowning at my back.

'Which pads?'

'These ones.' She patted a section of flesh behind me where it emerged from the bra strap.

'*Fat back*, that's what she called me,' I exploded down the phone to Pip that evening.

But now, wriggling stealthily into my new underwear in the beige hotel room, trying to keep my movements to a minimum to avoid attracting Saul's attention, I'm grateful for my new, cantilevered undergarments and the way they pull and hoist me into shape.

'Have you seen the price of room service?' asks Saul. He is now standing by the desk in the corner of the room, leafing through the hotel brochure in its padded leatherette cover. '£12.99 for a club sandwich. Who on earth would pay that kind of money?'

Saul is genetically programmed to be on the alert for scams and rip-offs. He is never happier than when he has foiled some real or imagined scheme to take him for a mug.

While he is engrossed in turning over the laminated pages, I slip the foolish dress off its hanger. I step into it and pull it up over my hips, contorting my body to zip it up. There was a time when I would have asked Saul to do that. In fact, there was a time when I wouldn't have had to, because he'd already have leapt up to do it – he always loved to watch me get dressed.

In front of the full-length mirror, I try to summon up some of the excitement I felt when I first tried the dress on, but it's no use. The woman in the mirror is not the woman I had in mind when I handed over my credit card and watched the dress being folded into tissue paper and sealed with dainty, customized tape.

Maybe with the shoes?

I pad over to my case on bare feet, conscious that Saul is now looking at me. But not speaking. Can there be anything more deflating than someone watching you dressed up in new finery and not commenting? Like when you have a major haircut and people pretend not to notice, or say, 'Oh, you've cut your hair,' without saying they like it.

'Are you wearing those shoes?'

I freeze in the middle of the room, the towering blue suede wedge sandals swinging from my right hand.

'Well, obviously I'm wearing these shoes. What's wrong with them?'

'Nothing wrong, *per se*.'

'*Per se*? Who the fuck says *per se*?'

'Clearly I do.' Saul adopts the clipped voice he always uses when I swear. 'All I mean is that those shoes are fun, but they're not really . . .'

'*Appropriate*?' I spit the word out. *Now* he tells me. Now, when we're here and they're all I've brought. 'I'll just wear my flip-flops, shall I?'

I'm angry, and newly flooded with doubt. After twenty-four years of marriage, I'm fluent in Saul subtext. What he means is the shoes are too young.

I'm sitting on the bed, angrily buckling them on to my feet, when a banging on the door announces the arrival of Katy and Pip.

45

'Grrr,' growls Katy when she sees me, making claw gestures in the air. 'My mother the cougar!'

'Is that a compliment?' I ask.

''Course it is,' says Pip.

'Not too mutton-dressed-as-lamb?'

'No way!'

I deliberately don't look at Saul or Katy, so I won't know if they're exchanging meaningful glances.

'What about me?' Katy wants to know. 'Do you like my dress? It's Vivienne Westwood. Cost more than a small house, but it was calling to me. I had to have it.'

Katy's dress is fuchsia-coloured taffeta, with a full skirt and tight-fitting bodice, over which her breasts spill fleshily. Her mouth is a slash of vibrant pink which makes her eyes appear preternaturally blue. She has a tiny fuchsia hat with a veil perched on top of her black hair. Fascinators, they're called, those things. I almost bought one myself – an eccentric construction of feathers and wires in navy blue – but bottled out at the last minute, convinced it would make me look quite ridiculous. Now, looking at Katy's – a witty statement of a thing sitting there on her head – I long for that unbought fascinator with every fibre of my being.

'It's very nice,' I say, and immediately wish I'd been more effusive.

'You look absolutely stunning,' says Saul. 'Both of you.' Then he corrects himself: 'All three of you.'

He stands between his daughters, an arm around each of them.

Pip looks pale in comparison with her sister. She is wearing a sage-green dress she's had for some time. It hangs loosely from her tiny frame, the hard ridge of her collarbone cutting across the thin spaghetti straps.

Worry fizzes inside me. How can she be pregnant when she's just a baby herself?

'You don't look too shabby yourself, Dad,' says Katy, eyeing her father with approval.

Saul has on a navy linen suit he bought in a sale in Italy when we were on holiday once, after a long lunch with one too many glasses of fine chianti. His shirt is crisply white and shows off the deep tan from his all-weather runs. There's not an ounce of fat on him, as he's always telling me. ('Pinch that,' he'll say sometimes, proffering a bicep or a taut stomach. 'Go on. Try.') His face is all planes and angles, the cheeks gently hollowed out. For a brief second I see him as a stranger might see him, a forty-nine-year-old man in peak physical condition, tall and trim, with a full head of dark curls threaded through with grey. A handsome man, that same stranger might conclude. A man who has not let himself go.

'Are we ready?' he asks now, looking over at me.

'Hold your horses. I still haven't done my make-up.'

I head for the bathroom, self-conscious in my over-high shoes. Saul's sigh follows me across the room.

'Do hurry up, Fran. The church is about twenty minutes away, apparently – more if we get lost, which we're bound to. All the roads around here look the same. We don't want to be late.'

Saul is never late to anything. I've lost count of the times we've turned up for parties or dinners and found the hostess still drying her hair, or the host just about to go and shave; the hours waiting in airport departure lounges after checking in too early.

As I start the whole laborious make-up process again, I hear Saul complaining to the girls.

'I don't know what she does in there. She never used to take so long to get ready.'

He waits by the door with our beautiful daughters, while alone in the bathroom I smear and smudge and rub and paint and make those insane faces I remember my mother making, folding lips over teeth to blot lipstick, looking to the heavens to apply mascara, sucking in my cheeks for the blusher.

The faces of women trying hard not to be who they are.

Saturday, 12 p.m.

Stepping out of the air-conditioned hotel lobby, I slam into the heat as if it's something solid. The towering wedge heels make me feel as if I'm walking with bricks strapped to my feet, and I grab on to Pip's arm for balance as we make our way to the car park.

'I'm so worried about you,' I say, low enough that Saul and Katy in front of us won't hear.

She puts her hand over mine and squeezes. 'I'm worried about me, too, Mum,' she says in a small, sad voice. 'But I don't want to talk about it now. I just want to forget about it this weekend. OK?'

It's not OK, but I nod, because what else can I do, and we continue to inch our way across the steaming tarmac. The hotel is a mid-sized, mid-range, mid-everything type of affair, its plaster facade painted that same distinctive honey colour as all the old stone buildings around here, so it is impossible to guess its real age. It has ivy growing up the walls in a slightly over-organized way, and an arched portico around the main entrance, which is flanked by two perfectly shaped ornamental trees in huge metallic pots. The car park is full of shiny Audis and 4×4s. It's the sort of place well-to-do people from neighbouring villages probably come for anniversaries and birthdays.

Not like that other hotel – that first one. It was not even a hotel really, but a jumped-up pub with rooms above and a fruit machine in the tiny lobby. 'Stay in the car until I call you,' he'd said, lust fighting with fear in his face. Of course that's something I only recognize with hindsight. At sixteen you don't expect to see fear on an adult's face. And I was still young enough to believe lust was just a manifestation of love.

I detect the hand of Lynn in the choice of hotel and am surprised. The Lucy I've created in my head would have very specific ideas about where she'd want her wedding reception to be. Have I misjudged her? I worry I'm becoming too unforgiving. I worry I'm turning into my mother.

'Hurry up!' Katy is leaning against Saul's dark-green Subaru, like a luridly coloured butterfly perched on a leaf. 'What were you talking about anyway?' she asks as we draw closer.

'Nothing,' says Pip.

Saul is anxious to be off. He has folded out the map of the area he insisted on buying, even though we have the Sat Nav. 'I like to see it laid out, so I get a feel for the geography of a place,' he'd said.

The truth is, Saul doesn't fully trust his gadgetry. The truth is, he doesn't really trust anything.

All of a sudden there's a kerfuffle at the hotel entrance.

'Wait!'

A small figure in sunflower yellow, with a huge-brimmed hat and skyscraper shoes, is advancing unsteadily through the car park towards us.

'Wait for me!'

Rosie is pink-faced and slightly breathless by the time she arrives.

'I'm so glad you're still here. I've been totally abandoned. I thought I was going to have to *walk*! In *these*!'

She is gesturing to her vertiginous shoes, which are made of sunflower-yellow suede with numerous straps criss-crossing her narrow little feet like a golden cage. Suddenly she spies Katy's dress.

'Oh my *God*! Is that Vivienne Westwood? I might actually have to kill you.'

Katy holds out the skirt of her dress and does a twirl like a little

girl. I remember her doing the same aged four in her school uniform on the first day of primary school, and again in a pink tutu
before her first ballet class. An unseen hand squeezes my heart like
an old dishcloth.

Saul is discomfited. 'Do you mean you need a lift to the church,
Rosie?' he asks, dubiously. 'Only, we've just got the two seatbelts
in the back, so I'm not insured to take you.'

'Oh, for goodness' sake, Dad. Live dangerously,' says Katy,
pushing Rosie in through the back door and climbing in after her.
Pip goes around to the other side.

'Where are your Mum and Dad?' I ask Rosie. 'And Jamie?'

My voice dries up on the last syllable of his name.

'Oh my days, you wouldn't *believe* the fuss they were making.'
Rosie rolls her brown eyes theatrically. 'They expected me to get
ready in like a nano-second and Mum got all cross when I got my
curlers out of my bag and started ranting about how she didn't
campaign for women's rights at university in the 1970s so that
her daughter could sit there with metal things in her hair. Yadda,
yadda, yadda. So then I showed her the Spanx and she nearly went
apoplectic. She said why didn't she just lace me into a corset like
Scarlet O'Hara and be done with it? I said that sounded like a
great idea and she completely lost it.'

'She's obviously stressed about the wedding.'

As we pull out of the car park, there's much squealing and giggling
from the back. Katy and Rosie – not natural allies, both being
too fond of the limelight – seem determined to forge a friendship.
Katy was always like this, forcing intimacy on new acquaintances
like an unwanted gift, then falling out with them over something and nothing. It was heartbreaking to see her bewilderment
when Annabel or Jessica or Ameera stopped returning her calls or
partnering her in science.

'Jammy is all over the place,' Rosie says.

I keep my eyes fixed on the windscreen, beyond which the winding country road unfurls like a green-edged ribbon. I feel my face
overheating and turn up the air-conditioning and fan myself with
Saul's map.

'Hot flush?' asks Saul, and chuckles. He doesn't realize we've gone past the point where such remarks are funny.

'What's up with him?' Pip asks. 'Wedding nerves?'

'I guess so,' says Rosie. 'Although he didn't seem nervous last night, or when we got up. Just since breakfast.'

My stomach jolts, and I have the strangest idea that Rosie is staring at me while she's saying this, her eyes burning holes through the back of the car seat, but when I glance in the rear-view mirror she's looking down, brushing at a speck of something on her dress.

Katy and Rosie begin talking about Liam, Jamie's best man – a web designer he's known since school whom Rosie describes as a 'dork'. I gaze out of the window, trying to clear my mind, or at least force it along a different track.

Inevitably, with Pip sitting behind me, incubating her secrets inside her, my thoughts turn again to Molly. For the first three months, I was on constant alert for things going wrong. Every stomach pang was the start of a miscarriage, the faintest twinge of nausea a sign that the baby wasn't thriving. When I went to the loo, I searched for tell-tale signs: streaks of blood that would signal the end of my foolishness.

Incredibly, it didn't happen. The nausea stopped and all of a sudden I wasn't tired any more, but filled with a fierce energy that saw me spending whole mornings in Ikea buying plastic storage boxes with coloured lids in which to store the detritus that had built up over the years in the little box-room – old school reports, yellowing bills, half-sewn sock puppets with black thread eyes, Saul's Padi licence, a whole forgotten folder of badly drawn nudes from my six-month life-drawing course.

My hair was thick and shiny, my skin positively glowed. I was ripe with purpose.

Where is that me now, I wonder? The one who strode purposefully around Ikea and efficiently sorted memories into boxes, kneeling for hours on the carpet in the spare room? The one who hummed along to the *Archers* theme tune as she cooked complicated dishes and surfed baby sites on the internet as furtively as porn, shutting them down the second Saul's key sounded in the lock?

Once I caught Saul staring at me strangely as I decanted dried pasta into specially bought jars.

'You're . . . different,' he said eventually.

'Different?'

He shrugged. 'I can't explain it. You're more . . . present.'

Funny to think that just two years separate that other, *present* me from the one who sits here in the front seat, so swollen with secrets I hardly dare open the window for fear of floating out and away, like a giant balloon.

'At the next junction, turn left,' says the Sat Nav woman.

Saul doesn't seem convinced. That's the problem when your instinct is to trust nobody but yourself. 'I'm sure if I go straight on it's more direct.'

He presses his lips together in deliberation before crossing straight over the junction, his face grimly set, hands stiff on the wheel, as if embarking on something perilous.

'Turn left,' says the woman. And again, emphatically, 'Turn left.'

'I hate her,' says Katy suddenly. 'She's so *bossy*!'

When we arrive at the church, there's already a line of cars strung out like bunting along the grass verge of the country lanes on either side of the little crossroads.

'Drop us off at the door,' Katy insists. 'We can't possibly walk in these shoes.'

Saul frowns slightly. I think he has been relishing the idea of walking into the church flanked by lovely young women. Still, he pulls up dutifully beside the path leading to the church, and there's a sudden flurry of activity in the back of the car – bags being opened, compacts extracted, lipstick refreshed, hair quickly brushed.

'I'll stay in the car and walk in with you,' I say, and am rewarded by a smile of gratitude.

'Thanks, darling,' says Saul, putting his hand on my knee.

I feel guilty then. Saul thinks I am staying for him, as a gesture of solidarity, but really I'm staying because I want to put off the moment when I walk into the church.

Because inside the church is Jamie.

Saturday, 1 p.m.

'Jammy looks nervous,' whispers Katy, leaning across her sister. We are sitting in a pew on the left-hand side of the church, midway back. Saul is on my left, Pip on my right and Katy at the far end, from where she is keeping up a running commentary as we await the arrival of the bride.

The thick stone walls of the quaint village church keep out the worst of the heat, but still the air sticks to my skin and I fan myself with the Order of Service booklet, on the cover of which Jamie's face smiles out next to that of a young blonde woman. I haven't let myself examine that photograph properly. I worry my face might give me away.

While Pip cranes to get a better look at Jamie's reported display of nerves, I find myself lost in my own reminiscences. Funny how weddings do that, catapulting us back in time to our earlier, wider-eyed selves.

Even as a teenager, I was never a big romantic. What I really wanted, now I look back on it, was to be rescued, whisked away from my dysfunctional family. I wanted rescuing from my mother's black moods that lasted for days on end, when she'd lie on her side, staring at the wall, while my brother and I tiptoed around her; and I wanted rescuing from my father's reproachful, disappointed eyes. He was a man who seldom strayed from the path of least resistance. Over the years when he lived with my mother, he developed an impressive arsenal of sighs and gestures of resignation. 'Your father is a saint,' people were forever informing me, and he would look abashed and shrug and say, 'What can you do?'

Now that I'm older than he was then, I realize my father must have been hugely frustrated. He'd married for love, but then found himself unequal to the demands that love placed upon him. Life was being lived somewhere else, while he padded softly around his wife in socks. He attended to our basic needs – cooking us meals (always the same dish on the same day of the week), ferrying us to doctors' appointments and piano lessons. But we always suspected there was somewhere else he really ought to be, something else he needed to be doing.

Even when my mother emerged from her moods, appearing suddenly on the stairs like the ghost of someone we used to know, things didn't improve. There was a madness about her then, a zealousness that made my chest tighten. She and my father argued in those phases: high-pitched intense exchanges coming up through the floorboards, marked by sudden alarming exclamations and the thudding disarrangement of furniture and utensils. She was forever coming up with impromptu plans, turning up at school in the middle of the day to take my brother and me off for a day-trip or to lunch in a ridiculously expensive London hotel. 'Isn't this *fun?*' she'd say, staring right through us, as if we were made of glass. We'd nod miserably, but it wasn't fun. I was the type of child who liked to be anonymous and keep my head down. Being called out of my lesson to find my mother standing impatiently in the head's office, car keys jangling, after spinning another story about ill relatives that no one was buying, was torture to me.

'There's so little joy in you, Francesca,' she said once, after we returned in stony silence from one of these interminable outings. And my father sighed heavily, upset with me for upsetting her.

After one of these episodes, her inevitable slide back into blackness would come almost as a relief.

'Look!' Katy hisses, interrupting my train of thought. 'Jammy's texting someone! Practically at the altar! Oh my God!'

'Relax,' says Pip. 'It'll just be Lucy. He'll be finding out where she is.'

At my feet, my handbag begins to vibrate.

I stare rigidly ahead, not looking either at the front of the church, where he is standing, or at my bag, which thankfully stops buzzing after a few seconds. I refuse to think about him, or what message he might have sent. This works until I feel my bag begin to vibrate again. For a few seconds, I can't breathe.

Then I force myself to calm down. Maybe it wasn't him, after all. Maybe he was texting Lucy at the same time as a message happened to come through on my phone. Two messages. It's possible. Think about something else. Anything else. Back to my childhood then. Was it really as awful as I remember?

There were good times, I think. When my mother's moods were stable, or she was taking her medication regularly without complaint, or my father, a lab technician who wrote unintelligible scientific features in his spare time, sold a piece to one of the specialist journals he subscribed to, there were family outings to the cinema, or even bowling. We had a holiday once in Brittany, where we rented a cottage near the sea and the sun shone, and we basked in the glow of our parents' approval and made friends with another family in a neighbouring house. But those occasions were so far apart as to stand out in my mind like jewels partly sunken in a sea of mud.

I escaped into an elaborately constructed fantasy world, or to friends' houses. Very rarely did I invite people home. 'It feels a bit like being at the dentist,' my friend Jade once said after a rare sleepover at mine. At the time I'd been mystified, wondering whether it was our dining chairs that looked like dentists' ones or the lacklustre prints on the walls. But later I decided what she meant was that it was like a waiting room. Our house felt as if we were all waiting for something to happen – we had no idea what it was, just that it was unlikely to be good.

I'm still thinking about my mother as the wedding music starts up, and we all get to our feet, turning as one to watch the bride walk down the aisle, on her mother's arm. ('How very modern!'

exclaims Christine, the old lady from the breakfast table, who is sitting in the row behind us.)

Lucy's mother is determinedly youthful-looking. Hair artfully sun-streaked, slim figure showcased in a figure-hugging, knee-length silver sheath dress and delicate silver strappy sandals. One of her brown, well-toned arms sports a plethora of dainty silver bangles which clink as she passes; the other is linked through her daughter's arm. Her smile fissures across her tightly smoothed face like crackle-glaze, and her expression is a fierce mixture of joy and pride, with an added dash of something akin to triumph. I stare at Lucy's mother for what feels like a very long time, noticing the fine wisps of baby hair around the parting and the way the little toe curls over its neighbours in the high shoes. Because the longer I look at Lucy's mother, the longer I can put off having to look at Lucy.

But everyone around me is oohing and aahing and cameras are being discreetly raised, the clicking of the shutters coinciding with the clicking of the women's heels as they make their slow progress down the aisle.

Up ahead I can see Jamie half-turned to watch his bride-to-be and my stupid heart splits open like a coconut at the rapture on his face. So then I have no choice but to look at her too.

And I am lost.

White-blonde hair falls loosely around her shoulders, held in place by a delicate wreath of interwoven daisies. A slim, almost boyish body, all long limbs and racehorse grace, setting off a long, simple white dress cut on the bias. Her face isn't conventionally pretty. Taken individually, none of her features would stand out – pale-blue eyes set slightly too close together, a long, narrow nose over a mouth whose lips are a little on the thin side. But together there is something magical about the configuration. She is luminous.

Saul takes hold of my left hand and squeezes. I glance over and am surprised to see his eyes filmy with tears.

'Remember ours?' he whispers.

I don't want to think about my own wedding. It feels oddly inappropriate while standing here in the cast-off glow of someone else's love story. Besides, the woman who stood at the front of Guildford registry office in borrowed shoes, holding Saul's hands in hers and looking into his brown eyes while making her vows (wondering, even then, *Is this right? Am I sure?*) isn't me, just someone I used to know well but lost touch with along the way.

I glance at Lynn, who is in the front row, wearing a nude-coloured linen dress, already badly creased. She is looking round, so I can see the smile that strains at the corners of her mouth, even while her eyes look stricken and a tear slowly snakes down her cheek.

I look quickly away, as if I have seen something I shouldn't have. Leaning down to get a tissue from my bag, I see my phone flashing. Keeping it hidden in the pocket, I slide it on. There are two messages in my inbox. One is from Jamie, as I knew it would be. The other is 'unknown'. The sound of my own swallowing is deafening as I click on both messages in quick succession. The first contains just one letter: 'x'. As I read the second, the air seems suddenly to go out of the church.

Leave him alone, it says. I glance around, a hard lump of fear lodged like a boiled sweet in my throat. My eyes scan the church, but everyone seems to be doing exactly what they're supposed to be, with their eyes on either the expectant groom or the bride. No one is furtively looking down at their laps, or sneaking glances at me to gauge my reaction.

Maybe the text isn't meant for me. Maybe someone has the wrong number and the real target of their intimidation is blithely going about their business, with a phone number one crucial digit away from mine. I switch off my phone and zip up my bag.

While the vicar talks about the nature of marriage and love, I try to put the messages from my mind. I am distracted by a faint noise to my right, an involuntary exhalation of breath, and to my surprise I realize that Pip is crying, her shoulders silently heaving.

I put my hand on her arm, shocked once again at its frailty. Pip has always worn her anxieties externally like a badge, inner turmoil revealed not by what she says or does, but by her shrinking frame and jutting shoulder blades. I'm transported back a decade to the dreaded Exam Years, when she wallpapered her room with

Post-it notes bearing dates and formulas and French verbs, and shut herself away, emerging at meal times, blinking as if unsure where she was, to push her food around her plate, hoping that by disarranging it she might fool me into imagining some of it had been consumed.

'She's got Swotorexia,' Katy informed us, leaning over the table to swipe extra roast potatoes from her sister's untouched plate. 'All her lot have it.'

By 'her lot' she meant the grafters, the girls who stayed up into the night revising rather than hanging out with boys. The ones who were disappointed with themselves when they got an A instead of an A*.

She grew out of it, thank God. But she's never far away, that miserable teenage girl who slouched around the house in bulky layers of jumpers and hoodies so we wouldn't notice her shrinking body.

She glances across at me now, and my heart shatters like eggshell. I put my arm around her and she leans her head into me, although her body remains stiff and rigid as if it's a completely separate entity.

One of Jamie and Lucy's friends has stood up to give a reading. It's something deeply traditional – the one from Corinthians about the greatest of these being love. I'm surprised at the conservatism of the choice: I'd expected something more challenging and unconventional. Jamie and Lucy are standing at the altar. Over the shoulder of the man in front, I can see that one of Lucy's legs is quivering as if in spasm. She is nervous, I realize, and this again comes as a shock. I'd imagined her to be invincible. Jamie is standing facing her. He glances across and catches my eye, and a jolt goes through me. We hold each other's gaze so long it seems as if everyone must be wondering what is going on. I look away, my cheeks burning, and when I look back Jamie once again has his face bent towards Lucy.

A woman in the second row, behind Lynn and Max, has a baby strapped to her chest, and a toddler next to her. The little girl has brown hair in bunches that stick straight out of her head like cocktail sticks in an orange and is already squirming restlessly in her seat. She is a little older than Molly would be now, I decide. Surprisingly, it comforts me to seek out children of a similar age. Seeing them helps me envisage my own daughter, the ghost child growing alongside these unknown infants like a photographic negative.

Saul didn't know whether to be embarrassed about my pregnancy or proud. It was, after all, a mark of his continued virility, a sign that his sperm, like him, were in the peak of physical condition, but then again there were the jokes, and the raised eyebrows and the 'rather you than me's. To give him credit, he never once let on that it hadn't been a joint decision – well, not in my hearing, anyway – but still I sensed as I got larger that he found the whole thing a little embarrassing.

'You are happy about it now, aren't you?' I asked him as we drove home from the twenty-week scan, me gazing damp-eyed at the printout of the black swirly image labelled Baby Friedman.

'Course,' he'd replied, taking his hand briefly off the wheel to squeeze my leg. Then he added, 'Which is just as well, seeing as you'd have done it anyway.'

The toddler with the bunches is starting to fidget properly now. Her mother leans down stiffly to pick up a bag the size of a small car, one hand shielding the sleeping baby in the pouch over her chest. After rummaging around in the bag, she extracts a packet of raisins. The little girl eyes them doubtfully. She was clearly hoping for something of higher value. She pops them into her mouth, one after the other, considering her options.

Pip shifts her head on my shoulder, leaving a damp patch where her tears have soaked through the silk fabric of my dress. I glance over and notice that Katy, on Pip's other side, has taken her older sister's hand and is holding it tight in both of hers, just as Saul is still clasping mine. For a moment, as we sit like this forming a chain of Friedmans inextricably linked together, I feel completely content. If we could just stay here, I think, not moving, not speaking, just being close to each other, we would be a perfectly happy family.

Saturday, 2 p.m.

We emerge into the sunlit churchyard like children released from school at the end of the day, all the pent-up emotion and exhilaration of the last hour erupting in a cacophony of laughter, frenzied greetings of old acquaintances only just encountered, and exclamations. 'So beautiful!', 'That dress!', 'Is my mascara all down my face?'

Saul has his arm around my shoulders. It feels inanimate and heavy in the stultifying heat, like a fur stole.

'I'm surprised Pip was so overcome,' he is saying. 'Usually it's Katy who goes in for the histrionics. Is she OK, do you think?'

For a moment, I'm tempted to tell him. Already Pip's secret has grown uncomfortable inside me. I long to be rid of it, to take it out and show it to Saul so we can both turn it over in our hands, inspecting it from all angles, holding it up to the light. Instead I shrug, the movement dislodging his arm from my shoulders.

'You know what weddings are like for bringing out the Kate Winslet in everyone.'

Saul smiles at the private joke I have given him like a small present. Ever since we watched the actress picking up an award and unable to speak for sobbing, her name has become a kind of catchphrase between us.

'Not going to do a Kate, are you, darling?' Saul said four months ago, when I opened the wedding invitation – *James, son of Lynn and Maxwell Irving, to Lucy, daughter of Madeleine Lesoer* – and my eyes were instantly blinded by tears.

There is a sudden murmuring and bustling around the church doors; women are reaching into their handbags and extracting little bags of confetti. The small girl I saw earlier has found a slightly older girl to play with and the two of them are charging in and out of guests' legs in their stiff, wide-skirted dresses. Now there's a flash of white and all the arms go up at once, confetti released like butterflies into the still air.

As the crowd around the doorway parts to let the couple through, I catch sight of Jamie's face lit up from within and something inside me tears apart like a worn pillowcase.

Outside in the pretty green churchyard, the guests have gathered into little knots, dotted around in their finery like posies of brightly coloured flowers. By the church doors, photos are now being taken. Jamie and Lucy are standing together, flanked by Max and Lynn on one side and Lucy's mother on the other.

Rosie, who has been busy talking to someone, comes hurrying up to barge in between her parents and her brother.

'Why didn't you tell me it was a family photo?' she exclaims, outraged.

I turn away to say something to Katy and find myself staring at her back as she talks animatedly into her mobile phone. 'How hard can it be?' she is asking someone – Rob, I assume. 'There are a gazillion wedding cards out there. All I'm saying is not too schmaltzy. How does that count as being demanding?'

I swap glances with Pip, who has recovered from her crying fit and is telling Saul about a case she has been working on. I still find it hard to believe my daughter is a trainee barrister, holding her own in a world I know nothing about. Saul is thrilled. 'She will have a job for life,' he says, which always makes me think of one of those heavy-duty supermarket bags. Bags for life, they're called. (As if you might want a plastic bag that could outlast you. *Bury me with my bag*, you might say.) But he's right. Pip won't have to know those dead midweek afternoons. She will always have a purpose. But, oh! With a jolt I remember that she's pregnant. What will happen to all her years of hard work now?

The little girl with bunches trips trying to run after her older new friend. For a second there is utter silence, while she decides how much it hurts, the air reverberating with expectation. When the wail comes, it is sharp and urgent. Suddenly something occurs to me. Of course! *I* will look after Pip's baby.

Everything happens for a reason.

Oh God, now I'm turning into one of *them*.

I'm sickened at the speed with which my imagination has slotted this unknown other child into Molly's place, as if she was an expired debit card.

It's interesting how people react to you losing a baby when you're in your forties. The sympathy is there, of course, but it's tempered. Having two healthy twenty-something daughters mitigated against me, limiting my entitlement to grief. 'The girls must be such a comfort to you,' people said. Or, 'At least you still have your daughters.'

Only one friend, a reception teacher from school, said the thing I suspect they were all thinking. And she isn't a friend any more. 'It must be a relief though, in a way.'

Those were her actual words. *A relief.*

'Fran! Pip! Katy!'

A shout has gone up, rising above the gradually subsiding sobs of the bunch-haired toddler, who is now clutching a raw carrot her mother has unearthed from the depths of her humungous bag.

'Fran! Pip! Katy! Come on!'

I turn to see Jamie waving at us, in his grey suit with the green tie that matches his eyes. Quickly I look away again, pretending not to have noticed.

'Come on, Mum.' Katy has hold of my arm and is propelling me towards the church steps. 'We're being requested!'

'I hate having my photo taken,' Pip protests. 'I always look like a serial killer.'

'I've never seen anyone who looks less like a serial killer,' says Jamie, laughing. 'What's your modus operandi, Pip? Do you *nice* people to death?'

The photographer arranges our little group with Jamie and Katy at the centre. I can tell from his face that he is already a little bit in love with Katy. And I can tell from hers that she knows this very well.

'Lady in pink, would you just move forward, and turn slightly towards the groom?' he asks, positioning her to the fore of the photo.

She grabs Jamie's arm, looking up at him in mock adoration, all blue eyes and dimples and tumbling black curls.

'Now if lady in green would stand on the groom's other side, with mum on the far right . . .'

'No, I want Fran to stand by me.' Jamie leans around Katy and takes my hand, pulling me so that I am on his other side, with Pip on the step in front. My palm burns where his fingers are. 'There. That's better, don't you think?'

Judging from the photographer's face, he clearly doesn't think, but he stays silent. I'm conscious of Jamie's arm around my back, his hand circling my waist.

'You look lovely,' he whispers.

'So do you,' I reply. 'Both of you,' I add hotly. 'Lucy's beautiful.'

I look around for Saul – he should be here in the photograph, too. My eyes scan the colourful knots of people in the churchyard until they alight on him chatting to the father of the bunch-haired child, a bearded man who has taken off his jacket to reveal a loud Hawaiian shirt. I wave to get Saul's attention and beckon him over.

He smiles, but shakes his head.

He knows. It hits me all at once. Saul knows about Jamie, or about the job in Spain, or the strange texts. Why else would he be hanging back? Saul loves having his photo taken. He says if he was on *Desert Island Discs* his one luxury item would be a picture with him in it. So he could remind himself that he's real, he says, not because he's vain.

'Say cheese,' the photographer commands.

'The trick is to smile with your eyes, apparently,' says Pip, facing the front so her words carry outwards.

'Like this?' Katy leans in front of Jamie, widening her eyes manically.

Lynn materializes by the photographer's side. She looks stressed. Her cheeks are the pink of freshly boiled lobster and her pale eyes are so watery it seems as though they might at any moment be washed entirely away, leaving her face as smooth as a bar of soap.

'Have you finished?' She directs her question to Jamie, as if the rest of us were inanimate props. 'Only we've got loads more photos to do and the reception starts at three.'

'We're nearly done,' says Jamie. 'Just one of Fran and me now.'

He is addressing the photographer, so he misses the look that flashes across Lynn's face. But I see it, and my cheeks flame as I stand woodenly, like something whittled.

The second I hear the click of the camera, I pull away, but my path is blocked by Lucy and her mother.

'Oh my *God*!'

Up close, Lucy's luminosity is almost uncomfortable. Like a bulb with too high a wattage. She looks as if she could burn me.

'You're Fran, right? I am, like, so fucking psyched to meet you at last.'

Is she speaking in tongues?

'*Lucy*!'

Her mother is mock-admonishing her daughter for her language, while at the same time staring rapturously at her as if trying to memorize her for a test.

I stick out my hand awkwardly, only to find it crushed against Maddie's alarmingly firm bosom as she leans in for a hug. 'Isn't it the most fabulous day?'

I agree that it is certainly the most fabulous day.

'Jam's told me so much about you – about all of you,' says Lucy. 'I could practically do an A level in you Friedmans.' She has stepped close to Jamie and is slipping her hands underneath his jacket, while all the time beaming her megawatt smile in my direction.

Jamie distractedly kisses the top of her head, and a skewer passes right through me.

'Are you having a lovely day?' My voice is prissy.

'I'm having the best fucking day.'

'*Lucy!*'

Maddie turns to me and shrugs theatrically in a 'what can you do?' type of way. 'Please don't judge me, Fran, for bringing up such a little guttermouth. She didn't get it from me.'

'Mum – you liar!'

'Oh, all right, she did get it from me. But I'm trying to mend my ways, aren't I, darling?'

'If you say so. Cunt!'

'*LUCY!*'

'It was a *joke!*'

Suddenly Lucy and her mother are convulsed with laughter. They hang on to each other, bent over double.

'I'm s-sorry,' gasps Lucy when she can speak. 'I think it's all the stress of the day, it's given me late-onset Tourettes.'

I watch them, a smile slapped on to my face like a reduced sticker. 'Must get back to Saul,' I mumble, striding off without waiting for a response.

Saul is still talking to the man in the Hawaiian shirt. Now I'm close to him I see he has a ponytail to match his beard. His wife is hovering near by. I ignore the baby strapped to her chest and focus instead on her enormous bag, out of which a packet of rice-cakes pokes unenticingly.

'His name is Bart,' Saul whispers, after finally tearing himself away. 'Can you believe that?'

'Like in *The Simpsons*?' I say.

'Exactly. And he asked me if I knew where he could get some drugs.'

Saul looks thrilled with himself.

'*You?* Are you sure he didn't mean Paracetamol, or Calpol or something?'

'No, he specified cocaine. And he said not to tell his wife.'

Saul is clearly loving this new image of himself as the sort of man who might know the best source of quality Class As, even though, to my certain knowledge, the last time he took drugs was in the mid nineties, when we shared a mysterious blue pill generously donated by a friend, and Saul spent the entire night convinced he was having a heart attack and pressing strangers' hands to his chest to feel his heart rate. Of course, that was in the pre-Marathon Man days, when his body wasn't yet a temple.

'I've just met Lucy.'

I intend my voice to be expressionless, but instead the name comes out tied to a laugh, making me sound incredulous – as if her being Lucy was the height of improbability and preposterousness.

'Lovely girl,' says Saul.

'Yes. Absolutely. But don't you think she seems a bit . . . full on?' I venture.

'Vivacious. There's nothing wrong with that.'

Again I hear my mother. *You have so little joy in you, Francesca.*

Katy and Pip have been chatting to various guests. I'm surprised how many people they know here, but I've forgotten how huge your social circle can be at that age. Katy had ninety-two Facebook posts on her last birthday. She showed them to me, scrolling interminably down. So many exclamation marks and smiley faces and rows and rows of xx's.

'I've just been propositioned for drugs!' Saul crows to them as we regroup.

The girls are agog and immediately demand to know who. Saul points out the pony-tailed man in the Hawaiian shirt.

'Oh, Bart,' says Katy, dismissively. 'He's a tosser.'

'Bart?' says Pip. 'As in *The Simpsons?*'

'It's his wife I feel sorry for,' says Katy, in the tone of one who knows. 'Every time they go out he disappears and she spends the whole time looking for him. Trailing round with all those snotty kids.'

'Only two, surely, and not so snotty . . .'

'Don't make excuses for him, Mum. He's a wanker, and she's a doormat.'

Lynn appears by Katy's shoulder, pink and slightly damp, her helmet head melting in the sun. 'Come along, come along. No time for pleasantries!' she says, making a brave stab at jolliness. 'The day is still young, even if I'm not!'

We smile dutifully and start to gather our things. In the corner of my vision the bunch-haired toddler, seeing her mother purposefully packing up her bag, makes a last dash for freedom.

'Bart?' I hear the woman cry faintly. 'Bart?'

All around us, guests are starting to drift towards their cars, brightly coloured petals caught on a listless breeze.

Saturday, 3 p.m.

'He's married, Mum.'
        'Ah.'
Pip's face, reflected in the mirror, is flushed.

'I know it sounds sordid, but it's not. We love each other. He says he's never felt like this, he didn't know it was possible to feel like this. And of course that makes him feel awful about his wife, because he's such a good person and he really loves her, it's just—'

'He's not *in* love with her.'

Pip glances over sharply as I finish her sentence for her. We are in the toilets in the 'orangery' in the grounds of our hotel, where the reception is being held – essentially a huge greenhouse filled with tables and exotic plants. All the windows and French doors are open, but it's still like a sauna – even the curly writing on the menu cards with which guests are fanning themselves seems to be wilting in the heat. The coolness of the dark, windowless toilets is a welcome relief and Pip and I have lingered, something about the occasion or the tropical heat or the glass of champagne on arrival making her uncharacteristically forthcoming.

'I know you probably think all married men say that, but he's different. *We're* different.'

'Darling, everyone thinks they're different.'

'You don't understand. We talk for hours every day. First thing in the morning I have an email from him to wake up to, and he calls me to talk me through my walk to work. When I was ill, he came in his lunch break to bring me soup from the deli, and when I drank too much the first time we went out because I was so nervous and was sick on the kerb, he sat beside me and rubbed my back. He is not just some married man.'

Useless to tell her no one is ever just some married man.

Before I can stop them, my thoughts peel back the last three decades like stage scenery and I'm sixteen again – and on the verge of meeting David. Until then, the only married man I'd known was my father and I'd imagined they were all like him – padding around their wives in socks and sighing a lot.

By this time, my mother had seen a new consultant and been given pioneering drugs which propelled her, glassy-eyed, out into the world, her face set to an alarming default smile that repelled all surprises, good and bad. Part of her treatment was twice-weekly in-depth therapy that saw her seeking me out in the early mornings to shake me awake and ask, had she been a terrible mother, had she ruined my life? These two new mothers – the one who was filled with angst about her shortcomings, and the plastic one with her plastic smile – were worse in a way than the one who lay with her face to the wall.

My mother's miraculous, pharmaceutically generated resurrection drove me to spend ever longer periods away from home. I joined every after-school society, not because I enjoyed debating or badminton or chess, but just to delay the inevitable return home. I lurked in the library until the librarian snapped shut the overdue fines tin, signalling closing time. Above all, I loitered at the house of my best friend, Jade.

Jade was actually Jane, but insisted on being called Jade in the manner of the time. The bleak 1970s were populated with plainly named children who believed being called something unusual was a shortcut out of the repressive brownness of life then. Looking back, everything about that decade seems brown, from the cover my parents bought for their very first duvet to the flared cords and scratchy jumpers we uniformly wore, and the rubbish-strewn streets. Now, of course, when every other child is called Apple or

Sunshine or Storm or Blue, children have to look for other ways to stand out from their surroundings, but to us Jade was the height of exoticism, a name that could transcend Reading, as we both longed to do.

Jade's family was everything mine wasn't. For a start, there were so many children. Now, all these years later, I can't remember how many brothers and sisters Jade had. Some of them lived at home, some didn't. But there were always extra people in the house as well: boyfriends and girlfriends, cousins, small children who would be there one week, playing in the garden on a rusty swingball set, and gone the next.

'Catholics,' my father said once, after he'd come to pick me up from her house, as if he was identifying a life-form in the lab.

While my house was in the suburbs, a bus-ride away from civilization, Jade lived thrillingly near the centre of town, in a shabby, woefully underheated Victorian terrace, where on winter evenings you could hardly hear her little portable television for the sound of the wind whistling through the cracks in the wooden window-frames.

While my parents seemed largely relieved by my absence and rarely questioned it, Jade's were too distracted to notice I was there.

'Hello, Fran, it's lovely to see you,' Jade's mother would greet me at the door. 'You'll be here to see our Jane . . . or is it our Karen you're after?'

'Sometimes I think she sees us all as one big joined-up child,' Jade said once, 'with lots of different heads.'

As Jade shared a room with her much younger sisters, there was never anywhere to go to be on our own, so we'd often sit outside on her front step, which is where we first met David.

David was different.

In Reading in the early 1980s, anyone who read novels, or travelled further than Alicante, or wore clothes that didn't come from the high street, was different. Just by dint of walking past Jade's front step in the middle of the afternoon, when all other men of his age were safely ensconced in their offices with their suit jackets hung over the backs of their chairs, David was remarkable. Add to that the fact that he always wore faded Levi's with either a white T-shirt or a black polo neck that set off his sweep of blond hair and diamond stud earring, and it was enough to capture the attention of two bored and impressionable teenage girls.

The first couple of times he walked past, he smiled. Those two smiles occupied hours of our time as we dissected and analysed them, subjecting them to one fanciful interpretation after another. The third time, he had a small boy on his shoulders and stopped to chat. He'd just moved in at the top of the road, he said. He and his son, Lennie. Named after Leonard Cohen, had we heard of him? We hadn't. But the very next afternoon we went to the record shop in the centre of town and listened on headphones to two whole albums, rhapsodizing about the lyrics, the poetry, the voice. We didn't understand a word of it, of course, but we absolutely believed that David did. David, we decided, was steeped in poetry and tragedy. A widower, we thought, or a maltreated divorcé.

The next time he came past, we discussed the famous Leonard Cohen song 'Suzanne', tossing it casually into the conversation as if we'd been listening to it for years, and David asked how old we were and said we seemed far more mature than sixteen. Then he asked if we'd be interested in babysitting so he and his wife could go out. Oh, hadn't he mentioned his wife?

Married men don't always lie. Sometimes they just omit.

Looking at Pip's face in the bathroom mirror as she tells me that hers is not just any old married man, I know she isn't ready to hear that.

We return to the orangery, still sweltering in the sun, picking our way carefully around the seated guests on our perilous heels.

By the time we get back to our table, Rob has arrived. He sits on Katy's left, fanning her with what looks like the wedding card they were arguing about on the phone earlier on. Katy looks cross. 'You've been ages,' she says before Pip and I have a chance to sit down. 'You two are always sneaking off.'

She thinks she is missing some drama. Katy has always been the most dramatic amongst us. 'When will something *happen*?' she would demand as a child, throwing herself down on to the sofa on those endless midwinter Sunday afternoons.

Now something is finally happening in her family and she feels sidelined. Poor Katy – she isn't made for the margins.

'So lovely to see you again, Fran,' says Rob, rising from his seat to wrap me in a hug. There are some hugs that feel awkward, like playing Twister with a stranger. But hugging Rob isn't like that. Hugging Rob feels like slipping into a favourite dressing gown. Already I'm thinking of how much I will miss him when he's gone. There's no use denying it – Rob is on borrowed time. But really he's been on borrowed time from the beginning.

'I'm going to deliberately choose against type next time,' Katy told us after a traumatic break-up with her first university beau. An actor called Phineas (we later discovered his real name was Justin), he had come into our living room, the first and only time we met him, and arranged himself on the sofa like a decorative throw.

'Isn't he gorgeous?' Katy demanded, hijacking us in the kitchen. 'Isn't he the most beautiful man you've ever seen?'

She wouldn't let up until she had our agreement that, yes, he was handsome, yes, he was beyond handsome. 'But what does Pip think? Does she think he's gorgeous?' Yes, Pip agrees he's gorgeous. 'But what do you *really* think?'

Katy has a tendency to value things only when she knows they're valued by others.

But Katy was true to her word about choosing against type. When she brought Rob home, a pleasant-faced bear of a boy-man, with huge hands and a surprising high-pitched giggle, I'd warmed to him immediately, while at the same time knowing instinctively that he was doomed. He was like one of those characters in plays who, as soon as they make an entrance, you just know will come to a sticky end. He was kind and dependable and he adored her. He didn't stand a chance.

The warning signs were there almost from the start. Katy imitated his Yorkshire accent, and yawned exaggeratedly whenever he talked about his electrical-engineering degree. She went to parties without him, and flirted with his friends. When they graduated a year ago, they broke up briefly, but at the last minute Katy bottled out of moving to London alone and penniless, and of course Rob came running, getting a job to pay the rent on their room in the south London house-share.

Already she is outgrowing him. After a succession of internships, she now has a paid job in the marketing department of a big publishing house. At night she goes out for drinks with her new friends from work without inviting him. 'He wouldn't enjoy it,' she tells Pip, who then tells me. 'He'd be out of his comfort zone.'

She thinks he's socially awkward, and yet the first time I saw Rob after Molly died, he hugged me, as he has just done now, and then, looking straight at me – not at a point above my head, or on the wall behind – he said, 'I'm so sorry.' And when the tears started rolling down my cheeks, he said, 'Oh, now I've upset you. I'm so clumsy. I just didn't want you to think I was ignoring what happened to you.'

I couldn't tell him I was crying because of all the friends who *had* ignored it, who'd thought that maybe if they didn't mention Molly she might just go away, who hadn't been brave enough to risk the unknown quantity of my reaction.

'Don't worry, Rob,' I'd said, squeezing his hand, as the tears spilled out quite unchecked and Saul raised his eyes to the ceiling, as if attempting to enter some other time/space dimension. 'You haven't upset me. The upset is in here all the time, I'm just glad to let it out.'

The thing about Rob was that he didn't understand but that didn't stop him wanting to. I'd love him and Katy to stay together, but all those years of standing at the school gates, trying gently to engineer my daughters' friendships – 'Wouldn't you like to ask Daisy to play?', 'Don't you think it would be fun to go to Jaswinder's house?' – has taught me that my children will like who they want to like, and there's nothing I can do to change that.

Sharing our table are a couple, around the same age as Saul and me, who introduce themselves as old friends of Lucy and Maddie – 'practically family, really' – and three assorted young people. One of these, a quite ridiculously handsome man in his thirties, is openly appraising Katy, and I feel a twinge of fear for Rob.

The Practically Family woman is asking Katy what she studied at university.

'Psychology?' she cuts in before Katy can finish her sentence. 'Pete's niece studied psychology.' Here she indicates her husband with a cursory wave of her hand. 'She's got a four-year-old child and I have to say she's the worst mother that ever lived. Spoils that child rotten. All those years of learning about the mind, you'd think she'd know the basics of child psychology, wouldn't you? Oh no. She thinks the Naughty Step is barbaric! Mind you, all Pete's family are a bit like that – won't be told anything.'

From the corner of my eye, I see poor Pete, a sandy-haired giant of a man with sad, red-rimmed eyes, looking pointedly at his wife's wine glass, and I wonder how long we will be stuck here at this table. In my mind, I imagine Lucy and Jamie drawing up the seating plan. 'Ugh, which poor sods will we put with the Practically Family? I know, let's stick them with the Friedmans.'

For some reason, this makes me feel fiercely protective of my little family group. We've always been a tight unit. After Saul's parents died and my brother moved abroad, we created our own family traditions. We always had an annual Christmas Eve party for anyone who wasn't rushing away to visit relatives, cramming their cars full of presents and cases of wine to sit on the motorway for hours on end. Friends would arrive at around six, with champagne (Cava in the early days), and small children already in their pyjamas, and we'd play silly games and eat baked potatoes and mince pies and the children would periodically run to the window to see if Father Christmas was arriving, before falling asleep on beds or sofas, their mouths still smeared with chocolate.

In later years, there'd be groups of teenagers piled into a bedroom watching DVDs and sneaking beers from the fridge, or heading out to the pub, while the adults swapped drunken stories about present-buying disasters and danced badly to songs from the 1990s that had somehow become old classics without us realizing. Sometimes Saul and I would look up to find Katy or Pip standing on the stairs convulsed in laughter, watching us throwing our hopeless shapes on the makeshift dance floor that was our living-room rug. Saul would grab my hand and we'd bow solemnly to our uninvited audience before taking up where we left off.

Even when Pip and then Katy left home, the Christmas Eve party tradition briefly continued. It became wrapped up in my mind with the excitement at having them back, a celebration of being a family again, even though by this stage unhappiness was already nibbling at my edges, driving a wedge between me and Saul.

The year I discovered Saul's correspondence with his old university girlfriend was the first without a party. 'But why?' Katy wanted to know. 'I don't feel like it this year,' I told her, glaring pointedly at my husband. 'Let someone else do it for a change.' By the next year I was just pregnant with Molly, and too exhausted to think about entertaining. And the year after that was when the celebrating stopped.

I look around at the neighbouring tables, heaped with bags and wide-brimmed hats and lightweight jackets as guests scramble to divest themselves of as much clothing as possible in the stifling heat. Each place setting has a phone next to it, like an extra item of cutlery, and disposable cameras have been scattered around so guests can record the proceedings. We are over to the side, at the opposite end to the top table, at which I can make out the white-blonde heads of Lucy and her mother, bent together. Next to Lucy, Jamie is leaning forward to talk to Rosie and Liam.

'He looks happy.'

Saul has covered my hand, resting on the table, with his own. I glance at him, searching for hidden meanings, but his face, turned towards Jamie, is smoothed out like a stone. (*And here I am displaying spontaneous affection to my wife,* goes Saul's internal monologue in my own head.)

'Yes.'

I slide my hand out from under his on the pretext of looking at the menu and notice he has constructed a mountain of potatoes on one side of his plate. I hope these strangers at the table will realize he is in training for a race, rather than just greedy.

'I'm so happy for Lucy,' says one of the young people, a girl with long brown hair and intelligent eyes and a dress that seems to be made from silver foil. 'At one stage we were worried she might not make it to the aisle.'

'What do you mean?' Pip is sitting back in her chair and I notice with a pang that she has already got into the habit of subconsciously placing a hand over her tiny belly.

'Nothing.' The girl is obviously worried that she might have spoken out of turn. 'Only that Jamie seems to have had kind of a turbulent time recently. That famous quarter-life crisis, I guess, only a few years late!'

I study the girl more closely. An old university friend, I decide, rather than a friend from Lucy's TV life. One of the other two, the not-so-handsome one, is her boyfriend. He has one hand on her silver thigh as he eats.

'Why turbulent?' Katy wants to know. 'Has he been upset by something?'

'Not upset – well, not according to Lucy.' The girl clearly wishes she'd never begun the conversation. 'Just . . . restless.'

Restless.

In my mind I see Jamie, pushing open a pub door and shaking the rain out of his hair as his eyes scan the tables. Looking for me.

Enough.

'Oh, yes.' Katy shrugs. 'But that's just him, isn't it?'

I see what she is doing. Claiming a greater knowledge. Letting it be known that she is more than a passing acquaintance. Katy is jealous of the girl, I think, with her intelligent eyes and her silver dress and her reports of Jamie's emotional wellbeing. I want to put my arms around my daughter and tell her it's OK to share, that you don't lose people by letting other people have them too. But the truth is, I'm jealous of the girl as well. I'm jealous of the history he has without me.

Restless. She said he's been restless. Almost didn't make it down the aisle. It could mean anything, of course. A million different things could make a man of twenty-eight feel restless.

And one of them could be me.

Saturday, 4 p.m.

The speeches have been going on too long.

Up until this point, goodwill has kept us all upright in our seats, but a combination of the rich food and Max's bombastic bonhomie and Maddie's saccharine, champagne-sloshed sentiments and Liam's sweet but rambling anecdotes, with the emphasis in all the wrong places, has done for us and we fidget this way and that, trying to cool down, hoping it will soon be over.

I remember my own wedding reception, so different from this one, all of us squashed into the upstairs room of an Italian restaurant. My mother, for once in sync with the prevailing mood, lurching between tears and laughter as is permissible only at weddings. My father gazing around as if he'd somehow stumbled into someone else's party and couldn't quite work out the most tactful way to leave. Saul's parents gamely seating themselves in the midst of our friends – funny, decent and blissfully unaware that within six years they'd both be dead, one from a brain aneurism and the other, shortly after, from a broken heart.

And me? An image comes unbidden into my head of me in a tiny toilet cubicle, sitting on the loo seat, biting on my own hand. Then Saul's voice coming through the door: 'It's OK, Fran. You're bound to feel weird. Come out. Come out and be with me.'

Liam finishes his speech with obvious relief and the guests rustle to attention, weighing up the quickest routes to bathrooms and fresh air, before being stopped in their tracks by Jamie rising to his feet.

'I know you're all desperate to escape,' he says, smiling, 'so I won't keep you long. But there are some people I must mention quickly.'

He is true to his word. The tributes are short and to the point. There are some names I don't recognize and I feel Mrs Practically Family stiffen beside me, clearly hoping to be singled out. Then, suddenly, Jamie's eyes are on me. 'And to Fran, and of course Saul, Katy and Pip. Just for being who they are.'

I feel the heat flush through me as people on the other tables turn towards us, craning to get a look. The moment seems to last for hours, although in reality it can't be more than a few seconds before Jamie has moved on to someone else. All of a sudden it is too much.

'I'm too hot,' I say to Saul, pushing my chair back abruptly. 'Why do they let it get so hot in here?'

I'm pushing past chairs and tables, glad now to have been seated on the outskirts of the room. Slipping through one of the open French doors, I find myself on the lawn, but the sun feels almost as oppressive as the heat inside the orangery. There's an oak tree round to the side, out of sight of the wedding party, its branches throwing out welcome shade, and I head for it, pausing to take off my ridiculous shoes. The dry grass feels scratchy under my bare feet and welcomingly cool.

As soon as I reach the shade, I drop down to the ground, suddenly aware of my wobbly legs and thumping heart and the blood surely boiling in my veins.

'Fran?'

He has arrived without me noticing, materializing by my side so unexpectedly that I wonder whether I have imagined him into existence.

'Jamie, your speech . . .'

'It's finished. Just Liam giving some spiel about practical things, what happens next, blah blah blah. I saw you leave. I needed to talk to you.' He is crouched down in front of me, one hand steadying him, fingertips pressed to the grass. I stare at his fingers, at the plain gold ring. 'Can't you look at me?' His voice sounds suddenly young. Choked. 'Can't you see how all over the place I am? I can't stop thinking about—'

'There you are!'

Katy stands with her feet apart, silhouetted against the sun.

'I've been looking all over. You two are very naughty, sneaking off like that. And at your own wedding too, young man. Poor show! Jammy, have you got a fag? I'm gagging. Don't look at me like that, Mother. I only have the occasional one.'

Katy throws herself down on the ground next to me as Jamie produces a packet of cigarettes from his jacket pocket.

I'm like a stone statue, rooted to the spot. Katy inhales deeply from the cigarette. At any other time, it would horrify me to track the progress of smoke and tar through her lovely mouth, down her throat, into her lungs – the lungs that must last her a lifetime. Then she looks at Jamie. 'So how does it feel to be married?'

He gets to his feet, brushing invisible blades of grass from his trousers so he doesn't have to look at either of us.

'It feels much like not being married – except that people in posh dresses and penguin suits keep plying me with champagne and expecting me to make speeches.'

'Sounds like hell.'

'Yep. And I suspect I'm being summoned back to it.'

He turns away and walks back towards the orangery, raising his left hand and fluttering his fingers in farewell. There's a brief glint of metal where the sun hits his ring.

For a few moments there is silence. I feel Katy formulating something to say, and I know suddenly that I must stop her before she says it.

'How's Rob?'

'Oh, you know, he's Rob.'

'You mustn't underestimate him, you know.' I ought not to be giving Katy advice. Me, of all people. Yet still I blunder on. 'He has . . . integrity.'

Katy is angry. 'For God's sake, Mum. I'm going out with him, not voting for him!'

We sit side by side, facing away from the hotel, both of us plucking at the grass like chicken feathers.

'The thing is,' says my daughter of twenty-two, 'I'm not the same person now that I was when I met him in second year.' From the corner of my eye I see her looking at me sideways. 'I can't believe you married Dad when you were only twenty-one. How did you know? How did you know you'd still love him when you were forty-five? How did you know you wouldn't be someone different entirely – in love with someone else entirely?'

Luckily she doesn't seem to expect an answer.

'I do love Rob,' she continues. 'It's just I think I need someone a little bit more . . . dynamic.'

'Darling, I know you think you want someone more like you, but can't you just settle for someone who allows you to be you? If there were two yous in the relationship, one of you would have to adapt to become someone else. Don't you see?'

But Katy is looking at me as if I'm talking Ancient Greek.

'I only got together with Rob in the first place because of you,' she says now. She has taken off her shoes and is rubbing the back of one ankle where the strap has left a deep red mark in her pale skin. 'You were always so scathing about my boyfriends. I wanted, just for once, to do something you approved of. I wanted to be in the cosy club for once with you and Dad and Pip.'

'Hang on a minute, darling. You can't start blaming us for your own choices.'

'I'm not blaming you. I'm just saying you have to take some responsibility too.'

I stare at my daughter. Is she seriously suggesting we have somehow coerced her into this relationship with Rob, that some silent conspiracy between the three of us has forced her down that particular path without her consent? I am angry with her suddenly.

'If you're having doubts, you ought to let Rob know.' My voice comes out more sharply than I'd intended and Katy flings herself backwards theatrically so she is lying on the grass.

'I know, I know, I know. You're right. It's just . . . Why do relationships have to be so hard? Why aren't we all born with some kind of detachable heart that you can take out whenever things get too horrible?'

The speeches inside must have finally ended because people are spilling out of the French doors on to the lawn, stretching and fanning themselves, gazing up at the sky as if it might contain the secret of how to turn down this unpalatable heat. Painfully pinching shoes are kicked off, wide-brimmed hats are removed and used as makeshift fans, suit jackets are carefully laid down in pockets of shade for women to sit on without risking their delicate dresses.

As Katy talks about detachable hearts, I spy a waiter weaving amongst the newly prostrate guests with a tray of champagne glasses and try to catch his eye without making Katy think I'm not listening. My head is full of Jamie. *Can't you see how all over the place I am?*

With irritating timing, Saul's arrival coincides with the waiter's.

'Hope you're pacing yourself,' he says as I take a glass from the tray. His smile is tight, his mouth a cut he doesn't want to risk splitting open.

Pip and Rob follow closely behind. It occurs to me suddenly that these are the two who really ought to be together. How different things would be if Rob was the father of Pip's baby, not this married other one. Maybe there wouldn't be much of a spark, but they would at least be kind to each other. And really, what more can we ask from someone?

They haven't even sat down before a flash of yellow announces the arrival of Rosie.

'Oh my God, I feel completely wrung out after those speeches. I sobbed all the way through, did you see? I bet I look a total wreck, don't I?'

We shake our heads dutifully and murmur dissent and I sip my champagne.

'I'm not really sure what we're supposed to be doing now,' says Rosie. 'I think we just sort of mill about aimlessly until the evening do starts.'

Rosie has never met Rob before, and as the two are introduced I see a flicker of surprise cross her face. She is quick to recover, stepping forward on her little twiggy legs to kiss him on both cheeks and then a third time for luck – a move which wrong-foots Rob entirely, so that her lips make contact only with his broad neck.

'Sorry,' he mumbles. 'I'm from Yorkshire, so I'm not used to these continental habits. We still bow and doff our caps up there when we meet new people.'

Everyone laughs, except Katy. I know she saw Rosie's expression and I know it rankled. Rosie was clearly expecting something different of Katy's boyfriend. Rob has in some way failed to measure up.

'They do look lovely together, don't they?'

I follow Pip's eyes across the lawn to where a group of people have gathered. In the middle stand Jamie and Lucy, holding hands in a blaze of sunshine.

'She's good for him,' Rosie says suddenly, serious for once, and I see a brief glimpse of a sensitive young woman lurking under that brittle surface. 'She doesn't let him take himself too seriously. She'll protect him.'

Protect him from what? I want to ask. But I can't speak because there is something big lodged in my throat. I think it might be my heart.

Saturday, 5 p.m.

The sun is no longer quite so hot, but the air is sticky and ill-tempered. I am trapped in conversation with Max and Maddie and Mrs Practically Family. This is not my fault. I went off in search of another glass of champagne, and found myself somehow corralled into their group. I feel I have been standing here for ever, listening to them talking about house prices and inheritance-tax loopholes and the delights of holidaying in Croatia.

Mrs Practically Family and Maddie are old friends. Their conversation is littered with 'do you remember the time . . . ?'s and 'wasn't it hysterical when . . . ?'s. Max, ever the academic, watches them both benignly as if he is conducting research. Mrs Practically Family obviously has the same thought, because she asks him if he will be writing her into his notes when he gets home.

'What do you think, Fran?' asks Maddie suddenly, and I see a sharpness to her that she has kept under wraps till now.

'About what?'

'About the wedding. Are you loving it? You must be loving it.'

She is quite drunk, but not drunk enough not to know exactly what she is saying.

I can't quite make my mind up about Maddie. She's much cleverer than she'd like to appear, I think. She's the kind of person you want on your side.

'It's wonderful.' I smile. 'Such a lovely day. Such a beautiful couple.'

'Of course, I've known Lucy since she was tiny,' says Mrs Practically Family, desperate to establish her credentials. 'She looks on me like an auntie really.'

'It's a fantastic match. We all couldn't be happier, could we?' Maddie hooks her arm through Max's and for a moment the two of them wobble as if in a heat haze, and the ground seems to lurch under my feet.

'Steady on!' Max's hand supports me under my elbow.

'Sorry,' I say. 'It's just so hot.'

Immediately Maddie is all concern. 'It is sweltering, isn't it? Especially for ladies of a certain age.'

I estimate that, underneath those gym-honed arms and the facial filler and the eyelashes she has had individually added to her own, Maddie must be getting on for ten years older than me.

'Excuse me,' I say. 'Just nipping to the loo. You know us ladies of a certain age and our bladders!'

I am hoping that the loos will be empty. I long to lean my head against the cool tiles, and close my eyes and be silent for a while. But as soon as I push open the door, I realize it's not going to happen.

'Mummy . . . Mummy! . . . Need wee-wee . . . *need wee-wee!*'

The little girl with the bunches is standing in the doorway of one of the toilet cubicles with her flowery pants around her ankles and her face puce with urgency.

Her harried mother has folded out the nappy-changing table and is attempting to put on a clean cloth nappy one-handed while keeping the baby from rolling off with the other hand. The baby is tiny, like a doll. I don't look at it.

'Crikey – you've got your hands full!'

I'm aiming for a jocular, all-women-together tone, but it comes out half-hearted and observational, like a voiceover on a nature programme.

'Mummy. Now!'

'I'll take her, shall I?' I say, stepping forward towards the little girl.

Instantly it's as though someone has cranked the volume on the television up to maximum.

'Not you! Mummy. I want Mummy!'

The woman looks up and forces her features into a smile. 'When you've got to go, you've got to go,' she says. 'Would you mind holding the baby? Just for a second.'

The baby.

I stand rooted to the spot. She has picked up the baby and is holding it out to me, but still I don't look at it, focusing instead on the enormous bag which is now open on the floor, revealing a jumble of eco-nappies and pots of herbal barrier cream and those awful rice cakes.

'Goin' do it now!' singsongs the little girl, and the mother lunges forward, thrusting the baby into my arms.

'I won't be a second,' she tells me. 'Don't worry, she's clean.'

She ushers the girl into the cubicle.

'Shut door, Mummy!'

'No, we have to keep an eye on Poppy, don't we?'

'SHUT DOOR. I BIG GIRL!'

There's a flash of the woman's exhausted, apologetic face, and then the door closes and I am left alone with the baby. The first baby I have held since Molly.

I hold her stiffly, this warm, living baby, with her gurgling noises and her open, blue eyes and hot, sweet-smelling breath.

Just a few seconds, and then the woman will be out and I can hand her over, like a bag of shopping I've been keeping an eye on. I just need to hold it together.

'It co-ming,' sings the little girl from inside the cubicle. 'Wee-wee co-ming.'

I won't look at the baby. I'll stare straight ahead at the wall.

But on the wall is a mirror and in the mirror is a woman. And the woman is me. And the woman is holding a baby.

There's a movement in the mirror, and I feel a tiny hand brush my face. I won't look down.

I look down.

I am back in the hospital, lying on my back with something cold and wet dripping over the preposterous mound of my belly and watching a screen on which a baby is moving; a perfect, everything-in-the-right-place baby.

'A girl,' says the radiographer, and I look at my daughter and know her immediately. The strangest feeling.

'Are you disappointed?' I ask Saul, whose eyes are fixed on the screen. 'Were you secretly hoping for a boy?'

Saul shakes his head and his hand finds mine. 'She's fine. That's all that matters.'

And now I'm holding someone else's baby. And my baby is nowhere. Again this baby who belongs to someone else puts her hands up to my face and, without meaning to, I look down, and feel like I'm falling. I want to throw the baby back down on the nappy table, turn round and run for the outside, and yet at the same time I want to crush her to me so tightly no one would ever be able to take her away.

The harassed mother has emerged from the cubicle without me noticing. Something in my face, as she glances at me, must alarm her, because she snatches her baby back, so it feels as though she is being torn from my arms.

'I did two wee-wees,' says the little girl, pushing past me to the sink. 'One was long and one was short.'

'Sorry,' says the woman. 'She's a bit toilet obsessed at the moment. Do you have any children?'

'Yes. Two girls. But they're grown up now.'

As soon as I've said it, I regret it. *Three girls*, I should have said. *I have three children, but one is dead.*

The woman is stroking her baby's soft, yielding body, running her fingers over the chubby arms and dimpled back and soft poached egg of belly, as if checking to make sure everything's still here, all the bits that go to make up her perfect, living baby, as if I might have pocketed a toe or a fat knee while she was gone.

I turn to leave.

'Don't you need the loo after all that?'

'No, not really. And I should be getting back.'

'Me too. I don't suppose you've seen my husband? His name's Bart. Ponytail? Loud shirt?'

'No. Sorry.'

Back in the orangery, the sun has passed overhead, bringing the temperature down to manageable levels. Chairs stand empty, still wearing the discarded jackets and pashminas of their one-time occupants. Impossibly young waiters and waitresses clear away the remains of the lunch, carrying outsized plates crusted with flakes of filo and brown smudges of gravy.

I want to go back to my room and lie down. In my head I see the big beige hotel bed with its freshly made-up sheets. I imagine kicking off these stupid shoes and climbing in fully clothed.

'Fran?' Lucy has come up behind me, one small, childlike hand warm on my arm. 'Is everything OK?'

I realize I must look quite strange, standing on the fringes of the room, gawping at the staff as they go about their business.

'Yes, fine. I mean everything's great.'

I wonder if my smile looks like a smile, or like those mouth-stretching exercises my mother used to do, convinced they would keep her skin youthfully supple.

'I've been looking for you. I wanted to apologize for earlier, outside the church. I think I was mildly hysterical with relief that it was over.'

'Don't be silly. There's nothing to apologize for.'

'Thank God for that. Jamie said you'd be cool about it, but I've been torturing myself worrying what you must think of me.'

Jamie said I'd be cool. They've talked about me. A wave of nausea rushes through me, bringing with it a faint aftertaste of the salmon en croute I had earlier.

'Such a lovely day,' I say. 'You've organized things so well.'

Lucy laughs unselfconsciously, throwing back her head to reveal the pinkness of the roof of her mouth and her white unfilled teeth. My daughters have the same teeth – straight and even, none crossing over, the result of years of traumatic braces and trips to the orthodontist in their mid teens. I wonder if mine was the last generation where no one bothered about overbites and underbites and incisors like vampire teeth, the last generation where our mouths are our own, rather than the product of wires and latex gloves and unfathomable charts filled in by people in white coats and swivel chairs.

'I'd love to take credit, but I'm afraid it's all down to Lynn and my mum. They're the ones who sorted everything out. I've been up to my eyes at work – as usual. Two big jobs back to back. One Morocco, the other South Africa. You know how it is.'

I smile again. Of course I don't know how it is, although I have a sudden, thrilling image of the contract tucked away in my bag, waiting to be signed. A year in Spain. It's not impossible. And who knows where that year could lead to?

'Sounds very exciting,' I say.

'Don't be fooled. It's just fucking hard work. Sorry about the language. Massively long days running around all over the place trying to keep everyone happy, and at the same time making sure they don't spend too much money. And all to advertise home insurance or fabric softener.'

'Sounds like you're doing very well though.'

'Oh, it'll do for now. I'm not intending to stay too long though. I wouldn't want to wake up and be *thirty-five* and still making ads for bloody cereal bars!' Lucy says 'thirty-five' as if it is the upper age limit she could possibly conceive of for herself, as if it stretches the boundaries of credibility. 'No – feature films. That's where I want to be,' she continues. 'That's my dream.'

'You're obviously very ambitious.'

'You have to be, don't you? You have to have goals, otherwise you'd fucking stagnate.'

Lucy glances at me and suddenly seems to remember who she's talking to.

'I don't mean that you have to have goals at work or anything. You probably have loads of goals of your own, Fran, don't you? To do with your kids, and your house and everything? Or I bet you're secretly writing a book – a memoir or something.'

I think of *Cash in the Attic*, and the endless afternoons watching the sky change colour through the living-room window, and the telephone that doesn't ring.

'I'm afraid it would be a very dull book.'

Lucy's glacially blue eyes do a funny thing now, seeming to harden in her head as she fixes them on mine. 'Oh, I don't know, Fran. I'm sure you have lots of secrets you could tell.'

'Secrets? Do tell.' Rob has come through the French window behind us. I am so relieved to see him, I could almost kiss him.

'I was just telling Lucy how incredibly boring my autobiography would be,' I say brightly.

'Oh, not half as boring as mine,' he says. 'Confessions of an Electrical Engineer! Anyway, Lucy, your mum's looking for you. Apparently there's cake to be cut somewhere.'

Lucy rolls her eyes. 'A bride's work is never done,' she says, hitching up her dress to step back outside, revealing a lightly tanned, muscular calf.

'Where's Katy?' I ask Rob, now it's just the two of us.

'I don't know. I was hoping you might have seen her.'

'Sorry. I've been lurking in the loo.'

Rob and I look at each other briefly, and I get the feeling there's a lot he would like to say. But in the end, he smiles a rather sad little smile.

'Drink?' he says. 'I feel like getting smashed.'

I take the arm he proffers.

'That sounds like a most excellent idea.'

Saturday, 6 p.m.

The first time I ever got drunk was with Jade. We were at David's house – the neighbour with the Levi's and the small son. And the wife he'd mentioned as an afterthought. We'd met her a couple of times by then, when we'd gone to babysit. She was a nervous woman with thin brown hair, through which her scalp showed pink and shocking. She'd trapped him into marriage, we'd decided. He was dying inside but couldn't leave his child.

We'd bumped into him and his son walking back from school, and he'd invited us back. He had a record to play us, he said, but I can't remember if he ever did. The boy was watching something on the television – and we were sitting in the kitchen, around a tiny table, with an extra leaf you could pull up for more than two people, when David produced a bottle of red wine from a cupboard.

'Do you fancy a drink, girls?'

'Yes,' said Jade, always the more adventurous.

That first sip was disgusting, like vinegar. At the time I thought it was because I wasn't used to it. Now I suspect it was just terrible wine. But I drank the whole lot because I didn't want to be rude, or to look like a baby.

At some point that afternoon David produced a guitar. He told us he was a songwriter – that's why he was at home during the day. And he mentioned a couple of bands we'd vaguely heard of.

Nowadays, in the era of *The X Factor* and *The Voice*, when people make music on their laptops in their bedrooms, everyone's a singer-songwriter, but in Reading in the early 1980s it was impressive.

I don't remember much about the song he played, except it didn't sound anything like Leonard Cohen. The alcohol made my head swim, and nothing felt real, so when Jade went upstairs to the loo and David suddenly lunged towards me and kissed me, his tongue huge in my mouth like a hard-boiled egg, I couldn't quite comprehend what was happening. By the time Jade returned, he was back in his chair, strumming his guitar, and I wondered if it had actually happened at all. But as we left, giggling and stumbling in the narrow hallway, he grabbed my arm and held me back to whisper, his warm, wine-soaked breath moist in my ear, 'How about coming on your own next time?'

Why didn't I tell Jade? Because, even then, I wasn't sure I'd interpreted him right. My own parents were so dysfunctional that the adult world remained a mystery to me. Was this how social interaction was between grown-up men and women – drunken kisses and barely heard whispers that might be forgotten by the next day? But that wasn't the only reason. I felt 'chosen'. Jade was the louder of us, more overtly pretty with her make-up and her unsuitably mature clothes, handed down from older sisters with Saturday jobs and disposable incomes who could afford to buy something on a whim and give it away because it wasn't just the right shade, or was too loose around the shoulders. Yet still he had chosen me over her, had seen something in me that was worthwhile, that she didn't have.

Embarrassing to say that about his mousy wife, and small, telly-watching son, I thought not at all. I like to tell myself that empathy is something you learn from others, and I had no one to teach me, but I think more likely I was just self-obsessed, as most teenagers are. I didn't know what the kiss meant in the long term – it was enough that, for a couple of hours in David's pokey terraced house, I'd been noticed and singled out. Just for a short while, I'd been special.

All this is passing through my mind as I sit on a grassy slope round the side of the orangery, sharing a bottle of purloined champagne with Rob while Pip nurses her third orange juice. Funny how these memories, so long-buried, have resurrected themselves today, unfolding themselves from the packing boxes in which they've been stored, giving themselves a good shake to get rid of the creases. I guess that's what weddings do: pluck out bits of the past like ingrown hairs.

Rob, it turns out, knows about Pip's pregnancy, and I am momentarily hurt, feeling myself to be on the tail-end of the confidences chain.

'So I'm the last to know?' I say, trying to make my voice light.

'No. Dad is,' says Pip. 'And it's not all about you, Mum. Remember?'

I smile. Absurdly, this makes me quite giddy with relief, as if I've been given a temporary pass from my life. Saul, Jamie, my daughters . . . I don't have to deal with any of it, because today it's not all about me.

'I know you don't want to tell us his name, but at least give us some background,' Rob says to Pip, and I hold my breath, wondering if she will close in on herself.

'I met him through work,' she says after a pause, her eyes shiny with the memory of it. 'He's really bright. You know those people who have a different take on everything, and once you've talked to them and seen things through their eyes you can't understand how you ever thought differently? And he's funny, too. I can't begin to tell you how much we make each other laugh. And we're so intellectually compatible. We just get each other. If we've both watched the same thing on television, or read the same book, we react to it in exactly the same way. We have a game where we read the papers online in the morning and then guess which three stories the other one read first, and they're always the same.'

'If you tell me you complete each other, I might just have to pour the rest of this bottle over your head,' says Rob.

Pip laughs and brings her arms up around her knees. She looks so happy, sitting there, that for a moment I allow myself to imagine that it will be all right. She met him through work, after all, so he must be a professional too. Couldn't this be the affair that bucks the stereotype? She is so lovely, my elder daughter. Would it be so strange for this married man to have seen in her what I see, and to have lost himself?

The image of David swims up through the past, his face a blur where time has rubbed away at the features. Angrily I slap it away. It's not all about me.

'And what about the baby?' ventures Rob.

But this is one question too many. 'I don't want to talk about it,' she says.

Sitting side by side on the slope, the three of us gaze out at the lawn, where the guests are throwing long shadows across the carefully watered grass.

'I am sorry though, Mum,' says Pip, still staring straight ahead. 'Don't think I'm not aware that this must be . . . difficult for you. After Molly and everything. Don't think I'm completely insensitive.'

'Where's Dad?' I ask, unsubtly switching the conversation into a different gear. 'I haven't seen him for ages.'

Pip shrugs. 'I saw him heading back towards the main building, but that was ages ago.'

'I'll go flush him out,' I say, climbing heavily to my feet. 'Who gave him permission to bunk off?'

I wince as I slip my shoes back on again. The heat has swollen my feet and they feel half a size smaller than when I first put them on. The straps are cutting into my skin like the string around a supermarket chicken.

As I pick my way around the clusters of people studding the grass under an ever-deepening blue sky, I catch a flash of fuchsia pink out of the corner of my eye. Peering through a flower-covered arch to the side of the orangery, I see Katy deep in conversation with the handsome man from our table earlier. They are not touching, or even standing particularly close, but something about the tilt of her head, and the placement of his hand high up on the wall between the two of them, his body propped up casually against it, makes me nervous for Rob.

For a second I think about joining them, trying just by my presence to jolt them out of whatever course they are set on, but I know it's pointless. Instead I continue onwards towards the main hotel building. With each step, my shoes feel more and more like they have razor blades embedded in the soles.

'They giving you trouble?' asks one of the receptionists as I hobble in, marking my painful progress through the lobby with a succession of sharp intakes of breath.

'Just a bit.'

'You want to try Fairy Feet.'

'Pardon?'

'Fairy Feet. Cushiony things you put in the soles of your shoes.'

'No. You mean Party Feet,' the other receptionist corrects her. 'Feet Fairies are the ones you fold up and bring along in your handbag.'

'Alternatively, some ladies bring a whole selection of shoes, so they can switch around when they need something more comfy,' says the first receptionist.

'Yes, but then you'd need a very big handbag,' observes the second one.

The hotel lift is mirrored inside and on the way up to the third floor I gaze at my reflection. My make-up has been almost entirely wiped away, exposing my own face underneath like a half-restored painting.

Saul has the room key so I knock on the door. Silence. I knock again.

Finally I hear some movement from within, and then the door opens. For a second I peer, disoriented, into unexpected gloom. The curtains have been drawn against the late-afternoon sun, and there's a fug in the air, like morning breath.

'Oh, it's you.'

Saul's expression isn't that of someone who has run eighteen miles and then spent the day smugly refusing drinks and saturated fats. He looks tired. For the first time, I notice how pronounced the lines are that run down the sides of his nose and mouth. His face is like a new T-shirt that's been over-aggressively folded into thirds.

'Are you ill?' I mean to be solicitous but it comes out like an accusation.

Saul turns and walks back towards the bed. 'Just tired,' he says, lying down on his back.

Saul doesn't do tired, at least not during the day. Occasionally he has been known to take a power nap, but even then he goes straight from alert to unconscious without passing through yawning, or weary, or 'just resting my eyes'.

'Are you sure you're all right?' I ask him.

I've sat down on the edge of the bed and am rubbing the soles of my feet. My shoes have left indentations in my flesh, so in the half-light it looks as if I am wearing some strange deep-red version of them.

'I'm fine,' he says. 'I didn't know where you'd got to. Jamie was looking for you.'

My face is turned away from him, down towards my aching feet, but still I wonder if he can feel the burning of my skin, or hear my heart thudding.

'Jamie seems to have been looking for you a lot today,' Saul continues, in the same even tone. 'You'd think he'd have more to do on his wedding day.'

'I think we're his Get Out of Jail card,' I say, scrutinizing my toes. 'Me and Pip and Katy.'

I am broadening us out, us Friedmans. I am spreading us Marmite-thin. I am making a unit out of me and my daughters so there's nothing wrong in Jamie seeking me out.

'You're probably right.'

There's silence then. We form a strange tableau, me and Saul. Him stretched out on his back, me bent over my own foot. Both of us alert and waiting – but for what?

'I keep thinking about us moving somewhere like this,' says Saul. 'I don't mean this bloody ridiculous hotel, but somewhere where there's beauty and history and culture and fresh air but you can still get a decent latte. You get so much more for your money in a place like this.'

'We've been through this. Why must you keep bringing it up?

I don't want to live in the countryside and knit little people for charity to go over the tops of drinks bottles.'

'Now you're just being silly.'

But I'm not. I think of the job offer in my bag – perhaps a little house in the Spanish hills with a view to the sea. Me on the terrace with a glass of wine and a book. Not cooped up in some poky country cottage with Saul and all our issues.

'It's not silly. I've told you how I feel.'

'When did you get so close-minded, Fran, so dogmatic?'

At last I look at Saul. This is not like him. Normally he avoids confrontation like the Dartford Crossing, preferring to incur long emotional detours, or even turn back altogether, than to face a conflict head-on. 'Are you sure you're all right?'

Lying in the semi-darkness, Saul gazes up at the ceiling. 'Next year I shall be fifty,' he says, apropos of nothing.

I wait, holding my breath, feeling we are on the verge of something and not quite knowing what that something is, or whether, now it has come to it, I really want to go wherever it is we are on the point of going.

But Saul doesn't say anything more, just carries on staring upwards while all the different implications of his words hang suspended for a moment in the air before settling around us like dust. I could push him on this. I could insist that he explains himself, burst through the door that he has opened just a crack. I could tell him about the strange texts from this morning. I don't know why I haven't mentioned them yet. But Saul and I have always had secrets. I used to imagine all couples were like that. My own parents were a mystery to one another. There used to be a TV show called *Mr & Mrs* where couples would come in and answer questions about each other. I was always astonished by the things they knew about their spouses – bathroom routines, favourite supermarket aisles, things other drivers did that most infuriated them. Sometimes I wondered if my parents even knew each other's names – it was always 'your mother' this, or 'your father' that.

So I come from a long tradition of marital secrets. Though I longed to have the kind of relationship other people boasted of, where they were soul mates who finished each other's sentences, I was genetically programmed to obfuscate and veil and cloud and fog.

Saul tried. He really did. Sometimes, in the early days, I'd wake up and find him lying on his side, his head propped up on his elbow, gazing at me in screwed-up concentration, as if trying to remember the combination to a safe. 'What are you thinking about?' he'd ask me, tapping his fingertips gently on my forehead; then, an hour later, or maybe two, 'What are you thinking about now?'

I cried about it once, in counselling, when Saul talked about how, when we'd first married, the thing he'd most been looking forward to was us getting to the nub of each other. 'Peeling each other apart like an onion' is how he put it, removing layer after layer until all that was left was the exposed heart. 'Sounds like a surgical procedure,' I joked, and then immediately I wept, because of the disappointment on the face of the middle-aged Saul sitting next to me, and of the younger Saul who'd dreamt of something different.

'I wanted to,' I said, through my tears, 'but I didn't know how.'

We'd held each other then, while Louise's lazy eye averted itself, discreetly, to the far corner of the room. And in the car on the way home, Saul had turned to me with something approaching excitement. 'It's not too late,' he said, his brown eyes locking on to mine, his broad hand warm on my thigh. But Saul didn't know how many things I wasn't telling him. And he certainly didn't know about all the things I hid from myself.

It had always been too late.

So rather than question his strange mood, I say, 'I held a baby just now.'

I try to sound casual, as if holding babies is something I do all the time, hardly worth mentioning.

Saul doesn't immediately respond. When he does it's merely to say, 'And?'

Disappointment sears into me. What was I hoping for?

Another silence. This time louder than the last. I try changing the subject.

'I'm worried about Katy. I think she has grown out of Rob.'

Saul makes a noise that's almost like a growl. 'He's not a bloody starter home, Fran, or a boy band or an old pair of shoes. You don't grow out of people you love.'

I am astonished. Saul is usually so restrained, so frustratingly measured, that I sometimes try to goad him into losing his composure. I don't recognize this new, easily riled husband, with his noises in the back of his throat and his staring eyes.

'But that's just it, I don't think she does love him any more – at least not in that way. It's horrible to think about her moving on, though, when we're so fond of him.'

'This is Katy's life, Fran. It's not about us, I'm afraid.'

'I know it's not about us. I just don't want her to make a mistake.'

'Did you never make mistakes when you were younger?'

I glance over, but he's still gazing into space, giving nothing away. I remember the two of us sitting on Louise's sofa a few weeks ago and me explaining how being with Saul was like being with a teacher or a mediator or someone trained in conflict resolution, so there was never a chance for things to come to a head, never one of those satisfying clearing-the-air blow-ups. But now we seem close to edging there, now I'm finally sensing the exposed nerve of him, I'm no longer so sure it's what I want.

There are some things you can never come back from. For a ghastly moment, I'm plunged back to that terrible time four years ago. What was it that told me Saul was cheating? ('Not cheating,' he insisted in counselling, practically in tears.) A guardedness that wasn't there before, a different way of looking at himself in the mirror, a new, private relationship with his mobile phone.

In the end, it was the mobile that did for him. A text message alert that came just that little bit later than was strictly acceptable, the look on his face as he glanced at me before reaching for his phone. Guilt, fear, dumb excitement. Of course I asked him, and of course he crumbled. Just like that. She was an old girlfriend from university (of course!). She was living in Edinburgh and was going through a divorce. Two teenagers, a thriving architect's practice, long evenings in on her own watching Scandinavian crime box sets and writing pithy updates on social media sites. She'd looked him up online and they'd started chatting.

'We never met in person!' he kept telling me, as if that mitigated against the 'I miss you' she'd sent in the text I saw, or the hundreds of long, increasingly intimate emails he later, ashen-faced, offered up to me.

'I love my wife,' he'd written in one.

'Of course you do,' she'd replied. 'That's what I love about you.'

Oh yes, they'd talked of love already, each of them trying the word on self-consciously like a new coat, attempting to appear nonchalant on the few occasions they wore it out in public.

No, I can't think of that now. Not with everything else that's happening.

'You're behaving oddly this evening,' I say briskly, to drive other thoughts from my mind. 'You haven't been listening to Coldplay again, have you?'

It's a poor joke.

'Come back to bed,' says Saul suddenly. 'I don't mean that in any kinky way, I just mean . . . come and lie down next to me, and let's just stay here and forget about the wedding, shall we? No one will notice we're gone. We've done our bit. We can watch crappy telly and order £12.99 sandwiches from room service. You're always saying you want me to be more spontaneous.'

'Don't be daft. I haven't spent all that money on a dress and shoes just to go to bed at half past six!'

I stand and cross to the window, putting as much physical distance as I can between me and Saul and his strange mood. Lifting the curtain, I can see more wedding guests arriving. The evening's intake is more sophisticated – there's a smattering of LBDs and silver strappy sandals and sequins that blaze when they catch the early-evening sun. Those of us who have been here since the morning will feel frumpy and over-fussy by comparison, with our stiff taffeta and jewel colours, like Christmas trees in January.

'I think I'll change,' I tell Saul.

He makes a noise then, like a kind of a snort. 'You're always changing, Fran. That's the problem.'

'What problem? What's got into you tonight?'

Saul heaves himself heavily out of bed, and begins putting on his shoes. 'Nothing. I'm just tired. Weddings are so draining, aren't they?'

He pauses and looks at me as if something has just occurred to him.

'You know how when people on television get married, they always have those cars with "Just Married" on the front, trailing tin cans and God knows what behind them in the road? Well, weddings are a bit like that, aren't they? You've got the great big happy celebration that we're all there to see, and then all these other emotions tied on to the back.'

For a moment we stay looking at each other, me and the husband who has never, in twenty-four years of marriage, talked this way, and then I turn back to the window.

'It's going to be another warm night,' I say.

Saturday, 7 p.m.

'You changed. Why did you change?'

Rosie is glaring at me and I have the distinct impression that I've broken the rules.

'My feet were killing me. I didn't think anyone would even notice.'

'You have to be uncomfortable at weddings. It's the law,' says Katy. 'Didn't anyone tell you that?'

I am wearing the outfit I'd been planning to wear tomorrow – slim black cotton trousers, a long white sleeveless top, very low at the back, and my silver flip-flops. Amid the sea of towering heels, I feel like a midget.

'I'm an Oompa Loompa compared with the rest of you,' I say.

'Yes,' says Katy. 'But at least you're an Oompa Loompa who can walk without crying.'

'You've missed all the drama,' says Rosie, and I notice for the first time that she is quite drunk. She is standing just that fraction too close, and talking louder than she needs to, with a drunkard's appreciation of their own wit.

'What drama?' Saul wants to know.

'Lucy and Jamie were arguing about something earlier on. They were round the side where they thought no one could see, but of course we were all *gawping*.' She makes her eyes go round and goggly to illustrate her point. 'They've made it up now, but still, it's not a great omen, is it, on their wedding day?'

'It'll just be wedding nerves,' says Rob, who has joined our group with Pip. 'That's pretty standard, isn't it?'

'And what makes you our resident wedding expert?' says Katy, tossing her head and turning slightly away. 'Am I missing something here? Was your degree Electrical Engineering with a module in Advanced Wedding Psychology?'

'All he's saying is it's natural for tempers to run a little high,' says Saul.

'Did you and Mum have a barney on your wedding day?'

'No. Our wedding day was pretty much perfect.'

'Ew, yuck!'

We are gathered around a long teak table on the terrace that divides the front of the orangery from the car park. The table is littered with empty glasses and handbags and phones in coloured cases, and cameras at the ready with their lens caps off. We stand around its edges, shifting our weight from foot to foot and eyeing up the newcomers as they arrive. Every so often, Rosie peels off from us to throw herself upon a new arrival.

'Oh my *God*, I *love* that dress! No, seriously, I *need* to have that dress in my life.'

I glance over at Pip, and see that, even in the deepening glow of the golden evening, she looks pale, her cheeks sunken smudges of dark shadow. I want to tell her to sit down, but can't risk drawing attention to her. A sudden burst of anger towards this unknown, nameless man who has hollowed out her lovely face causes my fingers to grip the stem of my glass more tightly, and once again I'm thinking of David, buried in the mudslide of my mind for so many years but now determinedly muscling back into the frame.

The first time I went to see him without Jade, I felt wooden with nerves. At home in my bedroom, I'd carefully applied a new blue cream eyeshadow that I thought brought out the colour of my eyes, but what had looked sophisticated in my wardrobe mirror felt clownish in the harsh light of a November afternoon. As I walked the long way round from the bus stop, so as not to pass Jade's house, I began to doubt I'd even heard him right. What if he hadn't said that after all, about me coming on my own? Or what if he'd been joking? Might he have just been drunk?

By the time I'd got to David's house, I'd convinced myself I'd made a huge and humiliating error, and had concocted a lame excuse should it turn out that I'd misinterpreted his intentions.

'I've just come to see if I can borrow that Roxy Music record,' I said before he'd had a chance to open the door fully. 'I was passing on my way to Jade's . . .'

At first, it had seemed that my doubts might be justified. David appeared distracted and ill at ease, his eyes constantly darting towards the door as he rifled through his record collection, looking for the one I'd asked for. 'I'm actually in a bit of a hurry,' he apologized. 'I have a song deadline to meet.'

'Oh, right. Me too. I can't stay long at all.' I felt my face burning through my cheap foundation.

But by the door, he'd taken my hand and turned me to face him. 'I've been thinking about you,' he said, lunging in to kiss me so unexpectedly I didn't have time to swallow first and immediately began panicking that I was going to suffocate, like in the dentist when they put that sucky thing in your mouth.

'I want to take you somewhere,' he murmured, his breath shockingly hot in my ear. 'So we can be on our own.'

And I remember the unfamiliar feeling of something turning liquid in my stomach and at the top of my legs, to the extent that when I walked back down the road towards the bus stop I had to pause, just out of sight, and lean against a wall. At the time I called it love and told myself it was all about how I felt, but who was I kidding? Really, it was about him, and how *he* felt and how I'd made him feel. For the first time in my life, I had power. He had chosen me, this grown adult man. Chosen me over my more effervescent, outgoing friend. I had what they both wanted. David, because he wanted me, and Jade, because she wanted him. It wouldn't have occurred to me, at sixteen, to think about what *I* wanted. Even the forty-five-year-old me, it occurs to me suddenly, still has difficulties with that one. It's a skill, I think, to allow yourself to want things.

'It's Freya, isn't it?'

One of the women from the breakfast table has materialized by my left elbow, wearing her husband at her shoulder like a particularly cumbersome bag.

'Fran,' I say. 'Lovely wedding, isn't it?'

'Oh yes. Lynn's done a wonderful job.' She has brown hair liberally threaded with silver and a strangely shaped blue-and-white-striped dress that balloons down from the bust before tapering in at the hem, reminding me of a biscuit barrel my parents used to have. When she leans in to speak to me, she fiddles with the necklace at her throat, rolling the pearls between her thumb and middle finger as if trying to gauge their value. 'All Lynn's hard work has really paid off,' she says, adopting a confidential tone as if we weren't complete strangers. 'It's not as if Max was much help.'

'Liz!' Her husband, who I now recognize as the oncologist, has a warning note to his voice, but his wife chooses to disregard it.

'Oh, we all know Max is Max,' she says, with a closed-lipped smile that lifts up her round cheeks until they all but obscure her tiny eyes. 'I'm just saying he wasn't exactly hands-on. Other things on his mind, probably.'

'Liz!'

'What? I'm not saying anything. Anyway, Fran's an old friend, isn't she? She knows the score.'

The oncologist gazes up to the side, as if imagining himself in his Happy Place, and I feel almost sorry for him. And for Lynn suddenly, with her pink face and her wrinkled dress and her friends handing out her secrets like Bombay mix.

'Fran's husband's in paper,' the oncologist suddenly announces to his wife, dredging up from somewhere this morning's conversation over the Danish pastries.

'In the papers?' she says, suddenly attentive. 'How interesting. What for?'

'No, in paper. His company sells paper.'

'They're the third-largest stationery company in the country,' I say loyally.

'Oh.' The woman looks slightly annoyed, as if Saul has deliberately misrepresented himself. 'I thought you meant in the newspapers.'

There's a silence, as we sip our drinks. Then I sense the woman has become alert to something.

'Oh my goodness,' she says, conspiratorially. 'I didn't know it was fancy dress!'

Following her gaze, I see that Lucy's mother Maddie has appeared, wearing a pair of tight white trousers teamed with a white low-cut satin waistcoat and spike-heeled gold sandals. She's accompanied by the handsome man from our table. Katy has been leaning lack-lustrely on the table, but now I feel her stirring to attention.

'Isn't it the most glorious evening?' Maddie says, indicating the magnified golden orb of the sun, suspended in a cobalt-blue sky.

'Gorgeous,' I concur.

'But don't you think it's a bit close?' ventures the oncologist's wife. 'A little bit oppressive? I wouldn't be surprised if there isn't a storm brewing.'

'Oh, I wouldn't mind that at all,' says Maddie gamely, and, despite everything, I warm to her and her relentless positivity. 'A bit of singing and dancing in the rain never hurt anyone. Reminds me of when I was at the Carnival in Rio de Janeiro a couple of years ago – boiling hot, then absolutely bucketed down, but no one minded in the slightest. Have you been?'

'No,' says the oncologist faintly. 'Although I did once attend a medical conference in Buenos Aires.'

'Is Lucy OK?' Rosie asks, resting one of her twiggy hands on Maddie's brown forearm. 'Only the newlyweds were getting a bit heated earlier.'

'Oh, I'm sure they're absolutely fine,' says Maddie firmly. 'They're both strong characters, that's all. Sparks will fly in that marriage, that's for sure. But better that than a dull, boring relationship. I couldn't think of anything worse, could you, Fran, than a dull, boring marriage to a dull, boring type, sat in front of the telly in the evenings watching *The Great British Bake Off?*'

'Oi, there's nothing wrong with *The Great British Bake Off*,' says Katy, newly animated now that the handsome man has arrived. 'We all love a soggy bottom.'

I smile, but inside I'm seething. A dull, boring marriage. Does she mean me? What was it Saul said that time in counselling – that an ideal marriage to him was like a warm, relaxing bath that he could immerse himself in? How angry I'd got. 'I don't want a Radox relationship!' I'd raged. Relationships ought to be challenging and stimulating, I told him. Great partners bounce off each other, spurring each other on.

'But don't you think,' Louise had said, 'it's rather lovely that Saul feels your relationship is his refuge? Mightn't it get tiring to be constantly stimulating and challenging?'

But Maddie has seen how it is. Maddie has got the measure of us. *I couldn't think of anything worse, could you, Fran?* We must have it written all over us, Saul and I.

Was that the reason Saul strayed, I wonder? Was predictability the back-story behind his short-lived dalliance with the architect in Edinburgh he'd last seen as a floppy-fringed twenty-three-year-old in a charity-shop overcoat?

Louise tried a few times to make us examine what she called 'the context of Saul's emotional affair' (how Saul bristled at that word 'affair'). Katy hadn't long left for university. We'd endured that dreadful journey back from dropping her in halls in Manchester, my vision blurred by tears and rain on the windscreen as we inched along the M6 in bumper-to-bumper traffic, only to arrive back to a house that seemed suddenly like an empty mock-up of the home it was when a family lived there.

We dealt with it in different ways. Saul bought some new vests and entered himself for two more marathons, while I threw myself into socializing, going out with friends straight from work, drinking far too much.

Saul did make an effort, suggesting we find a joint interest.

Mandarin, he thought, might be fun. I chuckled about that for days. Life drawing was my idea. I'd always loved art at school, but Saul wasn't keen. I think it reminded him too much of his lost architecture degree. So in the end we did separate things, comparing notes over a sandwich supper in the kitchen at nine or ten, which was fine, but somehow missed the point.

'I just hope Lucy knows what she's let herself in for,' Rosie is saying. 'Jamie can be a right moody git. It's all about giving him space, knowing when to leave him alone.'

Maddie's smile is tighter now as she replies. 'Oh, I'm sure Lucy has him under control, don't you worry. She may look like an angel, but she's tough as old boots. She'll lick him into shape.'

Rosie is not buying this. 'God help anyone who tries licking Jamie into shape. He's the most stubborn person I know, always has been. We're both a bit like that. We like to have our own way. We used to have the most fabulous rows.'

'Well,' said Maddie, in a bright, clipped voice, 'now he has Lucy to row with!'

From the orangery comes the sound of a microphone crackling into life, followed by a guitar tuning up. 'Testing,' booms a voice. Then again, slightly quieter, 'Testing.'

A live band. That's all I need. Motown classics and Queen anthems.

'Oh, they're here at last,' says Maddie, clapping her hands together. 'This lot are amazing. You'll *love* them. They did my friend Rupert's fortieth a couple of weeks ago. He had a *Wizard of Oz* theme. It was fabulous. We were dancing on the tables. The nightclub manager said he'd never had such a fun crowd. Let's go in and see.'

Maddie starts herding guests from the terrace towards the open doors of the orangery. 'Come on, party poopers,' she calls. 'Time for The Wedding, Round Two. Seconds away!'

Reluctantly, we gather up our things from the table, unhooking jackets from the backs of chairs, zipping up bags, emptying the last of the champagne into our glasses.

By now the sun is starting to bleed slowly into the sky, throwing the trees into dark relief and reflecting orange on the highlighted cheeks of female guests. As I pick up my glass, I feel Saul's hand under my elbow. 'I told you we should have stayed in bed,' he murmurs as we follow the throng inside.

I don't reply. I expect he wonders if I even heard.

Saturday, 8 p.m.

Inside the orangery, the tables from the front half of the room have been cleared away, leaving an expanse of floor free for dancing. A few small children are energetically jumping up and down as the band warms up and I find myself searching for the little girl with bunches.

In a far corner, I spy the mother sitting on her own, surreptitiously breastfeeding the baby, a scarf coyly positioned over its head. I scan the rest of the room, starting to feel bizarrely anxious, as if it were my own daughter unaccounted for, not some stranger's. Finally, just when I am starting to think about slipping outside to look for her, I spot her sitting under a table with two curly-haired boys. They have a plate piled high with cake and are busy nibbling the icing off the top and discarding the sponge on to the floor. Their faces are smeared with chocolate. I think of the girl's poor mother, with her rice cakes and her raisins, and feel a wave of sympathy for her. We try so hard to keep our children safe and healthy, convincing ourselves that our rules and restrictions will form a protective cage around them, refusing to acknowledge that the bars we've so lovingly fashioned are made of spun sugar and all it takes is the slightest puff of wind to rip them wide open.

The things I did to keep Molly safe. Folic acid, raspberry-leaf tea, yoga, meditation, massage, subliminal messages whispered through my belly, iron supplements, afternoon naps. I enfolded her in love like bubble wrap. I curated her with deference and awe, as if she was a masterpiece on loan from a gallery or museum. During the day, I curled up on the sofa, curving myself around her; at night I laid my hands flat over my bump, feeling her movements through my skin.

My new custodian role suited me. The woman who looked back at me from my mirror had plumper, smoother skin and a sexy, rounded shape. Being my daughter's keeper kept me fit and active and focused on the future. For a few short months, I was defined by happiness.

The little girl is sitting under the table in a cloud of taffeta, gorging herself on sugar, while in the far corner her mother gazes around her with that particular set smile that says, 'It doesn't bother me in the least that I have a breast exposed in a roomful of strangers.' I feel a pang of affection for her and her blind faith that her breast milk and her rice cakes will count for something in the end.

'Fran? Sorry I haven't had a chance to chat much today. It's been so frantic.'

Lynn has detached herself from a small knot of people near by and drifted towards me. Immediately I feel nervous, my mouth suddenly dry, my face muscles stiff and slow to comply. Guilt is doing horrible things to my insides, and yet I've done nothing to feel guilty about. Nothing has happened! I think again about mothers wanting to keep their children safe and something pinches inside me.

'I hear you've seen Jamie a couple of times recently.'

Lynn is aiming for casual, but she wears it awkwardly, like a fancy-dress costume someone talked her into against her better judgement.

'Yes. With him being in London and me visiting the girls so much, we have . . . coincided once or twice. It's lovely how well he gets on with Katy and Pip.'

I know what I'm doing, invoking my daughters to make it OK. I can't meet her eyes, but find myself staring instead at the red mark on the bridge of her nose where her glasses have worn a faint groove into her skin, then slip to her ears, which have turned purplish where her heavy, silver earrings are pressing into the flesh. Lynn isn't normally the jewellery type. I try to remember what subject she specializes in. Sociology? Social policy? Social anthropology? When I first met her she was still doing her doctorate and now she's running a department. Impossible to know where all the time goes, years tucked away inside hours, slipping past without notice.

'The thing is,' says Lynn, and a virulent pink stain spreads upwards and outwards from the neckline of her dress. 'The thing is, Jamie is married now. He needs to focus on his marriage. He doesn't need to be emotionally . . . invested anywhere else.'

'We just had coffee.'

Guilt makes me loud and over-expansive, holding up my hands in a pantomime gesture of innocent surprise.

Immediately Lynn backs off. 'I know. Of course. I'm not saying . . .' She blinks several times in rapid succession under her shellacked hair.

Her evident discomfort seems to draw Max over, as if some soundless secret alarm signal has passed directly from one to the other.

'Everything all right with you ladies? Can I get anyone another drink?'

Max puts his hand on Lynn's shoulder as if she's a convenient shelf to lean on, and I see how her body becomes alert at his proximity. I remember what the oncologist's wife said about *Max will be Max* and wonder again about the hidden lives of long-term couples and how you can never really guess what goes on between them. A few months ago, when Saul and I were in Barcelona for the weekend, we got talking to a couple in the hotel bar one evening. It was their anniversary, they told us. They'd been married thirty-five years. I remember looking at them and envying them their straightforward, easy life. This was when Saul and I hadn't long started counselling, when emotions were running high. What would it be like to be like them, I wondered? Newly retired, second home in Norfolk, grandchild on the way. How simple life would be. During the second brandy – practically a third of a bottle in true Barcelona style – the man had leaned forward to talk to Saul in low, animated tones, and afterwards Saul had been in such a rush to finish that we'd ended up leaving most of our drinks behind. 'That was so rude,' I said as the lift doors closed. 'Rude?' Saul turned to me. 'They were swingers, Fran. He asked if you minded being shared!' We'd collapsed laughing then, holding on to each other for support as we staggered back to our room.

That couple come back to me now, as I stand next to Max and Lynn. I look at Max more closely and realize with a jolt that he's quite handsome in a certain way, with his lightly tanned face and longish grey hair swept back from a high, domed forehead, his lips shockingly full and pink under his greying moustache. He's fiercely intelligent, and kind in his own distracted way. I can't imagine him being the type to fraternize with his students, but a junior colleague might find something to admire, or a visiting lecturer. Anthropology is Max's field. Even when we first met he'd already made modest history as the youngest member of the faculty in whichever institution he was at then.

'I'd love another white wine,' I say, at the exact same moment Lynn blurts out, 'I was just talking to Fran about Jamie.'

There is an awkward moment while we both stop and look at each other, wondering who has right of way.

'What about Jamie?' asks Max.

'Just how, now he's married, he needs to focus all his energy . . . his *emotional* energy . . . on Lucy.'

A look passes between Lynn and Max then, as if this isn't a new subject between them. As if what she's just said has somehow violated a prior agreement.

'I'm sure Fran understands that, darling.'

'It's just . . . I want him to be happy. He deserves to be happy.'

'And I'm quite sure Fran wants him to be happy, too. Come on, Lynn, it's a wedding, for God's sake. Let's enjoy ourselves, shall we? What was it you wanted, Fran? White wine?'

What I really want is to be away from here. Far away from Max, with his big pebbly teeth and his sympathetic eyes and his beefy hand on his wife's shoulder, and from Lynn, who is so loudly not saying what she came over to say. I want to stride over to where the band have started playing and snatch the guitar away from the red-headed singer with the witty T-shirt-printed-like-a-tuxedo and bring it smashing down on his freckled head. I want to push past all these people I don't know and don't want to know, past these lovely young things in their tiny spaghetti straps who don't think they will ever grow old. I want to look them straight in the face, so close they can feel my breath on their lips, and tell them that truth we keep hidden as if it's too much for them to bear – that one day you wake up and it's all behind you and you can never get it back, not ever. I want to leave them all behind – even the people I love. Because loving is too painful and too bloody and you can never get it right.

'White wine's lovely, thank you, Max.'

Saturday, 9 p.m.

The white wine is pretty awful, but still I have managed to down a fair few glasses. The first sip is the worst. After that, I've discovered, you get anaesthetized to the stuff.

I'm sitting at a table near the back with Rob and Pip. Rob is drunk, it's fair to say. He is building a tower on the table from menus and name cards. His jacket is long-since discarded, his shirt is open, and he is wearing his tie around his bare neck like a dandy's cravat. His heart is breaking.

'I always knew Katy was too good for me,' he says.

Pip and I look at each other, then away. This is the fifth or sixth time Rob has made this remark, and each time our protestations have been slightly less heartfelt.

'Sorry,' he says, seeing our expressions. 'I'm being boring. Rejection makes people boring.'

Pip sighs. 'All this is just conjecture,' she says. 'Last time I looked, you and Katy were still together. If you're so worried, you should just sort it out with her.'

'I would if I could find her.'

We all gaze around the room, hoping Katy might have sprung up from somewhere since the last time we looked just a few minutes ago.

'She's with that wanker who was on our lunch table.'

Rob drops another couple of name cards on to his tower and the whole edifice begins to wobble ominously. 'She's always so swayed by appearances,' he continues, as cards shower down around him. 'What's that all about?'

'Rob, you really should be talking to Katy about all this.'

'She's insecure, that's what it is.' Rob carries on as if Pip hasn't spoken. 'It took me years to realize that. You know, Fran, after you lost the baby, when we were still at uni in Manchester, she was distraught because she thought she'd been left out. When she found out Pip had been at the hospital and everything, she was absolutely beside herself. She said she felt like an outsider. You'd lost a baby, but somehow it was still all about her.'

'But that's ridiculous. Pip just happened to be near by. Katy had her exams.'

'I know. It's totally irrational. That's what I told her. But the thing is, Katy *is* totally irrational. She's a fucking nightmare. But she's *my* nightmare. I really love her, you know.'

'Yes, we know,' says Pip.

After what Rob has just said about the baby, I don't trust myself to speak. The truth is, after I lost Molly, I wasn't thinking about Katy. I wasn't thinking about anyone.

I'm so shocked, it takes me a while to realize something has changed. The band, which up to now has been playing a selection of up-tempo classics, has suddenly slowed right down and lowered the volume, only the faintest whisper of drum brushes accompanying a low acoustic guitar and piano. The lead singer steps up to the microphone. With his freckles and his red hair flattened against his head with sweat, he looks a lot younger than before – younger than my daughters, it strikes me now.

'Ladies and gentlemen,' he says, and his voice is a shock because it's so much higher-pitched than the one he sings with. 'A little bit later than planned – but then good things come to those who wait – please put your hands together for the first dance for the bride and groom!'

There's a deafening roar, and the sound of applause and the drumming of feet on the floor and people whooping and calling out. I don't want to look, but everyone is on their feet, and I can't stay seated.

Over the shoulder of the woman in front of me, I see Jamie and Lucy walk into the empty space that has cleared on the dance floor. They are both smiling and he is leading her by the hand. 'Aren't they just beautiful?' whispers the woman in front to her companion. And they are. Both of them are beautiful. And yet . . . as the revolving overhead light hits them, I notice imperfections that weren't there earlier. Lucy's long dress has a ring of dirt around the hem, and there's a redness around her eyes. Jamie has taken off his suit jacket, and his shirt is untucked at the back.

As the band play the opening chords to a love song I recognize from the radio a few summers ago, Lucy reaches up to hook her arms around Jamie's neck, and he puts his hands on each side of her tiny waist. There's a collective 'aah' from the guests and I force my face into a smile. They are looking at each other and laughing and then Lucy takes her hand from Jamie's neck and puts it gently up to his face to wipe something from under his eye. The smile stays on my face, but inside I feel something twist savagely. I don't want to see any more, yet I can't look away.

'Are you OK, Mum?' asks Pip, who is standing to my right.

'Yes, fine!' My voice is varnished hard and shiny.

Now other guests are crowding on to the dance floor to join Jamie and Lucy, and they are swallowed up in the throng.

'Steady on,' says Pip, as I pour myself a glass of wine so full it spills down the sides.

We have resumed our seats, me with my back to the dance floor, although the image of Lucy with her hand up to caress his face is still imprinted on my mind. Rob's mood, on the other hand, appears to have been lifted by the sight of Love's Young Dream. Perhaps he is thinking of Katy and happier times.

I think back to my own wedding, with all the guests squeezed into the Italian restaurant. No band, of course, but was there dancing? Yes, I believe there was. I have a flashback to my mother, medication augmented by alcohol, twirling amid the tables in her new red dress with her hands above her head while my father

117

looked away and pretended to be somewhere else. And Saul, tall and slight, at twenty-four still only just shaking off his adolescent gawkiness, encircling me from behind, with his boy's hands resting on my belly, where Pip was just beginning to make her presence felt. Whispering, 'Ignore them. From now on it's just us.'

'Tell us more about him.' Rob leans forward suddenly, looking up into Pip's face with his tired, brown eyes. 'Tell us about your man.'

I see Pip hesitate, caught between her fear of giving too much away and her desperation to talk about him – to analyse and describe and boast, until we acknowledge how special he is, how rare this thing they have together. Maybe she, too, is affected by the image of Lucy and Jamie clasped around each other, fingers stroking cheeks, because her face softens in the red disco lights.

'Well . . . he's really clever,' she says, and I remember how the younger Pip was forever attaching herself to worthy causes, leaning forward at the dinner table, just as she is now, trying to make Saul or me or sometimes Katy see just why this or that charity or political venture was so deserving, sure that if she could just find the right words we would embrace it, too.

Now the cause is a married man.

'And he's funny,' she adds. 'Not in-your-face funny, but quietly, drily funny. The kind of funny you only really appreciate afterwards. Do you know what I mean?'

She looks from me to Rob, and we nod, though I'm not sure I do.

'We met on a case. I walked into this room and I saw him and I knew. Isn't that odd? I just knew. Just like that. Not because he's so good-looking or anything, although I happen to think he is the most gorgeous man who ever lived, but there was something . . . oh, this is going to sound so cringy, but . . . there was something in me that recognized something in him. Oh, I know you don't know what I'm talking about.'

It's this more than anything that tells me Pip really is in love, this inability to believe that anyone else has ever experienced what she is going through, this utter conviction of uniqueness.

'Listen,' she says, still caught up in the flush of fervour. 'I know exactly how this sounds. I'm not stupid. If I were in your shoes, I'd think exactly the same. But if you could just meet him, if you could see us together, you'd understand. You know, one time we were in a restaurant and one of those guys came in selling roses, and he looked at us and said he'd never seen a couple more right for each other.'

Rob makes an explosive noise and flings himself back in his seat. 'Of course he'd say that, he's trying to sell you roses, for fuck's sake!'

Immediately Pip closes up. 'I knew you wouldn't get it,' she says.

The three of us fall silent now, gazing around the room. It occurs to me that I haven't seen Saul for a while, but I don't dare look behind me, towards the dance floor, even though the band has switched to a more up-tempo song.

I think about what Pip said and try to see it without the veil of cynicism. It does happen, after all – love does take people by surprise, despite their noblest intentions. Faithful, married men are sometimes blindsided by passion. They do occasionally leave their wives. It is sometimes a one-off, cataclysmic event rather than a pattern of predatory behaviour. Why shouldn't Pip be one of the exceptions? I picture them, two quiet, professional people, heads bent together over some complex legal paperwork, trying to suppress their own feelings until they are so devoured by them that they cannot keep pretending otherwise.

You can't help who you're attracted to. As soon as this thought comes to mind, I see a picture of Jamie in my head, as he was this morning when he emerged from the steam room, his smooth skin sweat-slicked and glistening, and I am flooded with a sense of shame. *What is wrong with me?* I drain the glass of wine in front of me, hoping to flush the image away.

'I loved Katy the moment I saw her,' says Rob. 'Mind you, so did most of the other blokes in our halls. I never for a minute imagined she might be interested in me. To be fair, she wasn't at first. Interested in me, I mean. Only in the second year, when we'd been friends for a while . . . I always knew she was too good for me.'

'Change the record, Rob.'

I glance over at Pip, surprised. She is always the patient one, ready to give the benefit of the doubt until proved comprehensively wrong. It's not like her to be so snappy.

Rob seems taken aback too. 'Sorry,' he says. 'I'm being boring, I know. Sorry.'

He pushes his chair back, lurches abruptly to his feet and barges his way past guests to get to the French windows, through which the dark shapes of the trees are just visible against the navy sky.

'Don't say it,' says Pip, before I can open my mouth. 'I know that wasn't kind. I'm so moody at the moment. I don't know what's the matter with me.'

'Er, maybe you're pregnant?'

Pip makes a face. 'Oh God, every time someone says that word, *pregnant*, I look around to see who they're talking to. It doesn't seem possible that it's me.'

'And how exactly *is* it possible? How did it happen, Pip? You're always so cautious about everything.'

Pip puts her face in her hands. 'Oh, this is so embarrassing – talking to my mother about my sex life! It must have happened the first time . . . we weren't planning . . . we had no . . . God, Mum, what am I going to do?'

I reach over and put my hand to Pip's hair, stroking it gently. 'You don't have to keep it, you know. No one would blame you.'

'Yes, but you don't understand. I love him.'

'And you think if you have his baby, he'll leave his wife?'

'Yes, maybe . . . No . . . I don't know. He has kids, you know.'

'Oh, Pip.'

'Two boys. Four and seven. He adores them. He's a brilliant dad, I can just tell.'

'So if you keep this baby, at least one child will grow up without a father.'

'I know. It's horrible. But Mum . . .'

'Here you are! Let me sit down. I've been dancing so much I think I might actually have done myself a permanent injury.'

Katy pulls out a chair and throws herself into it. Humidity has tightened up the curls in her black hair and her cheeks are flushed pink.

'You can't have been dancing that long,' says Pip. 'Rob was looking for you everywhere.'

'Well, he should have looked for me on the dance floor, because that's where I was.'

The sisters exchange a long look, each daring the other to go further.

'Anyway,' says Katy eventually, 'what were you two so deep in conversation about?'

I am about to tell Katy what we've been discussing – what harm can it do, seeing as Katy clearly knows all about it anyway? – when I feel a sharp jab in my shin. Looking down, I see that Pip has kicked me with the toe of her shoe. Glancing over, she shakes her head once, almost imperceptibly.

'Nothing.' I say. 'We weren't talking about anything.'

Saturday, 10 p.m.

Saul is deep in conversation with his new friend, Bart, the ponytailed AWOL dad who'd asked his advice earlier about procuring Class As. We are all spread out along the grassy slope outside the orangery. The sound of the band murdering Adele drifts out behind us, accompanied by a low murmur of chatter and the occasional shriek of laughter. Ahead, the darkness throws up the odd black shape of a tree or an ornamental signpost. I lie back and look up, hoping to see the stars, but the sky seems to have clouded over, although it's still unnaturally warm. Maybe she was right, the oncologist's wife, when she said the weather was turning.

'I just think marriage is an outdated concept,' Bart is saying. 'We live in a disposable era. Nothing lasts for ever. Got a perfectly good phone? Doesn't matter – six months later, bam, you want a new one. Started off in one job? Bet your life that in five years' time you'll be doing something completely different. Nobody does lifelong commitments any more. Better to have a renewable contract that runs out every five or ten years, so you have to make a choice whether to opt in again.'

'Yes, but children are a lifelong commitment,' Saul points out. 'You can't opt out of them every five years.'

It's the obvious argument, but I feel let down that he didn't say more to highlight the positives about marriage – in particular, about marriage to me. No matter that for weeks in counselling

I've been chipping away at the fabric of us; now that it is under external attack, I want Saul to leap to its defence.

'Children are resilient buggers,' says Bart. 'My parents split up and both remarried and it didn't hurt me. What doesn't kill you makes you stronger and all that shit. It teaches you adaptability and self-sufficiency.'

'Last I saw, your daughter was being terribly self-sufficient under a table with a plate piled with wedding cake,' I say.

Bart throws back his head and laughs. 'She's brilliant. She's just her own little person, you know? She has an old soul.'

'An old soul and a bad case of the trots, I'm afraid,' says Pip, who has just reappeared and dropped down on to the grass next to me. 'I just saw her in the loos with your wife – who, by the way, is looking for you.'

Bart remains prone, propped up on his elbow as if he hasn't heard, and, to my amazement, I find myself feeling sorry for him. Suddenly he appears to be every man who could never quite bear to grow up. You see them all over the place with their oversized headphones and their complicated shoulder-bumping handshakes. I even saw one in a onesie the other day, while I was on a bus – a grown man crossing the road, eating a McDonald's in an all-in-one grey romper suit.

Oh, I know he's preposterous, with his eagle tattoo and his thumb ring and that hideous disc thing stretching out a circular hole in the lobe of his left ear, and his refusal to acknowledge his parental responsibilities. But I recognize where it comes from, this stuckness. I know what it's like to be afraid to move on, afraid of what comes next, clinging stubbornly to what ought to have been left behind.

He reminds me of someone, I decide, with his rapt self-absorption, and his conviction that being controversial somehow equates with being entertaining, that being contemptuous of convention places you somehow above it. And now it comes to me: David, Jade's glamorous neighbour. All this time I have kept him at bay, yet once again he barges into my head through the fog of the intervening years. Not as he appeared then, to my sixteen-year-old self, but as he seems now that I have an adult framework to put him in.

He said he would pick me up in his car and we would 'go somewhere to get to know each other better'. I had no idea if that meant having sex, or genuinely getting to know each other better. And with Jade still out of the picture, I couldn't even ask her advice.

In the car he seemed nervous – very different from the suave, laid-back persona he'd projected in the past. I noticed he'd taken his earring out, and the hole in his ear looked angry and purple, as if it was slightly infected. Without it he looked conventional and a little bit old. We drove a few streets from the corner of my road, where he'd picked me up, and then he pulled into the side of the road. Anxiety blocked my throat as, leaving the engine running, he lunged in to kiss me so suddenly that my head was pinioned to the headrest. With his tongue in my mouth, he ran his hands roughly over my chest, as if he was feeling for lumps, which is when I understood that, yes, we were going to have sex. Crazy, now, to think that I just went along with it, without stopping to ask myself if it was what I wanted. The truth is, it never occurred to me to doubt that this was what I wanted. Or maybe I just believed that being wanted was what I wanted.

We drove to a part of town I'd never been to before, with rows of shabby terraced houses. On one corner there was a brightly lit pub with windows fronting on to the road and a little car park round the back where David pulled in. 'Public House and 2* Hotel' read a sign by the back door. I'd never been to a hotel before, and this wasn't at all what I'd imagined.

'You wait here,' he told me, and I saw fear mixing with the greed and the lust in his face. Already I was looking forward to it being over.

Inside there was a pink-chipped sink in the corner of the room and an air-freshener tree and a heavy plastic covering over the mattress, underneath the bobbly, static sheet. David produced a bottle of red wine from a plastic bag and we drank it out of tooth-mugs, even though I felt as if I might be sick. Then he lit a cigarette and offered me a puff and the room swam for a moment in front of my eyes, swirling like the multicoloured carpet under our feet.

'You're lovely, you are,' he said as he took off my clothes. But I didn't feel lovely. I felt as grubby as the net curtain over the window opposite the bed.

It hurt. That I do remember, the pain keeping time with the creaking of the plastic-covered mattress. Afterwards he kissed me on the forehead and rolled off. 'It gets better,' he said cheerfully, lighting up another cigarette. 'First time is always a bit hit and miss.'

This is what I am thinking of as Bart drones on about children being resilient and self-sufficient, while his little daughter suffers sugar overload, and his wife keeps watch with their baby, wanting to go home.

'Bart works with computers,' Saul informs me suddenly. 'It's something to do with software design in digital media. I don't understand any of it.'

Bart laughs again, as if he's being complimented. 'You've got to evolve with the times, Saul,' he says. 'Not much future in stationery once we're all working from a home hub. You want to diversify while you still can.'

All of a sudden I don't feel sorry for him any more, I loathe him. I loathe his loud shirt and his thumb ring and the tattooed eagle around his pudgy wrist. I loathe the way he is lying there daintily making himself a roll-up cigarette with his thick fingers, and I loathe the fat tongue that protrudes from his mouth when he licks the cigarette paper.

I loathe his fluffy ginger sideburns and his sloping shoulders and his wide hips.

But most of all, I loathe the way he is condescending to my husband, about whom he knows nothing – not the architecture degree he abandoned because I was pregnant with our daughter, nor the sick father he prioritized over his chance of heading up the company's new office in Australia.

I heave myself to my feet to go in search of another drink, and to escape Bart. There is a moment when I waver, on the threshold of the orangery, caught between the darkness to the back of me and the spinning lights and thumping bass and shrieking people to the front. Misgiving tugs at my hem.

I could go, it occurs to me. I could leave without saying anything, make my way back through the shadows to the main hotel building. I could slip into our room and close the door and wipe off my make-up and take off these silly clothes and lie under a cool sheet in the darkened room, imagining all the things that might have been, but aren't.

Instead I take a deep breath and step forward into the light and the noise and the people.

And Jamie.

Saturday, 11 p.m.

'I wouldn't be in a relationship again for all the tea in China. What do I need a man for? Between my neighbour Kamal, who puts up shelves and jump-starts my car, and my Rampant Rabbit, I have all bases covered. I'm quite happy on my own, thank you very much.'

Maddie is saying all this in a raised, breathy voice as she dances vigorously to the Black Eyed Peas. She has a very distinctive style of dancing which seems to involve keeping her feet, in their towering gold sandals, firmly planted on the floor, while gyrating from the hips and making elaborate movements with her hands in the air above her head.

'Sometimes, when I see couples who've been together for years and haven't got a thing to say to each other, sitting in restaurants in silence, just "Can you pass the salt?" and "Salmon's a bit dry", I thank my lucky stars to be going home on my own. Oh, don't get me wrong, Fran, I love company. I've loads of friends. Too many friends, really. All younger than me. I've a very young outlook. And I'm always busy. Lucy is constantly complaining that she can't get hold of me. "You're always out!" she says.'

At this point, Maddie mercifully breaks off and starts shimmying furiously on the spot, singing along to the song. Despite bristling at her dig at long-term couples, I can't help admiring her energy. There's something quite touching in her refusal to conform.

We have been dancing now for quite some time, or so it seems. It is that moment in the evening when the quantity of alcohol consumed intersects with the emotional intensity of the occasion and the sense that time is running out, and the dance floor is full of desperation and flailing limbs. Katy is in the middle, a blur of bright pink and whooshing hair, dancing with the three young people from our lunch table. She is very close to the handsome man and every now and then he leans in to say something, and she tilts her head to listen so his lips brush her ear.

Rob, meanwhile, is splayed out on his own at one of the tables, with a selection of shot glasses arranged in front of him. He is staring at Katy quite openly. Intensity radiates from him like a bad smell. The boorishness of the rejected lover is always a turn-off, no matter how fond you are of someone. *Get a grip*, I want to tell him. *Have some dignity*. But who am I to talk? Where is my own dignity? Where is my grip?

Dancing somewhere behind me, but close enough for me to sense him even through the crowd of people and the maelstrom of excitement, flirting and fatigue that hangs over the dance floor, is Jamie. I'm conscious of him in the same way you're conscious of the sun while holidaying somewhere warm. You might have your back to it, or even be completely in the shade, but you're always aware it's there.

'I'm very comfortable in my own skin,' Maddie is telling me, obligingly running a hand over her décolletage to indicate an example of said skin. 'I do a lot of Zumba and Salsa. I've even done a pole-dancing class. I have a fantastic relationship with my own self. I think that frightens men of my age. Not that men of my age interest me anyway – so boring and set in their ways, joining wine clubs and wanting a nap in the afternoon. And all those saggy bits and bald bits. No, thanks!'

Without warning, she flings her arms up in the air, causing me to step back in alarm, and executes a 360-degree spin. Then she resumes. 'Not that there aren't good ones. Saul keeps himself trim, doesn't he? It's just not my cup of tea. I get a lot of attention from men in their twenties and thirties. They're not scared of me. I like that, and I like how uncomplicated they are. And how fit! Do you like younger men, Fran?'

Maddie is still gyrating and flailing, but her eyes are firmly fixed on me, and she has a half-smile on her lips that could mean everything and nothing. The vat of champagne and wine that I have consumed is sloshing about inside me as I bob half-heartedly, transferring my weight from foot to foot in a poor approximation of dancing, unable to locate a rhythm.

'What? An old married woman like me?' I say.

Maddie keeps her eyes fixed on me, and the revolving coloured light above makes them glint intermittently red like an alarm sensor. 'Don't underestimate yourself, Fran. Rest assured, the rest of us don't.'

I smile. But something inside has come adrift from its moorings.

'Just going to the loo,' I say, clenching the muscles in my jaw so my smile doesn't slip off my face on to the dance floor.

Pushing through the dancers, I pause when I get to Katy. 'Go and talk to Rob, for God's sake,' I hiss in her ear. 'Can't you see the poor guy's upset?'

'The *poor guy* is pissed out of his head. I'm not ruining my night just because he can't hold his booze. He's being a complete wanker.'

Katy turns her shoulder to me to show she's angry, and I carry on weaving through the crowd, making sure I give Jamie and Lucy a wide berth.

The exchange with Katy has unnerved me, adding to the anxiety caused by Maddie's comment. The back of my mouth feels dry and there's a thudding in my ears, over and above the incessant beat of the music. I suddenly remember those weird texts from this morning. There haven't been any more. They must have been sent by mistake. Yet I can't completely shake off my niggling doubts. Could someone here be responsible? My eyes flick nervously around the room.

I spot Christine, the elderly lady from breakfast, sitting alone and make my way over to her. I remember how kind she seemed, and how much calmer she made me feel. Her silver head is bent and at first I think she's nodded off, but then I notice she is once again busy on her smartphone.

'Blogging again?' I ask her.

She looks up and smiles, distractedly. 'Not this time, dear. I'm actually live-streaming the party straight to YouTube. Some of Lynn's relatives couldn't make it, so they're watching as it happens.'

For a moment she seems on the verge of saying something else and I toy with the idea of flopping down next to her and letting everyone else just get on with it, but then I notice Rob brooding on a neighbouring table and feel duty-bound to move on. As I approach, I see he has three full shot glasses in front of him, and several more empty ones lie scattered about.

'Maybe you should go to bed, Rob. You've had a lot to drink. Things will look better in the morning.'

Rob hardly glances up, his gaze still intently fixed on the flash of pink that is my daughter. 'Don't worry, Fran.' His voice is thick, as if it has gobs of flour in it. 'I'm fine. I'm just keeping watch, that's all. That's what I do when we go out. Katy flits around like a butterfly on speed and I keep watch and then take her home. That's our deal. That's how it is.'

'And is that what you want, Rob?'

'I want *her*. I love her.'

Oh, let him not be about to cry.

'I know she's your daughter and everything, Fran, but Katy can be a right bitch sometimes. But then other times she's so lovely and other times she just needs looking after. Like when she found out about Molly.'

Once again, her name on someone else's lips brings a visceral reaction. She is real. Molly is real. Not a memory I carry around in my head, but a real person who meant something in other people's lives, not just mine.

'Katy was so upset then, about being left out . . .'

'We didn't . . .'

'Yes, but that's not what she felt. And the point is, I helped her. I was like her family.'

Why did I never know this was how Katy felt? I think back to that time, but can't see past my own agony.

She hadn't wanted a new sister. She'd been so set against it . . . But even as I'm thinking it, my own memory contradicts me.

I was around five months pregnant and Katy was home on holiday, so I'm guessing it was the Easter of that year. We were sitting on the sofa, side by side, watching something or other on the telly. Some rubbish probably. Katy and I like to watch crap – cooking programmes or reality shows or the occasional period nonsense – much to Pip and Saul's disdain. We get blankets and build ourselves a nest of cushions. I'd been feeling slight movements for a couple of weeks, but suddenly the baby gave an almighty kick and I let out a yelp of surprise, my hand automatically flying to my abdomen.

Immediately, Katy was alert. 'Was that the baby? Is it moving? Can I feel?'

My younger daughter has never been a respecter of personal space boundaries, and she didn't wait for a reply before scooting up next to me and laying both her hands on my bump. Obligingly, Molly kicked again and Katy squealed with pleasure.

'Oh my God!' she said. 'We're actually having a baby!' How could I have forgotten that?

I try to remember that last day. The day everything changed. Waking up as usual with my hands around my stomach, feeling the slow movements of my baby coming to consciousness inside me, imagining her fingers uncurling, her legs stretching. She'd slowed down a lot over the last few days. But that was normal. I was nearly thirty-seven weeks and huge. There wasn't a lot of space for her to move.

If I'd gone in then. If I'd gone in when her movements slowed instead of telling myself I was an old hand, I'd done it before. If I'd just listened to what she was telling me . . .

It's no use. I can't do this. I can't revisit this, not even for Katy. My palms are sweaty, my pulse racing as if it wants to run clear out of my body, and I can feel my breath coming in quick bursts.

'I'm sorry Katy felt that way,' I tell Rob, gripping the table. 'But I still think you should call it a day now.'

What I want to say is that whatever will happen will happen, whether he's there to watch over her or not. If not tonight, then tomorrow, and if not then, some other time. Because love isn't enough to make people stay. And love certainly isn't enough to bring them back.

But of course I don't say any of this.

Where on earth is Saul? He should be here, cajoling Rob to his feet and whisking him away, or talking some sense into Katy. She might listen to him. Although, looking at her now on the dance floor, her head thrown back with laughter, I'm not so sure. I'm cross with her for being so cruel. Yet, I suppose she's only doing what comes naturally. Dating has always been about survival of the fittest. Katy was never going to stay with Rob. She's only twenty-two. She is only just beginning to exercise her power. The break-up is inevitable, so is it so bad that it happens now?

Rob downs a shot and gazes straight ahead as if he hasn't heard me. 'I always knew she was too good for me,' he says.

Suddenly I can't listen to anyone. 'I'll be back in a moment,' I say, heading for the toilets.

In the cubicle – the one at the end, set slightly back, where I'm least likely to be noticed – I sit with my head in my hands, realizing I am drunker than I thought.

I think back to when I was in here earlier, with Bart's wife and the baby. I remember tiny fingers fluttering across my face, round blue eyes gazing up into mine. The solid bulk of the ridiculous cloth nappy, the soft back, like dough, gently dented by my fingertips, the plump pink lips, the upper one puckered into a blistered point from feeding.

When I felt Molly moving inside me that last morning, she wasn't much smaller than that baby. Slower movements than before, to be sure, but nothing to be worried about. *If I'd just double-checked. If I'd just presented myself at the hospital, saying, 'You'll think I'm paranoid, but can you just listen to her heartbeat and put my mind at rest?'* Could I have saved her?

I got up and showered, as I always did, enjoying the feeling of the warm water cascading over my huge belly, and dressed with care, within the limitations of the rapidly dwindling selection of clothes that still fitted. I was meeting Pip for lunch in Islington and was excited – I hadn't seen her for weeks.

Was that why I didn't pay more attention? Was I too focused on sea bream in a white-wine sauce in a grown-up restaurant with my daughter to listen to what Molly was trying to tell me?

In the train on the way into town, I upgraded to first class for an extra fiver, luxuriating in the respectful hush of the carriage and the extra space between the tables and the endless supply of free coffee from the trolley. Though I'd given up work a month before, I knew my days of long leisurely lunches and day-trips to London were numbered and I wanted to savour every moment. Now, of course, I can go to lunch whenever I want, making arrangements to meet a friend at a moment's notice. But instead I stay at home with *Homes Under the Hammer*, watching the seasons change through the living-room window.

'Blimey, Mum, you look fantastic. If that's what having a baby does for you, where do I sign up?'

Pip's compliment when I met her in the restaurant seems prophetic in the light of today's revelations. And I lapped it up, proud of my shiny hair and lustrous skin, my yoga-supple limbs and alcohol-free bloodstream. There I was, forty-three (and still got it!), having lunch with my accomplished daughter, the two of us attracting admiring glances from a nearby table of businessmen. I was breezing through late pregnancy without breaking a sweat. A quietly confident, efficient, modern woman. I almost drowned in love for myself.

And all the time my baby was dying inside me.

Someone comes into the toilets, the open door admitting a blast of noise, reminding me where I am. Out there people are singing along to the music, alcohol convincing them of musical abilities they don't possess. A child, up past his bedtime, is throwing a tantrum. 'I'm not tired,' he shrieks. Then, louder, 'Get off me, I said I'm *not tired*!' A woman is laughing like a car alarm, a high-pitched, grating noise.

'For anyone who hasn't copped off yet, no need to panic, we've a late licence until one,' comes the voice of the band's singer. The toilet door swings shut again on the whoops of delight from the assembled guests.

I am about to leave the cubicle when I hear sniffing sounds coming through the door from whoever just came in. Is someone taking drugs out there? The sounds continue and now I realize the person is crying. Now what do I do? My stomach feels suddenly tight, and my throat so dry that each swallow sounds amplified. The cubicle I am in is set back, so it's possible she thinks she's alone. Should I hide in here until she leaves? Or should I brazen it out, flushing loudly and confronting head-on the awkwardness of a stranger's tears? The cubicle feels suddenly very confined and I am on the point of pulling back the lock to release myself when the main toilet door opens again.

'Darling? Are you in here?'

I recognize that voice straight away.

'What on earth's the matter? Oh, my sweetheart, come here.'

The sniffing sounds are muffled now, and once again I hold my breath, not wanting to do anything to draw attention to myself. Because just beyond the door is Maddie. And unless I'm very much mistaken, sobbing into her mother's bosom is Lucy.

Saturday, midnight

How long have I been here in this cubicle?
Time seems to have been stretched beyond breaking point, and yet here I am still, listening to the oh-so-familiar sound of a mother comforting her child.

'Hush,' whispers Maddie. 'Everything will be OK.'

I stand stiffly in place, my back to the door.

'He does love you so, so much,' says Maddie, in a voice that's different from the one she was using earlier, as if it has taken off its party shoes and is padding around in bare feet.

Lucy makes a noise halfway between a snort and a cry. 'Then why is he—?'

Suddenly she's drowned out by a huge burst of sound from the party as the door opens again.

'Oh God,' says an unfamiliar voice. 'I'm so sorry. I'll come back later.'

'Don't be *silly*!' says Maddie, and the shoes are back on again, the voice hard and polished. 'Everyone knows the bride is expected to get emotional. It wouldn't be a proper wedding without a few tears! Are you ready to go back out again, darling, and face your adoring public?'

A brief moment of silence, then an audible intake of breath. 'Has my mascara run? Let me look in the mirror. Oh, I'm a complete mess!'

'Nonsense, darling. You're absolutely beautiful. Isn't she?'

There's an immediate murmur of concurrence from the unfortunate new arrival, whose opinion is clearly being sought. 'Radiant. Totally radiant.'

'There you are then. It's unanimous. You're gorgeous, Lucy. Now, shall we go?'

Another deep breath. Then: 'Yes. Lead on, Mother. Once more into the fray and all that.'

A peal of laughter, piercing and forced, followed by the creak of the door opening and slowly swinging closed again.

They are gone.

I slump against the door, weak with relief.

Purposeful now, I flush the toilet to alert the other occupant to my presence, and unlock the door. My face in the mirror is flushed, clashing with my fiery-coloured hair. Now that my make-up has faded, there are dark smudges under my eyes and an unsightly red patch which, on closer inspection, turns out to be where I have been pressing my forehead to the cubicle door.

As I leave the toilets, I'm acutely conscious of having only narrowly averted disaster. I need to get away now, while I am still intact, while I can still meet people's eyes and tell myself I've done nothing wrong.

Newly determined, I turn away from the door to the orangery, where the band have now entered the love anthems stage and a group of male voices are shouting along to a well-known song from *Grease*. Instead I take the fire exit out on to the terrace. I'm hoping to find it deserted, but I've reckoned without the commitment of the smoking contingent. The terrace tables where we sat earlier are humped with dark shapes, orange cigarette tips dancing in the darkness like fireflies.

No one here I recognize. I'll head round to the grassy slope where I last saw Saul and Pip. I'll let them know I'm going to bed.

As I move off around the side, one of the dark shapes detaches itself from the table and comes towards me.

'You're not going already?'

Jamie has his hand on my arm. We are just outside the halo of light thrown out by the doorway behind me, so it is too dark to see his expression.

'I'm just going to find Saul and Pip. I am getting a bit tired, actually. It's been a long day. Lovely, but long.'

His hand is stroking my bare arm, and now I feel it folding around my fingers.

'Have you had a lovely time? It must be such a wonderful feeling, knowing it's all passed off so well.' I'm babbling now, my voice shrill and silly, my hand burning in his.

'Don't go.' His lips are brushing my skin, his words hot and moist in my ear, and spiced with tobacco.

For a split second we sway together in the darkness, our hands touching. He is shorter than Saul, I think, but more solid somehow. I feel the heat coming off his skin even through the damp cotton of his shirt. Then I remember Lucy, sobbing in the toilets at her own wedding, and pull away.

'I really must find them. They'll be looking all over the place for me.'

I'm moving away as I speak, tossing words into the air behind me, my fingers still burning from his touch. I'm so hot I can hardly breathe. There are now solid banks of cloud overhead, obscuring the moon, but the air still feels hairdryer warm and there's an oppressive thickness about the night. Turning the corner to where the grass slopes away from the back of the orangery, the music is instantly louder, despite many of the French windows now being shut, no doubt due to some half-heartedly enforced noise-restriction law.

A few bodies are scattered on the ground, some of them casualties of the freely flowing alcohol. One man I walk past has lost his shoes, the dirt-blackened soles of his white socks starkly illuminated by the light from the French windows. Someone has thoughtfully put him into the recovery position and placed an empty ice bucket next to his head.

Other recumbent figures turn out to be people I half recognize. The young couple from our lunch table are lying in an embrace, one on top of the other, her silver dress glinting whenever she changes position. Their friend, the handsome man who was paying such attention to Katy, is nowhere to be seen.

Through the windows of the orangery, I see Bart's wife sitting with her coat on, gently rocking a baby buggy. Her face has lost its determined smile and is a carved mask of endurance. Her daughter is slumped fast asleep next to her, head resting on her little chubby arms, face still smeared with chocolate.

The guests on the dance floor have now formed a Conga and are snaking around the room. I spot Max and Lynn in there. Lynn is looking pinkly pleased, gamely kicking out a leg from time to time at interludes seemingly unconnected to the music. Her hands are planted firmly on either side of Max's thick waist and I wonder if she is deriving some measure of satisfaction from knowing that, for now at least, her husband is literally within her grasp.

I scan the line for a tell-tale flash of bright pink, but there is no sign of Katy, or Rob, or the handsome man. The table where I left Rob earlier is a graveyard of empty glasses and scattered name-cards.

I step away from the light and, peering blindly into the darkness, tread gingerly towards some shapes further away.

'Mum?' one says. 'Thank God for that. I thought everyone had abandoned me!'

'Pip?' I stumble towards her, grateful for my flip-flops. 'What are you doing, sitting here in the dark? Oh! Who on earth is that?'

'Three guesses. I'll give you a clue. He's very drunk and Katy is too good for him.'

I flop down heavily on to the grass next to the prostrate figure of Rob and put a hand on his shoulder, shaking him gently. Nothing. I shake a bit harder. Still nothing. 'How long has he been like this?'

'Probably about forty minutes, but it feels like an entire lifetime.'

'Poor Pip.' I put my arm around her and she leans her head on my shoulder. Usually it's Katy who's the more physically demonstrative, hurling herself upon you for a hug, or plonking herself down on your lap without warning or invitation, her adult weight soon becoming unbearable. Pregnancy has made Pip seek out human touch in a way she never did, even as a child.

'I'm so tired, Mum. I've been wanting to go to bed for ages, but I couldn't just leave him.'

'Katy?'

'God knows. She and Rob had this huge bust-up when she tried to make him go to bed, and he refused, and she said he was an embarrassment and stormed off. Then we brought him out here to calm down and he promptly passed out.'

'We?'

'Dad was here until a few minutes ago. He went off to find you. He's desperate to go to bed too.'

'I suppose he *was* up at the crack of dawn cantering across the countryside. And no doubt will do the same again tomorrow.'

'The legend that is Dad.'

'Quite.'

Snuggled up with Pip, I feel myself starting to calm down. Since my enforced incarceration in the toilet cubicle and the subsequent run-in with Jamie, I've been on edge, my pulse throbbing painfully, my stomach acidic and tight. But sitting with my daughter in the thick, muggy darkness, my heart begins to still.

'I don't think I could stand to have an abortion,' she says, out of the blue, aiming her words into the night. 'I know people do, and that's fine, but it doesn't feel right for me. I know that physically this isn't yet a baby, but in my head it's already a child, and I worry I might spend the rest of my life missing it. I know you understand, Mum. You know what it's like to lose a child.'

How strange to hear my usually reserved older daughter talk like this. I want to reply, but find my throat clogged with tears. Instead I squeeze her shoulders.

I remember sitting in that restaurant in Islington with her and feeling invincible. So smug with my shiny hair and my beautiful, clever daughter, and my huge, perfect belly. When did I start to become worried? Not immediately, I'm sure, though it was odd that she didn't move after the meal as she normally did. You don't go from invincible to anxious in one fell swoop. I told myself to be patient, that she'd move when she was ready.

Back home, I distracted myself, taking all the baby clothes out of the little chest of drawers we'd put in the spare room, unfolding them and laying them on the bed to gaze at. I'd held out against buying any as long as I could, but after the twenty-week scan, when I'd seen her moving around the screen, resistance was futile. Katy had bought her a tiny baby vest with a picture of a pram and the words 'that's how I roll'. I sat on the edge of the bed and held it up in front of me, imagining it filled out with the flour-soft skin of a newborn baby.

There are excuses you make when you're clinging on to normal by your fingernails. The rich food had sedated her. She'd inverted her sleeping patterns, so she'd now be awake all night instead.

When Saul came home, I greeted him with a face bright with denial. Yes, I'd had a lovely time with Pip. No, she wasn't too stressed over this new case. Oh, and Molly's playing silly-buggers, I said, with a little laugh to show it was nothing serious. She's gone into hibernation or something.

Because I didn't seem distressed, Saul wasn't either. He cooked dinner – some sort of stir fry, I think, Saul's culinary repertoire is largely wok-based – and, amazingly, when the time came to eat, I was hungry all over again. This time Molly would respond to the food, I convinced myself. She'd had her nap now. She'd be just waking up.

When the dinner produced no reaction, I ran myself a bath. Molly always came alive submerged in warm water, as if reacting to an environment she recognized. Lying back with my head resting on the edge of the bath, I willed her to send me a signal, my eyes glued to the mound of my stomach where it rose up out of the water, watching for that ghostly ripple, shapes made in skin.

I ran downstairs in a towel, water dripping a damp trail on the carpet. Saul was loading the dishwater in his usual mathematically precise way, as if he's trying to solve a Rubik's Cube.

'I can't find her, Saul!'

'What do you mean? What are you talking about?'

'Molly. I can't find her. She's not showing herself.'

Saul pulled me to him, water soaking his shirt, and stroked my wet hair. 'It'll be fine, Fran. She'll just be conserving her strength, that's all.'

'I want to go to the hospital.'

'But sweetheart . . .'

'I want to go to the hospital, Saul. I want to hear her. I won't sleep if I don't.'

In the A&E waiting room an extended Arabic-looking family was gathered – mother and grandmother in black headscarves, huge-eyed children staring at the mute television screen in the corner, following the subtitles with silently moving lips, a shrivelled old man in the centre of them all with a white beard and a bandage around his head through which blood seeped, shockingly red. Two loudly drunk women sprawled in the back row, one clutching a compress to an eye already turning black around the edges. 'He's not a violent person, d'you get me?' she said to her friend. 'He just gets a bit handy when he's had a few drinks.' There was a yellow-faced man sitting in front of us, with skin the texture of sweated onion. And me, staring at the TV with unseeing eyes, forcing myself to focus on how relieved I'd be when it was all sorted, when I heard Molly's heartbeat booming through the dome of my belly, the sublime embarrassment of being proved wrong.

'Mrs Francesca Friedman?'

The nurse who carried out the initial assessment looked exhausted, with violet shadows under her eyes.

'My wife just needs reassurance,' Saul told her when we were summoned to the cubicle off the main A&E waiting room.

She glanced at my bump, then up at my face. 'You'll have to go to the Labour Ward,' she said. 'I'll call up so they're expecting you.'

'I'm scared,' I whispered.

Saul bent down to kiss my forehead. 'It'll be fine,' he said. 'You'll see.'

'The thing is,' says Pip, wrenching me back to the present, 'part of me still feels it's not real. I mean, I still feel like such a baby myself. I spend half the time at work wondering when they're going to find out I'm a fraud who doesn't know anything. It doesn't seem possible that I'd be able to look after a baby.'

'Sorry to have to break it to you, Pip. That feeling never goes away.'

I think about my daughter at work, in the chambers I've never visited (in my mind they're wood-panelled), surrounded by serious-minded, public-school types, finding her place in a world completely alien to me, forming relationships that will move her further away.

'Oh, you're here. Thank God for that. I've been looking every-where. I'm really tired.'

Saul, a tall, lean black shadow against the charcoal sky, sounds put out, as if my not being in the places where he was looking is my fault. Immediately my hackles rise.

'Shall we go?' Saul has couched it as a question, but his body language says otherwise. His body language is already packed up and walking back to the room. His body language has put on its pyjamas and flossed its teeth.

'We can't leave Rob like this.' Pip is torn between her desire to do the right thing and her pressing fatigue. I can hear the dilemma in her voice. 'What if he chokes on his own vomit, or wakes up and doesn't know where he is and goes stumbling off into the darkness never to be seen again?'

'Rob's a big boy, darling. He'll be fine.' Saul has offered Pip his hand and is pulling her to her feet, but still she isn't sure.

'I just feel one of us should stay.'

'I'll stay.'

Only as the words come out do I realize I'm not ready yet to go to bed.

'I'll stay,' I repeat. 'It'll be finishing soon anyway. I'll stay until then to see if he wakes up, and if not, I'm sure the staff will help me get him back to the hotel.'

Saul's displeasure at this suggestion is palpable. 'It's ridiculous,' he says. 'This is Katy's mess. She ought to be sorting it out.'

'Well, maybe when you get back to the hotel you can find her and send her back out.'

Saul makes a snorting noise, but I talk over it.

'Pip's tired. She needs to go to bed. I won't be long.'

He isn't mollified, but his desire to be in bed exceeds his reservations.

'I'm aiming to be up by eight,' he says, as if he needs to explain himself. 'I want to finish my run in time for breakfast.'

'Don't forget the picnic.' The last word of Pip's sentence tails off into a wide yawn.

Saul looks up at the thick, sludge-coloured sky. 'Wouldn't be surprised if there was a storm overnight,' he says.

'Which is why they've brought gazebos,' Pip reminds him. 'That's what the invite said – Sunday-afternoon picnic, wet or dry. Make the most of the bank holiday weekend.'

The two of them are ready to go, yet they hover there as if waiting for permission to leave. Suddenly I have the strongest urge for them to be gone, to be here in the dark on my own.

'Off you go, you two. I'll follow in two minutes.'

'If you're sure. I still think it's ridiculous. Rob's a grown—'

'Go!'

Only after I have watched their two dark shapes disappear into the still lit-up hotel do I think to wonder how I'll get into our room if Saul, who has the only key, is already in bed.

But by then it's too late.

Sunday, 1 a.m.

The band has announced the last song and, somewhat predict-ably, a drunken chorus of 'Perfect Day' is ringing out from the orangery, where all the remaining windows have now been closed in deference to the hotel's other guests and the lateness of the hour.

'Is there anything to drink out here?'

Rob's voice, coming from his hitherto lifeless body, gives me a shock.

'I should think that's the last thing you need,' I say, although the truth is that while I've been sitting here keeping vigil, I've been berating myself for not bringing a bottle of wine to keep me company.

'Shit.' Rob raises himself heavily on to his elbows. 'I've been a nuisance, haven't I?'

'A bit.'

We remain for a while in companionable silence.

'Are you sure you've got nothing to drink?'

'Quite sure.'

It strikes me now that this is quite a bizarre situation, to be sitting in the darkness with my daughter's very drunk, potentially soon-to-be-ex-boyfriend.

'I've always liked you, Rob,' I say, and for some reason this makes us both laugh a lot, our giggles loud in the still, late-night air.

Rob rolls over on to his hands and knees and heaves himself up on to his feet.

'Where are you going?'

'To replenish our supplies.'

'But it's all finishing now, they'll be clearing everything away.'

'Exactly. Perfect time to collect up all the leftovers.'

He lurches up the grass slope towards the orangery.

'Don't—'

Too late, he is already rattling on the French windows, trying to work out why they won't open.

'There's a door around the side.'

Perhaps he can't hear, because he carries on rattling until one of the remaining guests finally takes pity and opens the catch to let him in.

I wonder if Katy's in there, and what will happen if she is. I should go in, just in case. A good mother would want to be sure there wasn't a scene. A good mother wouldn't loll drunkenly on the grass.

Yet I don't move. My limbs feel pleasantly welded to the ground. What will be, will be. Once that thought is in my head, it won't be budged. I sing a little to myself, in an experimental fashion. I'm not raging drunk, I decide. But I am buzzing in a nice, low-key way.

'Fran? Where are you? I can't see a bloody thing.'

Rob reappears suddenly, lurching around the side of the orangery, a bottle in each hand.

'Here,' I say. 'I've been singing.'

'Jolly good.'

He looms up over me, brandishing his spoils, before dropping back to the ground.

'What's going on in there?'

'Oh, you know, usual end-of-wedding stuff. Lights on, people snogging, aged aunts unconscious in corners.'

'Katy?'

'Katy who?'

Ah.

Rob hands me one of the bottles of wine. 'I couldn't carry glasses as well, so I got us a bottle each. We can just swig from the top.'

It belatedly occurs to me that I'm supposed to be looking after Rob, not indulging him.

'You really shouldn't be having any more.' My voice sounds prim and silly, even to me.

'Lucy and Jamie are still in there, saying their goodbyes. She's gorgeous. He's a lucky sod.'

I take a long swig from the bottle in my hand and almost gag. The wine tastes warm and thick and sweet, like blood.

'What on earth have you given me? It's vile. Wasn't there any of the Sauvignon Blanc left?'

'Oh, sorry. I forgot to say. I couldn't see any white, so I got you red. Don't you like it?'

'It's horrible,' I say, taking another long swig.

'There's a plan being hatched,' says Rob, 'to take all the excess booze to one of the hotel rooms and have an after-party.'

I imagine it. All the dregs of the wedding crammed into one of the beige rooms, guests splayed out across mushroom-coloured sheets, unwilling to admit it's all over.

'The bride and groom, of course, will be fucking off to their palatial bridal suite,' says Rob. 'Apparently there's a hot tub.'

A hot tub. There would be. The wine tastes acidic at the back of my throat, but I force it down. I won't think about it. Jamie and Lucy, bridal suites and hot tubs. I won't allow myself to go there.

'I'm game for the after-party,' I say. 'It might be fun.'

The idea of lying in bed next to Saul, listening to the noise he makes in his nose when he sleeps, watching the light change through the beige curtains, is intolerable.

Someone appears from around the side of the orangery.

'I'm going to have to move you folks, I'm afraid. We're finishing up here now.'

The boy in uniform seems too young to be up so late.

'No problem.'

I am obsequious to compensate for Rob because I worry about

him making a scene. At the moment he is passive, but desperation is throbbing under the surface like a volcano about to erupt.

'I'm not going back to my room,' slurs Rob. 'I don't want to see her again. My *ex*-girlfriend, I mean.'

There's an edge to his voice when he talks about Katy that wasn't there before, and for the first time I worry about her and whatever scene she has coming. She is so young still, without a sense of how lasting hurt can be, or the damage it can do. Hurt slides off her like water on oilskin. And yet when I was her age, I was already married. It hardly seems possible.

Rob and I are being ushered away from the orangery and in the direction of the hotel, but some sense of decorum makes me hesitate.

'We should go back in, to say thank you.'

Rob stands, swaying slightly, as he ponders this.

'Come on then,' he says eventually.

'We'll lose our late licence if people abuse it,' says the young boy who has been trying to move us on, his eyes wide and injured.

Rob finds this funny. 'We mustn't abuse the licence,' he tells me. 'The licence will need therapy.'

Entering the orangery feels like walking in on someone in the act of getting undressed. The harsh overhead lights have been turned on, revealing red-wine-stained tablecloths, littered with part-filled glasses and crumpled serviettes. A few of the disposable cameras that were left on each table at lunchtime are still scattered about, and in one corner a girl is using one to take photos of the blisters on her friend's foot.

There's a small crowd of guests on the dance floor, with jackets on and bags and toddlers draped over shoulders, performing the pantomime leave-taking of the pleasantly drunk. I see Lynn, exhausted but dimpling with pleasure, and Max, smiling bene-volently as if the credit for all of it lies with him. Maddie is tightly clutching the arm of Liam, the best man, and Lucy is returned to her former radiance, as if the girl sobbing in the toilets was someone else entirely. And next to her, holding her hand firmly as if she might at any moment blow away, is Jamie.

I stop, suddenly unsure about going on, but Rob, propelled by some inner momentum, continues on his set trajectory.

'Don't talk to us, we're licence-abusers,' he tells Lynn and Max, who smile gamely, as if they have the first clue what he's talking about.

'It's been so lovely,' I tell them. 'Thank you so much.'

'We're going to an after-party,' Rob announces. 'In someone's room. There's a hot tub.'

'No, Rob,' I say. 'There isn't.'

'Ha! You're right! The hot tub's in the bride and groom's room,' he says. 'Oi, Jamie! How about we all pile into your pad for a jacuzzi? We'll be quiet. You won't even know we're there.'

I feel my face burning as Lucy and Jamie look over, startled.

'He's just joking,' I say, refraining from miming drinking gestures behind Rob's back.

'Yes. Sorry,' says Rob. 'Ignore me. I'm the obligatory embarrassing jilted drunk. No wedding's complete without one.'

'Anyway, we're off now. We've had a fantastic day.' If my smile got any wider it would surely break my face.

'Well, you're not going without a hug.' Lucy opens her arms expectantly. What can I do except step towards her, the corners of my smile still lodged in my cheeks? I feel her exercise-hardened arms wrap around me. For such a slight little thing, she has surprising strength. My breath feels squashed inside me.

'It's been such a pleasure to meet you at last, Fran,' she says, finally releasing me and fixing me with her pale-blue gaze. 'I hope we're going to see lots of each other.'

'Absolutely,' I say.

'My turn,' says Rob, jolting me out of the way and grabbing hold of Lucy to sweep her into an embrace. For a moment the two of them sway together, he hulking over her tiny frame, and I worry he might crush her.

I feel a tap on my shoulder.

'So you're going to stay up some more, are you, you party animal, you?' says Jamie. His voice sounds unnatural, as if he's acting the part of himself.

'I don't know. We might look in, I suppose.'

'Sounds like fun. Maybe we'll—'

'Jamie!' Lucy is mock-slapping him on the arm. 'We are *not* going to crowd into one poxy room when we've paid a fucking fortune for the honeymoon suite. Either you come with me, or that's it. We're getting divorced.'

Lynn and Max and Maddie chortle at this, and I try to laugh along too, and turn away.

'I don't blame you,' I say to Lucy, grabbing hold of Rob's arm and steering him in the direction of the exit. 'Have a brilliant night.'

Halfway across the room, I stop, cringing. Did I really just tell them to have a brilliant night?

Rob glances down at me. In the harsh overhead light, his pale, broad face looks doughy and damp. Clearly I'm not looking much better because he says, 'Couldn't you at least look like you're enjoying it?'

He means it as a joke, but his words propel me right back to the 1980s and, once again, to David, my married seducer.

'Couldn't you at least try to look like you're enjoying it?'

It was the second time we'd had sex. A different hotel, but not much better.

'The room's cheaper than normal because it hasn't got any windows,' David had explained as we walked down the stairs to the lower level. 'I knew you wouldn't mind. It's not as if we're going to be hanging around long enough to admire the view.'

He was still nervous, this second time, but he was excited as well. His cheeks were flushed and I could hear him swallowing loudly. In the room, he'd produced the customary bottle of cheap red wine from his bag with a flourish, opening it with the corkscrew on the end of his penknife. But after he'd thrashed around on top of me for a little while on the quilted satin bed cover, he'd become tetchy.

'Couldn't you at least try to look like you're enjoying it?' he said, glaring down at me accusingly, as if I were a particularly dim student who wasn't even trying to get her algebra right. And later, 'You're supposed to *move*, you know.'

'Are you? Sorry, no one told me.'

'It's like having sex with a futon.'

I laughed then. It was Reading in 1984. I'd never heard the word 'futon' before. I thought he was making a joke. I thought Futons were something out of *Star Trek*, like Klingons.

But David, as I only really realize with hindsight, had little sense of humour.

We did it again, and I tried to move, but without any guidance as to exactly what form those movements were supposed to take, I was at sea. As David panted and thrust on top of me, I made experimental forays with my arms and legs, shifting them randomly in small jerky movements until he ground to a halt and rolled off, sitting on the edge of the bed to light a cigarette and stare moodily at the carpet tiles.

Afterwards, when he dropped me off, he stopped a few streets away from mine.

'It's probably best for you to get out here. So there's no chance of being seen. For your own sake. You know how people's minds work.'

I nodded, even though I knew I'd either have to walk the long way round to get home or else cut across the patch of wasteland where a girl had been raped a couple of years before, and where women regularly reported flashers. It wasn't late, but it was November and already pitch black. The top of my legs hurt and I was starting to feel hungover from the wine, although I didn't recognize it as that. I just associated that sick, thumping-head feeling with sex and with him.

'Oh, OK. Bye then,' I said, gathering up my bag.

He didn't get out of the car, just leaned across to peck me on the cheek without even taking his foot off the clutch.

'Fran?'

I turned, one foot already on the pavement, where a light drizzle had started to come down. For a moment I thought he'd say something nice then, something affectionate or at least kind.

'I think it'd be better if we didn't see each other for a bit. You're lovely and everything, but, you know, I've got to think about my wife and my son and what's best for them. You know how it is.'

'Oh, yes.' I nodded vigorously in the now pouring rain. 'That's fine.'

All this comes back to me now as Rob and I make our way back towards the main hotel building, where a couple of wall lights on either side of the entrance emit a welcoming yellow glow in the thick grey night. All these years without thinking of David, and suddenly he's lodged in my brain, with his reminders of things I don't want to face.

I shiver, and notice that the weather has changed. Impossible to believe that just a few short hours ago we were sweltering in the shade. Now banks of oppressive clouds swaddle the sky and there's a dampness in the air that carries an underlying chill.

'Did you feel that?'

'What?' Rob seems taken aback by my question, as if he's forgotten I'm even there.

'Rain. I'm sure I just felt some rain.'

'Nah. It's not going to rain on the golden couple's wedding. Don't be silly, Fran.'

We continue in silence for a few seconds as more spots of water land on my head, and I sense Rob brooding about something.

'I wonder if Katy's getting rained on in her love nest.'

I sigh silently, a deep, inward sigh that I swallow down.

'Don't jump to conclusions, Rob. She's probably back in your room right now, fast asleep. She just wasn't too impressed with your drinking, that's all. She's giving you a wide berth until you've slept it off.'

'I'm not stupid, Fran.'

'I never said you were. What do you—'

'He's disappeared as well, or hadn't you noticed? Pretty boy from our lunch table.'

'For God's sake, Rob, just drop it, hey?'

The rain is unmistakeable now, great big gobs of it splattering my bare shoulders and hair and rolling down my forehead.

'Sorry. I'm sorry. Ignore me. I'm an idiot.'

151

'You're not an idiot, Rob, you've just had a lot to drink. We both have. Maybe we should just go to bed.'

Part of me is hoping he says yes, and that the two of us will take the lift to the fourth floor and say goodnight in the corridor, before retiring to our respective rooms with our respective partners. But a bigger part can't bear the thought of being enclosed all night in that beige room with Saul, knowing that on the floor above – perhaps even in the room above – Jamie and Lucy are getting ready for their first night as husband and wife, testing out the hot tub, the sound of their giggles carrying down through our open window as I lie awake listening in the dark.

Sunday, 2 a.m.

The first person I see when we walk through the door of Room 34 is Bart.

'I thought you'd gone!' The words blurt from me like newly opened ketchup. 'Your wife was waiting all that time!'

'Oh, it's all right, she went home with the kids. It seemed stupid, both of us having to leave. I offered her the chance to stay out, said I'd take the kids home, but she said she was tired. They're all coming back tomorrow for the picnic. So . . . I've got a free pass!'

Bart seems genuinely delighted by this unexpected turn of events and touchingly convinced we'll all feel the same way. I take a deep breath and try to remember what it was about him earlier on that made me soften towards him.

'Hey, dude, did you find your girlfriend?'

Bart has turned his attention to Rob, and for the first time I notice that a change has come over him since I last saw him. His eyes are darting from side to side, and his whole body seems stiff and tense.

I glance rapidly around the room, where around thirty people are squashed into every neutrally coloured cranny. No flash of fuchsia pink, no black curls, no dimples or raucous laughter. It's both a worry and a relief.

'She's bound to be asleep,' I say, not believing it for a minute. Katy doesn't like to miss a party. Katy *is* the party.

'*He*'s not here either,' says Rob, and I don't have to ask him who he means. 'But those friends of his are.'

I see the couple from the lunch table wedged into one of the two armchairs by the window. She is on his lap and her silver-foil dress has ridden up her perfect brown legs. His eyes are fixed on her cleavage. They really ought to be in their own room.

The dressing table next to the door is crammed with bottles at various levels of fullness, purloined from the wedding party. Rob picks up the nearest one and takes a long swig.

'Er, we do have glasses, you know,' says a pinch-faced young woman whom I recognize as one of Lucy's bridesmaids. I'm assuming this is her room. She seems none too pleased to find it suddenly filled up with the wedding dregs. I look around for the partner whose idea this no doubt was and spot a tall, shaven-headed man, stripped to the waist, pouring shots into plastic cups and handing them out with a hostly air.

'That's bloody convenient!'

The raised voice is coming from over by the window, where the four-legged, four-armed creature that is the couple from lunch is sitting. It is Rob's voice.

'Brilliant! That's all we need!' mutters the pinch-faced brides-maid. 'A bloody fight.'

'There's not going to be a fight,' I tell her, moving off to collect Rob.

'They say they have no idea where Pretty Boy went. I say that's pretty bloody convenient.' Rob's face, as he speaks to me, is the colour of liver.

'Well, they probably don't.' I smile at the couple, trying to send *he's perfectly harmless* vibes. Meanwhile I steer Rob away. 'We'll have to leave if you carry on like this.'

'Sorry.'

'You've got to get a grip, Rob.'

'Sorry. I'm sorry, Fran. You don't deserve this. It's just . . . Oh, you won't understand, you've been happily married for years.'

'Try me.'

'It's just, you know that saying? If you love someone, let them go, and if they come back to you, they're yours, blah blah blah. Well, Katy wouldn't come back. Do you know how depressing that is? She's already taken off and I'm hanging on to her ankles like a bloody idiot, because she'd never fucking come back. And I feel so stupid. But I can't help myself.'

'Here you two are!'

I'm astonished that Maddie has arrived without more of a fanfare. She is wearing the same white suit, but has refreshed her make-up and her streaky blonde hair has been artfully mussed. I surprise myself by being pleased to see her.

'I'm so glad to see you, Fran. I thought I might be the oldest one here! Not that it bothers me in the slightest. Age is just an attitude, as far as I'm concerned.'

The oldest one here! The nerve of her!

'The newlyweds have gone up to their little love nest. They're so much in love, it warms your heart. Even an old cynic like me!'

'Yes,' I manage, because she is clearly waiting for a response. 'It's lovely.'

Maddie leans forward and I get a strong whiff of freshly applied Chanel No 5 mixed with a day's worth of champagne and perspiration – a heady, sweet smell that is all but overpowering.

'It sounds like such a cliché, but I think of Jamie as my son. I really do. You must feel the same about Rob here.'

I feel my head nodding up and down, as if it is being moved by some invisible hand. 'Oh yes. Rob's one of the family.'

Why on earth did I say that? When the chances are he won't be for much longer? I don't dare look at Rob's face. I have a horrible feeling he might be about to cry.

'Now, Fran, without being obvious about it, talk me through the talent in the room. Anyone interesting?'

'There's always Bart,' I say, with a tight smile. 'He's the one in the Hawaiian shirt.'

Maddie's own smile dims a notch. 'I don't think so,' she says. 'Not my type. I thought ponytails disappeared with the 1980s. Please don't tell me they're back again. I might have to leave the country.'

We all laugh prettily, but inside my head isn't pretty.

'Fran doesn't notice other men,' Rob says, ignoring the under-tones pulsing between Maddie and myself. 'She is married to Saul, and Saul is a saint.'

I feel myself go tense. A saint! Just what people used to say about my father. The idea of history repeating itself makes me feel queasy and I'm tempted to spill the secret of Saul's internet affair with the architect in Edinburgh. See, not so saintly, after all! But of course I keep quiet.

The corners of Maddie's mouth twitch. 'I'm sure he's not a saint all the time,' she says. 'Being married to a full-time saint would get a little dull, don't you think, Fran?'

Oh God, why did I agree to come here? There is no escape from this room, from these people. Only bed. Suddenly I remember the lack of a key. Going to bed would mean waking up Saul and suffering a day of pointed yawns tomorrow.

There are a lot of people crowded around the door to the bathroom. I watch them for a while, puzzling over their raucous conversation and loud shrieks of laughter.

'I see the coke's arrived,' says Rob. 'Don't tell Bart the Fart, he's been asking about it all evening.'

I observe more closely as the door opens and Rosie emerges with another girl. They are giggling and brushing their fingers under their noses. In the harsh bathroom light, Rosie's dress is the colour of industrially made curry. The couple from our lunch table slip in behind her, quickly locking the door.

'I don't need any of that stuff,' says Maddie, frowning. 'I've so much natural energy. People are always asking me where I get it from. If I had any of that, I'd be up for a week!'

'Good job Katy's not here,' says Rob.

'Why?' It comes out more sharply than I meant.

'Oh, nothing.'

'Rob?'

'Nothing. Nothing.'

'But what did you mean?'

'I didn't mean anything. Ignore me. Everyone else does.'

Rob is leaning against the wall, with his hands in his pockets. He looks like a child – a huge, drunk, broken-hearted child – and I want to put my arms around him and try to make him feel better. Imagine the field day Maddie would have with that one!

The couple from our lunch table emerge from the bathroom, laughing. The girl catches my eye and looks embarrassed, immediately turning her head as if she hasn't seen me.

There's a knock on the door and the pinch-faced bridesmaid gets up to answer it. The new arrivals tumble into the room in a whirl of raindrops and flushed cheeks and giggles – and fuchsia taffeta.

For a second the two of them stand shaking their hair and clothes, smiling around the room as if looking for applause from the audience. Then Katy sees us, standing over here by the far wall. Her face, which a moment ago was pink with excitement and rain and whatever it is the two of them have been doing in the rain, becomes first wide-eyed with surprise and then falls slack.

She glances up at the handsome man who has come in with her, similarly damp and shaking droplets of exhilaration from his hair, and gives the briefest shake of her head. A fleeting gesture, but telling.

'Oh, Jesus,' whispers Rob to himself.

Now Katy comes towards us, pushing the hair away from her face and smiling determinedly, as if being given directions from off stage.

'I wasn't expecting to see you here,' she says, mostly to me, although her body is partially turned towards Rob. 'Bit late for you, isn't it, Mum? Aren't you normally in bed with your sleepy-time tea hours before this?'

I know she's just casting around for something to say, but I'm still hurt.

Katy is still looking at me, but Rob reaches out and grabs her roughly by the arm to turn her to face him. 'Where've you been?'

'At the wedding. Not that you'd have any idea, seeing as you spent most of it in a drunken stupor, dribbling on the grass.'

'The wedding finished ages ago. Where've you been until now?'

'A few of us took a walk in the rain, to cool off. Anyway I don't have to explain myself to you. Not after the way you've behaved.'

I see what Katy is doing here, making a net of her guilt so that Rob's anger bounces off it straight back to him.

'It doesn't look like "a few of us". It looks like just two of you.'

Rob's voice has risen, and I glance around to see who is listening. The handsome man has joined some of his friends, but he keeps looking over. Our eyes meet and then immediately we look away. He seems nervous, but also half-dazed. For the first time, I soften towards him.

'Maybe we should go.' I'm appealing to Katy, but I mean Rob as well.

'And maybe you should stay out of it, Mum.'

Katy has her hand on her hip and her lower lip is jutting out. I notice she has recently reapplied her lipstick – the colour, perfectly matched to her dress, is fresh and even. I don't want to think about the circumstances in which you might need to reapply make-up in the company of a man you've not long met. Standing in that position, she looks so much like her childhood self that my throat catches. She was always so quick to imagine a slight, so premature in her reactions, attacking before she'd properly assessed the nature of the snub. And not just on her own behalf either. How many times have I seen her standing just this way, fronting up to someone she thought might have said something deprecating about one of her friends or, God forbid, Pip?

'I'll leave you two to chat,' I say, trying to keep my voice neutral. I'm so tired of it all now. Only the nagging worry that some dreadful scene might erupt while I'm gone, and the prospect of Saul's grumpy, woken-from-sleep face at the door, keep me from heading back to my own room. I make for the bed instead, intending to find a vacant patch of mushroom-coloured bedspread to sit on, but am intercepted.

'Is everything OK?'

It's the girl in the silver dress. I hardly recognize her without her boyfriend attached to her like a zip-on bag. She hooks her silky brown hair behind her ear nervously, then shakes it straight out again.

I remember that she is friends with the handsome man, and imagine that she, too, is trying to gauge the level of threat.

'Oh, everything's fine,' I say breezily. 'They'll sort themselves out.'

'We didn't really get a chance to meet properly at lunch. My name's Sasha.' She holds out a hand so delicate I hardly dare close my fingers around it, for fear of breaking it. 'You're friends of Jamie's, I'm guessing.'

'Well, friends of the family, really.'

'He's lovely, isn't he? Jamie?'

I get the feeling Sasha is testing me out, trying to get the measure of my allegiances. I smile and nod, not trusting my own voice.

'There's something quite mysterious about him. I think that's why Lucy fell for him. Because he's a challenge.'

Sasha is playing with the pendant around her slender neck, a free-floating silver heart that she slides up and down its delicate silver chain. I wonder if the man she's with gave it to her. I imagine her taking it out of its gift box and exclaiming, wondering secretly what it means to be given a silver heart by a man. Wondering what it means for her to wear it.

'Do you know,' Sasha leans forward conspiratorially, 'I once asked Lucy what she loved most about Jamie and she said, "I never know what he's thinking." Isn't that a strange thing to say about someone you're going to spend your whole life with? Don't you think there might be something else you'd love more?'

But I know what Jamie is thinking. I always know. Even though sometimes I wish I didn't.

'You two look like you're plotting something.' Rosie is standing next to us, her eyes darting between us. 'Come on, 'fess up. What are you talking about?'

'Nothing,' says Sasha. 'Just this and that.'

'Oh my *God*! I've been having the dullest conversations all day. Why does no one ever tell me anything juicy? Fran . . .' Rosie leans towards me and for a moment I think she's about to give me a hug, but no, she wants to whisper something. 'What's going on with Katy and Hugo? Is Rob going to start a fight?'

'Who's Hugo?' I take a small step backwards, hoping Rosie doesn't notice.

'You know.' Sasha looks personally affronted. 'My friend who was at our lunch table. The one over there.'

Of course, Hugo is the handsome man Katy has become so enamoured with. He *would* be called Hugo. I glance at Katy and Rob. They are talking to each other, but without looking at one another. Katy is addressing a spot on the floor by Rob's foot, while Rob is gazing upwards, lobbing the odd word up to the ceiling.

'My *God*, just everyone is falling out today,' continues Rosie. 'Earlier on Jamie and Lucy had that spat – on their *wedding* day, can you believe? And even Mum and Dad were arguing before they went to bed.'

Lynn and Max? I remember the pleasure on Lynn's face as she did the Conga, hands splayed around her husband's waist, and her quiet pride as she stood by Max's side, listening to departing guests effuse about the wedding. What can have happened between then and bed to cause an argument? It's depressing, the idea of all of us in our little beige bedrooms, having the same petty rows.

'You and Saul must be just about the only couple who *haven't* had an argument today,' Rosie goes on. 'Not that I could imagine anyone ever arguing with Saul. He's such a sweetie, isn't he? I can't believe he's even come along here to keep you company, when I know full well he was just *dying* to get to bed.'

'What do you mean, here?'

Rosie squints at me as if unsure whether I'm joking. 'Well, he's right over there, talking to Lucy's mother. He's been here, like, *ages*.'

I follow her gaze and, sure enough, there in a corner, deep in conversation with Maddie, is my husband of twenty-four years.

'I would go claim him if I were you,' says Sasha. 'Maddie's notorious!'

I smile, but all of a sudden I am having trouble breathing. There's no air in here. Someone has closed the window, I see now, maybe because of the rain, or perhaps they've had complaints about the noise. But the room is too hot, there are too many of us in here, breathing in each other's alcohol-soaked breath.

Why is Saul here? What made him get up and join the kind of party he'd normally do anything to avoid?

It comes to me with a certainty that feels physical, like a cricket ball in the stomach.

He doesn't trust me.

Sunday, 3 a.m.

'I woke up and remembered you didn't have a room key. And that was that. I couldn't go back to sleep. I lay there fretting for a while, hoping you'd come up, and then realized it was useless and came to find you.'

Saul is telling me all this in an avuncular voice (*And here I am at a party, being good-humoured, despite no sleep,* says Saul's internal monologue), but the expression on his face says he doesn't want to be here, fully dressed, in this airless hotel room, among all these strangers.

'See, what a sweetie!' says Rosie. 'Any of my exes would have been freaking out if I'd made them get out of bed in the middle of the night!'

'I didn't make him. He did it all of his own volition.' Resentment is bringing a sour taste to the back of my mouth. Or maybe it's the wine. I started drinking again practically the second I saw Saul, in some kind of bizarre Pavlovian response, but the dregs that are left taste a bit like salad dressing.

'Anyway, now you're here, we can both go up to our room, then you can go to bed and I'll come back with the key. Sorted!' I say.

Saul doesn't appear thrilled by this plan. 'I might as well stick around for a while, now I'm up.'

'Yay, Saul!' Rosie seems genuinely delighted at Saul's resurrection. She claps her hands together like a small child and does a little skip. It's rather unnerving. 'Bart will be so happy. He's been asking about you all night.'

Sasha is still standing with us, but her attention has wandered to the bathroom, where her boyfriend is standing, holding the door open and beckoning her over. 'I'm just being summoned, so I'd better . . .'

Rosie, craning to see what's happening, is not about to miss out. 'Me too!' She grabs hold of Sasha's hand and the two of them move hurriedly away.

'We'll be back!' Rosie calls over her shoulder.

Then it is just us. Saul and I. We gaze around the room in silence, and I have a flashback to Maddie talking about long-term couples sitting in silence in restaurants.

'There's another reason I couldn't sleep,' says Saul suddenly. He looks at me, as if weighing something up, and opens his mouth to speak. Then his expression shifts, as if he's changed his mind about whatever he was about to say. 'I'm worried about our daughter,' he says.

It's a funny thing, I've got one daughter who's pregnant by a married man and another who's in danger of having a very nasty public bust-up with her boyfriend, but when Saul says, 'I'm worried about our daughter,' the first thing I think of is Molly.

'My wife's worried about our daughter,' he told the midwife who opened the door of the Labour Ward the night Molly stopped moving. The midwife was small and plump, with frizzy ginger hair that escaped from the sides of the ponytail she'd pulled it back into, forming a soft orange fuzz around her head. Her shoes squeaked on the institutional green lino floor as she led us into a cramped side room.

'We're just after a bit of reassurance,' I told her, when I trusted myself to speak without choking. 'I expect you have that all the time, pregnant women coming in late at night, needing their minds put at rest?'

She nodded and smiled up at me, warmth crinkling up her face. 'It's not unheard of, yes.'

I felt better once she'd said that. Lots of women had scares like this. It was perfectly normal. They'd let us listen to our baby and then send us home, mortified but happy.

Nowadays, when I lie awake at night, in those scary dead hours between the last of the shouty late-night drinkers and the first of the early-morning commuters turning over car engines in the still, grey, pre-dawn light, I think back to that moment in that little room in the hospital, when everything was still possible. In my head, I rebuild the scene like Lego, detail by detail, remembering how the smell of antiseptic didn't quite mask the acrid whiff coming from the white plastic bin when the midwife pressed the pedal to throw something away. I remember the beeper on the desk that insistently flashed red, and how I felt embarrassed that we were keeping this busy woman from some more pressing emergency. I remember my file of notes next to it, reassuringly slim, and thinking that at least she would be able to see I wasn't a habitual time-waster, making a steady stream of unnecessary visits to the hospital on the slightest of pretexts.

I remember Saul's hand finding mine as we sat side by side, as if on a bus, waiting to be reassured, and the laminated poster on the wall opposite, giving a step-by-step guide to avoiding the spread of germs.

Sometimes when I lie awake beside Saul's lightly snoring body, I will myself back to that moment, re-creating every smell, every sound. The faint tapping of the blind against the window as the wind moved it, the occasional shouts from outside the window of the late-night drunks ejected from A&E. The voices of two nurses in the corridor outside, growing louder as they passed the door and then fading into the distance.

If I just concentrate enough, try enough, wish enough, I feel sure, on these long, lonely nights, that I can get myself back to that point, that moment when nothing had yet been decided, and then, once I'm back there, I can force another outcome. The midwife will get out her little CTG machine. No, even better, she'll just listen with her normal stethoscope and, because of the strength of Molly's heartbeat, that will be enough. 'Two heartbeats,' she'll say, straightening herself up and giving me her comforting smile. 'Now go home and get some rest.'

It never happens, of course. And after a sleepless night searching for the wormhole that will take me back in time to that little room, to the midwife smiling, to the laminated poster on the wall, the following day is always swollen with Molly's absence. Even though it's been two years, my life continues to be defined by the lack of her. So when Saul says he's worried about our daughter, I automatically think of my lost little girl.

But Saul is talking about Pip.

'She seems so wrapped up in herself,' he says. 'And she's lost weight. Have you noticed? I think it's starting again.'

He means the anorexia. When Pip was in the middle of it, slowly reducing herself to nothing, Saul could never call it by its name. 'My daughter isn't well,' he'd tell people. 'It's a nervous disease,' he'd add, if pressed for specifics.

I challenged him on it one day in counselling.

'Saul was ashamed that Pip had an eating disorder,' I said, while we were arguing about something else. 'He thought it reflected badly on him.'

Saul had turned to me then, open-mouthed.

'Is that really what you think?' he asked. 'That I cared what people thought of me?'

'Then why couldn't you ever admit it, if it wasn't because you didn't want people judging you?'

He looked at me as if I was being deliberately dense.

'Because I couldn't bear for people to be judging *her*. My daughter – my beautiful daughter – was attacking herself because she didn't think she was worthy of taking up space in the world. Do you really think I was going to let other people attack her too?'

I remember sitting in my customary spot on the left-hand side of the sofa in Louise's consulting room and being shocked at just how much Saul loved his daughter. No, that sounds wrong. Of course I knew Saul loved his children. How could I not know that? But what was shocking was the rawness of his love. What was shocking was the realization that Saul loved Pip and Katy just as much as I did.

Now, in this sweatbox of a hotel room, surrounded by these drunken semi-strangers, listening to Saul telling me why his worry about Pip is keeping him awake at night, that realization shocks me all over again.

Again I feel guilty for not telling Saul about Pip's pregnancy. My promise to my daughter, tossed out so easily with the puffed-up self-importance of the confidante, now feels burdensome. I want to shrug it off and hand it over to Saul so he can carry it for a while.

Frustration makes me tetchy. 'I don't think it's the *anorexia* again,' I say, emphasizing the word he finds so hard to say, just to prove a point. 'I think she has some . . . relationship troubles.'

Saul looks at me, and I notice how tired he seems. His naturally olive skin has a sallow tinge, and there are dark shadows under his eyes that I haven't seen there before. For a brief moment, I have a glimpse of how Saul will look in old age – the exaggerated hollow of his cheek making his slightly hooked nose more prominent. It makes me feel strangely protective of him, this old man hidden inside my husband's super-fit body.

'What do you mean by relationship troubles? I didn't even know Pip *had* a relationship. Oh, that's weird . . .'

Saul has broken off and is staring across the room at the closing bathroom door.

'What's weird?'

'Why is Katy going to the loo with Rosie?'

I watch him as realization dawns, settling over his features like a dark net.

'Oh.'

I cast around the room, looking for Rob, and am relieved to find he's not here. 'At least Rob's gone to bed.'

Saul, whose face is now set into hard lines, also looks around, his eyes finally coming to rest on a point near the floor. 'Sorry to disappoint you, darling,' he says.

Rob is sitting on the carpet, leaning back against the wall, his hair clinging damply to his skull, his face a sweaty mask of drunkenness and despair. His elbows rest on his knees, which are drawn up towards his chest, and his big, meaty hands hang down limply in between them.

'We can't leave until we've got him to bed,' Saul says. 'Otherwise things might kick off.'

Suddenly I'm tired, impossibly tired. The idea of going back on Rob duty fills me with weary dread. 'He won't leave. I've already tried.'

Now that the possibility of leaving has been snatched away, it's all I can think about. I stare mutely at the door, imagining opening it and heading out, making my way up to the next floor and bed.

I'm still staring at it when I hear a loud knocking noise, followed by a volley of smaller knocks.

'Oh my *God*,' squeals Rosie, who has just emerged from the bathroom, sniffing. 'It's the noise police, everyone shut up!'

'Don't answer it!' shouts Sasha's not-so-handsome boyfriend. 'Let's just pretend we're not here.'

Everyone obligingly quietens down, except a woman in orange who is lying across the end of the bed and thinks it hysterical to shriek out 'Coo-eee!'

Maddie breaks the silence as the knocking continues. 'There's no use pretending. They know we're in here.'

She pulls down on her waistcoat and runs her fingers through her tousled blonde hair, before straightening up and taking a deep breath. Then, shoulders thrown back, she opens the door a fraction, peering through the crack so the rest of us remain hidden from view.

'Oh,' she says, surprise causing her to take a small step backwards into the room. 'You? You're not supposed to be here! It's your bloody wedding night!'

Sunday, 4 a.m.

A m I talking too loudly? Saul is looking at me as if he's restraining himself from saying something. I'm hyperconscious of every sound I make, every move of my body. I feel Jamie's presence across the room from where he remains standing near the door.

'Lucy's fast asleep,' he explained when he arrived. 'I could hear you all down here, having fun, so I came to see what was going on. It's my wedding and if anyone's bloody well having fun it ought to be me, don't you think? I left her a note, don't worry.'

Rosie is hanging off his arm like a child's mitten on a string. She is transparently delighted that he's here, alone.

'Why should he be lying awake, missing out on everything? It's his bloody party, after all.'

Maddie, however, is unconvinced. 'What if she wakes up? You should be there when she wakes up.'

'She won't wake up. You know how soundly Lucy sleeps. Anyway, she'll see the note and come down. She won't mind. She'll be more cross that I didn't wake her up to come with me.'

I think of poor Lucy, waking up on her wedding night in some huge bridal bed, stretching out a hand to touch her new husband and encountering empty space. I force myself to imagine her confusion, hoping empathy will drown out that treacherous little voice at the back of my head asking, *Why would you leave your bride on your wedding night unless you're not happy?*

'He's being an utter twat,' Katy is saying.

She isn't talking about Jamie.

Since emerging from the bathroom, Katy has been in attack mode. When Saul told her, 'You don't need that stuff,' meaning whatever she'd been taking in the bathroom with Rosie, she rounded on him, cheeks flushed.

'I was just keeping her company. Don't judge me! Why are you here anyway?'

When we told her we were here largely because of Rob, she rounded on him as well.

'This is why I don't want to be with him any more,' she says, vindicated.

It's the first time she's voiced this out loud and, though it has been obvious for some time, it still hurts. She's right, Rob is being a twat. But he's principled and he's kind – *I'm so sorry about the baby* – and I will miss him.

'You haven't exactly behaved well today,' Saul says, primly. 'Where did you disappear to with that man?'

'Oh, honestly! We were just talking, OK? Or is that a crime now?'

Katy has always operated a boomerang approach to criticism, flinging it back in the face of whoever dished it out, without stopping to analyse its merits.

Right now is not the time to lecture her. Her blue eyes are round and glassy like a doll's and as she stands, she sways, listing to one side and then the other.

Looking at her, I contract with worry. What was Rob suggesting? Has Katy got a problem?

'It's very late,' says Saul, making a pantomime out of looking at his watch. 'Why don't we all get to bed and discuss it in the morning?'

'I'm not ready to go to bed,' I say. 'You go ahead though.'

'I'm not ready either,' says Katy, with a sideways look at the handsome Hugo.

Saul is growing frustrated. He has never been good at late nights. When we first got together, he'd preface every night out with 'It's not going to be a late one, is it?' until I told him it made him sound geriatric. I always thought that was one of the things he loved best about becoming parents when we were so young – that it signified the end of nights out. No more lurking around the edges of a club watching other people dance, or queuing for coats at two in the morning or waiting for taxis in the pouring rain. No more pretending he was having fun.

'Even in his twenties, Saul acted like a pensioner,' I once said to Louise.

Saul doesn't do two-in-the-morning confessionals or all-night poker. He doesn't do hangovers or lie-ins or long dark nights of the soul. Saul would do a short twilight evening of the soul, or better still a coffee morning of the soul.

'Some people are night owls and some aren't,' Saul appealed to Louise when I said that, about being a pensioner. 'Why does Fran have to make it a character failing that my body clock isn't the same as hers?'

Bart has spotted Saul and now makes his way over, throwing an arm around Saul's shoulder as if they are reunited brothers. 'Good to see you, dude.'

He has a silver tag chain around his neck, which I see is engraved with '*No place like home*', and the little mound of his beer belly strains against his flowery shirt.

'Respect to you, man,' he tells Saul. 'Quarter past four and still going strong. Hope I've got as much stamina at your age.'

Where do you start with a comment like that? I look at Saul's face and it is a mask of forbearance (*Here I am being a good sport*, says Saul's inner monologue). Meanwhile I seethe with indignation on his behalf, transformed suddenly into my husband's staunchest defender.

'Get a grip, Bart,' says Katy.

In spite of her smudged lipstick and blotchy, wine-sweated complexion, the look Katy gives to Bart is withering. I recognize it from many teenage spats – the look that says *give up, get lost, go away*. I have to hand it to my daughter – she can reduce grown men to rubble. But not Bart, apparently. He's like a puppy who just chewed the new rug and simply can't understand why everyone's cross.

'You know you love me really, babes,' he says, smiling at her.

'Oh, fuck off.'

'Katy!'

Saul is close to snapping. After nearly a quarter of a century with someone, you learn to read the signs. When was the last time he was up at this hour? When was the last time *I* was?

And now I'm thinking again of Molly and our late-night dash to the hospital and the little room with the poster on the wall of someone washing their hands. I won't think about it now. I won't. I won't.

'Come on, Fran.' I can feel Saul's brown eyes on me, already soft with sleep. 'Let's go to bed, hey?'

But Saul doesn't understand. He doesn't see that there's something keeping me here, even though my own eyes are drooping with exhaustion. I am tired of being around people who say 'babes' without being ironic and who, when you ask if it's still raining, consult an app on their phone instead of looking out of the window. But there's something keeping me rooted to the spot in this human sauna, with my smile sliding slowly down my face. Something that makes the thought of leaving impossible.

I'm not looking at Jamie, but I feel him in every part of me.

As if she can read my thoughts, Katy says, 'It's a bit weird about Jammy, though, isn't it? That he's down here on his wedding night. Without Lucy.'

Bart, predictably, disagrees. 'Why the fuck would you spend all this money on a party for all your mates and then miss it?'

He glances at me after he says 'fuck' as if I might be offended, and once again I find myself softening towards him.

'On our wedding night we stayed on the sofa bed at my parents' house,' says Saul, out of the blue.

'Romantic!' Katy is laughing. It's a loud, showy sort of laugh.

'They were giving us a lift to the airport the next day,' I say, surprised to find myself so defensive. 'For our honeymoon. And there were other wedding guests in the spare room.'

171

'Fran was pregnant and kept having to change position because the bed was so uncomfortable, and every time she did the whole thing made a loud creaking noise. It was all metal and springs, you see. And we were convinced that everyone else in the house was listening to this creaking noise and getting the wrong idea. By the end of the night we were crying with laughter.'

I've completely forgotten this – the little terraced house in Horsham full of sleeping relatives, the squeaking springs, the two of us giggling in the dark. Is that really how it was? How could you not love a couple who started off their married life like that? Even I am won over by the image of us, the young Saul and me, snorting with laughter on the creaky sofa bed.

So where does that other memory come from – lying in the darkness in the unfamiliar living room, surrounded by Saul's sleeping relatives, with Saul's arm leaden across me, listening to the ticking of the carriage clock on the mantelpiece and feeling the walls of the house pressing in? Is it only hindsight that has me feeling my way to the bathroom, with its pale-blue suite, pulling the light cord and gazing at my reflection in the mirror, realizing there was no turning back?

'Oi, Jam,' Katy is calling across the room behind me. 'Come over here and explain yourself.'

I don't want him to come nearer. My heart feels as if it will thump itself loose from its moorings.

Too late.

'Hello, Friedmans.'

I can't look at his face, so I gaze instead at his arm and the blond hairs there, soft against his tanned skin. He is wearing the grey trousers from his suit, slightly crumpled now, and a crisp white T-shirt. His wrists are surprisingly slight, feminine almost, and his fingers are long, with perfect white crescents on the nails. When my eyes alight on his wedding ring, gaudy in its newness, I stare at it for a long time.

Katy steps forward with her fake laugh and her extra-wide eyes. She takes his hand – the very hand I've been gazing at – in hers. I watch her pale slender fingers closing over the top of the bright ring. 'Are you on the run?' she asks, her smile wide. 'Are you going to get into trouble? Shall we hide you?'

There's a conspiratorial note in her voice, as if she and Jamie share some back story that the rest of us aren't privy to. Something burns in the pit of my stomach and I look abruptly away.

All of a sudden it's too much. Being in this room with these people, Katy's fingers closing around Jamie's hand, Jamie standing so close to me I could flick out my tongue and lick him.

'Where's the room key?' I ask Saul. 'I just need to go to the loo, and you can't get near the bathroom here.'

'I'll come with you,' Saul says, and for some reason his eagerness makes me prickle with irritation.

'Fine. But I'm coming back, I'm just warning you.'

Saul stares at me, tiredness fighting with something else in his brown eyes. 'I don't get it, Fran. Why are you making such an issue about staying? I can see you're exhausted.'

'Oh, for God's sake, Dad, live a little.' Katy has let go of Jamie's fingers and is standing with a hand on her hip. 'Or at least let Mum live a little.'

'Yeah, don't be killjoys,' says Jamie, although I still can't bring myself to look at his face. 'I've only just arrived. The party is just beginning!'

Spotting the key tucked into Saul's trouser pocket, I hook it out and make for the door. I need to be out of here.

'I'll be back in five minutes,' I call over my shoulder, not waiting to see if Saul will follow.

And now I am out in the beige corridor, where I tread the hush of the late hour into the thick carpet. The closed doors that lead into other people's rooms seem suddenly like gateways to another world, where life goes on as it should at four thirty-five in the morning, with sleeping and dreaming and soft, whispering snores.

In our own room, I look at the bed from which Saul emerged an hour or two ago. The covers are disturbed on the right-hand side, but the left side, my side, remains pristine. Is that how it will be when one of us dies, I wonder suddenly? The other one sleeping in half a bed for the rest of their life?

As I stand in the bathroom, swaying slightly over the basin, I feel almost giddy with tiredness. And yet a Mexican Wave of adrenaline is chasing after the tiredness and preventing it from settling. I long for sleep, but the thought of lying down on that bed seems impossible.

Using only the single light over the mirror, I reapply lipstick and work concealer into the dark rings under my eyes, then run a comb through my hair. My reflection looks grey in the spooky light.

Back out in the corridor, I take the stairs, scared of the loudness of the lift groaning into life in the deathly hush of the sleeping hotel. Nearing the bottom of the flight, I hear voices and, pushing through the fire door on the third floor, I'm surprised to see a gaggle of people spilling out of the room where the after-party was being held. The exaggerated shushing sound of drunken people trying to tell each other to be quiet reverberates along the corridor.

Saul comes towards me, his face slack with relief. 'We've all been turfed out, I'm afraid,' he whispers. 'Our hosts want to go to bed.'

Disappointment drops like a brick in my chest. 'Oh. I see.'

How foolish I feel now, with my newly rouged lips and my freshly combed hair.

Bart and Jamie are propping up Rob between them.

'I'm not going to bed!' he's shouting. 'Let's have a fucking party!'

I notice Katy lingering at the back of the group, whispering to Hugo. Her hand is on his wrist, her face slightly cocked to one side as she gazes up at him, so that her black hair tumbles down between them.

'Which floor?' asks Jamie, his green eyes finding mine. It feels as if a door is opening between us, revealing a landscape only we can see.

'Fourth. Just opposite us.'

Saul doesn't try to hide his relief to be going back to the room, with its half-made bed and his running things already laid out for the morning.

'I think I'll have a lie-in tomorrow,' he says, as if reading my thoughts. 'As long as I'm up by nine I can still go for a run and be back in time for the picnic. I'll skip breakfast. A piece of fruit will do me.' He grabs my hand and gives it a squeeze.

This is it. This is my life.

Bart and Jamie and Rob go up in the cramped lift, while Saul and I take the stairs. Katy stands in the doorway below, saying goodbye to her companion. There's the sound of giggling, followed by an ominous silence.

When we reach our floor, the others are there already and have been joined by Maddie. I didn't know she was on our corridor as well. The thought makes me uncomfortable.

At the door to Katy and Rob's room, we hesitate, waiting for Katy to catch us up with the key. She's a long time coming, and I sense Saul's disapproval snaking along the corridor to find her.

Finally she appears, smiling fixedly.

'Come on in,' shouts Rob as the door opens. 'Let's get this party started.'

The words clearly remind him of the lyrics to a song and he starts to sing at the top of his voice.

'Shut *up*!' hisses Katy. 'You're such a bloody embarrassment.'

Someone turns on the light and we all pile quickly inside, shutting the door behind us to keep the noise down. Though Katy has been here only one night the room is a mess, with clothes strewn across the bed and the floor, and make-up and toiletries littering the surfaces. I count three different pairs of shoes – not including the ones she has on. Even for Katy it seems excessive.

Rob throws himself on to the bed, on top of an emerald-green dress which still has its tags on it – clearly Katy's Plan B for the day.

'Be careful, will you?' she snaps, yanking it out from underneath him and holding it up in front of her, inspecting it for damage.

'Oops,' says Rob.

'Right. Well, if you're all sorted, we'll be getting to bed now.' Saul cannot wait to be gone. He is already turning, making for the door.

'Don't go,' calls Rob. 'We're having fun.'

'Will you be all right?' Saul asks Katy.

'Yeah, fine.' There's something triumphant about the way our daughter looks at us. Rob is showing his worst colours, strengthening her case against him. *You see?* says that arch of her eyebrows. *You see what I have to put up with?*

Katy will store up Rob's bad behaviour to mitigate her own, and my heart aches a little for him and for what he has ahead.

As we all shuffle towards the door, I feel the burning print of a hand on my arm. Jamie. It can only be Jamie.

'Please don't go to bed.' His voice is hot in my ear.

We walk on, my skin scorched where he touched it, and everything inside me thudding to get out.

Outside in the corridor, Saul asks for the key to our room.

The idea of going into that room with him, closing the door so it's just the two of us, sends a rush of claustrophobia through me, stoppering up my airwaves, constricting my throat.

As Saul inserts the key in the door, I open my mouth. I have to say something. My arm feels branded from the touch of Jamie's hand.

'I think I'll go for a walk.'

Everyone turns to stare – Saul, Maddie, Bart. I feel the blood rushing to my face, but there is no going back now.

'I'm not that tired and I just feel I need to walk off some of that alcohol.'

'But it's raining.'

Is that really all Saul is going to say? I daren't meet his eyes.

'It's stopped raining!' Jamie's voice is too eager. Everyone will know. 'I think it's a great idea. I'll join you, Fran.'

'Me too,' says Bart. 'I'm always up for anything. Ask anyone.'

'I don't *believe* you!' Maddie has stepped forward and is glaring at Jamie, her eyes like cut glass. 'Do I have to remind you, you got married to my daughter today! It's bad enough you came downstairs in the first place and left her alone. Now you want to go *walking* with *her*.'

Maddie says 'walking' as if it's a euphemism for something else, and my burning face smarts.

'It's fine. Look.' Jamie has taken his mobile phone from his pocket and is holding it under Maddie's nose. 'You know Lucy is surgically attached to her phone. If she wakes up and I'm not there, she'll call and I'll race back faster than a speeding bullet.'

'You're not seriously going to let this happen?' Maddie has turned her glare to Saul, who is still standing in the doorway of our room, half in, half out, gazing at me with a look I daren't analyse.

'What do you mean, "let this happen"?' I'm allowing myself to get angry now. 'All I'm doing is going for a walk. What's that got to do with Saul? He is not my keeper!'

The anger feels good, as if it's flushing out some of the heat and the embarrassment.

'Can I have the key, please?' My hand is out, and I'm daring Saul to refuse.

'This is crazy,' he says, shaking his head as he slaps the key into my hand.

I head off down the corridor. 'I'm going for a walk. If anyone else wants to come, fine. If not, that's fine too.'

'Wait for me,' says Bart.

I sense Jamie hanging back.

'I've got my phone,' he appeals to Maddie again. 'She won't know I'm gone.'

The door to the lift is still open and I step inside, followed by Bart, who seems oblivious to the tension.

Let him come now. Let him not be swayed by the force of Maddie's disapproval. Suddenly the thought occurs to me that I might be forced to take a walk in the middle of the night with only Bart for company. What on earth was I thinking?

Sunday, 5 a.m.

The three of us are crunching down the gravel drive in front of the hotel in the grey early-morning light. The rain has stopped, but there are puddles on the ground where the hard, baked earth has failed to absorb the water.

Bart has been talking about an exclusive festival he goes to in the grounds of a stately home, where you have to be invited and every other person has a trust fund.

'Oh, dude, you have to come. We were tripping for seventy-six hours straight, lying in the swimming pool with all our clothes on, thinking the trees were wearing petticoats. It was a blast.'

Bart reckons he can probably get us on the invite list. Bart knows someone who would sort it. Bart has no idea how much I wish he would go away.

'One time I thought I was a beetle,' he says.

Jamie stops walking.

'Bart. Mate. Please don't take this the wrong way . . .'

I freeze in anticipation of what he is going to say.

'. . . only there's something I really need to talk to Fran about, just on our own.'

He said it! I want the sodden ground to open under my feet, but at the same time I feel a wave of excitement that all but over-powers me.

Bart is flummoxed. He peers at us uncertainly through the grey mist of the new day. 'Oh, right. Only . . . I'm not really sure where I'm kipping tonight. I kind of thought I'd just hang out with you guys until breakfast time.'

My eyes are squeezed shut and my fingernails dig into my palms. Just seconds ago, I was wishing Bart every manner of ill and now I am guilt-ridden by the bewilderment in his guileless eyes.

'Listen, mate. I'm sure there are still people milling around. You're bound to come across someone still, you know, revelling.'

Jamie does an awkward jazz-hands gesture when he says 'revelling'.

Bart looks sorrowfully from Jamie to me and then back again.

'Whatever, man,' he says finally. 'Just remember you're married now. OK?'

He turns and walks slowly back towards the hotel, shaking his head, his Birkenstocks slapping lightly on the wet gravel.

'He's one to talk!' I say once he's out of earshot, just so there won't be a silence. 'The way he treats his poor wife.'

Jamie doesn't reply. We stand statue-like in the now pale-pink glow of the dawn, while the clouds overhead change colour and shape. The residual dampness in the air adds a chilly aftertaste to the passing breeze. Until now a mixture of alcohol and adrenaline has been driving me, but suddenly I sag under the weight of the realization of what we have just done, the line we have just crossed that cannot now be uncrossed.

'Jamie.' My voice sounds unnaturally loud in the static hush of the early morning. 'You should go back. What about Lucy?'

His eyes, when they finally meet mine, are hard and cold, glinting pink with the reflection of the rising sun. 'It's a bit late to talk about that, don't you think?'

The harshness of his voice makes me wince. He's right, though. What am I thinking of? It *is* a bit late for that.

'I love Lucy. I don't want you to get the wrong idea about that.'

Jamie has taken me roughly by the arm and is pulling me off the drive and towards the trees on the far side.

'I know.'

'*Do* you? *Do* you know, Fran?'

We have reached the shelter of the trees, which screen us from the drive and the building beyond. His breath is coming in short, angry bursts. This wasn't what I expected. What *did* I expect?

I turn to him. 'What do you want from me, Jamie? You know why this is impossible. Besides, I'm twice your age. I'm married. *You're* married.'

'I just want you to acknowledge it. That it's there. This feeling between us. I want to know I'm not imagining it. I feel like I'm going crazy.'

We have stopped behind a large elm and I lean back against the trunk, trying to absorb some of its solidity into my own shaky limbs.

'You're not imagining it,' I say, looking down at the ground, my voice so soft the wind could carry it clear away.

'What did you say, Fran?' He puts his hand under my chin and yanks my head up so that I'm looking at him. 'I need you to say it louder.'

'You're not imagining it.'

His other hand is around my arm, and his fingers tighten, pinching my skin. I feel suddenly afraid.

I'm sixteen years old again, standing in the rain watching David drive off, my legs still aching from the sex I hadn't known I didn't want, my cheeks stinging from cold and humiliation, knowing I should walk the long way round, but just wanting to be home. What was I scared of then? Surely not just the darkness or the being left alone? I think I was more scared of what I'd just discovered about how life works. That love was something that could be switched on and off like a cheap plastic light switch in a grubby hotel room. That sex was just an arrangement of bodies on a satin quilt, an orchestration of limbs without any involvement of the heart. That men could be desperate for you one minute, and the next they'd dump you on a street corner in the rain without a backward glance. I picked my way painfully around the puddles as I set off for home in the stupid ill-fitting shoes I'd sneaked out of the back of my mother's wardrobe, hoping they'd lend me some sort of understanding of what it takes to be an adult.

'Fran? Why are you always so elusive? All day I've wanted just a few moments alone with you, and now here we are, and yet you're not here. You're always somewhere else.'

Jamie's voice is choked like a child's. Looking up at him, I'm shocked at the smoothness of his jaw. Saul's would be bristly by now, thick hairs coming through – more white than dark now in this area, springing up in the soft crevices under his chin. I put up my hands to trace the right angle of his jawbone with my fingertip.

'You're trembling.'

His body is shaking. The tiny movements pass through my fingers, all the way down to the wet grass under our feet. His quivering hand burns on my waist.

'So are you,' he whispers, dipping his head so that his hair brushes my face, a wisp of silk against my skin.

He's right, I realize with surprise. My legs are quaking – the backs of my calves, my knees, the tops of my thighs.

Now his face is in my neck and his arms are around me, and mine around him. And we're holding on to each other as if we're the only things keeping each other from falling to the ground – which perhaps we are.

'We can't,' I whisper into his chest. 'You know we can't.'

For a moment I think he hasn't heard. My voice seems to belong to someone else entirely, a ghost voice that may or may not have spoken aloud.

Then, 'I know,' he says into the soft skin of my neck. 'I know. God, do you think I don't know? But can't we at least have this? Can't we at least have now?'

We stand swaying in the grainy light that turns from pink to grey and then gold as clouds pass overhead and the morning wakes up around us.

I remember Rob teasing Pip earlier about her lover and how she'd better not use the phrase 'he completes me'. Yet here with Jamie, I'm finding it hard to know where I finish and where he begins. Every single mawkish lyric memorized by every single love-sick schoolgirl isn't enough to contain how I feel.

If anyone was watching, they'd see a middle-aged woman in

flip-flops, leaning back against a tree with her eyes closed, and a young man in crumpled suit trousers bending over her with his arms wrapped around her and his face burrowing into her neck. They'd perhaps smile, even snigger. Well, it *is* a ludicrous pairing. They'd be entitled.

Yet from the inside, it feels perfect.

Eventually he raises his head and pulls away just enough to look into my eyes. We are inches apart.

I put my hands up to his hair and stroke it back from his face. My fingers pass over his nose, his eyelids, his lips. I read him like Braille, committing him to memory.

How long do we stand there, absorbing each other through our eyes and hands and skin?

He traces the shape of a heart on my face, and I remember the dark shadows under my eyes and the concealer streaked over the top.

'I look a mess.' I try to put my hands up to my face, but he intercepts them and replaces them around his waist.

'No, you don't. You're beautiful.'

We look at each other and the sun, which has been rising steadily into the high clouds, is reflected in his face and his eyes, so that he looks as if he is glowing, and for the first time in this endless day I feel completely calm.

Gradually, though, I become aware that Jamie has started shaking again, his left leg trembling violently against mine.

'What's wrong?'

Jamie has stepped backwards and is digging around in his pocket. He brings out his mobile phone. I can see it vibrating in his hand.

'Lucy.'

We both watch until the phone stops moving and is once again static in his palm. Almost immediately, it starts again.

'Oh Christ,' he says softly. 'I'm such a bastard.'

'You'd better go.'

'I know. I do love her, you know. It's just this is something . . . separate. Fran . . .'

I put my hand up to his lips. 'It's OK.'

'But Saul. How will he . . . ?'

'It's OK, Jamie. Really. You go.'

'I don't want to leave you.'

'I'm fine. Now go.'

I put my hand on his arm to give him a gentle shove, just as his phone begins to vibrate a third time.

'I'd better go,' he says finally.

The sun is spreading itself like butter along the undersides of the clouds as Jamie looks at me one more time, as if soaking me up, and then turns to walk back to the hotel.

From behind the tree, I watch him, a dark figure growing ever smaller until he disappears through the hotel doorway and there's nothing left to see.

Sunday, 6 a.m.

Outside the door to our hotel room, I hesitate, trying to gauge the emotional temperature inside. It's normally Saul who does this. I see him sometimes, walking down the front path at the end of the day and lingering in the porch just a little longer than strictly necessary, fussing over hanging up his coat.

It was worse immediately after Molly, of course. During those weeks and months when grief made me a stranger, even to myself.

Some days Saul would open the door to the smell of an elaborate meal I'd spent all day making, from one of those celebrity chef cookbooks where beautiful people eat beautiful food in beautiful homes. They're always laughing in those glossy colour photographs, as they pass the perfect food around. If I made that curry, I thought, or goulash or roulade, I'd learn how to smile again. The key to feeling whole again lay in a lovingly prepared lamb tagine.

Well, it's a lot of responsibility to place on a meal – and on the person eating it.

Saul could never eat enough, or be appreciative enough, or ask just the right questions, or make just the right noises. I never ate anything myself, just picked at the serving plate with an extra fork, and cleared away in stone-hearted silence.

Other times, when he came through the door, there'd be no smell of spices or roasting meat, just me curled up in a chair or on the bed, or, once or twice, in a corner of the kitchen, trying to make myself small enough to disappear altogether and slip through time and space so I could be with her again, counting her fingers and toes, fitting my fingertip into the dimple on her back.

So Saul is no stranger to the pause on the threshold, the unnecessary delay in turning the key. But it's a new feeling for me, this nervousness about what's behind the door. Saul is so consistent, so level.

'With Saul, I always know exactly what I'm going to get,' I once said to Louise, and he'd beamed with pleasure, taking it as a compliment.

Now I find myself hoping against hope that I'll walk into the room and find the same old Saul, predictable in his even-temperedness. I'm surprised by a sudden rush of love for the steadiness of him, his constancy in the face of all the fluctuations in our lives.

At first, when I open the door, my eyes struggle to adjust to the dimness. The early-morning light is barely filtering in through the curtains and the room is still plunged in gloom, the bed just a squarish shape in the darkness, Saul's outline an indistinct mound.

There's no sharp intake of breath, no tutting and no remonstrations. In the beige room, everything is still. Night-time pads the walls and surfaces, thickening the atmosphere.

The shape in the bed doesn't stir.

I creep in, glad now of the plush carpet. My flip-flops make a faint slapping noise and I slide them off, nudging them to the side of the door where they can't be tripped over. My bare feet sink gratefully into the deep pile and I realize for the first time how cold they've been.

I make my way to the bathroom, closing the door before turning on the light in case the noise of the extraction fan wakes Saul. I go straight to the mirror and stare at myself. Can it really be possible that those things happened to the woman in front of me – that scene under the tree? Surely such feelings would leave a mark – a purpling bruise, a vein-like scratch, the lightest burn-mark on delicate skin? But there is nothing.

I go through the motions. I remove every last scrap of make-up with a special wipe. I apply cream to nourish and rejuvenate my skin while I sleep. The last time I went to buy my usual pot from the make-up counter, the saleswoman suggested I try a different range 'for more mature skin' and I felt a sharp sense of loss, just like when I filled in a form at my bank and found I'd gone up an age bracket without realizing. I brush my teeth. I even floss. There's comfort in habit and routine. Familiarity counteracts the panic I feel lapping at my edges.

I turn the handle of the bathroom door silently and slip back out into the darkened bedroom. Sitting lightly on the edge of my side of the bed, I start stealthily manoeuvring off my clothes. Damn, what did I do with the T-shirt I always sleep in? I feel about on the floor for it. I'm so tired now, I just want to be horizontal, but getting into bed naked next to my husband would be unthinkable.

I just want to close my eyes and be alone with my thoughts. I want to take the memory of what just happened out of its bag like a brand-new dress, shake it from its tissue paper and lay it out so I can see it's real. I want to try it on and walk about in it and find out how it feels, how *I* feel. I want to bury my nose in it and breathe it in.

Most of all, I want to be under the covers when Saul wakes up.

'I wasn't gone long,' I'll tell him. 'Just a quick walk to clear my head and then straight back here.'

Saul will have been asleep the second his head hit the pillow. He's not the lying-awake kind.

But as I lower myself on to the bed and ease my legs in under the covers, I'm conscious of a certain stiffness about the body stretched out next to me. There's an alertness in the air, a sense of breath being held. I glance over and – oh, the shock – see Saul's eyes wide and glassy in the half-light.

'Where have you been?'

'I just got up to go to the loo, that's all. I've been back ages.'

It's the first thing that comes to mind. What are the chances, after all, that he's been lying here awake all this time? Far more likely he's just been woken up by me closing the bathroom door or coming to bed.

'Don't lie to me, Fran. Not on top of everything else.'

Saul's voice doesn't sound like his voice. It sounds tight and strangled.

Guilt makes me antagonistic.

'You know where I've been. I went for a walk with Bart and Jamie.' I emphasize 'Bart' without really meaning to. 'We watched the sun come up and had a chat and then came back. And now I'm tired.'

I move pointedly on to my side, my back to him, and bring my pillow around. After a quarter of a century with someone you recognize their shorthand. Saul knows this is my sleeping position. Adopting it in the past has called an immediate halt to countless long discussions and petty arguments.

'I bumped into Bart.' Saul is talking to my back, still in that strangely strangled voice.

'What do you mean?'

'He was in the lobby, waiting for the lift. He was going back to the room where the party was to ask if he could sleep there. He didn't seem too happy.'

'But why were you in the lobby? What were you doing? Were you following me?'

'Oh, for Christ's sake, Fran. I *saw* you. I was coming to find you and I *saw* you. Both of you. You and Jamie.'

There's a pounding in my head, and my mouth feels lined with sandpaper. Beneath the thin T-shirt, my heart slams into the mattress and I wonder if Saul can feel it too.

'I saw you, Fran,' Saul repeats. 'It's his wedding day, for God's sake.'

'But nothing happened,' I whisper, turning on to my back so that my words drift upwards and hang in the air.

Saul makes a noise that's halfway between a snort and a laugh. 'Get a grip, Fran. It's me, Saul. I *know* you. Remember?'

He is so controlled, even though I can feel how much this control is costing him and can sense the suppressed rage snapping at his heels.

This is how he was that night in the hospital, when the midwife with the ginger hair who'd introduced herself as Annie had gone off to fetch the CTG – the little hand-held machine the midwives always used to listen to the heartbeat.

'I know you think I'm being stupid,' I said. 'I just want to know she's OK.'

Saul had put his hand on my thigh, and squeezed. 'I don't think you're stupid. I'm just tired. It's been a long day.'

When Annie came back she asked me to get on to the trolley – she had to lower it with a remote control because I was too big by that stage to lift myself on. I lay back and pulled up my top and remember being embarrassed at how monstrous my distended stomach looked in that brightly lit place, an enormous walnut whip of flesh pushing up into the air.

'And Baby's due when?'

Annie was applying gel to the mound of my belly and the sudden cold caused me to take a sharp intake of breath before I replied.

'Just under three weeks.'

'And you last felt Baby move?'

'This morning.'

The exchange calmed me. I was conscious of the efficient way I was dispensing the details. I wasn't falling to pieces and therefore this wasn't a crisis.

'Baby probably knows it's nearly time for her to make an entrance, so she's taking it easy. Let's just have a listen, shall we?'

Saul stood next to my head, while Annie applied the machine over the cold liquid. We all listened to the faint flapping of the plastic slatted blind against the window, to the faraway voices in the corridor. She moved it slowly around, and we kept listening. She moved it up and down and around and around, and still we listened.

'I think the machine may be broken.' She addressed this to Saul, rather than to me. 'It happens sometimes. I'll go and fetch another.'

Edging past Saul, she went out of the room, leaving the door open and my glistening mountain of stomach foolishly exposed to the passing world. Then there was silence.

'Saul?'

'You heard what she said. The machine's broken. It happens all the time.'

That's when I heard it – the struggle for control in his voice, the breath straining against the constraints being forced on it.

When Annie returned, she said she would take me to a different room for an ultrasound scan, 'Just to be sure.'

'It's just being set up,' she said, and for a split second I found myself hoping there *was* something wrong, to justify all the time I was taking up when they were clearly so busy. Instantly, I was awash with guilt, sure that anything bad that happened now would be my own fault.

'Don't worry,' she said, seeing my face. 'The ultrasound is much more sophisticated. It'll pick up Baby's heartbeat no problem, I'm sure.'

'You see?' Saul said, squeezing my hand. 'It'll be OK.'

Annie led us to a bigger room, with a bed in the middle and all sorts of equipment on trolleys. She asked me to lie on the bed and again squirted cold gel on to my preposterous belly. Saul stood on the far side of me, watching the blank monitor the midwife hadn't yet switched on, as if waiting for a film to start.

The door to the room opened, admitting a short, furrow-browed man with glasses and a wide, fleshy nose that straddled his face like the yolk on a fried egg.

'I'm the senior registrar,' he said, holding up the plastic name badge attached to his white coat as if we might dispute this. He also said his name, but I've long since forgotten it. 'I've just come to make sure everything's all right.'

Until this point I'd been relatively calm, making myself believe what was being said about the faulty machine and the fact that it was going to be OK. But this man with his white coat and his plastic badge and his air of authority freaked me out. Why was he here?

I glanced up at Saul and he smiled at me, not giving anything away, not looking as if he was unnerved that a senior registrar had popped in to supervise a run-of-the-mill ultrasound scan.

'OK, Mrs Friedman, I'm just going to run this little gadget over your bump,' said Annie, taking an instrument off the trolley. 'Let's see what's going on in there, shall we?'

All of a sudden, I felt I couldn't breathe. I didn't want the cold metal of the machine near my skin, was terrified of what I'd see on the monitor.

'I'm scared,' I said again to Saul, gripping his hand.

He didn't reply, just gazed at the monitor as it flickered into life.

'There she is,' said the midwife, as our baby came into view, her back a perfect curve, her tiny fingers held up to her lovely face.

But while my heart melted at the picture on the screen, I was aware that the room was holding its breath. The walls with their countless plugs and laminated posters, the gleaming linoleum floor, the machinery with its entrails of cables, the plastic-covered mattress on which I lay, the senior registrar, the midwife, Saul, me. None of us breathing in case we missed it – the sound we were waiting for, the sound of my baby's heart beating inside her tiny, perfect chest.

Again and again, Annie ran the machine over my flesh.

'You're not holding it in the right place,' I said.

She had to be doing it wrong. She had to be. I glanced up at her face as I chastised her and saw a tear sliding down her cheek. No, no, no.

'Shall I?' The registrar took the machine from the now trembling midwife and started moving it slowly over my bump. There was a pause that seemed to stretch over time itself, stilling the whirring of the machines and the ticking of the white plastic clock on the far wall.

Come on! I silently urged my sleeping daughter. *Come on!*

The registrar's arm stopped moving. For a second he remained frozen, holding the instrument perfectly still, and then he gently laid it down on the bed next to me.

'I'm so very sorry,' he said, and his voice was sad and tired, 'but I have to tell you your baby has died.'

Something came tearing out of me then, screaming to the surface, something I couldn't control.

'No! You're wrong. Tell him, Saul.'

But Saul, standing beside me, still gripping my hand, just closed his eyes and took a long breath in. Later I'd bring that up in counselling again and again, how he hadn't lost control even then, even when we'd just discovered our daughter was dead. 'I couldn't,' he'd say. 'I had to be strong, for you.' But I'd accuse him of being afraid of his own feelings, or occasionally, shamefully, of not loving her enough.

And now here he is again, telling me he saw me with Jamie with that same enforced calm, that same infuriating suppression of his own feelings. It drives me into a fury.

'What do you want me to say, Saul?' My own voice is sharp compared with his, slashing the atmosphere in the room to ribbons. 'Nothing happened. How could it? Do you think I'm stupid? Do you think I don't know he's half my age? Do you think I don't know he's just got married? Huh?'

'And?'

Saul has raised himself to a sitting position and is leaning back against the padded headboard, his eyes glinting in the half-light.

'And what?'

'And what else, Fran? What else is he? Why else can nothing happen between you?'

'You know perfectly well why else.'

Saul's eyes are two lasers boring into me.

'Yes, but I want to hear you say it. Come on, Fran, say it. *Say it!*'

'All right.' My voice is high-pitched and breaking with anger and frustration. 'I'll say it.'

'Because he's my son.'

Sunday, 7 a.m.

I am on my side, pretending to sleep, while Saul lies awake next to me. My mind is reeling with memories I never wanted to revisit, mixing with the vinegary wine and exhaustion into one sickly, rolling mess.

'Don't judge me,' I hissed at Saul a short while ago, in the slowly brightening morning light. 'Don't you dare judge me.'

And now, of course, I lie here judging myself.

Shame colours everything red.

One time my mother, in one of her manic phases, bought us a tortoise for a pet and, on the advice of a children's television programme, decided it needed to hibernate. She supervised us filling a cardboard box with newspaper, settling the tortoise inside and then taping up the flaps before wedging it on a high shelf in the crammed garage. I was young, my brother younger still. Young children do not have much capacity for holding in mind things they can no longer see. We forgot about the tortoise. My mother retired back to her bed. Years later, after my mother had died and my father had remarried in spectacular haste, I went into the garage to sort through the stuff piled on the floor and the shelves – books, their yellowed pages mouldy with damp, broken vases, electrical appliances missing their plugs, random tools and bits for the car, rolls of leftover carpet smelling of mildew and mice. And there, right at the top, on the shelf where we'd put it twenty-eight years before, were the remains of the poor tortoise, just a hard carapace and tiny bones.

Some memories are so impossible to face that we hibernate them like tortoises. And if we're lucky, we forget about them altogether, tucked out of the way where no one ever looks. And then something happens – something that leads you back to that place you'd put out of your mind, to that box you'd sealed right up. And there is the memory – delicate and decaying around the edges, but still there. And then, what choice have you but to take it out and turn it over, looking for bones?

Lying on the bed in this hotel room, which I now hate with every fibre of my being, feigning sleep, with my insides churning and Saul's wakeful presence stirring up the air around us, I find myself back where I least like to go. The house on the outskirts of Reading, with my father sighing into his books and my mother facing the wall. Getting myself up for school, scraping together a packed lunch from whatever might be in the fridge. Avoiding Jade at break times now there's a huge, David-shaped barrier between us. Not wanting to think about the last time I saw him and what had taken place, telling myself I didn't care that he never contacted me again. Knowing all the time, deep down, what was happening inside me, but forcing myself to unknow it, making those deals that you conjure up when you're young and desperate – if I make a special effort with this essay, if I'm nice to my brother and try not to be rude to my father, then it will all go away, it will all go back to normal.

It's surprisingly easy to hide a pregnancy when you're not admitting it to yourself, and when you're sixteen or seventeen years old and your shape is still changing, and when your life is so devoid of intimacy that no one notices the tell-tale bump that a single cuddle might detect, or hears you when you're sick. Only at seven and a half months did my mother, suddenly up in every sense of the word, finally turn her attention to someone other than herself for long enough to notice that her daughter was not far off giving birth.

I gave David up to her like an offering to the Devil.

Even now, nearly thirty years later, I feel queasy thinking about the scene at David's house, with his hollowed-out wife and his wide-eyed young son, and how he denied it to my parents again and again, calling me a teenager with a crush, until my newly energized mother suggested we all go back to the hotels where I'd claimed we'd been to see if anyone recognized him. Then came the tears, and the apologies to the wife, who stood there in silence as if she'd seen it all before, the promises *on his son's life* that it would never happen again, that I'd done the chasing, that he'd been weak and foolish but he'd definitely, absolutely used a condom. That he couldn't understand what had gone wrong.

There were financial arrangements made, I think. David, of course, turned out not to be a songwriter after all, but an unemployed sales assistant who'd been sacked from his previous job for some unspecified breach of the rules. His wife kept the family afloat with two part-time jobs. No wonder she always looked so washed out.

The baby, considerately, was due in the summer holidays. The first time anyone called it that – *the baby* – I almost fainted from shock. I'd never allowed myself to believe that's what it was. I'd divorced myself from what was happening as if I was one person and my body was quite another. So when the doctor calmly said, 'Your baby is due in August,' I couldn't accept that he was talking about *my* body, *my* baby. It was someone else's mistake, someone else's nightmare.

My *situation*, as my parents always referred to it, seemed to give my mother a new lease of life. I'd never seen her so consistently committed to something. She liaised with doctors and social workers and adoption agencies, wheeling me in and out of depressing institutional offices like a piece of luggage, placing form after form in front of me to sign.

'Do you understand, Francesca?' these various officials asked, craning to see past my mother's commanding profile.

And I'd nod. What was there, after all, not to understand?

Occasionally one of these officials would ask my mother whether she mightn't consider raising the baby herself, and she'd look at them as if they were crazy. They had no idea that it was the process rather than the end result that was so enlivening her, giving her a reason to take her medication, a reason to be up and about and engaging with the world.

'I've done my mothering, thank you,' she'd reply, unaware of the irony.

Lying here now, I try to resist remembering that summer, choosing to see it only in snapshots. A girl who carried her late pregnancy around like a borrowed bag that had been strapped on but could soon be removed. Lying in the bath and watching in horrified fascination as the skin on my stomach moved by itself, wondering if there might be something not quite human in there. Being shown a photograph of a couple – she round-faced and pink, he shaggy-browed and smiling in the strained way of someone not used to it. 'They're a lovely couple,' said whichever of the interchangeable officials we were dealing with at that time. 'He's a lecturer and she's a mature student.'

I think my mother liked Lynn and Max because of the intellectual kudos they conferred. 'My husband's a writer,' she said, examining the picture. 'They sound like our sort.'

Next there's an image of the induction and my horror as I realized my mother was going to be with me at the birth – to see all my naked bits. That was almost worse than the labour itself.

Then, strangest of all – something I'd wonder afterwards whether I'd dreamt, or perhaps conjured up in a pethadine-induced haze – my mother's cool hand on my forehead, stroking my sweat-slicked hair back from my face in a room that smelt of sweat and blood, talking to me about her own childhood, her own mother, as the contractions came and went until pain blurred them all together into one long drawn-out howl.

The last snapshot: closing my eyes as the midwife came towards me, cradling something in her arms – something small and surprisingly long with mottled purple limbs that flung angrily into the air. Closing my eyes, closing my mind. If I couldn't see him, he wouldn't be real, and if he wasn't real it couldn't hurt, and whatever it was that was pressing on my heart would stop.

'I don't want to see him,' I said. 'He isn't mine.'

What happens when you have a child when you're still a child yourself? You play childish games, like What I Can't See Isn't There. You pretend what's happening is happening to someone else. You don't look, because if you looked you'd be lost. You tell the social workers, 'I just want to go back to school. I've a project due in September.' You say to your mother, 'Can I get new jeans now I'm normal-sized again?' You go with your parents to meet the pink-faced woman and her shaggy-browed husband and you tell them what A levels you've decided to take and the woman keeps her hand on the baby buggy the whole time as if you might try to snatch it from her. They promise to send photos every year, and for the first few years they do, only your mother doesn't show them to you because she says they'll upset you.

You tell yourself you've forgotten, that's what you do. You develop a skin that's tough as leather. You get a reputation for being emotionally robust, and no one knows it's because the part of you that's capable of the deepest feelings had to go into hibernation on the day your son was born or you'd surely have died from grief.

I'm lying on my side while my tears soak the mattress, angry with Saul for opening up the sealed box that contains my past. There are dark places in there, far darker even than this, where I cannot go.

'I know you're awake,' he says now, as if he can hear my thoughts. 'You might as well talk to me, Fran.' He doesn't sound bitter any more, just resigned. 'I've known there was something between you and Jamie, right from the start.'

'Of course there's something between us!'

'Aside from you being his mother, I mean. The way you two are with each other. I've heard about it before, when people separated by adoption develop strong feelings for each other. Sexual feelings even.'

'Ugh!' Saul's words make me recoil in disgust. 'You don't understand! You have no idea!'

'No? So tell me, Fran. Explain it to me. Explain what you were doing behind that tree, the two of you.'

I try to think back, try to take the memory of the glorious pink-washed morning out of its wrapping again, but when I do, it's soiled and grubby. My heart is racing. But it wasn't as Saul is implying. It just wasn't. We would never have . . . It wasn't like that.

'You wouldn't understand.'

'Try me.'

And now I'm furious. At what he's implying and the way he's judging without knowing anything about it. 'You wouldn't understand because you don't know the first thing about losing a child.'

I feel the mattress move as he shifts himself into a sitting position. 'How can you say that, Fran?'

'Because it's true. You never wanted Molly. It wasn't the same for you when we lost her.'

Even as I'm saying it, I'm wishing it unsaid. I feel the mattress move again as he gets up. I turn over and watch him walking about the room, picking up his running things from the chair.

'Where are you going?' My voice sounds whiny and petulant.

He doesn't look round.

'Where are you going?' I repeat, louder this time.

And now he does turn to look at me, and his face is the face of someone I don't recognize. I falter.

'I didn't mean—'

But whatever I was going to say is cut off by the sound of the door slamming shut behind him.

Sunday, 8 a.m.

Could this weekend get any worse? I mean, really? Could it? I knew it was never going to be easy. But this?

Alone in the hotel room, I sit up, leaning back against the padded headboard with my head in my hands. I imagine Saul streaking down the country lanes, listening to something rousing on his iPod and hearing my voice ringing in his ears. *'You don't know the first thing about losing a child.'*

I'm ashamed.

But he's done far worse things, whines the petty, childish voice in my head. *What about those emails to that woman? They even talked about love.*

And yet I never thought about leaving him. Not then, at any rate. If anything, the knowledge that Saul had wanted and been wanted by someone else made me cling to him as I'd never done before. For a few months, while the memory of what had been said between them was the first thing I thought of when I woke up every morning, I attached myself to Saul like one of those toy cats people stick on to car windows, suckered into place by their four paws. When we ate, I'd hold my fork in one hand, while the other was clamped to his arm. At night, for the first and only time in our relationship, I'd want him to fall asleep curled around my back. We had sex often and urgently, as though it was about to be rationed.

And all the time I asked him questions. Do you love me? Did you love her more? Would you have left me? Why? And again a hundred times: Why? Why? Why?

'Because I was weak . . . Because I was stupid . . . Because I was lonely . . . Because you were distant.'

Aha!

'So it's *my* fault!'

Funny how, though I've told Saul I forgive him and I'm over it, and though in the light of the last twenty-four hours I haven't a leg to stand on, it never quite leaves you, the visceral pain of betrayal.

I think about Jamie upstairs in the bridal suite with Lucy and hope they are sleeping peacefully. Already the person who stood with him under a tree in the just-born light of a new day feels like someone else. I am aghast at who I have been and what I have done. I tot up how much alcohol I consumed throughout the day yesterday. Enough, surely, to have skewed my judgement. More than enough. People will understand.

But I know they won't.

In the eighteen months since Jamie and I found each other, we have existed in a kind of bubble, just the two of us, and our feelings have grown and grown. Now that Saul has said what he's said, it's as though the bubble has burst.

I think about what Saul said about sexual feelings and I nearly gag. It wasn't like that. That first sight of him, on a bench in Regent's Park. The jolt of recognition. The astonishing familiarity of him.

But sexual? No, no, no. What, then? Obsessive, certainly. All those nights thinking about him, going over and over the things we'd said, the way he'd looked, the smell of him, the little muscle at the side of his jaw that twitches when he's nervous. Overwhelming, overpowering – all those 'over' words – over the top, overkill, overarching.

Over.

It's over. Whatever it is – was – it's over.

I don't have to put up with this, it occurs to me now. This confusion about Jamie, feeling judged by Saul. I have options.

My handbag is on the floor next to the bed and I rifle through it impatiently, looking for the letter from the school in Spain. The crisp white pages soothe me. I run a fingertip over the embossed letterhead. This doesn't have to be a fantasy. I could sign the contract and send it back. I could have a different life.

Then I remember Pip. Pregnant. *She'll be all right*, says a voice in my head. *She'll survive. Just like you did.* I could fly back for the birth. It's only two and a half hours away. My brother has a guest room at his house, with a view straight down the mountainside to the sea. I could live there and wake up to that view every morning. I could take up yoga and salute the sun. I'd be a different person in that place. I'd eat salad and drink two litres of water a day. I'd read *Wolf Hall* and take up photography. I'd find things to fill the empty spaces inside.

Saul won't like it, but once he gets used to it he'll realize it's for the best. We'll have a thoroughly modern separation, Skyping about the girls and meeting for coffee at Starbucks whenever I'm back in the UK. We'll learn how to be friends again.

I am so lost in this vision of my new life that the loud knock on the door startles me, and immediately my heart begins pounding painfully. Saul oughtn't to be back so soon. He's always so fastidious about his training routine. 'Marathons are one per cent sporting ability and ninety-nine per cent discipline,' he tells anyone who asks. 'Anyone can do it.'

I stand up and walk to the door, my legs wobbly, trying to remember if I've ever been so nervous about meeting my own husband. Our wedding? I recall how we got a taxi to the registry office from the flat we were renting. Was I nervous then, sitting next to Saul in the back of the cab on our way to be married? I don't think so. I do remember being shocked when he gave the driver ten pounds for a five-pound journey and told him to keep the change. It was the grandest gesture I'd ever seen him make.

It occurs to me that maybe he's back early because he's made some sort of momentous decision. Perhaps I'm not the only one whose mind has been running to separations. The thought makes me freeze. Recently I feel as though I've been lugging my marriage around like a heavy bag, yet faced with the real possibility of losing it I find myself stoppered up with fear.

I take a deep breath before opening the door a crack.

'Oh God, Mum, you've got to help me.'

Pip is wearing a pair of skinny jeans that accentuate her tiny legs and a baggy T-shirt she could well have slept in. Her hair is slightly matted on one side. She looks flattened – as if someone has tried to iron her.

'Rob's in my room. He's in a terrible state. Katy's kicked him out of their room. Apparently they've had a huge bust-up. Oh, why do people bother with relationships? They always turn out so badly.' Pip pushes her way into my room and throws herself down on the unmade bed. 'Where's Dad? Don't tell me – he's left you for Lucy's mother. He was powerless to resist that shimmy.'

'He's gone for a run.'

'Yeah. I guessed that. I didn't really think he'd done a bunk with Maddie.'

'Do you want me to come and talk to Rob?'

As if anyone needs relationship advice from me! Still, now that I've considered leaving this room, it seems suddenly imperative that I escape and not be here when Saul comes back, slaked and sweaty and having had two hours to dwell on things.

'Let's go.' I head out of the door, but Pip is looking at me strangely.

'Are you really going like that?'

Only now do I become aware that I am still wearing my night-time T-shirt and yesterday's tummy-toning pants. I pull on my jeans and rifle through my bag, realizing belatedly that I have exhausted my supply of clean clothes. Ransacking the drawers, I find a small pile of Saul's T-shirts sitting in freshly folded splendour in varying shades of navy and grey, like a Turner prize installation. I snatch one and disappear into the bathroom to change.

When we push open the door to Pip's room, I'm briefly dazzled by the daylight. This side of the hotel faces directly into the sun, which comes as a surprise after the dimness of my own room.

'Oh, I see you brought reinforcements. Hi, Fran.'

'Hi, Rob. How's your head?'

'Hideous. How's yours?'

'Marginally better.'

Rob is sitting in the armchair by the window with his head resting in his hands. His big frame dwarfs the chair, making it look as if it was made for a child. He is still wearing yesterday's clothes and his hair sticks out all over his head like the husk on a coconut.

'I just want you to know how sorry I am. About last night. I was such a prick. Feel free to throw stones at me. Or just punch me if that would help.'

His face, squinting up at us through the cup of his big hands, looks as if it might already have sustained a few punches. His skin is blotchy, his eyes sunken, and dark bristles sprout from his chin and upper lip.

'I don't think I'll punch you just now, if that's OK,' I tell him. 'The exertion might kill me.'

I flop down in the facing armchair, feeling the adrenaline of the last few hours drain from my body. We sit for a while, not speaking, while Pip bustles around filling the kettle to make tea.

'How much did I disgrace myself?' Rob asks. 'On a scale of one to ten.'

'Ten wouldn't even come up to the ankles of how much,' says Pip.

Rob sighs. 'That's kind of what I thought.'

My phone begins ringing in my bag, which I've brought, by force of habit, into Pip's room. I don't want to answer it, but Pip and Rob are looking at me expectantly.

'I'll take this outside,' I say, smiling, as I let myself out into the corridor.

'Can we talk, Fran?'

Jamie. I don't want to talk to him. And yet all I want to do is talk to him.

'Please, Fran?' His voice is soaked with misery, like overloaded trifle.

'Jamie, I don't know what to say.'

It's the truth, yet it's such a cop-out. He wants more from me. We want more from each other, and yet neither of us can – or will – define what exactly it is we want. My feelings for him came on so suddenly and powerfully they appeared unlimited. And yet if there's one thing I've learned over the last twenty-four hours, it's that there have to be limits. People need to be able to define and categorize relationships. They need to fit them into boxes that can be neatly filed. My relationship with Jamie is amorphous. It leaks from the containers we try to squash it into, snaking under doors and through walls. It confuses and upsets those around us, because no one knows how to classify it.

'Fran, I'm so fucking confused. What is this thing between us? You're my mother, but I'm not responding to you as a son. I'm responding to you as a—'

'Don't!'

My voice comes out more sharply than I intended and there is instant silence. I don't know what to say next, just that I need to stop him going any further. I need to stop the words that, once said, can never again be unsaid.

'But you feel it too. You said as much this morning. Tell me what you feel for me is just what a mother would feel.'

He sounds like a child, teetering on the edge of tears. But he *isn't* much more than a child. Why have I never really thought before of the toll this must all be taking on him? Have I really been too wrapped up in my own angst to pay any mind to his? I can't deny that my heart still lurches when I talk to him – it's doing it right now – and, deep down, I know Saul was right to say I've let my feelings for him blur the lines between love and passion and, yes, sex. I've been so selfish, but finally I see what I have to do. I have to set him free.

'Of course it's what a mother would feel,' I say, and I force my voice to stay steady. 'What else would it be?'

There's a long pause, and when I imagine how his lovely face will be clouding over with hurt and doubt, I almost can't stand it. But then I remind myself that it's for him and Lucy and Saul and all of us. If there's no box to fit us in, I must build a box around us.

'I love you, Jamie,' I tell him now, and I hear a little sound like air escaping, as if he's been holding his breath. 'But I think we shouldn't see each other for a little while.'

I prepare myself for his objections, but instead there is more silence and then a whispered 'yes', so quiet I almost think I might have invented it.

'And when we meet again, we can start over,' I blunder on. 'Do it properly this time.'

The 'yes' is louder this time. Unmistakeable. Without being able to see his face, I can't tell whether he's being bitter or sarcastic, but I choose to think not. I choose to think that while there's sadness, there's also relief. Something is over. A conclusion has been reached.

Finally, he speaks. 'And my father?' he says, in a voice that's different from before. 'Can you at least tell me something about him before we have this . . . break.'

He's asked me this before – that first time we met, and then later, sitting opposite each other in an over-heated pub, our fingers touching. He knows I won't talk about it. Although I want more than anything to give him something in exchange for all the hurt I've caused him, this is somewhere I can't go. Not now.

'I'm sorry,' I say. 'I have to go.'

Back in the room, Pip raises her eyebrows at me, but mercifully says nothing. Rob still has his head in his hands.

'I don't suppose I dare ask about Katy?' I say, burying my phone in my bag and sitting back down, hoping they won't notice my agitation.

Rob looks pained. 'No, best not. She's not happy with me. I don't blame her. She won't even let me back in the room. She says that's it.'

'Because of last night?'

'No.' If wretchedness were a competition, Rob might just have the edge. 'She's been saying it for ages, but I haven't wanted to listen. I thought if I pretended not to hear, and stayed put, it would eventually blow over and she'd forget all about it.'

'Rob, didn't it occur to you that if you act like a doormat, that's

204

how she'll end up treating you?' Pip hands out tea in two minia-ture mugs whose handles are too small for my fingers.

'Aren't you having any?' I notice Pip's own hands are now empty.

'No. I've gone right off tea and coffee.'

I've been so wrapped up in my own troubles that this reminder of Pip's pregnancy comes as a shock. I snatch another glance at her and it suddenly hits me that I am to become a grandmother. The thought is surprisingly painful. I ought to be mother to a toddler. I worry that Pip's baby will drive out the memory of mine. I worry that I will lose what I have left of Molly. And interwoven with this is worry for Pip herself, for my own living child. What if what hap-pened to me should happen to her?

Can there be anything worse than giving birth to a baby you already know is dead?

When the senior registrar told me that was what would have to happen, I didn't believe him. My body was already twisted and racked with grief. They couldn't be so cruel. Life couldn't be so cruel.

'I'm so sorry,' said Annie the midwife, who had by now recov-ered after the horror of the ultrasound. 'But it's far better for you to have a natural labour rather than a Caesarean. You'll heal so much quicker.'

She was talking about physical healing, of course.

Saul and I were sent home with pills to induce labour and a leaflet about stillbirth. That was the first time I realized that's what Molly was. A stillbirth. Seeing the word written down made me retch. It was too much like afterbirth – the by-product of a labour, rather than its endpoint, its prize.

We were told to present ourselves at the hospital the next day. We were urged to prepare family and friends, in case they wanted to see Molly in hospital once she was born. I remember feeling a sudden surge of hope when they said that, believing they were somehow suggesting there was a possibility that she might yet be all right. I didn't know that's how they do it now, encouraging extended families to be part of the process so they can mourn an actual child, not just a bump under someone's jumper or someone else's second-hand grief.

'Shall I call anyone?' asked Saul as we sank on to the sofa in our own suddenly freakishly empty living room.

I shook my head.

And the next day, the living nightmare of the birth. I was so terrified of how she would look that my body tried to keep her inside me, until finally she tore from me in a torrent of blood and pain and my own screaming voice echoing off the walls.

'No,' I yelled, when they asked if I wanted to hold her.

But then the image of Saul, cuddling his daughter, tears rolling down his face and splashing on to hers, gazing at her so intently as if he could pass his own breath into hers by the force of his will alone, stuff his own life into her through her pores, her nostrils, her mouth, her ears, until her tiny, muted heart spluttered into action.

'Here,' I whispered, holding out my shaking arms. 'Give her to me.'

This isn't what I want for Pip. I need to keep my children safe.

'Was it weird for you, yesterday?' Pip is lying on the bed, propped up by pillows, her calm blue eyes soft with kindness and fatigue. 'Not being acknowledged, I mean, as anything more than a "family friend".' She makes quote marks in the air with her small, childlike hands.

I shrug and stare at the coffee table between my armchair and Rob's. There's a Kindle on there, with a tiny light clamped to the top for reading in the dark. Who could have ever guessed, a few years ago, that we'd ever need such things? 'It was good of Lynn and Max to have us there at all. They needn't have.'

Rob takes his head out of his hands to scrutinize me. 'But I don't get it,' he says. 'Why wouldn't they just be upfront about it? It's not as if Jamie doesn't know, or Lucy, or anyone who matters. So Jamie's adopted. Big deal. Get over it.'

'They didn't want to make it public. It's their prerogative.'

I don't want to talk about Lynn and Max. I don't want to think about their reaction when they hear about my sunrise walk with

Jamie. I don't want to imagine the look on Maddie's face when she tells them or how they might get the wrong end of the stick. What is the right end of the stick? When did everything get so blurred?

A wave of nausea sweeps over me and I keep myself rigid in my chair, not daring to move.

And now there's some sort of commotion going on in the corridor outside. Doors are being banged and voices are raised. I recognize Katy's voice . . . and Saul's.

I suddenly remember that I have the room key. How long has he been out there, panting in the corridor in his sweaty black nylon?

Pip gets up and opens her door. 'Mum's in here,' she says. 'With Rob.'

'Sorry,' I say, holding out the key. 'I didn't think.'

'That's the problem, Fran,' says Saul softly as he takes it from my hand. 'You never do.'

Sunday, 9 a.m.

I don't want to go down to breakfast. Yet the thought of staying in this room with Saul and all the things we haven't yet said is too awful to contemplate.

Right now he is in the shower. I remember how, just yesterday morning, when he was freshly back from his run, I worried that he would want sex. Funny how I'm almost nostalgic for that now that he can't even bring himself to look at me, let alone touch me.

Perhaps I could initiate something? I slap the thought down before it has even properly formed.

'Fran never makes the first move,' Saul once complained to Louise, during one of our early sessions. 'I always feel like she's allowing sex to happen, rather than wanting it to.'

I'd refuted that, of course. Saul was the passive-aggressive one, not me. But now, when I consider the idea of overtly pushing for sex – taking my clothes off so I'm naked when he comes out of the shower, or even stepping in there with him – I find I can't.

'Perhaps Fran feels she would be giving too much away?' suggested Louise, tipping her head to one side. 'Perhaps she's worried that making a sexual move would make you believe that everything's all right.'

'But everything *is* all right,' Saul had replied, looking at me for confirmation. 'Isn't it, Fran?'

Now Saul's anger comes coiling under the bathroom door along with the steam from the shower. I wonder what incenses him most – the thing with Jamie (*What thing?* asks the outraged voice in my head. *Nothing happened*), or what I said about Molly. That unforgivable accusation.

'*You never wanted Molly,*' I said (can it be only an hour or so ago?). '*It wasn't the same for you when we lost her.*'

God, that was a terrible thing to say. Yet I realize now, I've been carrying those words with me for the last two years. If you'd just scratched a nail over the surface of everything else I've said since Molly died, you'd find those words hiding underneath.

I think about them now as I listen to the sound of Saul in the shower. Or, rather, the not-sound. For the first time I can remember, Saul isn't singing in the shower. The noise of his silence is deafening. For two years, those words about Molly have been like gallstones inside me. Now they are out and nothing in the world can make them go back.

I'm right, though. I try to relocate my sense of justification. He never wanted her.

But, sitting miserably on the edge of our bed, I acknowledge that's not entirely true. He never wanted a baby. But he always wanted *her*.

And again, there we are back in the labour ward, and I'm watching Saul cradling our daughter in his arms while he tries to will her to life. I remember a tear fall from his eye on to her cheek, so it looked, for a moment, as if she was crying.

'Here,' I said, holding out my arms. 'Give her to me.'

She was the most beautiful thing I'd ever seen. She had a cap of dark hair, just like her big sisters, and a plump, searching mouth. If her eyes were to have opened, I knew they'd be deep navy-blue. I longed to take a fingertip and softly lift her delicate lid where the skin was so transparent the veins showed through like the rivers on a map. Just one peep at her eyes . . .

But instead I busied myself with her hands, counting her tiny, slender fingers, just as I did with Pip and Katy when they were born. And after the fingers, I moved on to the toes, taking each one gently between my fingertips, making sure she was all there. It's what you do, isn't it, when you have a baby? Greedily laying claim to every inch of delicate skin, touching them all over, attempting to inventory every perfect part.

'She's lovely,' said Annie, the red rings around her eyes clashing with her orange hair. By the end of the labour there'd been two midwives, a student doctor and a consultant in the delivery suite. All of them were crying.

'You never get used to it,' the consultant said later, when she came to see us in the special little room they reserve for cases like ours. 'Even after twenty-eight years in this job, I'm still not used to it.'

I hadn't known what to expect after the birth. Of course, I hadn't even looked at the stillbirth leaflet they'd given me the night before. Just that word had been enough to stop me opening it. So I was shocked to discover we could stay in the room together, Saul and Molly and I, for as long as we wanted.

'Make sure you take lots of photos,' Annie told us as we sat on the bed, taking turns to hold our baby. 'Later on you'll be so glad to have those.'

She looked wrung out. Her shift had finished when I hadn't long been in labour, but I'd clung on to her hand and she'd promised to stay.

After she finally left, she was replaced by a woman with a soft Irish accent who came to take prints of Molly's feet. 'Dancing feet, she has,' she told me as we looked at the tiny black footprints on the white paper. 'Your little girl will be dancing up in Heaven.'

I saw the muscle in Saul's jaw twitch then, but I liked the woman's warm, musical voice, and wanted to hear more about Heaven and how my little girl would be tap-tap-tapping her way up there. I had her for such a short amount of time, I wanted to flesh her out with a thousand stories. I wanted enough anecdotes to fill a lifetime.

Saul, who *had* read the leaflet, phoned Pip. I was horrified when he told me she was on her way.

'She should have the chance to meet her sister,' he said.

But the idea made me nervous, although whether for Pip or

Molly I couldn't have said. I felt protective of both my eldest and youngest daughters, born more than twenty years apart but still my babies. Pip was so sensitive – was she ready to cope with this? And Molly, my perfect, sleeping child – how could I bear it if Pip was frightened of her, repulsed even?

In the end it was fine – two sisters meeting for the first and last time. A hello wrapped up in a goodbye. Now, in the light of what Rob said about how left out Katy had felt, I try to remember whether we talked about calling her, too, but I'm pretty sure we didn't. We just had the one night. How was Katy, in the midst of her exams in Manchester, going to fit in with that? It was about logistics, I tell myself. But is that entirely true? Did even the tiniest part of me worry that Katy might come and make it all about her, when we had such a short time to make it all about Molly?

Pip had brought a babygro for Molly that was like a tiny tiger costume – soft and fleecy with orange and black stripes and a hood with ears.

'Where on earth did you find a shop open at this time of night?'

Pip had looked at me as if I was crazy. 'I've had it for *months*. I couldn't resist it.'

For the first time, I realized that Molly wasn't just mine, something I'd grown in private like a forbidden plant. Other people had been forming their own relationships with her, while they waited patiently to meet her.

I watched jealously as Pip gently took off the plain white babygro Saul had brought from home (just as well he had read the leaflet – I'd never have thought about it). Molly's skin was white and milky, and marshmallow soft. Pip's fingers traced the slope of her little shoulders and the gentle rise of her tummy. Raising her up into a sitting position, she stroked the curve of her back, the tiny dent at the base. She was memorizing her, I realized, and it was a relief to know that the responsibility wasn't just mine, that if I ever forgot anything, someone else might know.

After Pip left, kissing Molly a tender goodbye, I dozed off, only to wake up abruptly, terrified that she'd been whisked away while I slept. Not seeing her on the bed beside me where she'd been, I raised myself up and was taken aback to see Saul standing by the window in the little room that, overnight, had become a world in itself. He was holding Molly in his arms, and he was whispering to her and pointing to things in the sky.

How could I have forgotten that image of Saul with our baby, whispering in the night? Only now, sitting here in this hotel room with him shut inside the bathroom with only his repressed fury for company, does it come back to me.

The door opens and my husband emerges in a cloud of steam and self-righteousness. He has a white towel wrapped around his waist and he doesn't look at me as he gathers fresh clothes from the neatly folded piles in the drawers.

'Aren't you going to at least talk about it?'

He doesn't reply immediately, just carries on selecting socks and boxer shorts. At the T-shirt pile, he pauses.

'I suppose that T-shirt you've got on is one of mine,' he says, without turning round.

The martyrdom in his voice sets me immediately on edge. The image of him standing at the window in that hospital room fades in the face of his infuriating conviction that he is the injured party. 'Oh, for God's sake, do you want it back?'

'No. I'm just wondering why you haven't got enough clothes of your own – you brought a big enough bag!'

How petty we are, after all, he and I.

'Look, let's go home, shall we?' I say. 'The day's ruined anyway. We should just make our apologies and leave now.'

Saul turns then, his mouth puckered as if sucking on a lemon. 'Oh, right. So because you can't face everyone after your romantic dawn stroll with the groom, who also happens to be your son, we've both got to sneak out with our tails between our legs. Is that right?'

Saul likes stock phrases such as 'tails between our legs' that come already stamped with accepted meaning, so he doesn't have to struggle to find the right words of his own. He applies these phrases to his conversation like decorative patches.

'It's got nothing to do with it. Jamie has nothing to do with it.'

To my annoyance, my voice starts wobbling as I say Jamie's name. And yet, though there's still a lurch inside me at the thought of him, is it my imagination or is it less visceral than it was? It's as though I'm finally able to see him from the outside, rather than from inside some secret pod that the two of us share.

Saul looks at me and then sighs. 'We can't leave, Fran.' His tone is gentler now. 'It's rude. And think of Pip and Katy. They're not going to stay here if we go, and why should they have their fun cut short?'

He's right. But the thought of the day stretching ahead – breakfast, the picnic, the endless conversations with people I don't really know, Lucy, Maddie, the whispering behind hands – makes me want to stay curled up here on the bed.

When Saul has collected all his clothes, he heads back into the bathroom to get changed, pointedly closing the door, and I try not to mind.

I lean back against the pillows and close my eyes, and wonder whether I might just drift back off to sleep. I imagine Saul coming out of the bathroom and deciding not to wake me and tiptoeing down to breakfast on his own. 'Fran's feeling a bit under the weather,' he'd say. And everyone would nod understandingly and tell him to pass on their good wishes.

But I know that he wouldn't leave me here, and no one would be understanding.

My phone beeps from somewhere in my bag. I try to ignore it, but when it beeps again I swoop down and rummage for it.

'Unknown' says the name in the inbox. A fibrous knot tightens inside me. With everything else that's been going on, I'd forgotten about yesterday's texts. But now my mouth is once again dust-dry as I click on the message.

'*What is it you don't understand about "go away"?*'

For a second, I close my eyes to block it out, before forcing my shaking fingers to press Delete. Ridiculously, I glance at the still-curtained window as if the anonymous texter might be out there, crouching on the sill. I take a deep breath, feeling my lungs inflate, and then exhale. That's it, nice and steady. Whoever it is, I won't give them the satisfaction of getting to me. I toss my phone back into my bag and zip it up. I'll pretend it's not even there.

'Right. Are you ready?'

Saul, fragrant from his shower and radiating rude health after his run, is dressed in perfectly uncreased clean clothes. His hair is damp and curly and his eyes bright after a night of not drinking. He is so wholesome he is practically organic.

'Do I look ready?'

'So get a move on. They stop serving breakfast at ten and I'm famished.'

Saul waits while I drag myself to the bathroom and brush my teeth. I hear him tapping the room key against the melamine surface of the dressing table. Tap tap tap. I come out and put a different top on, the same as on Friday night. And still he taps. I play a little game with myself. If he doesn't stop tapping by the time I've brushed my hair and put on some lipstick, I'll walk out of this room and I'll never come back. I'll keep walking and no one will find me. I'll be like those men who pop out for a loaf of bread and are never seen again. I'll head for Chile. I've always wanted to go to Chile.

When I'm finally ready, Saul is still tapping.

I don't go anywhere.

Sunday, 10 a.m.

'Did you know, in France it's legal to marry a dead person?' Katy's voice is unnaturally bright as she spears a fried tomato on her fork. Looking at her, fresh-faced and clear-skinned, wearing a simple white cotton dress, you'd never believe she'd been up half the night splitting up with her long-term boyfriend in a most public way.

'I'm sure that can't be right,' says Saul. He has a bowl of fruit salad in front of him and is methodically eating his way through all the cubes of melon first. Next he will tackle the orange segments. Watching him makes me want to scream.

'No, really. If you can prove you'd already planned the wedding, you can get married. Even if your fiancé is dead.'

'There might be some advantages in that,' says Rob from the other end of the table. He looks pale and pasty in the unforgiving light. He hasn't eaten anything, just drained three espressos in a row. 'Marrying a dead person must significantly reduce marital arguments.'

'And divorce would be so much easier,' Pip points out. 'No quarrelling over division of property or custody of the children.'

'Sounds perfect. I can't think why more of us don't marry dead people,' I say.

Saul looks at me across the table, then looks away again.

Unlike yesterday, we're not sharing a big communal table. By unspoken mutual consent, the wedding guests are dotted around the hotel lounge, grouped in smaller configurations of families and friends. No one is saying much and a thick layer of apathy hangs in the air.

Suddenly a shriek of laughter shatters the subdued mood. Glancing over, I see Maddie sitting with Mr and Mrs Practically Family, our neighbours from yesterday's lunch table. Maddie is wearing a tight, sleeveless denim dress with a low V at the front. Her hair looks gleaming and freshly washed and I wonder how she has found the time between now and the last time I saw her outside our hotel room just a few short hours ago. As soon as I've pictured her face, saying to Saul, 'You're not seriously going to let this happen?', I feel sick and have to put my fork down and keep perfectly still until it passes.

Maddie was already here when we came down and hasn't so much as glanced in our direction, as far as I can see. A few people looked up when we came in, and at first I felt myself burning under public scrutiny, but after we'd sat down I decided it was just my own paranoia. What's the big deal, after all? The few people here who know my real connection with Jamie surely won't find it odd for me to have a few minutes on my own with my son on his wedding day, and those who don't will just think I took a stroll with a groom who was finding it hard to sleep.

Lynn and Max arrive to a polite swell of greeting from the assembled guests. Lynn is wearing jeans with a lemon-yellow smock that clashes with her pink complexion, and mid-height cork wedges that pitch her forwards at an alarming angle when she walks. Max has gone for the casual look – a mint-green polo shirt tucked into high-waisted jeans. They both have the set smiles of people who have recently said, 'We just have to make the best of things.'

'Champagne, Lynn?' heckles Maddie, as they pick their way to a table near the windows, where Rosie is installed with a group of friends.

A dutiful titter of laughter goes around the room.

'Make mine a large whisky.' Max is attempting jollity in the same cautious but game way I imagine him approaching a particularly challenging piece of anthropological research.

I'm relieved to see there's no sign of either Jamie or Lucy. No doubt they'll be having a special honeymoon breakfast delivered to their suite. Perhaps they'll eat it in the hot tub. I deliberately force my thoughts down these avenues as if probing an ulcer with my tongue, waiting for the stab of pain, but it doesn't come. In its place is just a dull ache.

How strange it is, after eighteen months of emotional, post-reunion freefall, suddenly to feel some semblance of control. Although, now I think about it, hasn't it been longer than eighteen months? Didn't the rot really set in before Jamie? Ever since we said goodbye to Molly, my feelings have swung to and fro like a fairground swing, impossible to catch hold of, impossible to stop.

At the beginning, grief had me by the throat. When I was discharged from hospital, Saul left me outside in the pick-up area while he went to fetch the car, and while I stood there waiting, a young woman was wheeled up next to me, cradling a newborn baby on her lap.

'I could have walked but I'm so nervous about dropping the baby,' she said, catching me staring. 'I still can't believe he's mine. I keep thinking a nurse is going to come chasing after me and tell me to hand him back.'

By the time Saul pulled up, my face was wet with tears.

For weeks at home I wore only a dressing gown and howled into the cushions on the sofa whenever I was alone – and sometimes when I wasn't. Then grief became *like* the dressing gown, something familiar that I wore to cover up whatever was going on under the surface. Grief was the barrier between me and the emptiness that now lay at the heart of me, in that place where my baby had been.

When did I start becoming fixated on finding Jamie? Without a doubt, the loss of Molly prompted me to revisit, for the first time in years, that other lost baby. For decades I'd folded him away in a pocket inside me that was so secret even I didn't know it was there. But with her death he became unfolded and there was no way of getting him back in. My two lost babies became fused in my mind.

217

I had dreams where I chased them through deserted city streets, panting up stairs, hurling myself against locked doors, always sure that just beyond this wall, or over that crossing, I'd find them again. And then I'd wake up drenched with sorrow.

My mother had dealt with the adoption. Following her death – before he remarried swiftly enough to wear the same shiny leather shoes to both her funeral and his own wedding – my father had burnt most of her papers and donated her clothes to charity shops. One time I'd gone to visit him and been shocked to see, in the window of the local Cancer Research shop, the red dress my mother had worn when I got married. I'd remembered her twirling between the tables in the Italian restaurant where we had our reception, and been poleaxed by a sudden and savage sense of loss. Not for the mother I'd had, but for the one I could have had, the one she could have been if things had been different.

So the papers with the details of the agency, and Lynn and Max, and the photos they'd sent over the years, all went up in smoke. Afterwards my father denied there had been photos, or indeed anything important, among the things he'd burnt. 'It was just out-of-date tat,' he insisted. 'Things no one would have wanted.'

'Oh well, you tried,' Saul said.

But I needed to find my son, and the search for him distracted me from thinking about Molly. I'd never known Max and Lynn's surname, but I knew he was an anthropologist, so I started ringing around anthropology departments in universities across the country. 'Do you have a staff member called Max?' I'd ask bemused secretaries. 'In his late fifties?' Finally I found him, in a university in the south-west. Professor Irving was on six months' sabbatical, the secretary told me. Did I want to leave a message? I declined, but at least I now had a surname.

I tried Googling Max and found a few references to papers and books he'd written, and a photograph of him and Lynn standing with a group of others at an awards ceremony. I remember scrutinizing her face for hours, searching for clues as to what sort of mother she'd been. In the photo, she was wearing a pink formal dress that looked slightly too large, as if it was bought for someone else, but I was relieved to see that her face was kind. A Google search for Lynn herself threw up very little – a few academic papers she'd co-written, a couple of groups she'd chaired.

There was no clue as to an address, no mention of children.

I grew increasingly desperate, the dressing gown increasingly grubby. When I wasn't at the computer, I sat at the kitchen table playing Angry Birds on my phone. Saul told the girls he was worried about me. They'd always known about the adoption, that somewhere out there was an older half-brother they didn't know. When Jamie's eighteenth birthday had come and gone without him getting in touch, they'd been bereft. Pip showed me the 'Happy Birthday Bro' card she'd bought just in case. The Christmas after Molly died, Katy listened to me talking about what I'd found out about Max and Lynn, but how I still lacked any information about Jamie.

'I take it you've Facebooked him?' she'd said.

'Pardon?'

'I mean, you know his adoptive parents called him Jamie – or maybe James. And now you know their surname, so obviously you've Facebooked him, right?'

I had a Facebook account, of course. Katy set it up for me years ago, but at that time I knew very few other people who were on there, and soon became bored of checking in to find that an old school friend fancied a grilled panini for lunch, or that my brother's wife in Spain had posted another photo of their new dog, so I hadn't checked my account for months. As far as I was concerned, Facebook was for keeping in touch with people you knew. It never occurred to me that you could use it to find people you'd lost.

Let me tell you, there are a lot of Jamie/James Irvings in the world.

I spent a frustrating afternoon trawling through them until Katy showed me how to limit the search to the UK only.

Then it was a question of scrolling down, checking out the basic information available for public view. How I learned to love those people who were careless with their privacy settings. Whenever I came across a James Irving who allowed access to his comments and photo albums, my heart leapt a little, and even when I'd realized it couldn't possibly be the right James Irving, I still lingered, flicking affectionately through photos of people I didn't know, cavorting in swim-shorts on sun-kissed beaches or posing in stiffly positioned family groups. I looked at their birthdays and worked out their star signs, and was quietly pleased when they were 'in a relationship'.

When I finally found him, it wasn't by recognizing his photograph, but because there was a thumbnail profile picture of him on his graduation, flanked by Max and Lynn.

I gazed at the photograph in silence for a very long time. Whenever I'd allowed myself to imagine finding Jamie, I'd pictured myself screaming or running to find Saul or something similarly dramatic. But in the event, I was strangely numb. I surveyed the main photo on his page – him standing against a backdrop of the New York skyline – as if he was a celebrity in a magazine, someone with whom I had no personal connection but about whom I harboured a mild curiosity. I looked at his clothes, but couldn't tell much from the black hooded sweatshirt. His eyes were in shadow and impossible to make out. For hours I picked that page apart like the carcass of a chicken, looking for scraps of information. I scrolled through all 339 of his friends, trying to build up a picture of his life. From that I gleaned that he'd been to Durham University and was now living in London. A few of his friends had no privacy settings at all and I read through all their wall comments until I finally found one from Jamie himself. Just something throwaway about a party, but I re-read it several times anyway.

As my sense of Jamie built up from all this snooping, so my excitement increased. The more I found out, the more real he became – this grown man, walking around, being in the world.

'Why on earth haven't you messaged him?'

Katy was outraged when she discovered I'd known about Jamie's Facebook page for over a week yet hadn't done anything about contacting him.

'I can't barge into his life without any kind of warning,' I told her. 'It's not fair. He hasn't made any attempt to find me. Maybe he's happy the way he is.'

'Have you ever stopped to think it's not all about you?'

Katy's hands were on her hips and her cheeks were flushed pink. She looked like her own childhood self, demanding to be allowed to stay up late. She quivered all over with the conviction of injustice.

But wasn't she right in this instance? It wasn't all about me. Jamie had two sisters who could become a part of his life. The girls had the older brother they'd always fantasized about. Maybe contacting him wouldn't be a selfish act, but an act of generosity. A gift I could give to him, after all these years of giving him nothing.

In the end, the decision was taken out of my hands.

'I've done it,' Katy said over the phone, and I could hear in her voice that old stubborn defiance. This was always her way – dive in impetuously, then brazen it out to cover up her own latent misgivings.

'Done what?'

Although I knew instantly, of course, what she was talking about, I wanted to drag it out, postponing the moment when she told me and it became real and unstoppable.

'I sent Jamie a message. There's no use getting cross about it. He's my brother. I have the right.'

I imagined her talking to her friends, putting her side of the story impassionedly over a bottle of wine, getting their agreement that she was being treated unfairly. 'You should contact him,' I could imagine these friends saying, young faces flushed with indignation on her behalf. 'It's your right.'

I remember being so full of feelings when I put the phone down, all churning around inside me, that for a long time I couldn't separate them off from each other enough to work out what they were. Excitement, dread, guilt, fear, all going round and round like clothes in an overstuffed washing machine. When Pip rang me, just moments after I'd put the phone down to Katy, I was still no closer to working out how I felt.

'She shouldn't have done that,' my sensible older daughter said. 'But in a way, isn't it a relief? Now at least you'll know, one way or the other. We'll all know.'

Sitting here in the hotel lounge, I slowly pull apart the uneaten croissant on my plate. I'd thought I was hungry, but the gobs of gluey red jam and the greasy flakes are doing unpleasant things to my stomach. Remembering the heightened feelings triggered by Katy's phone call is like recalling a particularly powerful film or book. Impossible now to believe that happened to me.

Looking across the room, I notice Bart, sitting by the far wall. He is still wearing his crumpled Hawaiian shirt, and his face is the texture of the doughy centre of my croissant. His hair, still pulled back into its ponytail, appears greasy in the morning light. Glancing up suddenly, he catches my eye and for a moment we stare at each other and I remember that awkward dawn walk, and what Jamie said. I try to send a message to him telepathically. *That wasn't me. I'm not that woman.* But he looks away, frowning.

'Tosser,' says Katy, noticing our exchange of looks

I'm grateful to her. Yes, she's right. He *is* a tosser. But still I'm worried about what she'll say when she hears about my walk with Jamie. Though she won't understand – how can she, when *I* don't understand? – I know that Katy will feel she has missed out.

'You look tired, Dad.'

Pip, who herself looks as if she hasn't slept for a week, is frowning at Saul with her head to one side as if assessing a new crack in the bedroom wall. I follow her eyes and see, with a jolt, that she's right. I'm not really in the habit of looking at my husband. Of course, I look at him sometimes, but not really with a view to *seeing* him, if that makes any sense – more as a way of gauging his response to something I've said or done. I'm looking for a particular configuration of features, a creasing around the eyes or thinning of the mouth. I'm not looking at *him*. So now it comes as a shock to see the greyness of his skin and the way his face seems to be weighed down at the edges, and the deep crevices gouged through each cheek, from nose to mouth.

It's my fault.

Saul glances over at me, and then looks away again. 'I'm fine,' he says. 'I just have things on my mind.'

'You and me both,' says Rob.

222

Sunday, 11 a.m.

When did I start thinking about death all the time?

I've always thought about it periodically. Who doesn't? That sudden shocking realization that one day the world will still be here, but I won't be in it. But this is different. Nowadays I'll be trawling the supermarket aisles when all of a sudden it hits me. What's the point in getting the half-fat milk or the organic carrots or the low-salt baked beans? What's the point of agonizing over what to wear or how much I weigh or any of it? Sometimes I'm driving and I'll pass a new building that's just gone up and I'll think, *That'll still be here when I'm dead*, and it completely poleaxes me. I imagine all the people who'll live inside it, and then I imagine everything happening without me being in the world, and I can't breathe.

It just happened now, here on the grass outside the hotel, near where Jamie and I took our impromptu walk only a few hours ago. I was lying back, gazing up between the branches of the trees at the hazy blue-grey sky, and I felt myself beginning to lose that knotted feeling I've had all morning. I watched a cloud the colour of old pants drift slowly along above me and allowed myself to relax. Everything was fine until I started focusing on the tree overhead and idly wondering how old it was and how long it had been there, and all of a sudden I just thought: *why*? Why am I angsting about Saul and Jamie and Pip and Katy and Rob when

223

we're all going to die anyway, and it won't make the slightest difference to this tree or that one or the sky or the landscape, and the grass will keep on growing and people will come and go and nothing will change?

You'd think a thought like that might be soothing in a way, but it isn't. It has left me churned up again, and thinking of Molly and how there has to be some point to her. She can't have happened for no reason at all. I need to find a place to put her within the context of the world, but every time I try, I come up blank. The trees exist, the clouds, those blades of grass, but not my daughter.

'I have to talk to you, Mum.' Pip has raised herself on to one elbow next to me. I can see the veins protruding, blue, through her skinny wrist where it supports her head. With her other hand, she picks at the grass.

'About the baby?'

She nods. 'The baby,' she proclaims, putting on a deep, news-announcer type of voice. 'Sounds so bonkers, doesn't it? *The baby.*'

I look at her face – at hollows and shadows and things that turn downwards.

'Has he said anything about leaving his wife?' I ask her. 'The father, I mean.'

Her mouth twitches involuntarily at that word '*wife*' and I feel a sharp stab of hatred towards this unknown man, this married lawyer, who has impregnated my daughter. How dare he? How dare he be at home somewhere, with his wife and children, while Pip is here alone.

'He wants to,' she says. 'He says he feels guilty just thinking about it, but he can't help fantasizing about how it would be if we could be together all the time. They've been married fifteen years and this is the first time he's ever thought about leaving her. You can't imagine how torn it makes him.'

'So he is considering it, then?'

She pauses in her grass-plucking, as if to formulate her words carefully.

'He is putting in place an exit strategy. That's what he calls it.'

Before I can quiz her on just what an exit strategy consists of, a loud cheer goes up around us. Pip and I sit up. My stomach lurches as I see Jamie and Lucy approaching, crunching their way across the gravel. Lucy wears cut-off faded denim shorts with a pale-blue T-shirt and her hair is pulled back in a messy ponytail, with white-blonde silky tendrils already coming loose around her face. Jamie is also wearing shorts, dark-blue beach-style ones, with a loose white T-shirt over the top. His arm is hooked loosely around her waist. They are pulsing with youth.

So they've made it up then. I'm faint with relief.

I don't look at Jamie's face. There is still something there between us. Something that shouldn't be there. But it is less insistent now, since our phone conversation this morning, and I choose to ignore it, turning back instead to Pip, who is once again lying stretched out on her side.

'OK. And has he any ideas how long this "exit strategy" might take?'

She flushes and resumes her picking at the ground. 'You don't have to say it like that.'

'Like what?'

'Like it's never going to happen.' Pip presses her lips together, leaving a bloodless patch in the middle where they meet.

I'm just about to cave in and apologize when she bursts out, 'Jamie's father – he was married, wasn't he?'

Instantly the tight feeling is back again, the gnawing in the stomach. 'You can't compare the two, Pip. It was so long ago.'

'But you never talk about it. I really want to know, Mum. It might help me. Can't you see? Did you never talk about a life together?'

'I was sixteen, Pip, for God's sake.'

'Yes, but you must at least have thought you loved him? What about when the baby was born – didn't that win him round at all? Didn't he feel the slightest bond with his own child?'

I really don't want to think about what she's saying. I can't. And now there's something else as well, another thing making me uneasy.

'Pip, darling, promise me you wouldn't decide to go ahead with it just because of that? You wouldn't have a baby just because you thought it might win this man round.'

Pip's face immediately closes off. 'Of course not,' she says. 'What kind of idiot do you think I am?'

For a few moments there's silence between us, so thick that if you breathed in you'd choke on it. It's broken by a high-pitched voice.

'Is everybody happy?'

Rosie is standing on the lawn, in skimpy shorts and a vest. Her blonde hair is secured in two small, fat pigtails on either side of her head. She looks about five years old.

'Before we embark on yet more eating,' – cue dutiful groan from the assembled guests – 'we thought we'd give you a chance to work off a bit of yesterday's excess with a game!'

Rosie looks pleased with herself. She clearly enjoys being in the limelight and I wonder how it is for her, giving up the older brother she so plainly adores to an alpha woman like Lucy. It must take some getting used to.

'What could be better, on a nice relaxing summer day, than a nice relaxing . . . game of rounders!'

More groans.

Rosie claps delightedly. 'No excuses. Jamie and Lucy are team captains, so everyone has to give them, like, maximum respect.'

An 'oooooh' noise goes up from the audience.

'They're going to pick their teams and then we'll head down to that big lawn over there to play, so there's no risk of the huge hitters like me breaking any windows.' She points to a non-existent muscle on one of her twig-like arms.

Everything inside me is objecting. It has been thirty years since I played any kind of team sport. I've had no sleep.

'This is like some sick Japanese reality-TV show,' observes Pip. 'You know, where they keep piling on twisted challenges to see who cracks first.'

'Do you think we should run for it?'

I'm not altogether joking.

I'm not joking at all.

Jamie and Lucy are now standing on either side of Rosie and they take it in turns to call out names. There are whoops and claps as people jump up and sprint over to form a queue behind one or other of the newlyweds. Some people put on a show of having to be dragged upright and inch their way over, as if being drawn against their will. As more names are called, I feel once again the tension of a hundred childhood PE lessons spent twisted up in agony praying not to be the last, and remember the exquisite relief of being called and knowing that there was still someone else left waiting.

Lucy calls Saul and he springs to his feet as if he has had eight hours' sleep instead of two or three. He makes a Popeye gesture as he crosses to Lucy, flexing his biceps and earning a titter from the remaining guests. (*Here I am gamely joining in*, says Saul's inner voice.)

Jamie calls up Katy and she pantomimes 'Who, me?' before flashing him a huge smile and going to join him. Handsome Hugo is sitting with his friends and I see his eyes follow my younger daughter like a tracking device.

There are a smattering of children here. I notice that Bart's wife has rejoined the party and is sitting on a blanket next to the baby, who is lying on her back, little legs kicking in the air. Her little girl is staring at Lucy and Jamie with her eyes wide and her hand straight up, desperate to be picked.

The children are all chosen near the beginning and hop up and down behind their team leaders, eager to start. A couple of the older ones mime hitting a ball with a bat, as if getting in some imaginary practice, holding both hands behind one ear and swinging forward with an exaggerated motion.

Max and Lynn are divided up, with Lucy getting a slightly stiff-featured Max, while Lynn, looking as if this could possibly be the most spontaneous thing she's ever done, wends her way self-consciously towards her son.

'I'm warning you now, I might be a bit rusty,' says Max.

'Pip!' Lucy is looking over in our direction expectantly.

'Oh God.' Pip heaves herself heavily upright. 'I thought this kind of ritual humiliation was all in the past.'

'Are you sure you're up to it?'

She frowns at me. 'Didn't you hear about that woman soldier in Afghanistan who gave birth practically on the battlefield? I'm fine, Mum.'

Now Rob and I are left alone. We exchange nervous glances. The last two survivors on the life-raft, the last remaining prisoners in the camp. I feel as if we should be holding hands, singing gospel songs, standing shoulder to shoulder.

'Rob, get over here!'

Jamie is beckoning in our direction and I fix my eyes firmly upon Rob so as not to have to catch Jamie's eye, smiling as if the smile has been hurled at my face so hard it stuck there.

'And that leaves Fran for me,' says Lucy brightly. 'Yay!'

'Yay,' I repeat under my breath as I move forward to join her.

Even the certain knowledge that death will eventually render it all meaningless fails to help.

Sunday, 12 p.m.

I am a mid-fielder. Apparently my job is to stand a few metres back from the third base, ready to stop any balls that over-run the immediate rounders circle. In practice this means I do a lot of waiting, which suits me fine. Waiting is one of my strong points.

Lucy has organized us very efficiently. I got a glimpse as she was doing it of how she must be at work. Cheerfully bossy, cajoling people to do what she needs them to do – couching it as asking when really, once you scrape the surface of it, it's telling.

Although this has been billed as a relaxing, family-style game, it's pretty obvious from Lucy's attitude that she wants to win. She *really* wants to win.

'I'm not saying it matters to me whether we win or lose, but please bear in mind this is the first battle of my married life, and I want to set the right precedent,' she said, not altogether joking. When she lost the toss to see who would bat first, her face darkened briefly and I got a tight feeling inside, wondering what happened when Jamie got back to their room this morning.

'Right. Who's on base?'

Lucy lost no time looking for people to man the four bases, which have been marked out by short wooden posts brought specially for the occasion and driven into the grass at regular intervals. There was no shortage of volunteers. Bart is in our team, and Maddie, who of course commandeered a base for herself. Mrs Practically Family wanted to be on base and was aggrieved to be dispatched to out-field.

'I think you're missing a trick. I was always excellent at sports at school, and you know I like to keep myself in shape,' she pointed out.

'That's why we need you to cover the back,' said Lucy. 'We need a strong outer team.'

Saul has somehow wound up as backstop and is crouching down exaggeratedly low and swaying from side to side as though poised for action. He is doing this for comic effect, but it's starting to wear a bit thin now.

Pip is also a mid-fielder but she's hovering midway behind first and second base, so we can only wave to each other forlornly. Hugo is on fourth base. I'm relieved he and Katy are on separate teams.

Jamie is still organizing his team of batters. I watch him leaning over a small boy, showing him how to hold the bat, and something crumbles inside me. This is my son, it occurs to me suddenly. *My son.*

I think it is the first time since our reunion that I've fully believed it.

How do you prepare to meet a stranger you gave birth to?

I wasn't prepared. I know now that I ought to have done things differently – gone through the proper channels so that we'd both have had counselling and intermediaries. I know now that Facebook is the place for discovering party addresses and star signs, not long-lost children. I know now that emotions can't be clicked on and off with a mouse and that once you've called them into life, you can't minimize them or stash them away in a special file in your documents folder. I know all that now, but at the time, still half crazed with grief, I couldn't see beyond my own need.

'He got in touch!' That first, breathless phone call from Katy, the high pitch of her voice setting the phone handset vibrating.

My pounding heart expanded until it seemed to fill my chest completely, pushing out my ribcage, and pressing up into my throat. 'What did he say?' Was that really my voice, asking that as if it was a normal thing to ask, as if this was a normal conversation?

Jamie's message had apparently been short and non-committal, just confirming that, yes, he might be the person Katy was looking for. Katy read the message out, excited and triumphant, but even after she'd read it I still asked, 'Did he ask about me?'

How deluded we are, in the end. I'd listened to her read the message, I *knew* he hadn't mentioned me, and still I asked whether he had because I wanted the answer to be yes.

Because Katy had engineered the contact, she took ownership of the burgeoning relationship, meting out information to me and Pip like sweeties to children.

'She's doing my head in!' Pip said, when Katy announced she'd set up a meeting with Jamie, but that it was better she went alone, so as not to 'overwhelm' him. 'She's so possessive – it's like he's a new boyfriend or something.'

Saul was worried about the emotional ramifications.

'You know what Katy's like – she throws herself into things without stopping to think. What if he's a nutter?'

He apologized for that later, the 'nutter' comment. But by then the damage was done – Saul had become someone from whom I needed to protect my newly discovered son.

'It's not only Katy I'm worried about.' Saul tried to redeem himself then. 'How's Jamie going to react to all this? It must be such a shock. He hasn't been prepared. It's not fair on him.'

But Katy, as ever, did things her way. 'I'm an adult now, Mum. I'm entitled to make contact with my brother in my own right.'

So she went alone to that first meeting. They'd arranged to meet at six thirty on the South Bank, in a bar at the back of the British Film Institute. Katy had originally suggested the coffee shop but Jamie pointed out they might need a drink.

'You see!' Katy said before she went. 'That proves it – he's one of us!'

Saul had counselled her to keep the first meeting short, but two hours passed, and then three and four, with no word.

'It's so typical of her,' he said, pacing about the house. 'She doesn't know the meaning of holding back.'

I lay curled up on the sofa with the phone next to me. I didn't know I was rocking until Saul told me it was making him anxious.

Finally, at eleven thirty, she called, so giddy with excitement she could hardly speak. He was amazing, fantastic, she told me. They felt like they'd known each other all their lives. Oh, and by the way, he wants to meet you.

Only when she said that did I realize how much I'd been dreading rejection. How would I have coped if he'd said he wasn't interested, if he'd decided to turn his back on me the same way he must feel I'd turned my back on him?

Watching Jamie now, his long fingers gently covering the small hands of the little boy on his team as he shows him how to hold the bat high behind his shoulder and step forward as he swings, I remember how it was in those few days between Katy's meeting with him and my own. When Katy described him, how he looked, what he said, how he said it, everything was a readjustment. The baby I'd given birth to was now a man, walking around, taking up space in the world, with his own thoughts and opinions and prejudices and habits.

'He laughs just like you, Mum,' Katy said, relishing her role as the lynchpin of this new awkward triangle.

And that touched me too. Not just that there was a man who laughed like me, but that I even knew how to laugh at all.

'Shall we start?'

Rosie has produced a whistle and is blowing it impatiently, trying to get Jamie's team into line.

Lucy is bowling, of course. She keeps taking practice run-ups, circling her arm over her head. When she sees Saul studying her, she pretends to be doing it as a joke.

With the batsmen finally lined up in some sort of order, play begins. For a few minutes, I watch closely, smiling when the smallest of the children – the girl with the bunches – steps up to bat, the tip of her tongue protruding from her mouth in concentration. Lucy comes very close to her and throws the ball gently, aiming for the bat, which the girl can hardly lift off the ground, but at the last minute she moves it, so the ball fails to make contact with the wood. The same thing happens a second time. The girl's face starts to crumple and the chubby hands holding the bat shake. She misses a third time.

'She's out,' shouts the boy Jamie was coaching earlier. 'It's my turn now.'

'No, that was a bad throw,' lies Lucy. 'She gets another go.'

The little girl is sobbing now, big tears rolling down her cheeks, but she clutches the bat tight to her body.

'That's not fair,' shrieks the boy in the queue. 'She should be out.'

Jamie steps forward and positions himself behind the quivering girl, crouching down and reaching his arms around her so that he is holding her fingers over the bat. He whispers something in her ear and she quietens down, her body stilling with anticipation.

Jamie nods to Lucy, and she throws another ball.

Thwack!

'Hit it!' shrieks the little girl, jumping up and down. 'Hit it very long.'

'Very long,' agrees Jamie – this man who is my son – holding the girl's hand and running with her to first base.

Is it possible to sum up how I felt, waiting to meet him that first time? I was wearing clothes I'd decided on only after trying on every other possible configuration in my wardrobe. I'd bought a new outfit, of course – a fitted red woollen dress with a statement zip all the way up the back; long, wedge-heeled black boots. My hair was freshly cut, my make-up plentiful.

It was Pip who told me 'Too much.'

'He'll want to know who you are, Mum. This isn't you.'

So off it had come – the dress, the boots, the spray holding my hair stiffly into position. Instead I'd gone in jeans and a soft wool jumper, with Converse on my feet. To meet the man who was still only an abstract idea in my mind, a spot of sunlight dancing around on a wooden floor, impossible to pin down.

We'd arranged to meet in Regent's Park, on a bench in front of the boating lake. Jamie suggested it, and only much later did he admit he'd made a special trip to the park beforehand to scout around for the best spot.

I got there deliberately early, wanting to be in place when he arrived. You don't have to be a psychiatrist to guess it was a subconscious desire to make up for all the other times when I hadn't been there for him. So I sat there for half an hour in the cold, feeling my hands growing number and my nose getting redder, while an invisible hand sewed tiny, painful stitches across my heart.

'Remember, he's not a baby any more,' Saul had said before I left. 'He's not going to fill the gap left by Molly.'

I'd been furious. 'Do you think I don't know that? Of course he's not a baby. He's a man. He's a fully grown man.'

But when he finally appeared, I wasn't prepared. Neither for the foreignness of him, nor the familiarity. When I stood up to hug him, this six-foot stranger, I thought for a moment that I might faint. And when he sat down next to me, I felt the bench shift beneath us, as if it couldn't support such a weight of emotion.

We sat on that bench looking at each other in silence, and I was lost. I thought I'd prepared myself for him being an adult, but what I hadn't prepared for was how I would become a teenager again, how the me I'd constructed to get through my life would crumble away, leaving just that scared seventeen-year-old who'd shut herself down to get through.

And then there were the feelings. This wall of love that hit me out of nowhere for this man, this stranger. Who I was seeing through the eyes of a teenager.

You can see how that might be tricky.

'Are you nervous?' he'd asked, picking up my hand.

'Petrified.'

'Fran!'

Someone is calling my name. I jerk my head upright just in time to see a ball coming straight for me. Instinctively I duck out of the way, to a chorus of groans from my team.

'You're supposed to catch it, not dodge it,' says Lucy. Her smile is like tracing paper placed over her real mouth.

The game has moved on. Now Katy is in bat, my fumble allowing her to reach second base.

'Thanks, Mum,' she says, grinning back at me.

'Any time.'

I see Handsome Hugo watching from his position on fourth base. Katy doesn't look at him, but she shakes her curls and I know she knows he's watching.

Rob, who is up next, is also watching. His eyes flick back and forth between Hugo and Katy. He raises the bat, which looks like a toy in his huge hands. Instinctively all the fielders take a step backwards.

'Take no prisoners, Rob!' urges Jamie.

'Have mercy,' says Lucy, pretending to quake.

She bowls the ball.

Thwack!

The ball whistles over my head and disappears behind me. I hear Mrs Practically Family shouting 'Mine, mine,' and turn around to see her racing backwards, both hands raised to the sky, before tripping over and landing on her back. Meanwhile Rob is running. He's heavy, so he starts off slowly, but once he gains momentum there's something quite magnificent about him. Past first base, he looks ahead to make sure Katy is on the move. She is on third, now fourth. Her hand brushes Hugo as she runs home.

'I've got it, I've got it!' Mrs Practically Family is running with the ball in her hand.

'Throw!' shout the fielders as one. 'Throw it!'

She extends her arm behind her and, with a grunt of exertion, hurls the ball into the air.

By now Rob is midway to third base. As the third-base fielder steps forward to catch the ball, Hugo pushes him out of the way.

'Mine!' he yells, cupping his hands in the air.

He catches it and now it's just a straight race to fourth base. Rob is thundering down the home stretch as Hugo turns and flings himself, full length, at the wooden post. There is a loud crack, followed by a silence that mushrooms in the air like a nuclear cloud.

Sunday, 1 p.m.

'**K**eep your head tipped right back. No, further. That's it.'
Mrs A. Turner, the hotel's designated First Aider, is quietly bursting with self-importance. She is trying to suppress it but it exudes from her pores. It's in her shallow, fast breaths and her stiff, upright posture and the determinedly calm, efficient way in which she is taking charge. I get the feeling she doesn't get many situations of this magnitude to deal with.

I know she is Mrs A. Turner because it says so on the badge she wears pinned to the lapel of her dark regulation jacket. I wonder whether the A is short for Angela. She looks like an Angela. Or an Amanda. Not an Anna. Annas are soft and sensitive and have creative fingers. Mrs A. Turner's fingers, which are wrapped around a once-white hotel-issue towel, which in turn is pressed against Hugo's bloody nose, are fat and no-nonsense. The flesh around her wedding ring puffs out on either side of her finger like an hour glass.

Hugo is sitting on a chair and leaning his head back at a right angle to his neck. His nose is approximately three times fatter than it was this time yesterday. He no longer looks handsome.

'I think it's broken,' he moans, his words muffled under the towel.

Mrs A. Turner doesn't agree.

'If you'd broken your nose, there would probably be a crunching

236

sound when I do this,' she says, prodding his swollen cartilage. 'And there's often some sort of bruising under the eyes. You might not win any beauty contests for a while, but you'll live.'

Mrs A. Turner is attempting some humour but Hugo doesn't appear very appreciative. I imagine it's a shock for him – the idea of not winning beauty contests.

'It's definitely twice the size of the other one,' Katy is saying. She is standing in front of Rob, surveying both his outstretched wrists. Her eyes flick from one to the other as if weighing up the merits of two different cuts of beef.

We are all crowded into the compact hotel bar, which has been turned into a makeshift field hospital.

'A wedding's not complete without a few broken bones,' says Maddie gaily. I suspect Maddie is the kind of person who describes herself as 'calm in a crisis'. From the moment of the spectacular mid-air collision, caused by Hugo hurling himself headlong at the wooden post of fourth base at exactly the same moment as the human juggernaut that is Rob powered in for the touchdown, Maddie has thrown herself into taking charge.

While the rest of us adopted the universal hands-over-mouth, make-like-a-statue pose that inevitably follows any minor catastrophe, Maddie steamed into action, tipping Hugo's head back and asking for a towel or a cloth to be produced. Hugo's not-so-handsome friend obliged by donating the T-shirt off his back, only to be left self-consciously hugging his own pale torso, goose-pimply in the damp breeze.

Meanwhile Jamie was first on the scene to tend to Rob, who was lying on the ground with one arm bent under him. The rest of us crowded around being largely ineffectual. People called out suggestions. 'Roll him on to his side,' advised one. 'Don't move him, in case something's broken,' countered someone else. 'Is he dead?' asked a child. 'I think he is. I think he's dead.'

A hotel receptionist who'd been watching from her cigarette break ran over to help. By this time Rob had regained consciousness and was sitting up, cradling his arm. Blood dripped from a cut on his forehead, giving him a distinctly Hallowe'enish appearance.

'Why don't you bring them both inside?' the receptionist suggested. 'We've a highly trained First Aider who can help.'

She sounded touchingly proud when she said that, about the highly trained First Aider.

So here we are. Maddie, naturally, and Katy, on account of Rob, or maybe on account of Hugo. Me, partly because I happened to be pressing a tissue to Rob's head when we started moving inside, partly to avoid having to play any more rounders. Only when we were already crowded into the bar did I realize Jamie was with us too.

'I feel guilty,' he explained to Mrs A. Turner. 'It was my idea to have a game. And I was the one encouraging everyone to be competitive.'

'Accidents happen,' she said magnanimously.

'He was aiming right at me,' says Hugo from underneath the towel, his eyes still trained on the ceiling.

'Oh, don't be an arse,' says Rob.

Mrs A. Turner doesn't like this. Her mouth puckers into a thin flap that sits in the middle of her face like a gill.

'Well, you certainly weren't looking where you were going,' says Katy. 'You were so determined to score.'

'I don't think I'm the only one determined to score.'

They glare at each other, and there's so much going on in that glare that I can't look. Instead I glance away and happen to catch Jamie's eye. My stomach spasms, but I force myself to keep looking, and soon the tight feeling passes. I half smile and shrug my shoulders, and he does the same. Something passes between us that feels, for once, OK and calm. I sense Maddie looking at us, but I don't turn to face her.

Through the window of the bar, I see that the remaining rounders players have regrouped and are attempting to play on. Saul is in the queue to bat, chatting to Max, and I have a sudden flash of how he would look to a stranger. A tall man, at ease with himself. It's always disconcerting when this happens – when I come across my husband unexpectedly somewhere he's not supposed to be, and see him from the outside. One time I was on a bus coming home from the station. It was a Saturday and I'd been out shopping with a couple of friends from school. I was gazing through the window, watching the world go past in a pleasant blur, when I caught sight of a thin, black-clad figure running along the pavement. For a split second, before recognition dawned, I watched his long legs moving in an elegant, rolling motion and I envied him – this separate, self-contained man, progressing through the world at his own pace.

Afterwards, I'd thought about telling him I'd seen him and about feeling envious, but when he arrived home ten minutes or so after me the moment had already passed. 'You've been out for a run?' I said, as if surprised. 'You could have left a note.'

The jury is out on the question of Rob's wrist. He insists it's not broken, but Katy isn't convinced. Mrs A. Turner is erring on the side of a bad sprain, which pleases Maddie, who clearly feels a trip to A&E would be bad PR for the wedding.

'I'll take you to hospital,' I volunteer.

This doesn't go down well with Maddie. 'You'll miss the picnic,' she says.

Luckily for her, Rob decides it definitely isn't broken.

'It doesn't look broken to me either,' agrees Hugo. 'Just a bit fat.'

Now that the moment of crisis has passed, Mrs A. Turner is reluctant to let us depart. 'You really do need to keep a compress on that,' she says, fussing over Hugo, who has had enough of leaning back and is sitting upright, gingerly separating towel from face.

'I'm sure I'll live,' he says.

'We're incredibly grateful to you, though,' Maddie tells her, putting a hand on her arm and smiling benevolently at her. 'I don't know what we'd have done without you. You've been a total Florence Nightingale.'

'Just following procedure,' says Mrs A. Turner, but you can tell she's pleased. Her face, which is wide and strangely shallow, like a plate, turns pink at the edges, and she pats her short, curly brown hair like a pampered pet.

Rob and Hugo have to sign a form before we leave, some sort of health-and-safety thing, I suppose, to indemnify the hotel against either of them claiming future compensation. Rob has to sign with his left hand as he still can't move his wrist, which has now been bandaged up as far as the knuckles. The signature looks like a child's.

He and Katy are the first to leave the bar. Although they're walking side by side, they're not talking. It occurs to me that Katy hasn't touched him once since the accident, not even when he was lying on the ground. Looking at her dipped head and hunched shoulders, I see the struggle she's going through, torn between her loyalty to Rob and her need to be free, and, although I'm cross with her for how she's behaving, I can't help hoping she sees it through, whatever she's decided to do. If we were alone now, I'd tell her, 'Life's short, be happy.' I imagine myself saying it while we're having breakfast at home, or driving in the car, and grabbing hold of her hand. And it would be like a weight being lifted from her, or a light going on in her eyes.

But really I know I wouldn't say that. Really I know I'd say something like 'Couldn't you have been nicer?' There's always been such a huge gap between the mother I am in my imagination and the real one.

As I step out on to the gravel, Jamie materializes by my side. I swallow and glance around, wondering if Maddie is watching.

'Was it all right when you got back to your room this morning?' I ask.

He shrugs, and thrusts his hands into his pockets. 'Not really,' he says. 'But I'll make it up to her. How about you?'

'I've had better mornings.'

We walk a few steps in silence and I grow uncomfortable, wondering if he's remembering how we came this same way just a few hours ago, desperate to be alone. Something seems to have shifted since then. The strength of feeling is still there – my heart still sounds insanely loud in my own ears – but some of the urgency has gone. The phone call earlier has changed things, as has that horrible scene with Saul. The little bubble Jamie and I have existed in for the last eighteen months has finally burst and, exposed to the light of public scrutiny, the unspoken, primal feelings that we allowed to grow are already crumbling into dust. There's a calmness that wasn't there before.

'This whole getting-married thing has got me thinking about so much stuff.' Jamie looks away, as if the stuff he has been thinking about might be found in the cloud-spattered sky, or the gently swaying branches. 'I really want to know about my dad, Fran. I know you don't like to talk about him. You made that clear on our first meeting. But standing in the church yesterday, I couldn't stop wondering what kind of man does that to his wife, someone he made all those same vows to? What kind of man cheats on her with a sixteen-year-old?'

There's a whooshing noise in my head, making it hard for me to hear. *Stop*, I want to say. *Stop now.*

I think back to that first meeting, sitting on the bench in Regent's Park, and how he'd broached the subject and I'd been so shocked. Though, of course, I should have expected him to ask about his father, somehow I hadn't. I'd blocked it from my mind so effectively that hearing him ask the question brought on a panic attack just like the one I'm having now, and Jamie, seeing it, had backed down instantly.

'Don't worry,' he'd said then. 'We'll talk about it another time.'

But I don't want this to be that 'other time'. I'm not ready. I'll never be ready.

'I know his name was David,' Jamie goes on. 'And he was married, and a bit of a prick.'

'A total prick,' I manage.

'But isn't there anything else you can tell me? Anything at all?'

A shutter opens in my mind and I'm back there in the pouring rain, sixteen again. 'Bye then,' says David. 'Oh yeah, sure. Bye.' A car door closing . . .

The shutter slams shut.

'No.' My voice is terse. 'There's nothing more.'

I walk on another couple of steps before realizing that Jamie has stopped.

'Fine,' he says, when I look around. 'Thanks, Fran. Thanks for

241

all your help.' He raises a hand, and then drops it in a dismissive gesture.

I try to think of something I could tell him to make things better between us, but the whooshing noise is still going on in my head, and my insides hurt.

I turn around and carry on walking.

Sunday, 2 p.m.

'I've been to Sandwich.'

Bart is splayed across a rug with his wife and children tucked in around him. In front of him is a paper plate piled with a selection of crustless sandwiches neatly cut into triangles. We are once again sitting on the grass behind the orangery, where the hotel has laid out its version of a picnic across the outside terrace tables. Some of the older guests have seated themselves in proper chairs but most, like us, are kneeling or sitting cross-legged on a vast acreage of overlapping blankets and rugs, attempting to look at ease.

'It's actually a town in Kent,' Bart continues, as if someone has shown an interest. 'Went there on a total bender – in my younger days, of course.'

Bart is still wearing yesterday's clothes. He has kicked off his Birkenstocks, and his bare feet, which are resting on the rug alarmingly near his wife's plate, are blackened with dirt, through which the thick nails glisten yellow like fly paper. One of his nails looks to have some sort of fungal infection, with a raised white area surrounding one corner that has been eaten entirely away. I can't stop looking at it.

'The interesting thing about Sandwich,' he says, mistaking our silence for rapt fascination, 'is that it's not actually famous for the sandwich. What it's actually famous for is – get this – Viagra!' Bart chuckles appreciatively, spitting crumbs on to the rug as he does so.

'Fascinating,' mutters Katy, who is sitting behind my right shoulder. 'Knob.'

'Have you ever tried Viagra, Saul?'

I sense Saul tense up beside me at Bart's question, but his voice is relaxed as he answers, 'Can't say I have, no.'

'Oh, dude, you have to give it a go. We used to take it all the time in the clubs – mixed with other things, if you know what I mean. Coconut Pokes, we called them. Course, that was before I met my good lady wife.'

Bart flutters the fingers of one hand to indicate the woman who is sitting just behind him, rocking the baby robotically in one of those little chairs that convert to a car seat. She smiles weakly and I notice she is really quite pretty underneath the layers of exhaustion and disappointment.

'Need wee-wee.'

The little girl, who is now sporting a pink-and-white gingham hairband with a large ornamental bow in place of her bunches, is suddenly sitting up very straight. Her eyes flit urgently back and forth between her unresponsive parents.

'Need wee-wee,' she repeats, her voice louder.

'I believe it might be your turn, sweetie,' says Bart's wife.

'Sure. Just let me finish eating.'

'Need wee-wee *now*!'

'Sweetie, I don't think this can wait.'

'Just five minutes. I'm starving.'

'It coming. Wee-wee coming.'

'Oh, for fuck's sake.'

Bart scrambles to his feet and snatches up his daughter, whose blue eyes are wide with the effort of controlling her bladder. Without stopping to put on his shoes, he heads for the side entrance to the orangery. The French doors are all closed up today and the tables unmade. Clearly this is used as an occasional function room rather than a regular dining area.

For a moment there's a relieved silence, as we all continue to pick at the food on our paper plates. In addition to a couple of tuna and cucumber sandwiches on anaemic white bread, I have a few seedless grapes and a handful of crisps. In a plastic cup, teetering precariously on the woollen blanket next to me, are the remains of my second glass of white wine, lukewarm now and with an unpleasantly acrid aftertaste.

'Don't you get fed up?' Katy is addressing Bart's wife, and I stiffen when I hear the scarcely disguised belligerence in my daughter's voice.

'Sorry?'

'I know it's none of my business. Karen, isn't it? We've met before, but I'm completely hopeless with names . . .'

'Caro, actually. Short for Caroline.'

'Yes, that's it.' Katy sounds as if she's confirming the other woman's lucky guess. 'Caro. Don't you get fed up with the way Bart treats you?'

'Katy, I really don't think Caro needs your input.' Saul is smiling, but I can tell he's angry. If there's one thing Saul can't stand, it's people trespassing in other people's emotional space.

'Just tell her to mind her own business, Caro,' calls Pip from over to Saul's right.

'I'm just saying!' Katy is clearly not about to back down. 'Caro is obviously an intelligent woman, I don't understand why she lets him get away with it. That's all.'

I've got to hand it to her, it's a clever ploy – damning criticism dressed up as flattery. Katy has clearly been taking lessons in passive aggression from her father.

Caro's round eyes, a dulled version of her daughter's, blink rapidly as if deciding whether to cry.

'Ignore my daughter,' I tell her. 'She has a tendency to overstep the mark.'

'No, it's fine,' she says. Her voice wobbles on the word 'fine', as if underwater. 'I'd probably think the same if I was in your shoes. I bet you wouldn't believe I'm a qualified geophysicist, would you?'

That shocks us, all right. Mouths open and shut. 'Really?', 'Wow!' are some of the things we say in response to this surprising news.

'Yep. Postgraduate degree, then two years working in Australia studying tsunami and earthquake risk. I met Bart when I was home on vacation. We agreed we'd have a perfectly modern marriage – with each of us taking it in turn to focus on our careers. Two-year cycles, we said.'

'So this is Bart's two years?' asks Pip.

'Not exactly,' says Caro. 'Bart's two years seem to have turned into four. Children have a habit of throwing out calculations, don't they?'

'But Bart isn't at work now,' says Katy, reluctant to let go of her indignation, even in the face of this altered reality. 'Why don't you insist he takes more of the responsibility for looking after the kids? I wouldn't stand for it, if it was me.'

'Just as well it isn't you then.' Caro's voice has a new steely undertone. 'Look, I'm sure you mean well, but maybe you should try walking a mile in my shoes before you judge me. I don't know what movies you've been watching or books you've been reading, but marriage isn't an equal union of two perfectly harmonious individuals. It's one bloody compromise after another, day after day after day, like an endless yellow-brick road of compromises. At the moment I'm prepared to live with that, because the gains outweigh the losses. But you know what? If I decide I've had enough, that'll be all right, too. The less Bart helps out, the less I need him. His making himself redundant in our lives actually empowers me in the long run. Don't you see that?'

There's a peal of laughter to my left that I immediately recognize as Lucy's, followed by an answering giggle from her mother. On our section of rug, no one speaks as we try to reframe our perception of Caro as 'Bart's wife'.

It's Rob who is the first to break the silence. 'Good on you,' he says, raising his plastic cup in Caro's direction.

We all murmur an uncomfortable assent.

'I am returned.' Bart throws himself down on to the picnic

246

blanket as if just back from a hazardous exploratory expedition. 'Have I missed anything?'

Caro looks away and shakes her head.

'Where's Dolly?'

For a second I think she's said 'Molly' and the ground rocks underneath me. Then my mind catches up, but still the similarity unsettles me.

'She wanted to play with some of the other kids. She wouldn't take no for an answer. You know how she is.'

That this living reminder of my own ghost child should have almost exactly the same name is simply too much. I glance at Saul, but the coincidence doesn't seem to have registered with him. The unfairness of this rankles – that I should see my lost daughter everywhere, while Saul has buried her tidily away. Not for the first time, I wonder if it's a lack of imagination in Saul that leaves him impervious to Molly's visitations. How have I ended up with someone so literal, so requiring of physical proof?

'I can't share my thoughts about Molly with him,' I said to our counsellor, Louise, one time. 'He says we have to "start looking forward". We have to "move on".' I made speech marks in the air with my fingers as I spoke the words, as if talking about some cultish doctrine that everyone knew to be false.

'And you don't think that's a valid viewpoint?'

'Yes, but I need to be able to talk about my baby to the one other person who's supposed to understand.'

'You can,' Saul broke in. 'Just not all the time. Do you know,' he addressed this to Louise, 'last week she woke me up at five in the morning to ask if I would prefer that Molly hadn't been conceived at all and we had been spared her death, rather than have had her and lost her.'

The betrayal took my breath away. That he would tell that to Louise, with her neat, shiny bob and her pristine consulting room with the fringed yellow lamp and the coffee table with the tissues. What he didn't tell her, because he didn't know, was that by the time I asked him that question I'd been awake for hours, wrestling with my own grief and asking myself the same question

– would I rather be free of that grief, even if it meant being free of Molly? And it had been a revelation to realize the answer was no. I chose Molly – despite the pain and the loss and the constant empty space at the heart of everything I did and still do, I chose her over nothingness, over a world without her ever having been in it. I'd been so excited by this discovery that I'd woken Saul up, wanting to share it, wanting him to feel some of the euphoria I was feeling, but I hadn't communicated it well and Saul had been cross. 'I have to be up in an hour,' he'd said, looking at his clock.

Oh, I know Saul loved Molly. Once I nipped upstairs for my glasses and found him kneeling by our bed with his face buried in the little pink blanket she was first wrapped in at the hospital, which I keep in a box under the bed with all her other things – the print of her feet, her baby tag, that tiger babygro Pip bought for her, the photos we took. 'What are you doing?' I asked, snatching the blanket away. It was the last thing that really smelled of her, you see. All I could think of was that Saul, with his mixed scents of sandalwood soap and coconut shampoo and cool mint shaving gel, was rubbing away the last traces of her. Afterwards I said I was sorry, and I tried to explain, and he said he understood, but I'm not sure he did. So I know he did love her, but it wasn't the same. It couldn't be the same.

And that's why he can sit here and listen to this couple call their little girl by a name that's almost the same as our daughter's, and not flinch, or do anything to show he's noticed or been affected. I'm sitting right next to him – so close I can hear the creaking of his right knee (the one he's always had trouble with) as he shifts his weight – and everything in me is crying out, *I want her back, I want her back, I want her back,* but still he listens calmly to them saying 'Dolly' and sips from his bottle of water as if nothing is wrong. What was it Caro said, about marriage being an endless yellow-brick road of compromises, one after the other?

'Which kids is she playing with?' Caro is sitting up on her heels and craning her neck to see.

'Oh, you know. That little boy with the wild curly blond hair,

and his brother with the Superman cape. I don't know their names.'
Engrossed in his plate of sandwiches, Bart isn't even looking up.

'I can't see her though.'

'They're probably playing behind the trees or something.'

'No, I can see those boys you're talking about, but I can't see
her. She's not with them.'

'Course she is. They'll be playing hide and seek or something.
She'll be sitting behind a tree trunk. You know how she loves that
kind of thing.'

'No.' Caro's voice is rising in panic. 'The boys have gone and sat
down with their parents. She's not with them.'

'Oh, for fuck's sake, Caro. Will you just chill for once?'

But Caro is on her feet, gazing around, turning slowly in a circle.
And now she's calling out softly, 'Dolly,' and again, 'Dolly.'

And now she's shouting louder, 'Dolly,' and she's running over
to the little boys sitting on the picnic blanket next to their parents,
and they're shaking their heads, and the parents are raising their
eyebrows over their plastic cups and shrugging their shoulders.
And now they're all on their feet and shouting, and we're all
following suit. 'Dolly! . . . Dolly!'

And soon tears are streaming down my face because it sounds
so much like Molly, and because there's another little girl lost and
my heart is breaking all over again.

Sunday, 3 p.m.

After Molly died, I had dreams where I was looking for her everywhere, running through vast, empty buildings, where rooms opened on to more rooms, all of them empty, or through city streets and alleys, all leading on one from the other, but I never found her. I'd wake up with my heart racing, drenched with the panic of having lost the one thing you can never replace.

Looking for Dolly in the grounds of the hotel, I'm transported back to those dreams, to that time. The hospital arranged for Molly's cremation. There was a simple service. Katy and Pip both read poems, but I don't remember much of it. We had lunch in a gastropub afterwards and passed around the photos of her, and Katy kept crying and saying, 'Why didn't you call me?' and I remember feeling worried about the photographs and how long she was holding them. Of course, we could have made more copies if they'd been damaged, but somehow that didn't occur to me. We had so little left of Molly, I needed to conserve it.

I remember the waitress at that lunch coming over to take our order. 'Is it a birthday?' she asked, beaming around at our family group.

Pip was the first one to speak. 'No.' She shook her head. 'It's more of a wake actually. My baby sister died.'

The waitress froze with her pencil hovering over her pad. I saw her look at me, noticing my yellow skin and sunken face. I saw her take in the two grown-up daughters next to me, and calculate how old that would have made me when I conceived. I saw what effect that had on her sympathy-ometer. 'Sometimes these things happen for a reason,' she said. And then she read us the list of specials.

All of the picnickers are now involved in the search for Dolly. Paper plates and napkins lie abandoned on the sea of rugs, a smattering of crisps ground into tartan wool. There are pashminas and jackets and nappy-changing bags and children's shoes. Just one figure remains seated, dark-clothed and solitary. Saul has volunteered to stay and keep watch over Caro and Bart's sleeping baby, oblivious in its baby chair. I was surprised when I'd heard him make the offer, more surprised still when the parents had agreed, running off to search for their daughter without a second glance, the way people do when they haven't yet learned how transitory life is, and how sometimes you don't get a second chance.

Katy and I pair off, heading without consultation towards the main hotel building. Everywhere there are guests on their own, or in twos and threes, walking slowly, swivelling their heads from side to side. 'Dolly,' they call. 'Dolly!'

'I keep hearing Molly,' I say to my daughter, turning my head away so she won't see my reddened eyes.

'You hear her?' Katy says, misunderstanding. 'What does she say?'

'No. When they shout "Dolly", I hear "Molly". They would be around the same age. Don't you think that's weird?'

'It's a zeitgeist name,' says Katy. 'Molly, Polly, Dolly – they're all names of the moment. Tilly, Millie, Lily.'

I feel a sharp stab of pain. I wanted to give her a timeless name, this daughter of mine who will never age. But have I instead given her a trendy name that will soon become stale? Have I consigned her to this moment, when I need so much for her to be universal, to grow with me and not be left behind?

'What was your name for Jamie when he was born? Before Lynn and Max called him Jamie?'

I don't want to talk about it. Thinking about Jamie floods

me with confusion, pumping round and round inside me until I overheat with it.

'I didn't have a name for him. I only knew I was pregnant a few weeks before he was born, and I knew from the start he would be adopted. I guess I disassociated from him. I didn't want to name him, or see him when he was born. I didn't want him to be real.'

I want to talk about something else, but my mind whirs like a fruit machine through other possible subjects without alighting on a single one.

'I gave you Jamie as a present,' Katy says.

'Pardon?'

'When I sent him that message on Facebook and went to meet him – that was for you. I was trying to give you something because you were so sad about Molly.'

I don't know what to say. I walk on without speaking, my footsteps deafening on the gravel.

'I regretted it for a while,' Katy goes on. 'When I saw how you were with him, how intense. I was jealous, I suppose.'

I don't want to talk about this. And yet I must. Katy keeps shooting me sideways glances and I know she won't rest until she gets something from me.

'Things with Jamie were complicated,' I say. 'They were always bound to be, I suppose. Having a son who is also a stranger. My feelings for him are – were . . . confused.'

Katy shrugs. 'Of course they're confused. You always say you fell in love with me and Pip and Molly at first sight, so it makes sense that you fell in love with him at first sight too. Except that first sight happened when he was twenty-six. It's bound to feel a bit odd.'

As she speaks, something falls into place inside me. *Of course. That's exactly how things happened.* I remember that rush of love for my three girls – the two living and the one not living. How could I not have expected to feel that same rush of love for my son? And once it was there, how could I not have agonized over what to do with it? All those feelings, for someone I didn't even know – someone fully grown who didn't need my protection, who didn't need me to feed him, or keep him warm and safe. She's right. How could that not be confusing?

We push through the doors into the lobby. I recognize one of the receptionists from last night.

'How are your feet?' she asks, and I remember the conversation we had about shoes and the little cushions you can put inside them to stop them from hurting. It seems impossible that was just a few hours ago. It feels like years. Wouldn't it be great, I think, if you could put a cushion around your heart, to stop it from hurting? I imagine inventing one, and presenting it on *Dragon's Den*.

We tell the receptionist about Dolly, and she looks sympathetic but says they'll probably have found her by now. She says her children were always giving her scares when they were younger. 'But they always turn up, don't they?' she says. 'They never stay lost.'

I want to tell her she's wrong – sometimes children *do* stay lost, no matter how hard you look for them – but I just smile and ask her to keep an eye out anyway.

As we leave the lobby, a grey cloud that has been blocking the sun shifts, bathing us in a sudden bright light as if we've just stepped on to a stage.

I'm still thinking about what Katy said, about giving Jamie to me as a present because I was so sad about Molly. I decide she isn't talking about replacing one lost child with another, but rather about trying to fill up some of the empty space that Molly left behind. Like Saul, Katy always wants to find solutions, even when there is nothing to be done.

So often I focus on Katy's failings – how she speaks without thinking things through and hurts people without realizing, how she puts herself at the centre of every frame, every drama, even when it isn't hers to own – that I forget about her strengths. Then out of the blue it will flay me all over again, the knowledge that this daughter of mine, made from my own cowardly genes, is the most fearless and honest person I know.

I don't tell my daughters often enough how amazing they are, although I think it all the time. Sometimes I'll be thinking about how big-hearted and loyal Pip is, or how fabulously, flamboyantly reckless Katy is, and be so overwhelmed by love and pride that I imagine the girls must feel it without being told, that it must radiate out through my skin and into theirs. Yet of course they don't, and it doesn't. *You have so little joy in you, Francesca,* my mother said to me all those years ago. Why don't I praise my children every day?

'Thanks for what you said about Jamie,' I say now, linking arms with my daughter impulsively.

Katy hugs my arm to her side, smiling, and I realize how rarely I make the first move physically towards her. Usually there's no need. She is so tactile herself, it's more a question of disengaging than connecting.

I remember what Rob was saying last night about Katy feeling excluded when Molly died, because we didn't summon her down from Manchester to meet her baby sister at the hospital. Suddenly I feel I have to explain.

'I'm so sorry you never got to meet Molly,' I say now. 'We never meant to leave you out. We were just so wrapped up in what was happening. We never thought.'

'But you called Pip. You asked Pip to come.'

'Yes, but you were so far away. And you had exams.'

It sounds feeble, even to me.

'You never gave me the option though, Mum. How do you think it felt to find out you'd all been there together, all three of you – all four of you when you count Molly – and I'd been left out?'

As always when she's angry, Katy's stroppy childhood self comes to the fore – the little girl who threw herself upon your leg when you tried to leave home without her, and who was once sent home from school for biting a girl who wouldn't let her join in her game. I'll miss her, if I take that job in Spain, I realize suddenly.

'I'm sorry,' I repeat now. 'I didn't realize how it would affect you.'

'She was my *sister*. Of course it affected me.'

When Katy says this, I think that maybe it's me who has an issue with putting myself at the centre of the world. I've been so sure this was my tragedy, the loss of Molly, I haven't allowed for the possibility of it being anyone else's.

We carry on walking, arm in arm, and though it feels awkward, it also feels good.

As we round the side of the orangery, we spot handsome Hugo further down the slope. He lifts one hand to wave, then thinks better of it and turns quickly away.

Katy sees him, but says nothing.

'Rob's a lovely man. Be careful with other people's hearts,' I tell her impulsively.

'Ha. Like you are with Dad's, I suppose!'

I'm shocked by this sudden flash of vitriol.

'I will be careful,' she continues, pulling my arm further through hers. 'But you know, Mum, sometimes the long goodbye isn't the kindest way.'

'What's that supposed to mean?'

But now we are back at the lawn, and the answer gets lost at the sight of the still-deserted picnic rugs, with their scattered debris, and the lone figure of Saul still there, mechanically rocking the baby.

'Don't tell me they haven't found her.'

Saul shakes his head. 'Apparently there's a pond over there, behind the overflow car park,' he says, pointing. 'That's where they've all gone. They've looked everywhere else.'

'Oh my God!' Katy claps her hand over her mouth.

I think about the little girl with the bunches, who is now the little girl with the gingham hair-band, who is now lost. I think about how she's nearly the same age as Molly. I think about her being called Dolly. I think about Jamie and how much of him is lost to me and how much of him I'll never know. I don't want there to be any more lost children in the world.

I start walking back towards the orangery side entrance.

'It's not there,' says Saul. 'The pond's the other way.'

But I don't listen to him.

I have a purpose, finally. After all this time, all these months, all those wasted afternoons, I have a purpose.

I need to find the lost children.

Sunday, 4 p.m.

Caro is still crying, great noiseless sobs that cause her daughter's tiny body to shake.

'Mummy sad,' says Dolly. 'S'all right, Mummy.' Clumsily, she pats her mother's head. 'All better now, Mummy.'

Caro is kneeling on the picnic rug with her arms around Dolly and her head buried deep in her daughter's neck. She has kept up this posture since being summoned from the fruitless trip to the pond some ten or fifteen minutes ago to find her child happily installed between Saul and me, eating forbidden crisps from a family-sized packet.

'I remembered how my own daughters were obsessed with toilets at that age,' I tried to explain. 'How we'd get back from one loo trip and they wouldn't even let us sit down before insisting they needed to go again. They're so pleased with themselves, aren't they, when they first ditch the nappies?' I addressed Caro directly. 'It's their first real measure of control.'

Pip and Katy's toddler faces flash into my mind, wide-eyed with wonder at the thing they'd just produced. 'Come see,' they'd say, tugging at my arm and pulling me towards the toilet. 'Come see what I did.'

'I remembered seeing Dolly in the toilets yesterday afternoon,' I continued, 'and I thought she might have gone back there on her own, just to prove she could.'

'But I checked,' said Maddie, ruffled. 'I opened the door and saw the loos were empty. You saw me, didn't you?' She appealed to Lucy as a witness, as if she might not be believed.

'But there's one toilet stall set back from the others,' I said. 'I noticed it yesterday. You wouldn't have been able to see it from the door.'

I didn't mention yesterday's scene with Lucy sobbing. I hoped she wouldn't put two and two together.

'She'd locked the door,' I told the throng of relieved searchers who'd gathered around, hungry for the happy ending, the reward for their efforts. 'And then, of course, she couldn't open it again. She was OK, though. She's a tough little cookie.'

Tough little cookie! When did I ever use phrases like that? It was the heightened emotion of the situation that did it, I think.

'But how did you get in, if it was locked?'

Maddie just wanted to get things straight, I reminded myself. She didn't mean to sound like a police interrogator.

'I crawled underneath the door!' I smiled, to show I realized how preposterous an image that must conjure up – me crawling on my belly, commando style, on the toilet floor. 'Dolly almost had a heart attack at this strange woman appearing at her feet!'

I left out the bit about finding her blotchy-faced and spent with crying, and how her mouth had turned down at the corners when she'd looked at the person coming to rescue her and realized it wasn't her mummy or her daddy. And how, when she'd let me pick her up and carry her out, she'd stayed stiff in my arms, so I hadn't, even for one moment, imagined she was my Molly.

All around us, people are flopping heavily down on to the rugs, or into chairs, wrung out by the worry of the last half-hour. Bart has taken the baby out of her chair, waking her to hug her floppy, pliant body to his chest. My heart softens momentarily towards him. Sometimes we all need to grab hold of the things we most love, just to prove they are real. All the same, I can't help wondering how pleasant it can be for the baby, to be pressed up against Bart's unwashed shirt.

I wander over to the terrace and sink down into a chair. I'm glad Dolly is safe. I'm glad Jamie's wedding is saved.

'Thank God for that,' Lynn says, as if reading my mind. 'May I?' She sits herself down in the seat next to me without waiting for a reply.

'Surely you weren't expecting everything to go to plan? It *is* a wedding, after all!' I'm setting the tone at light, hoping Lynn picks it up like a baton and runs with it.

Lynn is not the running type.

'I really am so grateful that you found her, but I was hoping we could have a little chat anyway.'

I continue gazing straight ahead at the picnic scene. I haven't slept in over thirty hours. I'm too tired for whatever Lynn has to say.

'It's been quite . . . unsettling for Jamie to have you back in his life these last eighteen months. Lovely, I'm sure, but unsettling nevertheless. In fact, it's been quite unsettling for all of us.'

Lynn is picking at the hem of her yellow smock as if she would unravel it. I don't have to look at her face to know it will be as pink as the sun on the bottom of the clouds this morning when Jamie and I stood behind the trees.

'I'm sorry,' I say to her. 'I know we should have gone through the right channels. It wasn't fair to barge into your lives like that.'

'Don't get me wrong, Jamie is very fond of Pip and Katy. And you, of course. Only . . .'

'Only you'd rather we'd stayed out of it.'

I mean it to be a statement of fact, but it comes out sounding like an accusation.

'No. I didn't say that.'

It's the closest I've heard Lynn come to raising her voice, and it has the effect of instantly shaming me. I wonder what it must have been like to grow up with her as a mother, how Jamie and Rosie must have dreaded upsetting her. In that respect, she's not so different from my own mother. The thought horrifies me – that I could have given away my son to a version of my own mother. But as soon as I've thought it, it's gone. Lynn isn't my mother. She has warmth, where my mother had self-interest. And more than that, she has love, where my mother had blame.

'All I mean is that it could have been handled better, the whole thing. You and Jamie needed someone to help you . . . contain yourselves.' She flushes deep red. 'No, not contain yourselves, I didn't mean that. I meant contain your feelings. You needed someone in between you, some intermediary, to absorb the excess of what you have both been feeling. Sometimes it's just too much. Sometimes feelings are just too much.'

I'm astonished by Lynn's passion and, more than that, by her understanding. I realize, belatedly, that I have misjudged her.

'Max and I argued about it last night.'

I remember Rosie saying something about a quarrel between her parents.

'Max thinks we should ask you to stay away from Jamie for a bit, just while he settles into married life. But I feel that would be counter-productive.'

Now it's my turn to feel my face burning. 'I think we've sorted some things out,' I say. 'We're into a new phase now.'

'I hope so,' says Lynn. 'Jamie's a smashing boy. He deserves to be happy.'

Smashing? Who says 'smashing'? The same kind of person who says 'tough little cookie', perhaps.

'He is,' I say. 'A smashing boy. You've done a fantastic job bringing him up. He couldn't have done any better.'

From the corner of my eye, I see Lynn hold back a smile, and I'm glad I said it. She deserved to hear that. It was my wedding present to her.

'I know you want the best for him,' she says now. 'So I wonder if I couldn't prevail on you just to let him know something about his father. I know it must be hard. I know you were young and he was married, but isn't there anything you could give him to go on, any crumb of information?'

Again that feeling of things tipping inside me, that noise in my head. I remember the pain between my legs. I don't want to remember any more.

'I can't talk about it,' I say. 'I'm sorry.'

'Oh, well. At least I tried.'

She's gone back to the bright, social voice I remember from yesterday's reception, painting it on top of her real voice like varnish. It's as if the emotional exchange we've just had never took place.

'That looked pretty intense,' whispers Pip, slipping into the seat that Lynn has just vacated.

'Don't ask.'

The thing about Pip is she has always had some kind of sixth sense about when you want to talk and when you don't. My stomach is still churning after the conversation with Lynn, and I don't feel like chatting, so we sit in silence, watching the others. Caro has finally unglued herself from her daughter and is sitting with both her babies on her lap. Bart is hovering near by, unusually attentive, but his wife's body language isn't encouraging. Every time he moves towards her, she blocks him by turning slightly away. I wonder if she might have reached that point of no return she spoke about earlier.

Saul is talking to Rob, who cradles his bandaged hand awkwardly in his lap. Behind them, Katy and Rosie whisper conspiratorially, their heads close together.

At the far side of the group, Jamie is sitting up, chatting to someone I don't know, while Lucy reclines in front of him with her head resting in his lap. His hand gently strokes her hair as he talks. It occurs to me that I've been panicking about losing Jamie just as I've found him again, but that even if I'd known him all his life, like Lynn, I'd still be facing losing him and it would still hurt. Let's face it, there's no easy time to lose a child.

'Mum?' Pip's voice cuts into my thoughts. She lays her head on my shoulder. 'Can I come back home with you and Dad tonight?'

'Of course, but what about work?'

'Duh! Bank holiday?'

With the casual disregard of the unemployed, I'd forgotten there's a day off tomorrow. That's why they decided to let the wedding spill over into Sunday. So everyone will have a day to recover, and Max and Lynn and Maddie get to spend Sunday night winding down at the hotel with the newlyweds before they fly off on honeymoon tomorrow.

'You'll have to let Katy know. Weren't you due to get a lift back with her and Rob?'

'If she goes back with Rob. I wouldn't bet on it, though, the way things are at the moment.'

We sit a while longer, looking at Rob, and then at Katy. I try to forget about Lynn's clipped voice when she asked about Jamie's father, and the tightness in my chest.

'I used to love bank holidays,' Pip says softly. 'Now they're the longest days ever.'

It takes a second or two for me to understand.

'Because he's with his wife?'

She nods.

'Oh, darling.'

What else is there to say?

Sunday, 5 p.m.

Can a wedding ever have lasted so long? I think of other eras and cultures, where wedding feasts go on for weeks, and feel weak with relief that we will shortly be going home. Everything feels unravelled, like an expensive new jumper with a snagged thread at the hem.

Pip and I have been trying to leave for ages, but Saul is being elusive, although I can see how tired he is by the deepening crevices in his face, each one marking an hour's lost sleep, like rings in a tree trunk.

It struck me a few minutes ago that Saul hasn't looked at me directly all day.

For months – years, really – I've been the one cold-shouldering, turning away when he tries to get near, replying to his questions with one-word answers that drop like stones into the gap between us. Now it's Saul's turn to present to me a polished, shiny surface that everything slides off, and I find myself full of dread.

I long to talk to him about Pip and the baby. The thought of what she's going through, and what she has to face, fills me with sadness – history repeating itself, when I dreamed of so much better for her.

At least she'll have support though. She won't have to be alone, like I was – until Saul. I think of the letter in my bag. A new life in Spain, while my daughter is back in England, needing her mother.

'How come Pip is coming back with you?'

Katy has appeared by my side. We're all back in the hotel lounge, where we repaired to escape a sudden shower. Tea is being served, but I don't want any tea. I just want to go home.

'I don't know, darling. She just said she wanted to come home for the night.'

'She was supposed to be getting a lift back with us.'

'Does it matter?'

'Yes, actually! I don't want to be on my own with Rob all that time. Things are . . . difficult. Anyhow, I'd been meaning to ask you and Dad if I could move home for a bit.'

It shouldn't be a surprise, but it is. My tired mind struggles to reconfigure our domestic routine, Saul's and mine, with Katy back in the picture.

'Of course you can move back. We'd love to have you, but don't you think you should sort things out with Rob first?'

'Things are sorted, Mum. Rob's a lovely bloke, but it's been over between us for ages. He just hasn't wanted to face it. I'm going to tell him now that I'm coming home with you.'

'Hang on. You mean you're literally moving back in right now?'

But she has already gone. I remember what she said earlier on about long goodbyes not always being the kindest way. Oh, poor Rob.

Saul approaches. I'm nervous around him today, I realize, and my stomach is fizzing unpleasantly. I just want to be at home on our own.

'I hear we have the pleasure of both our daughters' company back home,' he says.

I nod, mute. I want to lean my head on his shoulder. I want to take his hand. But I don't dare.

'I expect you'll be relieved to have someone else in the house,' he says. 'Diluting the atmosphere.'

I don't understand what he's saying. I look at him, but he doesn't meet my eyes.

'I've been talking to Lynn,' Saul continues. 'She's upset that you won't give Jamie any information about his father. I have to say,

I think you're being unfair, Fran. I know you don't like talking about it, but fathers do matter, you know, especially at times like this.'

I'm so tired, and everything is churning, and for a second I think I might cry.

'I can't,' I say to him. 'I just can't.'

Saul's features harden, but he says nothing. We sit in silence, gazing around the room. Over by the door, Bart and Caro and their children are taking their leave with maximum fuss, working their way around the table where Jamie and Lucy sit with Maddie and Max and Lynn. They have so much paraphernalia with them that progress is slow. When Bart leans down to kiss Lucy on the cheek, the corner of a nappy, which is sticking out of the duck-decorated bag on his shoulder, pokes Maddie in the eye and she makes a big show of borrowing a tissue from Lynn to dab at it. Caro catches my eye across the room and raises the hand that isn't attached to her daughter. I think something might have shifted in her face. Does she look slightly less defeated?

'You know, Fran, I love you very much, but you can be very selfish. I always knew it, but this weekend has really hit it home. First that business with Jamie, and now this refusal to speak about his father, about David. You might try, just for once, thinking of someone other than yourself. You might try taking some responsibility.'

Saul is hissing in my ear, but I don't answer him. I can't. Something has broken inside me – a vial smashing, liquid leaking, toxic, over the shards of shattered glass. I don't want to think about David, but now that Saul has said his name he's right here in front of me, leaning across the front seat of the car, explaining why he can't take me to my door. *It's probably best for you to get out here. So there's no chance of being seen. For your own sake. You know how people's minds work.* And even at sixteen I knew it was all about him, about him not being seen, about him returning to his wife and his child and his own little world without any risk of comeback.

The whooshing noise in my head is back, louder than ever.

I haul myself to my feet without saying a word to Saul and head towards the door. I'm conscious of various people smiling up at me from their tables, but everything is lurching around me, the walls seem to be wobbling, and I don't stop. There's a fire starting in the pit of my stomach. I can feel the embers igniting and I'm frightened of where it will end.

I stumble to the hotel bar and order a whisky, before realizing I don't have any money. The barman says he'll add it to the tab, and I say thank you and I don't ask him whose tab.

I take my drink outside, but it's raining. Rosie is here, her narrow shoulders hunched over a cigarette, the blades jutting through the skin like Toblerone segments. She looks like a small child.

'Oh,' she says, looking up in surprise. 'It's you.'

I watch as she slides her other self over this naked one, straightening up, arranging her face into a smile. But it's too late. I've seen the naked hostility in her face. And now it's my turn to be shocked.

'It's *you*,' I say, repeating her own words back to her.

She frowns. 'Sorry?'

'The text messages. Warning me to keep away. It's you.'

'I don't know what you mean.'

Ordinarily I might have backed off, but exhaustion has dissolved my social restraint, and the burning in my stomach won't leave me alone.

'I think you do.'

She stares into my eyes, the denial dying on her lips. Then she shrugs. 'OK, it was me. There, happy now?'

Absurdly, I feel my eyes watering. 'Why? I didn't do anything to you.'

'Didn't you? Didn't you really? Oh, come off it, Fran. Take a bit of responsibility, will you? We were a happy family. Then you march in and, like, staple your family on to ours without ever thinking about the rest of us or asking us what we want. How do you think Mum felt when Jamie got all starry-eyed about meeting you? How do you think *I* felt, when, just like that, he's suddenly got two shiny new sisters?'

Her tiny body is quivering and, despite everything, sympathy courses through me.

'I'm sorry. I can see it must have been very hard. I know we could have handled things better. But Rosie, don't you think Jamie deserves to know that we're here and we never forgot him?'

'And what about me?'

'Pardon?'

'Don't I deserve that, too? Bet you didn't know that I tried to contact my birth mother when I was eighteen and she didn't want anything to do with me. Does that make me less deserving than him?'

'No, of course not.'

'You're not good for him, Fran. There's something kind of creepy about the way you two are with each other. He was happy before, and now he's stressed all the time. I just think you need to give him some space.'

I feel my skin tingling, blood rushing to my face. 'He has the right to know,' I repeat, but my voice carries little conviction. All I can think about is that word 'creepy'. 'I'm going to go now,' I say. 'I'm sorry about your birth mother. I really am. That must have been awful for you.'

She shrugs again, her bony shoulders jabbing the air. She's a child still, I see now, storing rejections like a squirrel's winter nuts.

Back in the lounge, I have to walk past Jamie's table to get back to Saul, who has now been joined by Pip and Katy. I hear someone say 'Fran!' – either Lucy or Maddie – but I don't respond. The fire inside me has taken light, and I feel the flames building. The walls are still moving and I want to close my eyes, but every time I do, I see David's car driving off, leaving the sixteen-year-old me standing alone in the dark drizzle.

I take a seat next to Saul and Katy starts immediately. 'It's all sorted. I'm coming home with you. And don't start lecturing me about Rob, I can—'

'Are you OK?' interrupts Pip, leaning across her sister to put a hand on my leg. 'You look absolutely awful.'

'Can we leave now?' I ask. 'I just really want to go home.'

267

But now I'm conscious of another figure looming beside us – Lucy, her small, delicate features set hard with determination.

'I need to talk to you, Fran.' She's trying to keep a smile on her face, but it's more like a crack than a smile, a fissure in plaster through which words are coming out.

'I'm sorry, Lucy. We're just about to leave. We're all so tired.'

'I'm not surprised you're tired, after your early-morning stroll with *my husband*.'

Her face flushes dark red as she says '*my husband*' and I wonder if it's the first time she's used that phrase. The flames are high now inside me, the sound of the heat crackling at my ribs joining with the whooshing in my head. I wish Lucy would go away. I wish they'd all go away.

'Lucy, I think Fran's not feeling too good.'

Saul is trying to defuse things and I want to thank him, but Lucy is talking over him, and I can tell she doesn't care how I'm feeling.

'I just think . . .' she says, and stops for a moment. 'I just think Fran owes him, do you know what I mean?' She is addressing the others. 'She gave him up without a second thought. And he's given her a second chance – given you all a second chance – because that's what Jamie's like. He sees the best in everyone. He wants to believe everyone means well. We invited you all here in good faith, because we want you to be a part of our lives. And the one thing he asks of her in return, the one bloody thing, she refuses to give him.'

'I can't,' I say. 'I can't.'

'Of course you can. Just something. So his name's David. David what? What did he do? Where did he live? What colour was his hair? How did you feel about him?'

And now there's a blaze where my body used to be, and the noise is all around me and inside me, and I'm thinking about Jamie and about Molly and about all the lost children. Including me. Because at sixteen, you're still a child. I was still a child. And I'm thinking about that child, standing in the rain watching the car driving away, and I don't want to go further, but now I can't stop. I'm remembering how it was dark and wet and cold and I just wanted to be at home, so I took the short cut, even though no one ever took the short cut because we'd all been told so many times.

'Come on, Fran.' Lucy's voice is cajoling now. 'Just something. Anything!'

And now there's no going back, and there I am picking my way home in my mother's too-big shoes, wondering if this was what happened when you grew up – men had sex with you and then dropped you on a street corner without a backward glance. Maybe this was why my mother was the way she was. Because of disappointment – because of the gulf between what you read about in magazines and this tawdry reality. And I see him ahead, but by then it's too late, because there's nowhere to run to, and besides, maybe he's just waiting for a friend or tying his shoelace, or whatever else a man could be doing in the darkest corner of a patch of wasteland. And by the time I notice his eyes, wide and staring and shining in the semi-darkness, and how his hand, closed around a bottle of something, is shaking, it's already happening.

'Oh, this is pointless.' Lucy again.

On some level I'm conscious of her walking away, but my mind is still there, in that dark place, reliving the things I pushed down so far inside me I thought they'd never find their way back to the surface. Even now, the very worst is blocked to me – the physical details of the attack, the fear, the pain – but the little things, I do remember. The pungent smell of cheap aftershave overlapping the fetid sweetness of his breath; the label sticking up from the back of his jumper and how I imagined him putting on that jumper in the morning and wondered if he knew, even as he pulled it over his head, that he was going to do this, or whether he thought this was going to be just a normal day; the way, afterwards, he helped me find the shoe that had come off and asked me if I'd like another 'date', quite as if we'd just come back from a trip to the movies, and told me to meet him in the same place the next day; how I let myself into my house with my key and wished just for once there'd be the smell of dinner cooking and someone asking where I'd been and why I looked so pale and what had happened to my tights.

'Mum? Mum, what's wrong? Ignore her, she's out of order. You don't have to say anything if you don't—'

'It was rape.'

The voice that comes out of my mouth isn't mine, it's like the whisper of a child.

'Pardon?'

Three heads – Saul, Pip, Katy – bend towards me, not understanding, but wanting to understand, like kind strangers in a foreign country wanting to help you when you're lost.

'I was raped,' I repeat, my voice stronger now.

'But that's not true.' Saul is looking at me as if I'm a child who has got the wrong end of the stick and needs to be put right. 'The father was that married man. David. He had a wife and a child and a polo-necked jumper. He confessed. You told me.'

'No.'

'What do you mean, no?'

'That's what I wanted people to believe, because that's what *I* wanted to believe. But that's not how it was.'

And I tell them how it was, even though my daughters' eyes fill with tears and my husband looks at me as if I'm someone he doesn't know.

'I never told anyone,' I say. 'I just blotted it out.'

And the fire inside me is out now, and it feels as if something has been shifted, furniture moved around so everything feels lighter and more spacious. And someone is holding my hand, but I don't know who it is, and someone else is saying, 'We should tell them the truth,' but I don't know who that is either.

All I know is that I just want to go home.

Sunday, 6 p.m.

The oncologist and his wife, who we had breakfast with yester-day morning, step up behind us at the reception desk, where we are queuing to pay our bill. I hope they'll be too exhausted for chitchat, but they smile expectantly as they approach.

'Wonderful wedding, wasn't it?' says the oncologist's wife, her eyebrows arching as if she is expecting to be contradicted. I re-member our conversation last night, and how she said 'Max will be Max' with those same arched brows.

'Yes, lovely,' says Saul. He takes my hand and squeezes it hard, and I stare at a point on the ceiling to stop myself from crying.

'Bit of an endurance test, though,' grimaces the oncologist. 'Liz would insist on staying right till the bitter end.'

'I don't like to miss anything. It's just how I am.'

We stand in silence while the receptionist deals with the woman in front. I can feel Saul searching for something to say. He has always been scared of silences.

'We're paying our daughters' bills, too,' he says eventually. 'Funny, no matter how old they are, they're never too old for the Bank of Mum and Dad.'

He is trying to lighten the atmosphere. In actual fact, Pip has always been fiercely independent, refusing to take handouts from us since the day she graduated from university. Katy is less so. But still – the Bank of Mum and Dad!

'Do you have children?' Saul must be desperate to resort to that one. Small talk is usually my terrain, but the scene in the hotel lounge has drained me of all social niceties, so it is left to him to feel his way.

The oncologist (it occurs to me that I never asked his name) exchanges a look with his wife. 'We have two children,' he says eventually. 'But one of them died.'

Oh. I look at him more closely, and now I see it. The grief that lives behind his eyes. How did I not notice it before?

'Our son,' says his wife. 'He fell off a balcony in a resort in Crete two years ago when he was on holiday with friends. He was twenty-three. Drunk as a skunk, of course. Silly sod.'

How have I so misjudged them? I have assumed I know them because of how they talk and dress. But I know nothing about them at all.

'One never knows how to answer that question of how many children,' says the oncologist quietly. He has his hand in his jacket pocket and is moving it about as if jiggling his mobile phone. 'One imagines it will get easier, but so far it hasn't.'

'I'm so sorry,' says Saul, and for a moment I fear he is going to offer up Molly as some sort of compensation, and I know if he does I won't be able to bear it. It was Katy, I think, who came up with the term Grief Olympics, complaining that when she told people at university about Molly they'd often invoke a death of their own in response. 'I'll see you one dead baby sister and raise you a dead grandparent,' was how she put it. She'd called it Competitive Grief, but I know now it's more complicated than that – it's more like discreetly raising a trouser leg to reveal the sock that proves you're a member of the same club. But still, I'm grateful when Saul keeps quiet.

'Mr and Mrs Friedman?' says the receptionist, handing Saul the bill. She looks at me. 'Don't forget. Fairy feet,' she says.

Saul looks startled.

'We're paying the bill for our daughters, too,' I say. Heat rushes to my face as I imagine how that might sound to the couple behind us, as if we're boasting that we still have our children. Just for a moment I wish Saul *had* told them about Molly, so they'd know the context. *Our* context.

'Blimey, that's a bit steep.' Saul has put his glasses on to examine the bills, and he is frowning, so that they slip down his nose, giving him a schoolteachery look.

'I can double check it if you like, sir,' says the receptionist.

Saul sighs. 'No, I'm sure it's correct. It's just a bit of a shock, that's all.'

He gets out his credit card and puts it into the machine, and I close my eyes automatically as I always do, in case anyone should accuse me of spying on their pin number. Even my own husband.

Back in the hotel lounge, we look around for Katy and Pip to signal that we're leaving. They are standing close together, whispering furiously, and when they return the gesture straight away, I know they've been talking about me. My daughters' eyes are clouded with worry and I'm already regretting what I revealed to them earlier. I shouldn't have burdened them with that.

Katy had been all set to march across to Jamie's table to repeat what I'd just told them.

'They think Mum's being obstructive,' she said. 'They ought to be told what happened to her. They ought to know why she gave him away, that it wasn't her fault.'

Thankfully the others managed to talk her out of it, though judging by Katy's face I can see she still doesn't agree. My daughter is itching to right wrongs. She doesn't yet understand that some wrongs can never be made right.

'Right, let's say our thank yous and get going,' says Saul when Pip and Katy have joined us.

By this time the assembled guests have thinned out considerably, sprayed across the tables in the lounge like the last stubborn blooms on a branch.

'Are you OK?' asks Pip, for the hundredth time since my meltdown.

'I'm fine,' I tell her. 'I'd just like to get out of here.'

We begin doing the rounds of the tables. Rob is sitting alone at one, with his coat on, and I go over to him.

'I suppose you've heard,' he says as I approach. 'Katy's leaving me.'

'Well, I know she's coming home for a little bit. But I've no idea what her long-term plans are.'

Rob looks up at me, not looking away until I've finally met his eye. 'Yes, you do.'

What can I say to that?

'Will you be all right?' I ask feebly, for of course he will be all right, although he probably doesn't believe it at the moment.

'Oh yes, I shall be dandy. I'll save myself a fortune. Katy has expensive tastes.'

He is angry. Not surprisingly. But not bitter, I think. I'm glad.

'Will you keep in touch with us?'

Rob starts to nod his head and then stops, smiles a sad little smile. 'I don't know. I've so enjoyed being part of your family, Fran.'

My eyes instantly fill with tears. Must we really lose Rob too? Isn't there some way he could stay? But I know there isn't.

I remember that early-morning revelation I woke Saul up to tell him about. How I'd realized that, despite the pillow cases chewed through with grief, if I was offered the choice of not knowing Molly, and therefore not knowing the pain of her loss, I'd still choose her. I'd always choose her.

So, too, I choose Rob, though there's a good chance I might never see him again. And I choose Jamie, who might or might not be still speaking to me. And I choose Pip and Katy and Saul. Just as the oncologist and his wife choose their son, the silly sod who fell to his death one balmy, drunken night in Crete. Our choices become our losses, but they make up who we are.

After hugging Rob (how I'll miss that big bear hug of his), I turn to say goodbye to the couple at the next table. It takes me a few seconds to realize it's Mr and Mrs Practically Family, the friends of Maddie and Lucy who sat next to us at lunch yesterday. They fall silent when I approach and I have the feeling I've interrupted an argument.

'We must stay in touch,' says Mrs Practically Family. 'I always say I'm a collector of people, don't I, Pete? I love picking up waifs and strays. Here's my card.'

She gives me a black business card with pink writing on it that says *Suzy Scholten, Life Coach: Arranger, Fixer, Sorter*, followed by a telephone number.

'Maybe you could sort me,' I say. I was going to say 'fix me', but changed my mind at the last minute. I suspect it would be beyond even Suzy Scholten's powers to fix me.

'I'm sure I could,' she says. 'Don't you think I could, Pete?'

'She could,' mutters Pete.

Saul is saying his goodbyes at the other side of the room, but I catch him glancing over at me from time to time. I think Saul would like to fix me if he could.

'Give me your email,' says Suzy Scholten. 'I'll add you to my mailing list.'

Watching this exchange is Christine, the elderly woman we met at breakfast yesterday. For once she is without her phone, and she fixes me with sympathetic eyes when I approach to take my leave. 'This wedding hasn't been easy for you, has it?' she asks.

I'm taken aback. Lynn and Max had told us that most people at the wedding didn't know anything about our relationship with Jamie. Or is she referring to something else?

'Just remember, whatever you're going through, you're not the first and you certainly won't be the last,' she says. 'Like I told you yesterday, there's nothing new under the sun.' She reaches out her small, soft hand, wraps it around mine and gives the lightest of squeezes, and I feel some of the tension of the last few hours begin to lift. Impulsively I lean forward to hug her.

Finally we're all regrouped at Jamie and Lucy's table to say goodbye. Lynn and Max are there, and Maddie, of course.

'I'm sorry I've been a bit full on,' says Maddie, noticing something in my face perhaps. 'Sometimes I go over the top. You just have to ignore me.' She puts her hand out to stroke my arm, and for once I don't recoil.

Max and Saul have entered into a detailed discussion concerning the most direct route home. 'It's six of one, half a dozen of the other,' Saul is saying. I inhale through my teeth to stop myself getting irritated at the phrase.

'We're so glad you could come,' says Lynn, linking her arm through Max's as if in a three-legged race.

'It was lovely of you to invite us,' I say, when I can trust myself to speak.

Lucy gets up and gives me a perfunctory hug. 'I'm glad we met at last,' she says, her fine white-blonde hair tickling my cheek. 'Sorry if it got a bit heated back there. You'll like me when you get to know me, I promise. I'm fun when I'm not getting married.'

By the time I get around to Jamie, I'm tired of hugging and saying goodbye. As ever, there's something tugging inside me, pulling me towards him, but, thank God, it's manageable. I know I won't see him for a while. And when I do see him again, things will be different. It couldn't have continued, that intensity. We step forward, both of us, and put our arms around each other, and I can feel his heart thudding against mine, just as it did twenty-eight years ago during those few months when we were one. And I know that he is who he is because of Lynn and Max and Rosie and the whole life he has lived, and that has little to do with me and nothing to do with what happened on a patch of wasteland a long time ago.

I sense everyone watching us, in that way people do when they're trying not to look like they're interested. We pull away self-consciously.

'Have a fantastic honeymoon,' I say.

'We'll do our best,' he replies.

Sunday, 7 p.m.

'It's not fair though,' Katy says for the millionth time. 'Jammy needs to have the facts.'

That's not what she means. What she means is that the others need to have the facts. So they won't judge me.

'But who will it help?' I ask. 'Even if I wanted to, I'd never find the man who attacked me, to ask if he's got a grandfather with diabetes, or a mad aunt in the attic, or a pigeon-toed cousin. So Jamie can't ever find out anything about hereditary stuff. So how will it help him to know?'

'Because it's the truth,' Katy splutters. 'Everyone deserves to know the truth about who they are.'

'Catkin,' says Saul from the front seat, and her old pet name soothes my tired heart, 'sometimes the truth can do a lot of damage.'

'Sometimes the truth is an arse,' says Pip.

I glance at her in the rear-view mirror, but she is giving nothing away. At least on the way out to the car I got her to promise she'll tell Saul about the baby tomorrow. 'And the father?' I asked. She nodded. 'After your story this afternoon, it doesn't even seem so awful any more,' she said.

The girls both have iPods and after a while they plug their head-phones into their ears and lean back and close their eyes.

It feels good to have them there in the back of the car, just as

277

they were when they were children, when Saul and I would drive them home from parties or sleepovers or grandparents' houses and they would argue for the first few minutes about whose arm or leg was intruding into the other person's half, before drifting off to sleep. I've forgotten the quiet thrill of being enclosed in the car together, us four, while the world carries on outside – of sitting in the front with Saul and knowing that our children are behind us and safe.

I try not to imagine how Molly, at two, might have insisted her car seat went in the middle of her two grown-up sisters, or how it would be to glance in the rear-view mirror and see the top of her sleeping head. I try to concentrate on the two I can still protect, rather than the one I couldn't.

Saul is uncharacteristically quiet. I'm aware we still haven't talked properly about my walk with Jamie this morning, or my revelations just now, or about Pip and the baby he doesn't even know about yet, or Katy and Rob. The things we haven't talked about are like a third person who sits wedged between us, perched awkwardly on the hand brake, balancing out our ghost child in her car seat in the back. My handbag, containing the letter with the job offer from Spain, is in the footwell and I lean down to zip it up, feeling oddly lighter once it is closed off from view.

'At the next junction, turn right,' says the Sat Nav woman. And then again, 'Turn right.'

'Do we need her? I thought you and Max had the route covered between you?'

Saul glances at the tiny screen on the dashboard where a blue arrow is tracing a route across a brightly coloured map. 'I suppose we could turn her off,' he says reluctantly. 'As long as we keep the screen on. I don't want to leave anything to chance.'

Usually that's the kind of phrase that drives me mad, but tonight I find it comforting.

'That was exhausting, wasn't it?' I say.

Saul nods. 'I've had more relaxing weekends.' He glances in the mirror, at our sleeping children. 'I wish you'd told me,' he says. 'About the . . . attack.'

Is it any wonder he can't say the word 'rape' when it's taken me nearly thirty years to admit it?

'I couldn't. I couldn't let it be real.'

'I'm so tired of all the secrets, Fran. The counselling was supposed to be making us more transparent to one another, but instead it seems to have just made things worse.' He stops, as if struck by something, then continues, 'Do you remember that family photo last Christmas where you kept trying to Photoshop out your wrinkles and in the end you'd rubbed yourself almost completely away? That's how I feel now. I feel you're becoming more and more blurred and indistinct, and I'm just so tired of trying to keep you in focus. Do you understand?'

I can't remember the last time Saul made a speech like this.

I remember that photo though. It was one that had been taken on Saul's iPhone and uploaded to the computer – a close-up of the four of us. I'm sitting on the sofa with Katy and Pip on each side, and Saul is leaning over the back, with his arms stretched around us. Rob took it on Christmas Day last year, and we all have that over-stuffed, glazed, quasi-hysterical look of people who have eaten and drunk excessively and taken insufficient exercise. Saul loved it because we're all smiling and wanted to print it out to take it into his office, but before I'd allow it I insisted on 'doctoring' the picture. There was a lattice of lines around my eyes and mouth that I didn't like, and my skin texture reminded me of the yellowing doilies I'd seen in Saul's grandmother's house the one time I went there before she died. I'd only just discovered how to airbrush photos on screen, and was still carried away with the thrill of being able to erase years, even decades, with a few clicks of the mouse.

I started with a few small lines around the eyes, but then that made the lines in the lower part of my face more obvious, so I erased a few of those just for balance. The function was a fairly crude one, so every time I made a change it rubbed away the definition in that area, until, when I finally stopped to survey the full effect, I found I'd rubbed myself mostly away. All that re-mained was a fuzzy, almost faceless woman in a pink paper hat.

Saul had been furious, particularly when he realized I hadn't made a copy before I carried out my 'improvements'. He's not angry now, but in a way this grim-faced resignation is worse.

'No more secrets,' I say in a small voice. 'I promise.'

Once again I'm reminded of what Caro said about marriage being an endless yellow-brick road of compromises, one after the other, day after day. Maybe that's as good as it gets. Maybe that's good enough.

'What if you're not the only one with secrets?' Saul has his eyes fixed firmly on the road ahead, his hands in the 'ten to two' position on the steering wheel as advocated by a million driving instructors the world over.

For a moment I think he might not have spoken, after all, that it's just my own over-heightened emotions playing tricks on me. 'Pardon?'

'What if I've got a secret? Have you ever even considered that possibility, Fran?'

My heart feels as if it's being juiced like an orange. He's leaving me. The ex-girlfriend in Scotland. What else could it be?

My hands grow damp and begin to shake. *Please let him not say anything more. I will promise to be different. I will promise to be less opaque.*

'I'm being made redundant.'

It isn't what I expected him to say.

'I'm losing my job, Fran. I've known for months, but I haven't been able to tell you.'

He doesn't want to leave me.

'Surely you must have guessed. I've been dropping so many hints about downsizing and you going back to work. You must have had some inkling?'

I shake my head slowly. 'I thought you'd had enough of me – I thought you'd gone back to her.'

'Who?'

'That woman in Edinburgh.'

'Jesus, Fran, that was years ago. I don't even think about her any more. It was always you. It'll always be you.'

I open my mouth to say something waspish about how it wasn't always me, and then close it again.

'I'm so scared, Fran. I'm forty-nine. What if I don't get another job? How will we manage? Who will I be without my job?'

It's horrible hearing Saul – who, it occurs to me now, is probably the strongest person I know – sounding so small suddenly, so un-Saul-like.

'I'm ready to go back to work now,' I say. 'It feels like the right time. And you'll find something else. I know you will.'

Saul is silent, leaning slightly forward, gripping the wheel. 'I always hated that job anyway,' he says eventually.

'What? But you always said you enjoyed it.'

'What else was I going to say? It was my life. How could I admit I was spending all those hours on something I couldn't stand?'

We sit in silence while I try to make sense of this new information.

'You should have told me you hated it,' I say after a while.

'We should both have told each other a lot of things.'

Again we lapse into silence, and for the first time in years I find myself wondering what Saul is thinking.

Finally he sighs.

'We're going to have a lot to talk about with Louise on Thursday,' he says, and he smiles, and I release the breath I wasn't even aware I'd been holding and smile back at him.

We settle back into our seats and I think about Jamie, and how by now he'll be sitting down with Lucy and their parents and sighing with relief that it's all over, and looking forward to the honeymoon tomorrow, and I wish him well and hope he knows that. And I think about our lost little Molly and just how much we loved her. Looking in the mirror, I see my two sleeping daughters and I think about how much, though they're completely grown, they still need me. I think about the letter in my bag, and how I will reply.

I reach into the glove compartment and take out the slim leather box that houses the spare glasses that Saul hates. I click it open and lean over to slide the tortoiseshell frames on to his nose. 'You're supposed to be wearing these,' I remind him.

'Whatever,' he says.

On the dashboard, the blue arrow of the Sat Nav points insistently upwards as, our eyes fixed on the road ahead, we join the motorway that will lead us home.

Acknowledgements

Thanks to:

Felicity Blunt, Jane Lawson, Marianne Velmans, Kate Samano, Lynsey Dalladay, Suzanne Bridson, Becky Ritchie, Katie McGowan, Rikki Finegold, Mel Amos, Roma Cartwright, Fiona Godfrey, Juliet Brown, Natalie Greenwold, Louise Millar, Amanda Jennings, Jacky Hyams, Michael Fawcett, Billie Fawcett, Jake Fawcett, Otis Fawcett.

Tamar Cohen is a freelance journalist who lives in London with her partner and three teenage children. She is the author of the acclaimed *The War of the Wives* and *The Mistress's Revenge*. Follow her on twitter @mstamarcohen